THE EXPEDITION OF

HUMPHRY CLINKER

Mod. Lib. 10 —

THE MODERN LIBRARY
OF THE WORLD'S BEST BOOKS

THE EXPEDITION OF

Humphry Clinker

BY

TOBIAS SMOLLETT

INTRODUCTION BY

ARTHUR MACHEN

THE
MODERN LIBRARY
NEW YORK

THE MODERN LIBRARY
is published by RANDOM HOUSE, INC.

Manufactured in the United States of America

INTRODUCTION

A good many years ago—forty-five to be exact—I lived in a quiet and retired street called Clarendon Road, in a western quarter of London then called Notting Hill Gate, now, more superbly, Holland Park. I earned a bare living and no more by teaching children their elements, and paid out of my wages five shillings a week for a very small and narrow room on the top floor of the house. In London I was friendless, or all but friendless. I had no money for amusements and (I think) no capacity for being amused. I had nothing to do but read, and being bookish by nature, I passed most of my leisure in reading. My library appointments were original, though not luxurious. Against the wall of the landing, outside my door, there hung on nails a step-ladder, as a means of escaping to the roof in case of fire. Between the steps of this ladder, I had arranged my small collection.

It was a mixed lot. There was the Odyssey of Homer. I was reading it when I left school three years before, and I finished it in Clarendon Road. There was the "Bad Boy's Diary", a funny American book which I am afraid you have forgotten in America, as you have forgotten "Out of the Hurly Burly" and "Elbow Room". There was Carlyle's "Sartor Resartus" and "Essays", Disraeli's "Curiosities of Literature", "Don Quixote", the "Earthly Paradise", "Songs Before Sunrise", Tennyson, Poe, Chaucer, De Quincey, Burton's "Anatomy of Melancholy", a series of logical text books, and Smollett. There were, no doubt, other books there that I have forgotten, but these that I have cited I read over again and again and loved them the better I knew them.

Not the least favored in the step-ladder collection was the tall green book, published, I think, by Nimmo, which contained all of Smollett's best work. It held "Roderick Random", "Peregrine Pickle", "Humphry Clinker", the portentous and unreadable tragedy called "The Regicide", a nautical farce, "The Reprisal", and a satire called, if I remember, "Reproof". The tragedy, as I say, was unreadable, the farce not much better, the satire negligible; but the three novels were a perpetual resource, and by the time my residence in Clarendon Road was over and I "went down", as they say at the University, I believe I could have graduated with honours in all three tales. It is curious that Fielding, who is always coupled with Smollett, never much attracted me. I have read "Tom Jones" and "Amelia" once only, and I shall never read them again! But if you hold that Dickens was a mighty genius, and that Thackeray was an extremely clever fellow; then you will love Smollett and leave Fielding.

I hesitated for some time when I was asked by the publisher of this volume to select a tale of Smollett's for re-issue. There seemed a great deal to be said for "Roderick Random". There is a rough vigour and fertility of invention about it, an unseemly joy of rampant youth that make it, I will not say a highly attractive, but certainly a highly arresting book. It was written when Smollett was twenty-six; and I should think is comparable with that dread drink of the Irish mountains and wastes that they call *potheen*, raw, white whiskey, hot from the still, reeking of peat smoke and those oils of distillation, which are over-rich for tender stomachs. One cannot deny that this is a fearsome beverage; and yet it is whiskey in its most genuine and undoubted state, a more veracious and characteristic drink than the elegant, blended, softened, refined product that they put into fancy bottles and deck with attractive labels. So with "Roderick Random"; it is hot from the skill of Smollett's hot brain, lustful, furious, reeking with the fervour of unbroken youth, all raw and burning with the loves and hates of this perfervid Scot. And I can think of no book which depicts with such a biting burin the dark alleys of the eighteenth century, the black, sordid, appalling side of the life which in certain aspects was courtly, leisurely, elegant. Pope lived exquisitely with Whig nobles, and looked down from a height into the pit of Grub Street: he must have perfumed himself with rare essences after writing the "Dunciad". But the pit was black indeed; part of a map of London which contained Beer Lane and Gin Alley, a city whose inhabitants starved one day and vomited their surplus of drink the next, where unclean vessels were emptied out of window, where Johnson signed his letters, *Impransus*, "Dinnerless", whose river was not so much Thames as Fleet Ditch, "Roaring Mother of Dead Dogs", where all but naked men starved to death in the Debtors' Prisons; a city of dreadful *night*, indeed. Such was "the town" that Smollett saw in the 'thirties and 'forties of the eighteenth century: the stench of its brothels and garrets and black byways, the harsh cries of its lusts, and its agonies reek and scream in the pages of "Roderick Random".

And then, again, a formidable case might be made out in favour of "Peregrine Pickle", having regard, above all, to the group of which the inimitable Commodore Trunnion is the centre. In "Roderick Random", with all its tremendous vigour, Smollett's *heart* is both hard and cruel, without a touch of real tenderness. Roderick himself is, as Dickens said, a young ruffian; nay, he is much worse, he is a thankless wretch, without gratitude, without a spark of decent feeling in his breast. There is plenty of roughness and hardness in "Peregrine Pickle"; but Smollett's heart is beginning to melt, and when Hatchway writes the Commodore's epitaph, there are tears flowing, and they are not the tears of sensibility which bedewed a good many pages in the late eighteenth century. And there is rare comedy, too, in "Peregrine Pickle". "Roderick Random" is too brutal for true laughter; but read in "Pickle" how Commodore Trunnion rode to his wedding, and was delayed by reason of the wind changing. And read, too, that famous chapter which treats of the Banquet after the Manner of the Ancients. It is horseplay fun, no doubt; but it is learned and curious fun and nobody took any serious hurt by it; though the French marquis was made somewhat unwell by partaking of the soup flavoured with assafetida.

But in spite of these strong claims my choice fell on "Humphry Clinker". It lacks the ferocious vigour of "Roderick Random", it has nothing quite so good as Trunnion and his friends; but it is the most agreeable book of the three; and perhaps I chose it in something of a missionary spirit, hoping that those who knew nothing of Smollett might be led by "Humphry" to desire a more thorough acquaintance. For the brutality, the hardness, the cruelty have been almost purged away by the catharsis of life. Smollett has been a fighting man for thirty years, giving hard knocks and taking them, drudging tremendously at dreary, weary work of compiling and translating, continually in hot water, seeing very little of the pleasant side of literary life in London. He was not of the Johnsonian circle, though the two men knew each other, as appears by the letter which Smollett wrote to Wilkes in the affair of Frank Barber, Johnson's black servant. Johnson, says Smollett, "was humble enough to desire my assistance on this occasion, though he and I were never cater-cousins". The novels are not mentioned in Boswell, but as Johnson thought Fielding a low writer, it is not difficult to infer his judgment on Smollett.

Smollett's life, then, had been troubled and laborious and quarrelsome. His associates were chiefly the Grub Street drudges who toiled under him at translation and compilation; and allowing for the flowing line and high colour in which Smollett always dealt, we may see what manner of men these were in Jeremy Melford's Letter of June 10.

It had been a rough life and a hard life, and Smollett had taken it hardly; but in 1769 he felt that the battle was almost over. He was forty-eight; in the estimation of the eighteenth century an old gentleman. He was ill, and perhaps he felt that the end of things was upon him; and so he began to write his last book, "Humphry Clinker".

As a young man, the central figures, the heroes, if we can call the rascals by such a name, were young men. The elderly Smollett chooses an elderly man, Matthew Bramble, as the largest character in his last book. I do not know whether any ingenious person has traced the connection between Smollett and Wales. Such connection there certainly was; witness the admirable sea doctor, Morgan, one of the great successes and one of the few amiable characters in "Roderick Random". And so, Matthew Bramble in "Humphry Clinker" is a Welsh squire, with a place somewhere near Abergavenny (pronounce it as Winifred Jenkins spells it, "Abergány"). Smollett evidently knew something of Wales and the Welsh: it may be noted that young Melford had been at Jesus College, Oxford, and that his friend, still "up", is Sir Watkin Phillips, and that another friend, mentioned several times, is Mansel, a good name and an ancient name in South Wales. I do not know where Smollett got his love of Welshmen and his fondness for writing about them; but he was certainly not a profound Welsh scholar. For he makes his good Matthew Bramble member of Parliament for Dymkymraig. Now that word signifies "no Welsh", which would certainly not be a just description of any constituency near Abergavenny in the middle of the eighteenth century: in those days *Dymsaesneg*, "no English", would have been far closer to the mark. And again, as appears from the introductory letter of the publisher, Smollett thought that toasted cheese could be sent by post: a monstrous error, indeed.

But to tell the truth, Matthew Bramble, born Loyd—I think Smollett meant "Lloyd"—is not very much of a

Welshman. He is generous, as Morgan was generous, and proud, as Morgan was proud; but he does not possess that typical Welsh quality which in Morgan is resplendent: the quality of boiling with fury over a trifle at a moment's notice. Matthew, in fact, is Smollett himself; a good man and a kind man, but a little soured over with age and illness, a little disenchanted, somewhat valetudinarian. How his nephew and niece, "Jery" and Lydia enjoy the Hot Wells and Bath and London, and relish the manner and manners of their time as I suppose young people do now, though for the life of me—I am ten years older than Matthew—I can't see how they do it. Thus Lydia on the Hot Wells:

"Then, for variety, we go down to the *nymph of Bristol Spring*, where the company is assembled before dinner, so good natured, so free, so easy; and there we drink the water, so clear, so pure, so mild, so charmingly maukish."

Hear Matthew Bramble on the same:

"The man deserves to be fitted with a cap and bells, who for such a paultry advantage as this spring affords, sacrifices his precious time . . . and exposes himself to the dirt, the stench, the chilling blasts, and perpetual rains, that render this place to me intolerable."

So it is all through the book: we have Lydia's raptures, Jery's enjoyment; and then the subacid comment of the old squire. Not that Matthew Bramble is ill-natured; he is one of the best of men: but he is getting on in years and misses his comforts. Nothing is more diverting than Lydia in London. She can have no idea that any earthly temple can be more grand or magnificent than St. Paul's, there is such an infinity of gay equipages in the streets that one's head grows giddy and one's imagination is confounded as you gaze. Then, the river is spanned by three stupendous bridges that seem to be the work of giants, Ranelagh is like "the enchanted palace of a genie", Vauxhall dazzles and confounds by the variety of its beauties: and, on the whole, London realises the Arabian Nights and the Persian Tales, and it is extremely like Bagdad in the golden days of Haroun al Raschid.

Old Matthew does not feel like that. He finds the London mutton frowsy; he longs for the thyme fed mutton of his Monmouthshire hills; and as for Vauxhall:

"When I see a number of well-dressed people, of both sexes, sitting on the covered benches, exposed to the eyes of the mob; and, which is worse, to the cold, raw, night air, devouring sliced beef, and swilling port, and punch, and cyder, I can't help compassionating their temerity; while I despise their want of taste and decorum."

And he finally concludes that Vauxhall and all such places must be subsidised by the doctors and undertakers; their "damp and gloomy walks" being, evidently, pathways and short cuts to disease and death.

And, there is one very remarkable achievement in "Humphry Clinker". For once, the young people, the "juvenile leads", as actors would call them, are put in their right place, that is, the background. There can be no doubt that, save in very few instances, the hero and heroine of a story are sheer nuisances. Who cares about Waverley, or Montrose (in the "Legend of Montrose") or Nicholas Nickleby, or Kate Nickleby, or Madeline, or young Martin Chuzzlewit, or Little Nell? We have to endure all these tedious folk for the sake of the delightful and enchanting people that they meet; we must walk with Little Nell because Quilp is on her track; we must bear with the vacuous Nicholas to get an introduction to Squeers, and the Kenwigs family, and the Crummles Company: and we have to pretend all the while that the fortunes of the insipid young people are the chief interest in the several books. In "Humphry Clinker" there is none of this. The emotions and enthusiasms of Lydia and Jery are but a background for the humours of Matthew Bramble, of that cross old maid,

Sister Tabitha, of the delightful Winifred Jenkins, and of the cantankerous and whimsical Scot, Lismahago.

Smollett could not depict either a hero or a heroine. His "Roderick Random" and "Peregrine Pickle" are tolerable precisely because they are rather blackguards than heroes. In "Humphry Clinker" he wisely expends all his strength on his humorous characters, and even though Lydia Melford be deep in love, she continues to be entertaining.

ARTHUR MACHEN.

LONDON, 1929.

To Mr. Henry Davis, Bookseller, in London

RESPECTED SIR,

I have received your esteemed favour of the 13th ultimo, whereby it appeareth, that you have perused those same Letters, the which were delivered unto you by my friend the reverend Mr. Hugo Behn; and I am pleased to find you think they may be printed with a good prospect of success; in as much as the objections you mention, I humbly conceive, are such as may be redargued, if not entirely removed——And, first, in the first place, as touching what prosecutions may arise from printing the private correspondence of persons still living, give me leave, with all due submission, to observe, that the Letters in question were not written and sent under the seal of secrecy; that they have no tendency to the *mala fama,* or prejudice of any person whatsoever; but rather to the information and edification of mankind; so that it becometh a sort of duty to promulgate them *in usum publicum.* Besides, I have consulted Mr. Davy Higgins, an eminent attorney of this place, who, after due inspection and consideration, declareth, That he doth not think the said Letters contain any matter which will be held actionable in the eye of the law. Finally, if you and I should come to a right understanding, I do declare *in verbo sacerdotis,* that, in case of any such prosecution, I will take the whole upon my own shoulders, even *quoad* fine and imprisonment, though, I must confess, I should not care to undergo flagellation: *Tam ad turpitudinem, quam ad amaritudinem pœna spectans*——Secondly, concerning the personal resentment of Mr. Justice Lismahago, I may say, *non flocci facio*—I would not willingly vilipend any Christian, if, peradventure, he deserveth that epithet: albeit, I am much surprised that more care is not taken to exclude from the commission all such vagrant foreigners as may be justly suspected of disaffection to our happy constitution, in church and state——God forbid that I should be so uncharitable, as to affirm positively, that the said Lismahago is no better than a Jesuit in disguise; but this I will assert and maintain, *totis viribus,* that, from the day he qualified, he has never been once seen *intra templi parietes,* that is to say, within the parish church.

Thirdly, with respect to what passed at Mr. Kendal's table, when the said Lismahago was so brutal in his reprehensions, I must inform you, my good Sir, that I was obliged to retire, not by fear arising from his minatory reproaches, which, as I said above, I value not of a rush; but from the sudden effect produced by a barbel's row, which I had eaten at dinner, not knowing, that the said row is at certain seasons violently cathartic, as Galen observeth in his chapter περὶ ἰχθύς.

Fourthly, and lastly, with reference to the manner in which I got possession of these Letters, it is a circumstance that concerns my own conscience only; sufficeth it to say, I have fully satisfied the parties in whose custody they were; and, by this time, I hope I have also satisfied you in such ways, that the last hand may be put to our agreement, and the work proceed with all convenient expedition; in which hope I rest,

Respected Sir,
Your very humble servant,
JONATHAN DUSTWICH.

P.S. I propose, *Deo volente,* to have the pleasure of seeing you in the great city, towards All-hallowtide, when I shall be glad to treat with you concerning a parcel of MS. sermons, of a certain clergyman deceased; a cake of the right leaven, for the present taste of the public. *Verbum sapienti, &c.*

J. D.

To the Revd. Mr. Jonathan Dustwich, at——.

SIR,

I received yours in course of post, and shall be glad to treat with you for the MS. which I have delivered to your friend Mr. Behn; but can by no means comply with the terms proposed. Those things are so uncertain——Writing is all a lottery——I have been a loser by the works of the greatest men of the age——I could mention particulars, and name names; but don't choose it——The taste of the town is so changeable. Then there have been so many letters upon travels lately published——What between Smollett's, Sharp's, Derrick's, Thickness's, Baltimore's, and Baretti's, together with Shandy's Sentimental Travels, the public seems to be cloyed with that kind of entertainment—— Nevertheless, I will, if you please, run the risque of printing and publishing, and you shall have half the profits of the impression——You need not take the trouble to bring up your sermons on my account——No body reads sermons but Methodists and Dissenters——Besides, for my own part, I am quite a stranger to that sort of reading; and the two persons, whose judgment I depended upon in those matters, are out of the way; one is gone abroad, carpenter of a man of war; and the other has been silly enough to abscond, in order to avoid a prosecution for blasphemy——I'm a great loser by his going off——He has left a manual of devotion half finished on my hands, after having received money for the whole copy——He was the soundest divine, and had the most orthodox pen of all my people; and I never knew his judgment fail, but in flying from his bread and butter on this occasion.

By owning you was not put in bodily fear by Lismahago, you preclude yourself from the benefit of a good plea, over and above the advantage of binding him over. In the late war, I inserted in my evening paper, a paragraph that came by the post, reflecting upon the behaviour of a certain regiment in battle. An officer of said regiment came to my shop, and, in the presence of my wife and journeyman, threatened to cut off my ears———As I exhibited marks of bodily fear more ways than one, to the conviction of the byestanders, I bound him over; my action lay, and I recovered. As for flagellation, you have nothing to fear, and nothing to hope, on that head——There has been but one printer flogged at the cart's tail these thirty years; that was Charles Watson; and he assured me it was no more than a flea-bite. C— S— has been threatened several times by the House of L—; but it came to nothing. If an information should be moved for, and granted against you, as the editor of those Letters, I hope you will have honesty and wit enough to appear and take your trial———If you should be sentenced to the pillory, your fortune is made——As times go, that's a sure step to honour and preferment. I shall think myself happy if I can lend you a lift; and am, very sincerely,

Yours,

HENRY DAVIS.

LONDON, *Aug.* 10*th.*

Please my kind service to your neighbour, my cousin Madoc——I have sent an Almanack and Court-kalendar, directed for him at Mr. Sutton's, bookseller, in Gloucester, carriage paid, which he will please to accept as a small token of my regard. My wife, who is very fond of toasted cheese, presents her compliments to him, and begs to know if there's any of that kind which he was so good as to send us last Christmas, to be sold in London.

H. D.

THE EXPEDITION OF HUMPHRY CLINKER

To Dr. Lewis

DOCTOR,

The pills are good for nothing—I might as well swallow snow-balls to cool my reins—I have told you over and over, how hard I am to move; and at this time of day, I ought to know something of my own constitution. Why will you be so positive? Prithee send me another prescription —I am as lame and as much tortured in all my limbs as if I was broke upon the wheel: indeed, I am equally distressed in mind and body—As if I had not plagues enough of my own, those children of my sister are left me for a perpetual source of vexation—what business have people to get children to plague their neighbours? A ridiculous incident that happened yesterday to my niece Liddy, has disordered me in such a manner, that I expect to be laid up with another fit of the gout—perhaps, I may explain myself in my next. I shall set out to-morrow morning for the Hot Well at Bristol, where I am afraid I shall stay longer than I could wish. On the receipt of this send Williams thither with my saddle-horse and the *demi pique.* Tell Barnes to thresh out the two old ricks, and send the corn to market, and sell it off to the poor at a shilling a bushel under market price.—I have received a sniveling letter from Griffin, offering to make a public submission and pay costs. I want none of his submissions, neither will I pocket any of his money—The fellow is a bad neighbour, and I desire to have nothing to do with him: but as he is

1

purse-proud, he shall pay for his insolence: let him give five pounds to the poor of the parish, and I will withdraw my action; and in the mean time you may tell Prig to stop proceedings.—Let Morgan's widow have the Alderney cow, and forty shillings to clothe her children: but don't say a syllable of the matter to any living soul—I'll make her pay when she is able. I desire you will lock up all my drawers, and keep the keys till meeting; and be sure you take the iron chest with my papers into your own custody.—Forgive all this trouble from,

Dear Lewis,
Your affectionate
M. BRAMBLE.

GLOUCESTER, *April* 2.

To Mrs. Gwyllim, house-keeper at Brambleton-hall

MRS. GUILLIM;

When this cums to hand, be sure to pack up in the trunk male that stands in my closet, to be sent me in the Bristol waggon without loss of time, the following articles, viz. my rose collard neglejay, with green robins, my yellow damask, and my black velvet suit, with the short hoop; my bloo quilted petticot, my green manteel, my laced apron, my French commode, Macklin head and lappets, and the litel box with my jowls. Williams may bring over my bum-daffee, and the viol with the easings of Dr. Hill's dock-water, and Chowder's lacksitif. The poor creature has been terribly constuprated ever since we left huom. Pray take particular care of the house while the family is absent. Let there be a fire constantly kept in my brother's chamber and mine. The maids, having nothing to do, may be sat a spinning. I desire you'll clap a pad-luck on the wind-seller, and let none of the men have excess to the strong bear—— don't forget to have the gnte shit every evening before dark.

—The gardnir and the hind may lie below in the landry, to partake the house, with the blunderbuss and the great dog; and I hope you'll have a watchful eye over the maids. I know that hussy, Mary Jones, loves to be rumping with the men. Let me know if Alderney's calf be sould yet, and what he fought——if the ould goose be sitting; and if the cobler has cut Dicky, and how the pore anemil bore the operation. No more at present, but rests,

Yours,
TABITHA BRAMBLE.

GLOSTAR, *April* 2.

To Mrs. Mary Jones, at Brambleton-hall

DEAR MOLLY,
    Heaving this importunity, I send my love to you and Saul, being in good health, and hoping to hear the same from you; and that you and Saul will take my poor kitten to bed with you this cold weather. We have been all in a sad taking here at Glostar—Miss Liddy had like to have run away with a player-man, and young master and he would adone themselves a mischief; but the squire applied to the mare, and they were bound over.——Mistress bid me not speak a word of the matter to any Christian soul— no more I shall; for, we servants should see all and say nothing——But what was worse than all this, Chowder has had the misfortune to be worried by a butcher's dog, and came home in a terrible pickle——Mistress was taken with the asterisks, but they soon went off. The doctor was sent for to Chowder, and he subscribed a repository, which did him great service——thank God he's now in a fair way to do well—pray take care of my box and the pillyber, and put them under your own bed; for, I do suppose, madam Gwyllim will be a prying into my secrets, now my back is turned. John Thomas is in good health, but sulky.

The squire gave away an ould coat to a poor man; and John says as how 'tis robbing him of his parquisites.——I told him, by his agreement he was to receive no vails; but he says as how there's a difference betwixt vails and per-quisites; and so there is for sartain. We are all going to the Hot Well, where I shall drink your health in a glass of water, being,

> Dear Molly,
>
>   Your humble servant to command,
>   W. JENKINS.

GLOSTAR, *April 2d.*

To Sir Watkin Phillips, Bart. of Jesus college, Oxon.

DEAR PHILLIPS,

As I have nothing more at heart than to convince you I am incapable of forgetting, or neglecting the friendship I made at college, I now begin that correspondence by letters, which you and I agreed, at parting, to cultivate, I begin it sooner than I intended, that you may have it in your power to refute any idle reports which may be circu-lated to my prejudice at Oxford, touching a foolish quarrel, in which I have been involved on account of my sister, who had been some time settled here in a boarding-school. When I came hither with my uncle and aunt (who are our guard-ians) to fetch her away, I found her a fine tall girl, of seventeen, with an agreeable person; but remarkably simple, and quite ignorant of the world. This disposition, and want of experience, had exposed her to the addresses of a person —I know not what to call him, who had seen her at a play; and, with a confidence and dexterity peculiar to him-self, found means to be recommended to her acquaintance. It was by the greatest accident I intercepted one of his letters; as it was my duty to stifle this correspondence in its birth, I made it my business to find him out, and tell him very freely my sentiments of the matter. The spark did not like the stile I used, and behaved with abundance of mettle. Though his rank in life (which, by the bye, I am ashamed to declare) did not entitle him to much deference; yet as his behaviour was remarkably spirited, I admitted him to the privilege of a gentleman, and something might have happened, had not we been prevented.—In short, the business took air, I know not how, and made abundance of noise—recourse was had to justice——I was obliged to give my word and honour, &c. and to-morrow morning we set out for Bristol Wells, where I expect to hear from you by the return of the post.——I have got into a family of originals, whom I may one day attempt to describe for your amusement. My aunt, Mrs. Tabitha Bramble, is a maiden of forty-five, exceedingly starched, vain, and ridiculous.—My uncle is an odd kind of humorist, always on the fret, and so unpleasant in his manner, that rather than be obliged to keep him company, I'd resign all claim to the inheritance of his estate.—Indeed his being tortured by the gout may have soured his temper, and, perhaps, I may like him better on further acquaintance; certain it is, all his servants and neighbours in the country are fond of him, even to a degree of enthusiasm, the reason of which I cannot as yet comprehend. Remember me to Griffy Price, Gwyn, Mansel, Basset, and all the rest of my old Cambrian companions. ——Salute the bed-maker in my name—give my service to the cook, and pray take care of poor Ponto, for the sake of his old master, who is, and ever will be,

> Dear Phillips,
>> Your affectionate friend,
>>> and humble servant,
>>>> JER. MELFORD.

GLOUCESTER, *April* 2.

To Mrs. Jermyn at her house in Gloucester

DEAR MADAM,

Having no mother of my own, I hope you will give me leave to disburden my poor heart to you, who have always acted the part of a kind parent to me, ever since I was put under your care.——Indeed, and indeed, my worthy governess may believe me, when I assure her, that I never harboured a thought that was otherwise than virtuous; and, if God will give me grace, I shall never behave so as to cast a reflection on the care you have taken in my education. I confess I have given just cause of offence by my want of prudence and experience. I ought not to have listened to what the young man said; and it was my duty to have told you all that passed, but I was ashamed to mention it; and then he behaved so modest and respectful, and seemed to be so melancholy and timorous, that I could not find in my heart to do any thing that should make him miserable and desperate. As for familiarities, I do declare, I never once allowed him the favour of a salute; and as to the few letters that passed between us, they are all in my uncle's hands, and I hope they contain nothing contrary to innocence and honour.——I am still persuaded that he is not what he appears to be: but time will discover——mean while I will endeavour to forget a connexion, which is so displeasing to my family. I have cried without ceasing, and have not tasted any thing but tea, since I was hurried away from you; nor did I once close my eyes for three nights running.——My aunt continues to chide me severely when we are by ourselves; but I hope to soften her in time, by humility and submission.——My uncle, who was so dreadfully passionate in the beginning, has been moved by my tears and distress; and is now all tenderness and compassion; and my brother is reconciled to me on my promise to break off all correspondence with that unfortunate youth;

but, notwithstanding all their indulgence, I shall have no peace of mind till I know my dear and ever honoured governess has forgiven her poor, disconsolate, forlorn,

Affectionate humble servant,

till death,

LYDIA MELFORD

CLIFTON, *April* 6.

To Miss Lætitia Willis, at Gloucester

MY DEAREST LETTY,

I am in such a fright, lest this should not come safe to hand by the conveyance of Jarvis the carrier, that I beg you will write me, on the receipt of it, directing to me, under cover, to Mrs. Winifred Jenkins, my aunt's maid, who is a good girl, and has been so kind to me in my affliction, that I have made her my confidant; as for Jarvis, he was very shy of taking charge of my letter and the little parcel, because his sister Sally had like to have lost her place on my account: indeed I cannot blame the man for his caution; but I have made it worth his while.——My dear companion and bed-fellow, it is a grievous addition to my other misfortunes, that I am deprived of your agreeable company and conversation, at a time when I need so much the comfort of your good humour and good sense; but, I hope, the friendship we contracted at boarding-school, will last for life——I doubt not but on my side it will daily increase and improve, as I gain experience, and learn to know the value of a true friend.——O, my dear Letty! what shall I say about poor Mr. Wilson? I have promised to break off all correspondence, and, if possible, to forget him: but, alas! I begin to perceive that will not be in my power. As it is by no means proper that the picture should remain in my hands, lest it should be the occasion of more mischief, I have sent it to you by this opportunity, begging you will either keep it safe till better times, or return it to Mr. Wilson himself, who, I suppose, will make it his business to see you at the usual place. If he should be low-spirited at my sending back his picture, you may tell him I have no occasion for a picture, while the original continues engraved on my——But no; I would not have you tell him that neither; because there must be an end of our correspondence——I wish he may forget me, for the sake of his own peace; and yet if he should, he must be a barbarous——But it is impossible——poor Wilson cannot be false and inconstant: I beseech him not to write to me, nor attempt to see me for some time; for, considering the resentment and passionate temper of my brother Jery, such an attempt might be attended with consequences which would make us all miserable for life——let us trust to time and the chapter of accidents; or rather to that Providence which will not fail, sooner or later, to reward those that walk in the paths of honour and virtue.——I would offer my love to the young ladies; but it is not fit that any of them should know you have received this letter.——If we go to Bath, I shall send you my simple remarks upon that famous center of polite amusement, and every other place we may chance to visit; and I flatter myself that my dear Miss Willis will be punctual in answering the letters of her affectionate,

LYDIA MELFORD.

CLIFTON, *April* 6.

To Dr. Lewis

DEAR LEWIS,

I have followed your directions with some success, and might have been upon my legs by this time, had the weather permitted me to use my saddle-horse. I rode out upon the Downs last Tuesday, in the forenoon, when the

sky, as far as the visible horizon, was without a cloud; but
before I had gone a full mile, I was overtaken instantaneously by a storm of rain that wet me to the skin in three
minutes—whence it came the devil knows; but it has laid
me up (I suppose) for one fortnight. It makes me sick to
hear people talk of the fine air upon Cliftondowns: How
can the air be either agreeable or salutary, where the demon
of vapours descends in a perpetual drizzle? My confinement
is the more intolerable, as I am surrounded with domestic
vexations.—My niece has had a dangerous fit of illness,
occasioned by that cursed incident at Gloucester, which I
mentioned in my last.———She is a poor good-natured simpleton, as soft as butter, and as easily melted—not that
she's a fool—the girl's parts are not despicable, and her
education has not been neglected; that is to say, she can
write and spell, and speak French, and play upon the
harpsichord; then she dances finely, has a good figure, and
is very well inclined; but, she's deficient in spirit, and so
susceptible—and so tender forsooth!—truly, she has got a
languishing eye, and reads romances.———Then there's her
brother, squire Jery, a pert jackanapes, full of college-
petulance and self-conceit; proud as a German count, and
as hot and hasty as a Welch mountaineer. As for that fantastical animal, my sister Tabby, you are no stranger to her
qualifications—I vow to God, she is sometimes so intolerable, that I almost think she's the devil incarnate come to
torment me for my sins; and yet I am conscious of no sins
that ought to entail such family-plagues upon me—why
the devil should not I shake off these torments at once? I
an't married to Tabby, thank Heaven! nor did I beget the
other two: let them choose another guardian: for my part
I an't in a condition to take care of myself; much less to
superintend the conduct of giddy-headed boys and girls.
You earnestly desire to know the particulars of our adventure at Gloucester, which are briefly these, and I hope they
will go no further:—Liddy had been so long cooped up in

a boarding-school, which, next to a nunnery, is the worst kind of seminary that ever was contrived for young women, that she became as inflammable as touch-wood; and going to a play in holiday-time,—'sdeath, I'm ashamed to tell you! she fell in love with one of the actors—a handsome young fellow that goes by the name of Wilson. The rascal soon perceived the impression he had made, and managed matters so as to see her at a house where she went to drink tea with her governess.—This was the beginning of a correspondence, which they kept up by means of a jade of a milliner, who made and dressed caps for the girls at the boarding-school. When we arrived at Gloucester, Liddy came to stay at lodgings with her aunt, and Wilson bribed the maid to deliver a letter into her own hands; but it seems Jery had already acquired so much credit with the maid (by what means he best knows) that she carried the letter to him, and so the whole plot was discovered. The rash boy, without saying a word of the matter to me, went immediately in search of Wilson; and, I suppose, treated him with insolence enough. The theatrical hero was too far gone in romance to brook such usage: he replied in blank verse, and a formal challenge ensued. They agreed to meet early next morning and decide the dispute with sword and pistol. I heard nothing at all of the affair, till Mr. Morley came to my bed-side in the morning, and told me he was afraid my nephew was going to fight, as he had been over-heard talking very loud and vehement with Wilson at the young man's lodgings the night before, and afterwards went and bought powder and ball at a shop in the neighbour-hood. I got up immediately, and upon inquiry found he was just going out. I begged Morley to knock up the mayor, that that he might interpose as a magistrate, and in the mean time I hobbled after the squire, whom I saw at a distance walking at a great pace towards the city gate—in spite of all my efforts, I could not come up till our two combatants had taken their ground, and were priming their pistols. An old house luckily screened me from their view; so that I rushed upon them at once, before I was perceived. They were both confounded, and attempted to make their escape different ways; but Morley coming up with constables, at that instant, took Wilson into custody, and Jery followed him quietly to the mayor's house. All this time I was ignorant of what had passed the preceding day; and neither of the parties would discover a title of the matter. The mayor observed that it was great presumption in Wilson, who was a stroller, to proceeed to such extremities with a gentleman of family and fortune; and threatened to commit him on the vagrant act.——The young fellow bustled up with great spirit, declaring he was a gentleman, and would be treated as such; but he refused to explain himself further. The master of the company being sent for, and examined, touching the said Wilson, said the young man had engaged with him at Birmingham about six months ago; but never would take his salary; that he had behaved so well in his private character, as to acquire the respect and good-will of all his acquaintance, and that the public owned his merit as an actor, was altogether extraordinary.——After all, I fancy, he will turn out to be a run-away prentice from London.—— The manager offered to bail him for any sum, provided he would give his word and honour that he would keep the peace; but the young gentleman was on his high ropes, and would by no means lay himself under any restrictions: on the other hand, Hopeful was equally obstinate; till at length the mayor declared, that if they both refused to be bound over, he would immediately commit Wilson as a vagrant to hard labour. I own I was much pleased with Jery's behaviour on this occasion: he said, that rather than Mr. Wilson should be treated in such an ignominious manner, he would give his word and honour to prosecute the affair no further while they remained at Gloucester—Wilson thanked him for his generous manner of proceeding, and was discharged. On our return to our lodgings, my nephew ex·

plained the whole mystery; and I own I was exceedingly incensed—Liddy being questioned on the subject, and very severely reproached by that wild-cat my sister Tabby, first swooned away, then dissolving in a flood of tears, confessed all the particulars of the correspondence, at the same time giving up three letters, which was all she had received from her admirer. The last, which Jery intercepted, I send you inclosed, and when you have read it, I dare say you won't wonder at the progress the writer had made in the heart of a simple girl, utterly unacquainted with the characters of mankind. Thinking it was high time to remove her from such a dangerous connexion, I carried her off the very next day to Bristol; but the poor creature was so frightened and fluttered, by our threats and expostulations, that she fell sick the fourth day after our arrival at Clifton, and continued so ill for a whole week, that her life was despaired of. It was not till yesterday that Dr. Rigge declared her out of danger. You cannot imagine what I have suffered, partly from the indiscretion of this poor child, but much more from the fear of losing her entirely. This air is intolerably cold, and the place quite solitary—I never go down to the Well without returning low-spirited; for there I meet with half a dozen poor emaciated creatures, with ghostly looks, in the last stage of a consumption, who have made shift to linger through the winter like so many exotic plants languishing in a hot-house; but in all appearance, will drop into their graves before the sun has warmth enough to mitigate the rigour of this ungenial spring.—If you think the Bath-water will be of any service to me, I will go thither so soon as my niece can bear the motion of the coach.——— Tell Barns I am obliged to him for his advice; but don't choose to follow it. If Davis voluntarily offers to give up the farm, the other shall have it; but I will not begin at this time of day to distress my tenants, because they are unfortunate, and cannot make regular payments: I wonder that Barns should think me capable of such oppression——As for Higgins, the fellow is a notorious poacher, to be sure; and an impudent rascal to set his snares in my own paddock; but, I suppose, he thought he had some right (especially in my absence) to partake of what nature seems to have intended for common use;——you may threaten him in my name, as much as you please, and if he repeats the offence, let me know it before you have recourse to justice.——I know you are a great sportsman, and oblige many of your friends: I need not tell you to make use of my grounds; but it may be necessary to hint, that I am more afraid of my fowling-piece than of my game. When you can spare two or three brace of partridges, send them over by the stage-coach, and tell Gwyllim that she forgot to pack up my flannel and wide shoes in the trunk-mail—I shall trouble you as usual, from time to time, till at last I suppose you will be tired of corresponding with

Your assured friend,
M. BRAMBLE.

CLIFTON, *April* 17.

To *Miss Lydia Melford*

Miss Willis has pronounced my doom——you are going away, dear Miss Melford!— you are going to be removed, I know not whither! what shall I do? which way shall I turn for consolation? I know not what I say—all night long have I been tossed in a sea of doubts and fears, uncertainty and distraction, without being able to connect my thoughts, much less to form any consistent plan of conduct—I was even tempted to wish that I had never seen you; or that you had been less amiable, or less compassionate to your poor Wilson; and yet it would be detestable ingratitude in me to form such a wish, considering how much I am indebted to your goodness, and the ineffable pleasure I have derived from your indulgence and approbation—Good God! I never heard your name mentioned without emotion! the most distant prospect of being admitted to your company, filled my whole soul with a kind of pleasing alarm! as the time approached, my heart beat with redoubled force, and every nerve thrilled with a transport of expectation; but, when I found myself actually in your presence;——when I heard you speak;—when I saw you smile; when I beheld your charming eyes turned favourably upon me; my breast was filled with such tumults of delight, as wholly deprived me of the power of utterance, and wrapt me in a delirium of joy!——encouraged by your sweetness of temper and affability, I ventured to describe the feelings of my heart—even then you did not check my presumption—you pitied my sufferings and gave me leave to hope—you put a favour-able—perhaps too favourable a construction, on my appear-ance—certain it is, I am no player in love—I speak the language of my own heart; and have no prompter but nature.——Yet there is something in this heart, which I have not yet disclosed.——I flattered myself—But, I will not——I must not proceed—Dear Miss Liddy! for Heaven's sake, contrive, if possible, some means of letting me speak to you before you leave Gloucester; otherwise, I know not what will—But I begin to rave again.—I will endeavour to bear this trial with fortitude—while I am capable of reflecting upon your tenderness and truth, I surely have no cause to despair—yet I am strangely affected. The sun seems to deny me light——a cloud hangs over me, and there is a dreadful weight upon my spirits! While you stay in this place, I shall continually hover about your lodgings, as the parted soul is said to linger about the grave where its mortal comfort lies.——I know, if it is in your power, you will task your humanity—your compassion—shall I add, your affection?—in order to assuage the almost intolerable disquiet that torments the heart of your afflicted,

WILSON

GLOUCESTER, *March* 31.

To Sir Watkin Phillips, of Jesus college, Oxon.

HOT WELL, *April* 18.

DEAR PHILLIPS,

I give Mansel credit for his invention, in propagating the report that I had a quarrel with a mountebank's merry Andrew at Gloucester: but I have too much respect for every appendage of wit, to quarrel even with the lowest buffoonery; and therefore I hope Mansel and I shall always be good friends. I cannot, however, approve of his drowning my poor dog Ponto, on purpose to convert Ovid's pleonasm into a punning epitaph,—*deerant quoque Littora Ponto:* for, that he threw him into the Isis, when it was so high and impetuous, with no other view than to kill the fleas, is an excuse that will not hold water—But I leave poor Ponto to his fate, and hope Providence will take care to accommodate Mansel with a drier death.

As there is nothing that can be called company at the Well, I am here in a state of absolute rustication: This, however, gives me leisure to observe the singularities in my uncle's character, which seems to have interested your curiosity. The truth is, his disposition and mine, which, like oil and vinegar, repelled one another at first, have now begun to mix by dint of being beat up together. I was once apt to believe him a complete Cynic; and that nothing but the necessity of his occasions could compel him to get within the pale of society—I am now of another opinion. I think his peevishness arises partly from bodily pain, and partly from a natural excess of mental sensibility; for, I suppose, the mind as well as the body, is in some cases endued with a morbid excess of sensation.

I was t'other day much diverted with a conversation that passed in the Pump-room, betwixt him and the famous Dr. L——n, who is come to ply at the Well for patients. My uncle was complaining of the stink, occasioned by the vast quantity of mud and slime, which the river leaves at low ebb under the windows of the Pump-room. He observed, that the exhalations arising from such a nuisance, could not but be prejudicial to the weak lungs of many consumptive patients, who came to drink the water. The Doctor overhearing this remark, made up to him, and assured him he was mistaken. He said, people in general were so misled by vulgar prejudices that philosophy was hardly sufficient to undeceive them. Then humming thrice, he assumed a most ridiculous solemnity of aspect, and entered into a learned investigation of the nature of stink. He observed, that stink, or stench, meant no more than a strong impression on the olfactory nerves; and might be applied to substances of the most opposite qualities; that in the Dutch language, *stinken* signified the most agreeable perfume, as well as the most fetid odour, as appears in Van Vloudel's translation of Horace, in that beautiful ode, *Quis multa gracilis*, &c.—The words *liquidis perfusus odoribus*, he translates *van civet & moschata gestinken*: that individuals differed *toto cœlo* in their opinion of smells, which, indeed, was altogether as arbitrary as the opinion of beauty; that the French were pleased with the putrid effluvia of animal food; and so were the Hottentots in Africa, and the Savages in Greenland; and that the Negroes on the coast of Senegal would not touch fish till it was rotten; strong presumptions in favour of what is generally called *stink*, as those nations are in a state of nature, undebauched by luxury, unseduced by whim and caprice: that he had reason to believe the stercoraceous flavour, condemned by prejudice as a stink, was, in fact, most agreeable to the organs of smelling; for, that every person who pretended to nauseate the smell of another's excretions, snuffed up his own with particular complacency; for the truth of which he appealed to all the ladies and gentlemen then present: he said, the inhabitants of Madrid and Edinburgh found particular satisfaction in breathing their own atmosphere, which was always impregnated with stercoraceous effluvia: that the learned Dr. B——, in his treatise on the Four Digestions,

explains in what manner the volatile effluvia from the in-
testines stimulate and promote the operations of the animal
economy: he affirmed, the last Grand Duke of Tuscany,
of the *Medicis* family, who refined upon sensuality with
the spirit of a philosopher, was so delighted with that odour,
that he caused the essence of ordure to be extracted, and
used it as the most delicious perfume: that he himself (the
doctor) when he happened to be low-spirited, or fatigued
with business, found immediate relief and uncommon satisfaction from hanging over the stale contents of a close-stool,
while his servant stirred it about under his nose; nor was this
effect to be wondered at, when we consider that this substance abounds with the self-same volatile salts that are so
greedily smelled to by the most delicate invalids, after they
have been extracted and sublimed by the chemists.——By
this time the company began to hold their noses; but the
doctor, without taking the least notice of this signal, proceeded to shew, that many fetid substances were not only
agreeable but salutary; such as *assa fœtida*, and other medic-
inal gums, resins, roots, and vegetables, over and above
burnt feathers, tan-pits, candle-snuffs, &c. In short, he used
many learned arguments to persuade his audience out of
their senses; and from *stench* made a transition to *filth*,
which he affirmed was also a mistaken idea, in as much as
objects so called, were no other than certain modifications
of matter, consisting of the same principles that enter into
the composition of all created essences, whatever they may
be: that in the filthiest production of nature, a philosopher
considered nothing but the earth, water, salt, and air, of
which it was compounded; that, for his own part, he had no
more objections to drinking the dirtiest ditch-water, than he
had to a glass of water from the Hot Well, provided he was
assured there was nothing poisonous in the concrete. Then
addressing himself to my uncle, 'Sir (said he) you seem to
be of a dropsical habit, and probably will soon have a confirmed *ascites:* if I should be present when you are tapped,

I will give you a convincing proof of what I assert, by drinking without hesitation the water that comes out of your abdomen.'——The ladies made wry faces at this declaration, and my uncle, changing colour, told him he did not desire any such proof of his philosophy: 'But I should be glad to know (said he) what makes you think I am of a dropsical habit?' 'Sir, I beg pardon (replied the Doctor) I perceive your ancles are swelled, and you seem to have the *facies leucophlegmatica.* Perhaps, indeed, your disorder may be *oedematous,* or gouty, or it may be the *lues venera:* If you have any reason to flatter yourself it is this last, sir, I will undertake to cure you with three small pills, even if the disease should have attained its utmost inveteracy. Sir, it is an arcanum which I have discovered, and prepared with infinite labour.—Sir, I have lately cured a woman in Bristol —a common prostitute, sir, who had got all the worst symptoms of the disorder; such as *nodi, tophi,* and *gummata, verrucœ, cristæ Galli,* and a *serpiginous* eruption, or rather a pocky itch all over her body.——By that time she had taken the second pill, sir, by Heaven! she was as smooth as my hand, and the third made her as sound and as fresh as a new born infant.' 'Sir (cried my uncle peevishly) I have no reason to flatter myself that my disorder comes within the efficacy of your nostrum. But this patient you talk of may not be so sound at bottom as you imagine.' 'I can't possibly be mistaken (rejoined the philosopher) for I have had communication with her three times—I always ascertain my cures in that manner.' At this remark, all the ladies retired to another corner of the room, and some of them began to spit.—As to my uncle, though he was ruffled at first by the doctor's saying he was dropsical, he could not help smiling at this ridiculous confession, and, I suppose, with a view to punish this original, told him there was a wart upon his nose, that looked a little suspicious. 'I don't pretend to be a judge of those matters (said he) but I understand that warts are often produced by the distemper; and that one upon your

nose seems to have taken possession of the very key-stone
of the bridge, which I hope is in no danger of falling.'
L——n seemed a little confounded at this remark, and assured him it was nothing but a common excrescence of the
cuticula, but that the bones were all sound below; for the
truth of this assertion he appealed to the touch, desiring he
would feel the part. My uncle said it was a matter of such
delicacy to meddle with a gentleman's nose, that he declined
the office—upon which, the Doctor turning to me, intreated
me to do him that favour. I complied with his request, and
handled it so roughly, that he sneezed, and the tears ran
down his cheeks, to the no small entertainment of the company, and particularly of my uncle, who burst out a-laughing for the first time since I have been with him; and took
notice, that the part seemed to be very tender. 'Sir (cried the
Doctor) it is naturally a tender part; but to remove all
possibility of doubt, I will take off the wart this very night.'

So saying, he bowed with great solemnity all round, and
retired to his own lodgings, where he applied a caustic to
the wart; but it spread in such a manner as to produce a
considerable inflammation, attended with an enormous
swelling; so that when he next appeared, his whole face was
overshadowed by this tremendous nozzle; and the rueful
eagerness with which he explained this unlucky accident, was
ludicrous beyond all description.——I was much pleased
with meeting the original of a character, which you and I
have often laughed at in description; and what surprizes
me very much, I find the features in the picture, which has
been drawn for him, rather softened than over-charged.

As I have something else to say; and this letter has run
to an unconscionable length, I shall now give you a little
respite, and trouble you again by the very first post. I wish
you would take it in your head to retaliate these double
strokes upon

Yours always,

J. MELFORD.

To Sir Watkin Phillips, of Jesus college, Oxon.

HOT WELL, *April* 20.

DEAR KNIGHT,

I now sit down to execute the threat in the tail of my last. The truth is, I am big with the secret, and long to be delivered. It relates to my guardian, who, you know, is at present our principal object in view.

T'other day, I thought I had detected him in such a state of frailty, as would but ill become his years and character. There is a decent sort of woman, not disagreeable in her person, that comes to the Well, with a poor emaciated child, far gone in a consumption. I had caught my uncle's eyes several times directed to this person, with a very suspicious expression in them, and every time he saw himself observed, he hastily withdrew them, with evident marks of confusion —I resolved to watch him more narrowly, and saw him speaking to her privately in a corner of the walk. At length, going down to the Well one day, I met her half way up the hill to Clifton, and could not help suspecting she was going to our lodgings by appointment, as it was about one o'clock, the hour when my sister and I are generally at the Pump-room.—This notion exciting my curiosity, I returned by a back-way, and got unperceived into my own chamber, which is contiguous to my uncle's apartment. Sure enough, the woman was introduced but not into his bed-chamber; he gave her audience in a parlour; so that I was obliged to shift my station to another room, where, however, there was a small chink in the partition, through which I could perceive what passed.—My uncle, though a little lame, rose up when she came in, and setting a chair for her, desired she would sit down: then he asked if she would take a dish of chocolate, which she declined, with much acknowledgment. After a short pause, he said, in a croaking tone of voice, which confounded me not a little, 'Madam, I am truly concerned for your misfortunes; and if this trifle can be of any service to you, I beg you will accept it without ceremony.' So saying, he put a bit of paper into her hand, which she opening with great trepidation, exclaimed in an extacy, 'Twenty pounds! Oh, sir!' and sinking down upon a settee, fainted away—Frightened at this fit, and, I suppose, afraid of calling for assistance, lest her situation should give rise to unfavourable conjectures, he ran about the room in distraction, making frightful grimaces; and, at length, had recollection enough to throw a little water in her face; by which application she was brought to herself: but, then her feeling took another turn. She shed a flood of tears, and cried aloud, 'I know not who you are: but, sure ——worthy sir—generous sir!—the distress of me and my poor dying child—Oh! if the widow's prayers—if the orphan's tears of gratitude can ought avail—gracious Providence!—Blessings!—shower down eternal blessings!'—— Here she was interrupted by my uncle, who muttered in a voice still more and more discordant, 'For Heaven's sake be quiet, madam—consider—the people of the house—— 'sdeath! can't you.'——All this time she was struggling to throw herself on her knees, while he, seizing her by the wrists, endeavoured to seat her upon the settee, saying, 'Prithee—good now——hold your tongue'——At that instant, who should burst into the room but our aunt Tabby! of all antiquated maidens the most diabolically capricious— —Ever prying into other people's affairs, she had seen the woman enter, and followed her to the door, where she stood listening, but probably could hear nothing distinctly, except my uncle's last exclamation; at which she bounced into the parlour in a violent rage, that dyed the tip of her nose of a purple hue,—'Fy upon you, Matt! (cried she) what doings are these, to disgrace your own character, and disparage your family?'——Then, snatching the bank-note out of the stranger's hand, she went on——'How now, twenty pounds!——here is temptation with a witness!—— Good-woman, go about your business——Brother, brother,

I know not which most to admire; your concupissins, or
your extravagance!'————'Good God (exclaimed the poor
woman) shall a worthy gentleman's character suffer for an
action that does honour to humanity?' By this time, uncle's
indignation was effectually roused. His face grew pale, his
teeth chattered, and his eyes flashed————'Sister (cried he,
in a voice like thunder) I vow to God, your impertinence is
exceedingly provoking.' With these words, he took her by
the hand, and, opening the door of communication, thrust
her into the chamber where I stood, so affected by the scene,
that the tears ran down my cheeks. Observing these marks
of emotion, 'I don't wonder (said she) to see you concerned
at the back-slidings of so near a relation; a man of his
years and infirmities: These are fine doings, truly————This
is a rare example, set by a guardian, for the benefit of his
pupils —— Monstrous! incongruous! Sophistical!' — I
thought it was but an act of justice to set her to rights; and
therefore explained the mystery—But she would not be
undeceived, 'What! (said she) would you go for to offer
for to arguefy me out of my senses? Did'n't I hear him
whispering to her to hold her tongue? Did'n't I see her in
tears? Didn't I see him struggling to throw her upon the
couch? O filthy! hideous! abominable! Child, child, talk
not to me of charity.————Who gives twenty pounds in charity?—But you are a stripling—You know nothing of the
world————Besides, charity begins at home—Twenty pounds
would buy me a complete suit of flowered silk, trimmings
and all—' In short, I quitted the room, my contempt for
her, and my respect for her brother, being increased in the
same proportion. I have since been informed, that the person, whom my uncle so generously relieved, is the widow
of an ensign, who has nothing to depend upon but the
pension of fifteen pounds a year. The people of the Well-
house give her an excellent character. She lodges in a garret, and works very hard at plain work, to support her
daughter, who is dying of a consumption. I must own, to

my shame, I feel a strong inclination to follow my uncle's example in relieving this poor widow; but, betwixt friends, I am afraid of being detected in a weakness that might entail the ridicule of the company, upon,

Dear Phillips,

Yours always,

J. MELFORD.

Direct your next to me at Bath; and remember me to all our fellow-jesuits.

To Dr. Lewis

HOT WELL, *April* 20.

I understand your hint. There are mysteries in physic, as well as in religion; which we of the profane have no right to investigate—A man must not presume to use his reason, unless he has studied the categories, and can chop logic by mode and figure—Between friends, I think, every man of tolerable parts ought, at my time of day, to be both physician and lawyer, as far as his own constitution and property are concerned. For my own part, I have had an hospital these fourteen years within myself, and studied my own case with the most painful attention; consequently may be supposed to know something of the matter, although I have not taken regular courses of physiology *et cetera et cetera.*——In short, I have for some time been of opinion (no offence, dear Doctor) that the sum of all your medical discoveries amounts to this, that the more you study the less you know.—I have read all that has been written on the Hot Wells, and what I can collect from the whole, is, that the water contains nothing but a little salt, and calcarious earth, mixed in such inconsiderable proportion, as can have very little, if any, effect on the animal economy. This being the case, I think, the man deserves to be fitted with a cap and bells, who for such a paultry advantage as this spring affords, sacrifices his precious time, which might be employed in taking more effectual remedies, and exposes himself to the dirt, the stench, the chilling blasts, and perpetual rains, that render this place to me intolerable. If these waters, from a small degree of astringency, are of some service in the *diabetes*, *diarrhœa*, and *night sweats*, when the secretions are too much increased, must not they do harm in the same proportion, where the humours are obstructed, as in the *asthma*, *scurvy*, *gout* and *dropsy?*—Now we talk of the *dropsy*, here is a strange fantastical oddity, one of your brethren, who harangues every day in the Pumproom, as if he was hired to give lectures on all subjects whatsoever—I know not what to make of him—Sometimes he makes shrewd remarks; at other times he talks like the greatest simpleton in nature—He has read a great deal; but without method or judgment, and digested nothing. He believes every thing he has read; especially if it has any thing of the marvellous in it; and his conversation is a surprizing hotch-potch of erudition and extravagance.——He told me t'other day, with great confidence, that my case was dropsical; or, as he called it, *leucophlegmatic:* A sure sign, that his want of experience is equal to his presumption; for, you know, there is nothing analogous to the dropsy in my disorder——I wish those impertinent fellows, with their ricketty understandings, would keep their advice for those that ask it——*Dropsy*, indeed! Sure I have not lived to the age of fifty-five, and had such experience of my own disorder, and consulted you and other eminent physicians, so often, and so long, to be undeceived by such a—But, without all doubt, the man is mad; and, therefore, what he says is of no consequence. I had, yesterday, a visit from Higgins, who came hither under the terror of your threats, and brought me in a present a brace of hares, which he owned he took in my ground; and I could not persuade the fellow that he did wrong, or that I would ever prosecute him for poaching—I must desire you will wink hard at the practices of this rascalion, otherwise I shall be plagued with his presents, which cost me more than they are worth.——If I could wonder at any thing Fitzowen does, I should be surprized at his assurance in desiring you to solicit my vote for him at the next election for the county: for him, who opposed me, on the like occasion, with the most illiberal competition—You may tell him civilly, that I beg to be excused. Direct your next for me at Bath, whither I propose to remove to-morrow; not only on my own account, but for the sake of my niece, Liddy, who is like to relapse. The poor creature fell into a fit yesterday, while I was cheapening a pair of spectacles, with a Jew-pedlar.——I am afraid there is something still lurking in that little heart of hers, which I hope a change of objects will remove. Let me know what you think of this half-witted Doctor's impertinent, ridiculous, and absurd notion of my disorder— So far from being dropsical, I am as lank in the belly as a grey-hound; and, by measuring my ancle with a pack-thread, I find the swelling subsides every day—From such doctors, good Lord deliver us!—I have not yet taken any lodgings in Bath; because there we can be accommodated at a minute's warning, and I shall choose for myself—I need not say your directions for drinking and bathing will be agreeable to,

Dear Lewis,

Yours ever,

MAT. BRAMBLE.

P.S. I forgot to tell you, that my right ancle pits, a symptom, as I take it, of its being *oedematous*, not *leuco-phlegmatic*.

To Miss Letty Willis, at Gloucester

HOT WELL, *April* 21.

MY DEAR LETTY,

I did not intend to trouble you again, till we should be settled at Bath; but having the occasion of Jarvis, I could not let it slip, especially as I have something extraordinary to communicate——O, my dear companion! What shall I tell you? for several days past there was a Jew-looking man, that plied at the Wells with a box of spectacles; and he always eyed me so earnestly, that I began to be very uneasy. At last, he came to our lodgings at Clifton, and lingered about the door, as if he wanted to speak to somebody——I was seized with an odd kind of fluttering, and begged Win to throw herself in his way: but the poor girl has weak nerves, and was afraid of his beard. My uncle, having occasion for new glasses, called him up stairs, and was trying a pair of spectacles, when the man, advancing to me, said in a whisper——O gracious! what d'ye think he said?—'I am Wilson!' His features struck me that very moment——it was Wilson, sure enough! but so disguised, that it would have been impossible to know him, if my heart had not assisted in the discovery. I was so surprised, and so frightened that I fainted away, but soon recovered; and found myself supported by him on the chair, while my uncle was running about the room, with the spectacles on his nose, calling for help. I had no opportunity to speak to him; but looks were sufficiently expressive. He was paid for his glasses, and went away. Then I told Win who he was, and sent her after him to the Pump-room; where she spoke to him, and begged him in my name to withdraw from the place, that he might not incur the suspicion of my uncle or my brother, if he did not want to see me die of terror and vexation. The poor youth declared, with tears in his eyes, that he had something extraordinary to communicate; and asked, if she would deliver a letter to me: but this she absolutely refused, by my order.——Finding her obstinate in her refusal, he desired she would tell me that he was no longer a player, but a gentleman; in which character he would very soon avow his passion for me, without fear of censure or reproach——Nay, he even discovered his name and family, which, to my great grief, the simple girl forgot,

in the confusion occasioned by her being seen talking to him
by my brother, who stopt her on the road, and asked what
business she had with that rascally Jew—She pretended she
was cheapening a stay-hook, but was thrown into such a
quandary, that she forgot the most material part of the
information; and when she came home, went into an
hysteric fit of laughing. This transaction happened three
days ago, during which he has not appeared, so that I suppose he has gone. Dear Letty! you see how Fortune takes
pleasure in persecuting your poor friend. If you should see
him at Gloucester—or if you have seen him, and know his
real name and family, pray keep me no longer in suspence
——And yet, if he is under no obligation to keep himself
longer concealed, and has a real affection for me, I should
hope he will, in a little time, declare himself to my relations.
Sure, if there is nothing unsuitable in the match, they won't
be so cruel as to thwart my inclinations—O what happiness
would then be my portion! I can't help indulging the
thought, and pleasing my fancy with such agreeable ideas;
which after all, perhaps, will never be realized—But, why
should I despair? who knows what will happen?—We set
out for Bath to-morrow, and I am almost sorry for it; as
I begin to be in love with solitude, and this is a charming
romantic place. The air is so pure; the Downs are so agreeable; the furz in full blossom; the ground enamelled with
daisies, and primroses, and cowslips; all the trees bursting
into leaves, and the hedges already clothed with their vernal
livery; the mountains covered with flocks of sheep and
tender bleating wanton lambkins playing, frisking, and skip-
ping from side to side; the groves resound with the notes of
black-bird, thrush, and linnet; and all night long sweet
Philomel pours forth her ravishingly delightful song. Then,
for variety, we go down to the *nymph of Bristol spring,*
where the company is assembled before dinner; so good
natured, so free, so easy; and there we drink the water so
clear, so pure, so mild, so charmingly maukish. There the

fun is so chearful and reviving; the weather so soft; the walk so agreeable; the prospect so amusing; and the ships and boats going up and down the river, close under the windows of the Pump-room, afford such an enchanting variety of moving pictures, as require a much abler pen than mine to describe. To make this place a perfect paradise to me, nothing is wanting but an agreeable companion and sincere friend; such as my dear miss Willis hath been, and I hope still will be, to her ever faithful

LYDIA MELFORD.

Direct for me, still under cover, to Win; and Jarvis will take care to convey it safe. Adieu.

To Sir Watkin Phillips, of Jesus college, Oxon.

BATH, *April* 24.

DEAR PHILLIPS,

You have, indeed, reason to be surprised, that I should have concealed my correspondence with miss Blackerby from you, to whom I disclosed all my other connexions of that nature; but the truth is, I never dreamed of any such commerce, till your last informed me, that it had produced something which could not be much longer concealed. It is a lucky circumstance, however, that her reputation will not suffer any detriment, but rather derive advantage from the discovery; which will prove, at least, that it is not quite so rotten as most people imagined—For my own part, I declare to you, in all the sincerity of friendship, that, far from having any amorous intercourse with the object in question, I never had the least acquaintance with her person; but, if she is really in the condition you describe, I suspect Mansel to be at the bottom of the whole. His visits to that shrine were no secret; and this attachment, added to some good offices, which you know he has done me, since I left *Alma-mater,* give me a right to believe him capable of saddling me with this scandal, when my back was turned——Nevertheless, if my name can be of any service to him, he is welcome to make use of it; and if the woman should be abandoned enough to swear his bantling to me, I must beg the favour of you to compound with the parish: I shall pay the penalty without repining; and you will be so good as to draw upon me immediately for the sum required——On this occasion, I act by the advice of my uncle; who says I shall have good-luck if I pass through life without being obliged to make many more compositions of the same kind. The old gentleman told me last night, with great good-humour, that betwixt the age of twenty and forty, he had been obliged to provide for nine bastards, sworn to him by women whom he never saw—Mr. Bramble's character, which seems to interest you greatly, opens and improves upon me every day.— His singularities afford a rich mine of entertainment; his understanding, so far as I can judge, is well cultivated; his observations on life are equally just, pertinent, and uncommon. He affects misanthropy, in order to conceal the sensibility of a heart, which is tender, even to a degree of weakness. This delicacy of feeling, or soreness of the mind, makes him timorous and fearful; but then he is afraid of nothing so much as of dishonour; and although he is exceedingly cautious of giving offence, he will fire at the least hint of insolence or ill-breeding.—Respectable as he is, upon the whole, I can't help being sometimes diverted by his little distresses; which provoke him to let fly the shafts of his satire, keen and penetrating as the arrows of Teucer—Our aunt, Tabitha, acts upon him as a perpetual grind-stone.— She is, in all respects, a striking contrast to her brother— But I reserve her portrait for another occasion.

Three days ago we came hither from the Hot Well, and took possession of the first floor of a lodging-house, on the South Parade; a situation which my uncle chose, for its being near the Bath, and remote from the noise of carriages.

He was scarce warm in the lodgings when he called for his night-cap, his wide shoes, and flannel; and declared himself invested with the gout in his right foot; though, I believe it had as yet reached no farther than his imagination. It was not long before he had reason to repent his premature declaration; for our aunt Tabitha found means to make such a clamour and confusion, before the flannels could be produced from the trunk, that one would have imagined the house was on fire. All this time, uncle sat boiling with impatience, biting his fingers, throwing up his eyes, and muttering ejaculations; at length he burst into a kind of convulsive laugh, after which he hummed a song; and when the hurricane was over, exclaimed 'Blessed be God for all things!' This, however, was but the beginning of his troubles. Mrs. Tabitha's favourite dog Chowder, having paid his compliments to a female turnspit of his own species, in the kitchen, involved himself in a quarrel with no fewer than five rivals, who set upon him at once, and drove him up stairs to the dining-room door, with hideous noise: there our aunt and her woman, taking arms in his defence, joined the concert; which became truly diabolical. This fray being with difficulty suppressed, by the intervention of our own footman and the cook-maid of the house, the squire had just opened his mouth, to expostulate with Tabby, when the town-waits, in the passage below, struck up their music (if music it may be called) with such a sudden burst of sound, as made him start and stare, with marks of indignation and disquiet. He had recollection enough to send his servant with some money to silence those noisy intruders; and they were immediately dismissed, though not without some opposition on the part of Tabitha, who thought it but reasonable that he should have more music for his money. Scarce had he settled this knotty point, when a strange kind of thumping and bouncing was heard right overhead, in the second story, so loud and violent, as to shake the whole building. I own I was exceedingly provoked at this new alarm; and before my uncle had time to express himself on the subject, I ran up stairs, to see what was the matter. Finding the room-door open, I entered without ceremony, and perceived an object, which I cannot now recollect without laughing to excess—It was a dancing master, with his scholar, in the act of teaching. The master was blind of one eye and lame of one foot, and led about the room his pupil; who seemed to be about the age of threescore, stooped mortally, was tall, raw-boned, hard-favoured, with a woollen night-cap on his head; and he had stript off his coat, that he might be more nimble in his motions—Finding himself intruded upon, by a person he did not know, he forthwith girded himself with a long iron sword, and advancing to me, with a peremptory air, pronounced, in a true Hibernian accent, 'Mister What d'ye callum, by my saoul and conscience, I am very glad to sea you, if you are after coming in the way of friendship; and indeed, and indeed now, I believe you are my friend sure enough, gra; though I never had the honour to sea your face before, my dear; for becaase you come like a friend, without any ceremony at all, at all'—I told him the nature of my visit would not admit of ceremony; that I was come to desire he would make less noise, as there was a sick gentleman below, whom he had no right to disturb with such preposterous doings. 'Why, look-ye now, young gentleman (replied this original) perhaps, upon another occasion, I might shivilly request you to explain the maining of that hard word, *prepasterous:* but there's a time for all things, honey'—So saying, he passed me with great agility, and, running down stairs, found our foot-man at the dining-room door, of whom he demanded admittance, to pay his respects to the stranger. As the fellow did not think proper to refuse the request of such a formidable figure, he was immediately introduced, and addressed himself to my uncle in these words: 'Your humble servant, good sir,—I'm not so *prepasterous*, as your son calls it, but I know the rules of shivility—I'm a poor knight of Ireland,

my name is sir Ulic Mackilligut, of the county of Galway;
being your fellow-lodger, I'm come to pay my respects,
and to welcome you to the South Parade, and to offer my
best services to you, and your good lady, and your pretty
daughter; and even to the young gentleman your son,
though he thinks me a *prepasterous* fellow—You must know
I am to have the honour to open a ball next door to-morrow
with lady Mac Manus; and being rusted in my dancing, I
was refreshing my memory with a little exercise; but if I
had known there was a sick person below, by Christ! I
would have sooner danced a hornpipe upon my own head,
than walk the softest minuet over yours.'—My uncle, who
was not a little startled at his first appearance, received his
compliment with great complacency, insisted upon his being
seated, thanked him for the honour of his visit, and repri-
manded me for my abrupt expostulation with a gentleman
of his rank and character. Thus tutored, I asked pardon of
the knight, who, forthwith starting up, embraced me so
close, that I could hardly breathe; and assured me, he loved
me as his own soul. At length, recollecting his night-cap,
he pulled it off in some confusion; and, with his bald-pate
uncovered, made a thousand apologies to the ladies, as he
retired—At that instant, the Abbey bells began to ring so
loud, that we could not hear one another speak; and this
peal, as we afterwards learned, was for the honour of Mr.
Bullock, an eminent cowkeeper of Tottenham, who had just
arrived at Bath, to drink the waters for indigestion. Mr.
Bramble had not time to make his remarks upon the agreeable nature of this serenade, before his ears were saluted
with another concert that interested him more nearly. Two
negroes, belonging to a Creole gentleman, who lodged in
the same house, taking their station at a window in the
stair-case, about ten feet from our dining-room door, began
to practise upon the French-horn; and being in the very
first rudiments of execution, produced such discordant
sounds, as might have discomposed the organs of an ass——

You may guess what effect they had upon the irritable
nerves of uncle; who, with the most admirable expression of
splenetic suprize in his countenance, sent his man to silence
these dreadful blasts, and desire the musicians to practise in
some other place, as they had no right to stand there and disturb all the lodgers in the house. Those sable performers,
far from taking the hint, and withdrawing, treated the messenger with great insolence; bidding him carry his compliments to their master, colonel Rigworm, who would give
him a proper answer, and a good drubbing into the bargain;
in the mean time they continued their noise, and even endeavoured to make it more disagreeable; laughing between
whiles, at the thoughts of being able to torment their betters
with impunity. Our squire, incensed at the additional insult,
immediately dispatched the servant, with his compliments
to colonel Rigworm, requesting that he would order his
blacks to be quiet, as the noise they made was altogether
intolerable—To this message, the Creole colonel replied,
that his horns had a right to sound on a common staircase;
that there they should play for his diversion; and that those
who did not like the noise, might look for lodgings elsewhere. Mr. Bramble no sooner received this reply, than his
eyes began to glisten, his face grew pale, and his teeth chattered. After a moment's pause, he slipt on his shoes, without
speaking a word, or seeming to feel any further disturbance
from the gout in his toes. Then snatching his cane, he opened
the door and proceeded to the place where the black trumpet-
ers were posted. There, without further hesitation, he began
to belabour them both; and exerted himself with such astonishing vigour and agility, that both their heads and horns
were broken in a twinkling, and they ran howling down
stairs to their master's parlour-door. The squire, following
them half way, called aloud, that the colonel might hear
him, 'Go, rascals, and tell your master what I have done;
if he thinks himself injured, he knows where to come for
satisfaction. As for you, this is but an earnest of what you

shall receive, if ever you presume to blow a horn again here, while I stay in the house.' So saying, he retired to his apartment, in expectation of hearing from the West Indian; but the colonel prudently declined any farther prosecution of the dispute. My sister Liddy was frighted into a fit, from which she was no sooner recovered than Mrs. Tabitha began a lecture upon patience; which her brother interrupted with a most significant grin, exclaiming, 'True, sister, God increase my patience and your discretion. I wonder (added he) what sort of sonata we are to expect from this overture, in which the devil, that presides over horrid sounds, hath given us such variations of discord——The trampling of porters, the creaking and crashing of trunks, the snarling of curs, the scolding of women, the squeaking and squalling of fiddles and hautboys out of tune, the bouncing of the Irish baronet over-head, and the bursting, belching, and brattling of the French-horns in the passage (not to mention the harmonious peal that still thunders from the Abbey steeple) succeeding one another without interruption, like the different parts of the same concert, have given me such an idea of what a poor invalid has to expect in this temple, dedicated to Silence and Repose, that I shall certainly shift my quarters to-morrow, and endeavour to effectuate my retreat before Sir Ulic opens the ball with my lady Mac Manus; a conjunction that bodes me no good.' This intimation was by no means agreeable to Mrs. Tabitha, whose ears were not quite so delicate as those of her brother——She said it would be great folly to move from such agreeable lodgings, the moment they were comfortably settled. She wondered he should be such an enemy to music and mirth. She heard no noise but of his own making: it was impossible to manage a family in dumb-shew. He might harp as long as he pleased upon her scolding; but she never scolded, except for his advantage; but he would never be satisfied, even tho'f she should sweat blood and water in his service—— I have a great notion that our aunt, who is now declining into the most desperate state of celibacy, had formed some design upon the heart of Sir Ulic Mackilligut, which she feared might be frustrated by our abrupt departure from these lodgings. Her brother, eyeing her askance, 'Pardon me, sister (said he) I should be a savage, indeed, were I insensible of my own felicity, in having such a mild, complaisant, good-humoured, and considerate companion and house-keeper; but as I have got a weak head, and my sense of hearing is painfully acute, before I have recourse to plugs of wool and cotton, I'll try whether I can't find another lodging, where I shall have more quiet and less music.' He accordingly dispatched his man upon this service; and next day he found a small house in Milsham-street, which he hired by the week. Here, at least, we enjoy convenience and quiet within doors, as much as Tabby's temper will allow; but the squire still complains of flying pains in the stomach and head, for which he bathes and drinks the waters. He is not so bad, however, but that he goes in person to the pump, the rooms, and the coffeehouses; where he picks up continual food for ridicule and satire. If I can glean any thing for your amusement, either from his observation or my own, you shall have it freely, though I am afraid it will poorly compensate the trouble of reading these tedious insipid letters of, Dear Phillips,

Yours always,
J. Melford.

To Dr. Lewis

Bath, April 23.

Dear Doctor,

If I did not know that the exercise of your profession has habituated you to the hearing of complaints, I should make a conscience of troubling you with my correspondence, which may be truly called the lamentations of Matthew Bramble. Yet I cannot help thinking I have some right to discharge the overflowings of my spleen upon you, whose province it is to remove those disorders that occasioned it; and let me tell you, it is no small alleviation of my grievances, that I have a sensible friend, to whom I can communicate my crusty humours, which, by retention, would grow intolerably acrimonious.

You must know, I find nothing but disappointment at Bath; which is so altered, that I can scarce believe it is the same place that I frequented about thirty years ago. Methinks I hear you say, 'Altered it is, without all doubt: but then it is altered for the better; a truth which, perhaps, you would own without hesitation, if you yourself was not altered for the worse.' The reflection may, for aught I know, be just. The inconveniences which I overlooked in the high-day of health, will naturally strike with exaggerated impression on the irritable nerves of an invalid, surprised by premature old age, and shattered with long-suffering—But, I believe, you will not deny, that this place, which Nature and Providence seem to have intended as a resource from distemper and disquiet, is become the very centre of racket and dissipation. Instead of that peace, tranquillity, and ease, so necessary to those who labour under bad health, weak nerves, and irregular spirits; here we have nothing but noise, tumult, and hurry; with the fatigue and slavery of maintaining a ceremonial, more stiff, formal, and oppressive, than the etiquette of a German elector. A national hospital it may be, but one would imagine that none but lunatics are admitted; and truly, I will give you leave to call me so, if I stay much longer at Bath.——But I shall take another opportunity to explain my sentiments at greater length on this subject—I was impatient to see the boasted improvements in architecture, for which the upper parts of the town have been so much celebrated and t'other day I made a circuit of all the new buildings. The Square, though irregular, is, on the whole, pretty well laid out, spacious, open, and airy; and, in my opinion, by far the most wholesome and agreeable situation in Bath, especially the upper side of it; but the avenues to it are mean, dirty, dangerous, and indirect. Its communication with the Baths, is through the yard of an inn, where the poor trembling valetudinarian is carried in a chair, betwixt the heels of a double row of horses, wincing under the curry-combs of grooms and postilions, over and above the hazard of being obstructed, or overturned by the carriages which are continually making their exit or their entrance—I suppose after some chairmen shall have been maimed, and a few lives lost by those accidents, the corporation will think, in earnest, about providing a more safe and commodious passage. The Circus is a pretty bauble, contrived for shew, and looks like Vespasian's amphitheatre turned outside in. If we consider it in point of magnificence, the great number of small doors belonging to the separate houses, the inconsiderable height of the different orders, the affected ornaments of the architrave, which are both childish and misplaced, and the areas projecting into the street, surrounded with iron rails, destroy a good part of its effect upon the eye; and, perhaps, we shall find it still more defective, if we view it in the light of convenience. The figure of each separate dwelling-house, being the segment of a circle, must spoil the symmetry of the rooms, by contracting them towards the street windows, and leaving a larger sweep in the space behind. If, instead of the areas and iron rails, which seem to be of very little use, there had been a corridore with arcades all round, as in Covent-garden, the appearance of the whole would have been more magnificent and striking; those arcades would have afforded an agreeable covered walk, and sheltered the poor chairmen and their carriages from the rain, which is here almost perpetual. At present, the chairs stand soaking in the open street, from morning to night, till they become so many boxes of wet leather, for the benefit of the gouty and rheumatic, who are transported in them from place to place. Indeed this is a shocking inconvenience that extends over the whole city; and,

I am persuaded, it produces infinite mischief to the delicate and infirm; even the close chairs, contrived for the sick, by standing in the open air, have their frize linings impregnated like so many spunges, with the moisture of the atmosphere, and those cases of cold vapour must give a charming check to the perspiration of a patient, piping hot from the Bath, with all his pores wide open.

But, to return to the Circus; it is inconvenient from its situation, at so great a distance from all the markets, baths, and places of public entertainment. The only entrance to it, through Gay-street, is so difficult, steep, and slippery, that in wet weather, it must be exceedingly dangerous, both for those that ride in carriages, and those that walk a-foot; and when the street is covered with snow, as it was for fifteen days successively this very winter, I don't see how any individual could go either up or down, without the most imminent hazard of broken bones. In blowing weather, I am told, most of the houses in this hill are smothered with smoke, forced down the chimneys, by the gusts of wind reverberated from the hill behind, which (I apprehend likewise) must render the atmosphere here more humid and unwholesome than it is in the square below; for the clouds, formed by the constant evaporation from the baths and rivers in the bottom, will, in their ascent this way, be first attracted and detained by the hill that rises close behind the Circus, and load the air with a perpetual succession of vapours: this point, however, may be easily ascertained by means of an hygrometer, or a paper of salt of tartar exposed to the action of the atmosphere. The same artist who planned the Circus, has likewise projected a Crescent; when that is finished, we shall probably have a Star; and those who are living thirty years hence, may, perhaps, see all the signs of the Zodiac exhibited in architecture at Bath. These, however fantastical, are still designs that denote some ingenuity and knowledge in the architect; but the rage of building has laid hold on such a number of adventurers, that one sees new houses starting up in every out-let and every corner of Bath; contrived without judgment, executed without solidity, and stuck together with so little regard to plan and propriety, that the different lines of the new rows and buildings interfere with, and intersect one another in every different angle of conjunction. They look like the wreck of streets and squares disjointed by an earthquake, which hath broken the ground into a variety of holes and hillocks; or, as if some Gothic devil had stuffed them altogether in a bag, and left them to stand higgledy piggledy, just as chance directed. What sort of a monster Bath will become in a few years, with those growing excrescences, may be easily conceived: but the want of beauty and proportion is not the worst effect of these new mansions; they are built so slight, with the soft crumbling stone found in this neighbourhood, that I shall never sleep quietly in one of them, when it blowed (as the sailors say) a cap-full of wind; and, I am persuaded, that my hind, Roger Williams, or any man of equal strength, would be able to push his foot through the strongest part of their walls, without any great exertion of his muscles. All these absurdities arise from the general tide of luxury, which hath overspread the nation, and swept away all, even the very dregs of the people. Every upstart of fortune, harnessed in the trappings of the mode, presents himself at Bath, as in the very focus of observation——Clerks and factors from the East Indies, loaded with the spoil of plundered provinces; planters, negro-drivers, and hucksters, from our American plantations, enriched they know not how; agents, commissaries, and contractors, who have fattened, in two successive wars, on the blood of the nation; usurers, brokers, and jobbers of every kind; men of low birth, and no breeding, have found themselves suddenly translated into a state of affluence, unknown to former ages; and no wonder that their brains should be intoxicated with pride, vanity, and presumption. Knowing no other criterion of greatness, but the ostentation of wealth, they discharge their affluence without taste or conduct, through every channel of the most absurd extravagance; and all of them hurry to Bath, because here, without any further qualification, they can mingle with the princes and nobles of the land. Even the wives and daughters of low tradesmen, who, like shovel-nosed sharks, prey upon the blubber of those uncouth whales of fortune, are infected with the same rage of displaying their importance; and the slightest indisposition serves them for a pretext to insist upon being conveyed to Bath, where they may hobble country-dances and cotillons among lordlings, squires, counsellors, and clergy. These delicate creatures from Bedfordbury, Butcher-row, Crutched-friers, and Botolph-lane, cannot breathe in the gross air of the Lower Town, or conform to the vulgar rules of a common lodging-house; the husband, therefore, must provide an entire house, or elegant apartments in the new buildings. Such is the composition of what is called the fashionable company at Bath; where a very inconsiderable proportion of genteel people are lost in a mob of impudent plebeians, who have neither understanding nor judgment, nor the least idea of propriety and decorum; and seem to enjoy nothing so much as an opportunity of insulting their betters.

Thus the number of people, and the number of houses continue to increase; and this will ever be the case, till the streams that swell this irresistible torrent of folly and extravagance, shall either be exhausted, or turned into other channels, by incidents and events which I do not pretend to foresee. This, I own, is a subject on which I cannot write with any degree of patience; for the mob is a monster I never could abide, either in its head, tail, midriff, or members; I detest the whole of it, as a mass of ignorance, presumption, malice, and brutality; and, in this term of reprobation, I include, without respect of rank, station, or quality, all those of both sexes, who affect its manners, and court its society.

But I have written till my fingers are crampt, and my nausea begins to return——By your advice, I sent to London a few days ago for half a pound of Gengzeng; though I doubt much, whether that which comes from America is equally efficacious with what is brought from the East Indies. Some years ago a friend of mine paid sixteen guineas for two ounces of it; and, in six months after, it was sold in the same shop for five shillings the pound. In short, we live in a vile world of fraud and sophistication; so that I know nothing of equal value with the genuine friendship of a sensible man; a rare jewel! which I cannot help thinking myself in possession of, while I repeat the old declaration, that I am, as usual,

Dear Lewis,

Your affectionate

M. BRAMBLE.

After having been agitated in a short hurricane, on my first arrival, I have taken a small house in Milsham-street, where I am tolerably well lodged, for five guineas a week. I was yesterday at the Pump-room, and drank about a pint of water, which seems to agree with my stomach; and to-morrow morning I shall bathe, for the first time; so that in a few posts you may expect farther trouble; mean while, I am glad to find that the inoculation has succeeded so well with poor Joyce, and that her face will be but little marked ——if my friend Sir Thomas was a single man, I would not trust such a handsome wench in his family; but as I have recommended her, in a particular manner, to the protection of lady G——, who is one of the best women in the world, she may go thither without hesitation as soon as she is quite recovered and fit for service——Let her mother have money to provide her with necessaries, and she may ride behind her brother on Bucks; but you must lay strong injunctions on Jack, to take particular care of the trusty old veteran, who has faithfully earned his present ease by his past services.

To Miss Willis, at Gloucester

BATH, *April* 26.

MY DEAREST COMPANION,

The pleasure I received from yours, which came to
hand yesterday, is not to be expressed. Love and friendship
are, without doubt, charming passions; which absence serves
only to heighten and improve. Your kind present of the
garnet bracelets, I shall keep as carefully as I preserve my
own life; and I beg you will accept, in return, my heart-
housewife, with the tortoise-shell memorandum-book, as a
trifling pledge of my unalterable affection.

Bath is to me a new world——All is gayety, good-
humour, and diversion. The eye is continually entertained
with the splendour of dress and equipage; and the ear with
the sound of coaches, chaises, chairs, and other carriages.
The merry bells ring round, from morn till night. Then
we are welcomed by the city-waits in our own lodgings; we
have music in the Pump-room every morning, cotillons every
forenoon in the rooms, balls twice a week, and concerts
every other night, beside private assemblies and parties without number——As soon as we were settled in lodgings, we
were visited by the Master of the Ceremonies; a pretty little
gentleman, so sweet, so fine, so civil, and polite, that in our
country he might pass for the prince of Wales; then he
talks so charmingly, both in verse and prose, that you would
be delighted to hear him discourse; for you must know he
is a great writer, and has got five tragedies ready for the
stage. He did us the favour to dine with us, by my uncle's
invitation; and next day squired my aunt and me to every
part of Bath; which, to be sure, is an earthly paradise. The
Square, the Circus, and the Parades, put you in mind of the
sumptuous palaces represented in prints and pictures; and
the new buildings, such as Princes-row, Harlequin's-row,

Bladud's-row, and twenty other rows, look like so many enchanted castles, raised on hanging terraces.

At eight in the morning, we go in dishabille to the Pump-room; which is crowded like a Welsh fair; and there you see the highest quality, and the lowest trades folks, jostling each other, without ceremony, hail-fellow well met. The noise of the music playing in the gallery, the heat and flavour of such a crowd, and the hum and buz of their conversation, gave me the head-ach and vertigo the first day; but, afterwards, all these things became familiar, and even agreeable.—Right under the Pump-room windows is the King's Bath; a huge cistern, where you see the patients up to their necks in hot water. The ladies wear jackets and petticoats of brown linen, with chip hats, in which they fix their handkerchiefs to wipe the sweat from their faces; but, truly, whether it is owing to the steam that surrounds them, or the heat of the water, or the nature of the dress, or to all these causes together, they look so flushed, and so fright-ful, that I always turn my eyes another way—My aunt, who says every person of fashion should make her appear-ance in the bath, as well as in the abbey church, contrived a cap with cherry-coloured ribbons to suit her complexion, and obliged Win to attend her yesterday morning in the water. But, really, her eyes were so red, that they made mine water as I viewed her from the Pump-room; and as for poor Win, who wore a hat trimmed with blue, what betwixt her wan complexion and her fear, she looked like the ghost of some pale maiden, who had drowned herself for love. When she came out of the bath, she took assa foetida drops, and was fluttered all day; so that we could hardly keep her from going into hysterics: but her mistress says it will do her good; and poor Win curtsies, with the tears in her eyes. For my part, I content myself with drink-ing about half a pint of the water every morning.

The pumper, with his wife and servant, attend within a bar; and the glasses, of different sizes, stand ranged in order before them, so you have nothing to do but to point at that which you choose, and it is filled immediately, hot and sparkling from the pump. It is the only hot water I could ever drink, without being sick—Far from having that effect, it is rather agreeable to the taste, grateful to the stomach and reviving to the spirits. You cannot imagine what wonderful cures it performs—My uncle began with it the other day; but he made wry faces in drinking, and I'm afraid he will leave it off—The first day we came to Bath, he fell into a violent passion; beat two black-a-moors, and I was afraid he would have fought with their master; but the stranger proved a peaceable man. To be sure, the gout had got into his head, as my aunt observed; but, I believe, his passion drove it away; for he has been remarkably well ever since. It is a thousand pities he should ever be troubled with that ugly distemper; for, when he is free from pain, he is the best tempered man upon earth; so gentle, so generous, so charitable, that every body loves him; and so good to me, in particular, that I shall never be able to shew the deep sense I have of his tenderness and affection.

Hard by the Pump-room, is a coffee-house for the ladies; but my aunt says, young girls are not admitted, insomuch as the conversation turns upon politics, scandal, philosophy, and other subjects above our capacity; but we are allowed to accompany them to the booksellers' shops, which are charming places of resort; where we read novels, plays, pamphlets, and news-papers, for so small a subscription as a crown a quarter; and in these offices of intelligence (as my brother calls them) all the reports of the day, and all the private transactions of the Bath, are first entered and dis-cussed. From the bookseller's shop, we make a tour through the milleners and toymen; and commonly stop at Mr. Gill's, the pastry-cook, to take a jelly, a tart, or a small bason of vermicelli. There is, moreover, another place of entertainment on the other side of the water, opposite to the Grove, to which the company cross over in a boat——It is called Spring-garden; a sweet retreat, laid out in walks and ponds, and parterres of flowers; and there is a long-room for breakfasting and dancing. As the situation is low and damp, and the season has been remarkably wet, my uncle won't suffer me to go thither, lest I should catch cold: but my aunt says it is all a vulgar prejudice; and, to be sure, a great many gentlemen and ladies of Ireland frequent the place, without seeming to be the worse for it. They say, dancing at Spring-gardens, when the air is moist, is recommended to them as an excellent cure for the rheumatism. I have been twice at the play; where, notwithstanding the excellence of the performers, the gayety of the company, and the decorations of the theatre, which are very fine, I could not help reflecting, with a sigh, upon our poor homely representations at Gloucester—But this, in confidence to my dear Willis—You know my heart, and will excuse its weakness.——

After all, the great scenes of entertainment at Bath, are the two public rooms; where the company meet alternately every evening—They are spacious, lofty, and, when lighted up, appear very striking. They are generally crowded with well-dressed people, who drink tea in separate parties, play at cards, walk, or sit and chat together, just as they are disposed. Twice a week there is a ball; the expence of which is defrayed by a voluntary subscription among the gentlemen; and every subscriber has three tickets. I was there Friday last with my aunt, under the care of my brother, who is a subscriber; and Sir Ulic Mackilligut recommended his nephew, captain O Donaghan, to me as a partner; but Jery excused himself, by saying I had got the head-ach; and, indeed, it was really so, though I can't imagine how he knew it. The place was so hot, and the smell so different from what we are used to in the country, that I was quite feverish when we came away. Aunt says it is the effect of a vulgar constitution, reared among woods and mountains; and, that as I become accustomed to genteel company, it will wear off.—Sir Ulic was very complaisant, made her a great many high-flown compliments.; and, when we retired, handed her with great ceremony to her chair. The captain, I believe, would have done me the same favour; but my brother seeing him advance, took me under his arm, and wished him good night. The Captain is a pretty man, to be sure; tall and strait, and well made; with light-grey eyes, and a Roman nose; but there is a certain boldness in his look and manner, that puts one out of countenance— But I am afraid I have put you out of all patience with this long unconnected scrawl; which I shall therefore conclude, with assuring you, that neither Bath, nor London, nor all the diversions of life, shall ever be able to efface the idea of my dear Letty, from the heart of her ever affectionate

LYDIA MELFORD.

To Mrs. Mary Jones, at Brambleton-hall

DEAR MOLLY JONES,

Heaving got a frank, I now return your fever, which I received by Mr. Higgins, at the Hot Well, together with the stockings, which his wife footed for me; but now they are of no survice. No body wears such things in this place— O Molly! you that live in the country have no deception of our doings at Bath. Here is such dressing, and fidling and dancing, and gadding, and courting and plotting—O gracious! if God had not given me a good stock of discretion, what a power of things might not I reveal, consarning old mistress and young mistress; Jews with beards that were no Jews; but handsome Christians, without a hair upon their sin, strolling with spectacles, to get speech of Miss Liddy. But she's a dear sweet soul, as innocent as the child unborn. She has tould me all her inward thoughts, and disclosed her passion for Mr. Wilson; and that's not his name neither;

and thof he acted among the player-men, he is meat for
their masters; and she has gi'en me her yallow trollopea,
which Mrs. Drab, the mantymaker, says will look very well
when it is scowered and smoaked with silfur——You
knows as how, yallow fitts my fizzogmony. God he knows
that havock I shall make among the mail sex, when I make
my first appearance in this killing collar, with a full foot
of gaze, as good as new, that I bought last Friday of madam
Friponeau, the French mullaner——Dear girl, I have seen
all the fine shews of Bath; the Prades, the Squires, and the
Circlis, the Crashit, the Hottogon, and Bloody Buildings,
and Harry King's row; and I have been twice in the Bath
with mistress, and na'r a smoak upon our backs hussy——
The first time I was mortally afraid, and flustered all day;
and afterwards made believe that I had got the heddick;
but mistress said, if I didn't go I should take a dose of
bumtaffy; and so remembering how it worked Mrs. Gwyllim a pennorth, I chose rather to go again with her into
the Bath, and then I met with an axident. I dropt my petticoat, and could not get it up from the bottom.——But what
did that signify; they mought laff, but they could see nothing; for I was up to the sin in water. To be sure, it threw
me into such a gumbustion, that I know not what I said,
nor what I did, nor how they got me out, and rapt me in a
blanket—Mrs. Tabitha scoulded a little when we got home;
but she knows as I know what's what——Ah Laud help
you!—There is Sir Yury Micligut, of Balnaclinch, in the
cunty of Kalloway——I took down the name from his gentleman, Mr. O Frizzle, and he has got an estate of fifteen
hundred a year—I am sure he is both rich and generous——
But you nose, Molly, I was always famous for keeping
secrets; and so he was very safe in trusting me with his
flegm for mistress; which, to be sure is very honourable; for
Mr. O Frizzle assures me, he values not her portion a brass
varthing——And, indeed, what's poor ten thousand pounds
to a Baron Knight of his fortune? and, truly, I told Mr.

O Frizzle that was all she had to trust to——As for John Thomas, he's a morass fellor—I vow, I thought he would a fit with Mr. O Frizzle, because he axed me to dance with him at Spring Garden—But God he knows I have no thoughts eyther of wan or t'other.

As for house news, the worst is, Chowder has fallen off greatly from his stomick—He eats nothing but white meats, and not much of that; and wheezes, and seems to be much bloated. The doctors think he is threatened with a dropsy—Parson Marrofat, who has got the same disorder, finds great benefit from the waters; but Chowder seems to like them no better than the squire; and mistress says, if his case don't take a favourable turn, she will sartinly carry him to Aberga'ny, to drink goat's whey—To be sure, the poor dear honymil is lost for want of axercise; for which reason, she intends to give him an airing once a-day upon the Downs, in a post-chaise—I have already made very creditable connexions in this here place; where, to be sure, we have the very squintasense of satiety——Mrs. Patcher, my lady Kilmacullock's woman, and I are sworn sisters. She has shewn me all her secrets, and learned me to wash gaze, and refrash rusty silks and bumbeseens, by boiling them with winegar, chamberlye, and stale beer. My short sack and apron luck as good as new from the shop, and my pumpydoor as fresh as a rose, by the help of turtle-water—But this is all Greek and Latten to you, Molly——If we should come to Aberga'ny, you'll be within a day's ride of us; and then we shall see wan another, please God——If not, remember me in your prayers, as I shall do by you in mine; and take care of my kitten, and give my kind sarvice to Sall; and this is all at present, from your beloved friend and sarvent,

W. JENKINS.

BATH, *April* 26.

To Mrs. Gwyllim, house-keeper at Brambleton-hall

I am astonished that Dr. Lewis should take upon him to give away Alderney, without my privity and concurrants—What signifies my brother's order? My brother is little better than noncompush. He would give away the shirt off his back, and the teeth out of his head; nay, as for that matter, he would have ruinated the family with his ridiculous charities, if it had not been for my four quarters—What between his willfullness and his waste, his trumps, and his frenzy, I lead the life of an indented slave. Alderney gave four gallons a-day, ever since the calf was sent to market. There is so much milk out of my dairy, and the press must stand still: but I won't lose a cheese pairing; and the milk shall be made good, if the sarvents should go without butter. If they must needs have butter, let them make it of sheep's milk; but then my wool will suffer for want of grace; so that I must be a loser on all sides—— Well, patience is like a stout Welsh poney; it bears a great deal, and trots a great way; but it will tire at the long run. Before its long, perhaps I may shew Matt, that I was not born to be the household drudge to my dying day—Gwyn rites from Crickhowel, that the price of flannel is fallen three-farthings an ell; and that's another good penny out of my pocket—When I go to market to sell, my commodity stinks; but when I want to buy the commonest thing, the owner pricks it up under my nose; and it can't be had for love nor money—I think every thing runs cross at Brambleton hall—You say the gander has broke the eggs; which is a phinumenon I don't understand: for when the fox carried off the old goose last year, he took her place, and hatched the eggs, and partected the goslings like a tender parent—Then you tell me the thunder has soured two barrels of beer in the seller. But how the thunder should get there, when the seller was double-locked, I can't comprehend. Howsomever, I won't have the beer thrown out, till I see it with my own eyes. Perhaps, it will recover——At least it will serve for vinegar to the sarvents.——You may leave off the fires in my brother's chamber and mine, as it is unsartain when we return.————I hope, Gwyllim, you'll take care there is no waste; and have an eye to the maids, and keep them to their spinning. I think they may go very well without beer in hot weather——it serves only to inflame the blood, and set them a-gog after the men. Water will make them fair and keep them cool and tamperit. Don't forget to put up in the portmantel, that cums with Williams, along with my riding-habit, hat, and feather, the viol of purl water, and the tincktur for my stomach; being as how I am much troubled with flutterencies. This is all at present, from

Yours,
TABITHA BRAMBLE.

BATH, *April* 26.

To Dr. Lewis

DEAR DICK,
    I have done with the waters; therefore your advice comes a day too late——I grant that physic is no mystery of your making. I know it is a mystery in its own nature; and, like other mysteries, requires a strong gulp of faith to make it go down——Two days ago, I went into the King's Bath, by the advice of our friend Ch————, in order to clear the strainer of the skin, for the benefit of a free perspiration; and the first object that saluted my eye, was a child full of scrophulous ulcers, carried in the arms of one of the guides, under the very noses of the bathers. I was so shocked at the sight that I retired immediately with indignation and disgust ——Suppose the matter of those ulcers, floating on the water, comes in contact with my skin, when the pores are all open,

I would ask you what must be the consequence?———Good Heaven, the very thought makes my blood run cold! we know not what sores may be running into the water while we are bathing, and what sort of matter we may thus imbibe; the king's-evil, the scurvy, the cancer, and the pox; and, no doubt, the heat will render the *virus* the more volatile and penetrating. To purify myself from all such contamination, I went to the duke of Kingston's private Bath, and there I was almost suffocated for want of free air; the place was so small, and the steam so stifling.

After all, if the intention is no more than to wash the skin, I am convinced that simple element is more effectual than any water impregnated with salt and iron; which, being astringent, will certainly contract the pores, and leave a kind of crust upon the surface of the body. But I am now as much afraid of drinking, as of bathing; for, after a long conversation with the Doctor, about the construction of the pump and the cistern, it is very far from being clear with me, that the patients in the Pump-room don't swallow the scourings of the bathers. I can't help suspecting, that there is, or may be, some regurgitation from the bath into the cistern of the pump. In that case, what a delicate beveridge is every day quaffed by the drinkers; medicated with the sweat and dirt, and dandriff; and the abominable discharges of various kinds, from twenty different diseased bodies, parboiling in the kettle below. In order to avoid this filthy composition, I had recourse to the spring that supplies the private baths on the Abbey-green; but I at once perceived something extraordinary in the taste and smell; and, upon inquiry, I find that the Roman baths in this quarter, were found covered by an old burying ground, belonging to the Abbey; through which, in all probability, the water drains in its passage; so that as we drink the decoction of living bodies at the Pump-room, we swallow the strainings of rotten bones and carcasses at the private bath—I vow to God, the very idea turns my stomach!—Determined, as I

am, against any farther use of the Bath waters, this consideration would give me little disturbance, if I could find
any thing more pure, or less pernicious, to quench my thirst;
but, although the natural springs of excellent water are
seen gushing spontaneous on every side, from the hills that
surround us, the inhabitants, in general, make use of well-
water, so impregnated with nitre, or alum, or some other
villainous mineral, that it is equally ungrateful to the taste,
and mischievous to the constitution. It must be owned, indeed, that here, in Milsham-street, we have a precarious and
scanty supply from the hill; which is collected in an open
bason in the Circus, liable to be defiled with dead dogs, cats,
rats, and every species of nastiness, which the rascally populace may throw into it, from mere wantonness and brutality.———

Well, there is no nation that drinks so hoggishly as the
English———What passes for wine among us, is not the
juice of the grape. It is an adulterous mixture, brewed up
of nauseous ingredients, by dunces, who are bunglers in the
art of poison-making; and yet we, and our forefathers, are
and have been poisoned by this cursed drench, without taste
or flavour—The only genuine and wholesome beveridge in
England, is London porter, and Dorchester table-beer; but
as for your ale and your gin, your cyder and your perry,
and all the trashy family of made wines, I detest them as
infernal compositions, contrived for the destruction of the
human species.———But what have I to do with the human
species? except a very few friends, I care not if the whole
was———.

Heark ye, Lewis, my misanthropy increases every day—
The longer I live, I find the folly and the fraud of mankind grow more and more intolerable—I wish I had not
come from Brambleton-hall; after having lived in solitude
so long, I cannot bear the hurry and impertinence of the
multitude; besides, every thing is sophisticated in these
crowded places. Snares are laid for our lives in every thing

we eat or drink: the very air we breathe, is loaded with contagion. We cannot even sleep, without risque of infection. I say, infection—This place is the rendezvous of the diseased—You won't deny, that many diseases are infectious; even the consumption itself, is highly infectious. When a person dies of it in Italy, the bed and bedding are destroyed; the other furniture is exposed to the weather and the apartment whitewashed, before it is occupied by any other living soul. You'll allow, that nothing receives infection sooner, or retains it longer, than blankets, feather-beds, and matrasses—'Sdeath! how do I know what miserable objects have been stewing in the bed where I now lie!—I wonder, Dick, you did not put me in mind of sending for my own matrasses—But, if I had not been an ass, I should not have needed a remembrancer——There is always some plaguy reflection that rises up in judgment against me, and ruffles my spirits—Therefore, let us change the subject.

I have other reasons for abridging my stay at Bath—You know sister Tabby's complexion—If Mrs. Tabitha Bramble had been of any other race I should certainly have considered her as the most —But, the truth is, she has found means to interest my affection; or, rather, she is beholden to the force of prejudice, commonly called the ties of blood. Well, this amiable maiden has actually commenced a flirting correspondence with an Irish baronet of sixty-five. His name is Sir Ulic Mackilligut. He is said to be much out at elbows; and, I believe, has received false intelligence with respect to her fortune. Be that as it may, the connexion is exceedingly ridiculous, and begins already to excite whispers. For my part, I have no intention to dispute her free-agency; though I shall fall upon some expedient to undeceive her paramour, as to the point which he has principally in view. But I don't think her conduct is a proper example for Liddy, who has also attracted the notice of some coxcombs in the Rooms; and Jery tells me, he suspects a strapping fellow, the knight's nephew, of some design upon the girl's heart. I shall, therefore, keep a strict eye over her aunt and her, and even shift the scene, if I find the matter grow more serious—You perceive what an agreeable task it must be, to a man of my kidney, to have the cure of such souls as these.—But, hold, you shall not have another peevish word (till the next occasion) from

Yours,

BATH, *April* 28.   MATT. BRAMBLE.

To Sir Watkin Phillips, of Jesus college, Oxon.

DEAR KNIGHT,
    I think those people are unreasonable, who complain that Bath is a contracted circle, in which the same dull scenes perpetually revolve, without variation—I am, on the contrary, amazed to find so small a place so crowded with entertainment and variety. London itself can hardly exhibit one species of diversion, to which we have not something analogous at Bath, over and above those singular advantages that are peculiar to the place. Here, for example, a man has daily opportunities of seeing the most remarkable characters of the community. He sees them in their natural attitudes and true colours; descended from their pedestals, and divested of their formal draperies, undisguised by art and affectation—Here we have ministers of state, judges, generals, bishops, projectors, philosophers, wits, poets, players, *chemists, fiddlers,* and *buffoons.* If he makes any considerable stay in the place, he is sure of meeting with some particular friend, whom he did not expect to see; and to me there is nothing more agreeable than such casual rencounters —Another entertainment, peculiar to Bath, arises from the general mixture of all degrees assembled in our public rooms, without distinction of rank or fortune. This is what my uncle reprobates, as a monstrous jumble of heterogeneous principles; a vile mob of noise and impertinence, without

decency or subordination. But this chaos is to me a source
of infinite amusement.

I was extremely diverted last ball-night to see the Master
of the Ceremonies leading, with great solemnity, to the
upper end of the room, an antiquated Abigail, dressed in her
lady's cast-clothes; whom he (I suppose) mistook for some
countess just arrived at the Bath. The ball was opened by a
Scotch lord, with a mulatto heiress from St. Christopher's;
and the gay colonel Tinsel danced all the evening with the
daughter of an eminent tinman from the borough of South-
wark—Yesterday morning, at the Pump-room, I saw a
broken-winded Wapping landlady squeeze through a circle
of peers, to salute her brandy-merchant, who stood by the
window, propped upon crutches; and a paralytic attorney
of Shoe-lane, in shuffling up to the bar, kicked the shins of
the chancellor of England, while his lordship, in a cut-bob,
drank a glass of water at the pump. I cannot account for
my being pleased with these incidents, any other way, than
by saying they are truly ridiculous in their own nature, and
serve to heighten the humour in the farce of life, which I
am determined to enjoy as long as I can.

Those follies, that move my uncle's spleen, excite my
laughter. He is as tender as a man without a skin; who
cannot bear the slightest touch without flinching. What
tickles another would give him torment; and yet he has
what we may call lucid intervals, when he is remarkably
facetious—Indeed, I never knew a hypochondriac so apt to
be infected with good-humour. He is the most risible misan-
thrope I ever met with. A lucky joke, or any ludicrous
incident, will set him a-laughing immoderately, even in one
of his most gloomy paroxysms; and, when the laugh is over,
he will curse his own imbecility. In conversing with strangers, he betrays no marks of disquiet—He is splenetic with
his familiars only; and not even with them, while they keep
his attention employed; but when his spirits are not exerted
externally, they seem to recoil and prey upon himself——He

has renounced the waters with execration; but he begins to find a more efficacious, and, certainly, a much more palatable remedy in the pleasures of society. He has discovered some old friends, among the invalids of Bath; and, in particular, renewed his acquaintance with the celebrated James Quin, who certainly did not come here to drink water. You cannot doubt, but that I had the strongest curiosity to know this original; and it was gratified by Mr. Bramble, who has had him twice at our house to dinner.

So far as I am able to judge, Quin's character is rather more respectable than it has been generally represented. His *bon mots* are in every witling's mouth; but many of them have a rank flavour, which one would be apt to think was derived from a natural grossness of idea. I suspect, however, that justice has not been done the author, by the collectors of those *Quiniana;* who have let the best of them slip through their fingers, and only retained such as were suited to the taste and organs of the multitude. How far he may relax in his hours of jollity, I cannot pretend to say; but his general conversation is conducted by the nicest rules of propriety; and Mr. James Quin is, certainly, one of the best bred men in the kingdom. He is not only a most agreeable companion; but (as I am credibly informed) a very honest man; highly susceptible of friendship, warm, steady, and even generous in his attachments, disdaining flattery, and incapable of meanness and dissimulation. Were I to judge, however, from Quin's eye alone, I should take him to be proud, insolent, and cruel. There is something remarkably severe and forbidding in his aspect; and, I have been told, he was ever disposed to insult his inferiors and dependants. ——Perhaps that report has influenced my opinion of his looks——You know we are the fools of prejudice. Howsoever that may be, I have as yet seen nothing but his favour able side, and my uncle, who frequently confers with him. in a corner, declares he is one of the most sensible men he ever knew——He seems to have a reciprocal regard for old

Squaretoes, whom he calls by the familiar name of Matthew, and often reminds of their old tavern-adventures: on
the other hand, Matthew's eyes sparkle whenever Quin
makes his appearance—Let him be never so jarring and
discordant, Quin puts him in tune; and, like treble and
bass in the same concert, they make excellent music together—T'other day, the conversation turning upon Shakespeare, I could not help saying, with some emotion, that I
would give an hundred guineas to see Mr. Quin act the
part of Falstaff; upon which, turning to me with a smile,
'And I would give a thousand, young gentleman (said he)
that I could gratify your longing.' My uncle and he are
perfectly agreed in their estimate of life; which Quin says,
would stink in his nostrils, if he did not steep it in claret.

I want to see this phenomenon in his cups; and have
almost prevailed upon uncle to give him a small turtle at
the Bear. In the mean time, I must entertain you with an
incident, that seems to confirm the judgment of those two
cynic philosophers. I took the liberty to differ in opinion from
Mr. Bramble, when he observed, that the mixture of people
in the entertainments of this place was destructive of all
order and urbanity; that it rendered the plebeians insuffer-
ably arrogant and troublesome, and vulgarized the deportment and sentiments of those who moved in the upper
spheres of life. He said such a preposterous coalition would
bring us into contempt with all our neighbours; and was
worse, in fact, than debasing the gold coin of the nation.
I argued, on the contrary, that those plebeians who discovered such eagerness to imitate the dress and equipage of
their superiors, would likewise, in time, adopt their maxims
and their manners, be polished by their conversation, and
refined by their example; but when I appealed to Mr. Quin,
and asked if he did not think that such an unreserved mixture would improve the whole mass?—'Yes (said he) as
a plate of marmalade would improve a pan of sirreverence.'

I owned I was not much conversant in high-life, but I

had seen what were called polite assemblies in London and elsewhere; that those of Bath seemed to be as decent as any; and that, upon the whole, the individuals that composed it, would not be found deficient in good manners and decorum. 'But let us have recourse to experience (said I)— Jack Holder, who was intended for a parson, has succeeded to an estate of two thousand a year, by the death of his elder brother. He is now at the Bath, driving about in a phaeton and four, with French horns. He has treated with turtle and claret at all the taverns in Bath and Bristol, till his guests are gorged with good chear: he has bought a dozen suits of fine clothes, by the advice of the Master of the ceremonies, under whose tuition he has entered himself: he has lost hundreds at billiards to sharpers, and taken one of the nymphs of Avon-street into keeping; but, finding all these channels insufficient to drain him of his current cash, his counsellor has engaged him to give a general tea-drinking to-morrow at Wiltshire's room. In order to give it the more eclat, every table is to be furnished with sweet-meats and nosegays; which, however, are not to be touched till notice is given by the ringing of a bell, and then the ladies may help themselves without restriction. This will be no bad way of trying the company's breeding.'

'I will abide by that experiment (cried my uncle) and if I could find a place to stand secure, without the vortex of the tumult, which I know will ensue, I would certainly go thither and enjoy the scene.' Quin proposed that we should take our station in the music-gallery, and we took his advice. Holder had got thither before us, with his horns perdue, but we were admitted. The tea-drinking passed as usual, and the company having risen from the tables, were sauntering in groupes, in expectation of the signal for attack, when the bell beginning to ring, they flew with eagerness to the desert, and the whole place was instantly in commotion. There was nothing but justling, scrambling, pulling, snatching, strug-

gling, scolding, and screaming. The nosegays were torn
from one another's hands and bosoms; the glasses and china
went to wreck; the tables and floors were strewed with
comfits. Some cried; some swore; and the tropes and figures
of Billingsgate were used without reserve in all their native
zest and flavour; nor were those flowers of rhetoric unat-
tended with significant gesticulation. Some snapped their
fingers; some forked them out; some clapped their hands,
and some their back-sides; at length, they fairly proceeded
to pulling caps, and every thing seemed to presage a general
battle; when Holder ordered his horns to sound a charge,
with a view to animate the combatants, and inflame
the contest; but this manœuvre produced an effect quite
contrary to what he expected. It was a note of reproach that
roused them to an immediate sense of their disgraceful
situation. They were ashamed of their absurd deportment,
and suddenly desisted. They gathered up their caps, ruffles,
and handkerchiefs; and great part of them retired in silent
mortification.

Quin laughed at this adventure; but my uncle's delicacy
was hurt. He hung his head in manifest chagrin, and seemed
to repine at the triumph of his judgment—Indeed, his victory was more complete than he imagined; for, as we afterwards learned, the two amazons who singularised themselves most in the action, did not come from the purlieus
of Puddledock, but from the courtly neighbourhood of St.
James's palace. One was a baroness, and the other, a wealthy
knight's dowager—My uncle spoke not a word, till we had
made our retreat good to the coffee-house; where, taking
off his hat and wiping his forehead, 'I bless God (said he)
that Mrs. Tabitha Bramble did not take the field to-day!'
'I would pit her for a cool hundred (cried Quin) against
the best shake-bag of the whole main.' The truth is, nothing
could have kept her at home but the accident of her having
taken physic before she knew the nature of the entertainment. She has been for some days furbishing up an old suit

of black velvet, to make her appearance as Sir Ulic's partner at the next ball.

I have much to say of this amiable kinswoman; but she has not been properly introduced to your acquaintance. She is remarkably civil to Mr. Quin; of whose sarcastic humour she seems to stand in awe; but her caution is no match for her impertinence. 'Mr. Gwynn (said she the other day) I was once vastly entertained with your playing the Ghost of Gimlet at Drury-lane, when you rose up through the stage, with a white face and red eyes, and spoke of *quails upon the frightful porcofine*—Do, pray, spout a little the Ghost of Gimlet.' 'Madam (said Quin, with a glance of ineffable disdain) the Ghost of Gimlet is laid, never to rise again'——Insensible of this check, she proceeded: 'Well, to be sure, you looked and talked so like a real ghost; and then the cock crowed so natural. I wonder how you could teach him to crow so exact, in the very nick of time; but, I suppose, he's game——An't he game, Mr. Gwynn?' 'Dunghill, madam.'—'Well, dunghill, or not dunghill, he has got such a clear counter-tenor, that I wish I had such another at Brambleton-hall, to wake the maids of a morning. Do you know where I could find one of his brood?' 'Probably in the work-house at St. Giles's parish, madam; but I protest I know not his particular mew.' My uncle, frying with vexation, cried, 'Good God, sister, how you talk! I have told you twenty times, that this gentleman's name is not Gwynn.'——'Hoity toity, brother mine (she replied) no offence, I hope—Gwynn is an honourable name, of true old British extraction————I thought the gentleman had been come of Mrs. Helen Gwynn, who was of his own profession; and if so be that were the case, he might be of king Charles's breed, and have royal blood in his veins.'————'No, madam (answered Quin, with great solemnity) my mother was not a whore of such distinction ——True it is, I am sometimes tempted to believe myself of royal descent; for my inclinations are often arbitrary

—If I was an absolute prince, at this instant, I believe I should send for the head of your cook in a charger——She had committed felony, on the person of that John Dory, which is mangled in a cruel manner, and even presented without sauce——*O tempora! O mores!*'

This good-humoured sally turned the conversation into a less disagreeable channel——But, lest you should think my scribble as tedious as Mrs. Tabby's clack, I shall not add another word, but that I am as usual

Yours,

J. MELFORD.

BATH, *April* 30.

To Dr. Lewis

DEAR LEWIS,

I received your bill upon Wiltshire, which was punctually honoured; but as I don't choose to keep so much cash by me, in a common lodging house, I have deposited 250*l.* in the bank of Bath, and shall take their bills for it in London, when I leave this place, where the season draws to an end——You must know, that now being a-foot, I am resolved to give Liddy a glimpse of London. She is one of the best hearted creatures I ever knew, and gains upon my affection every day——As for Tabby, I have dropt such hints to the Irish baronet, concerning her fortune, as, I make no doubt, will cool the ardour of his addresses. Then her pride will take the alarm; and the rancour of stale maidenhood being chafed, we shall hear nothing but slander and abuse of Sir Ulic Mackilligut——This rupture, I foresee, will facilitate our departure from Bath; where, at present, Tabby seems to enjoy herself with peculiar satisfaction. For my part, I detest it so much, that I should not have been able to stay so long in the place if I had not discovered some old friends; whose conversation alleviates my disgust ——Going to the coffeehouse one forenoon, I could not help contemplating the company, with equal surprize and compassion.———We consisted of thirteen individuals; seven lamed by the gout, rheumatism, or palsy; three maimed by accident; and the rest either deaf or blind. One hobbled, another hopped, a third dragged his legs after him like a wounded snake, a fourth straddled betwixt a pair of long crutches, like the mummy of a felon hanging in chains; a fifth was bent into a horizontal position, like a mounted telescope, shoved in by a couple of chairmen; and a sixth was the bust of a man, set upright in a wheel machine, which the waiter moved from place to place.

Being struck with some of their faces, I consulted the subscription-book; and, perceiving the names of several old friends, began to consider the groupe with more attention. At length I discovered rear-admiral Balderick, the companion of my youth, whom I had not seen since he was appointed lieutenant of the Severn. He was metamorphosed into an old man, with a wooden leg and a weatherbeaten face, which appeared the more ancient from his grey locks, that were truly venerable—Sitting down at the table, where he was reading a news-paper, I gazed at him for some minutes, with a mixture of pleasure and regret, which made my heart gush with tenderness; then, taking him by the hand, 'Ah, Sam (said I) forty years ago I little thought'— I was too much moved to proceed. 'An old friend, sure enough! (cried he, squeezing my hand, and surveying me eagerly through his glasses) I know the looming of the vessel, though she has been hard strained since we parted; but I can't heave up the name'———The moment I told him who I was, he exclaimed, 'Ha! Matt, my old fellow cruizer, still afloat!' And, starting up, hugged me in his arms. His transport, however, boded me no good; for, in saluting me, he thrust the spring of his spectacles into my eye, and, at the same time, set his wooden stump upon my gouty toe; an attack that made me shed tears in sad earnest ———After the hurry of our recognition was over, he pointed out two of our common friends in the room: the bust was what remained of colonel Cockril, who had lost the use of his limbs in making an American campaign; and the telescope proved to be my college chum, sir Reginald Bently; who, with his new title, and unexpected inheritance, commenced fox-hunter, without having served his apprenticeship to the mystery; and, in consequence of following the hounds through a river, was seized with an inflammation of his bowels, which has contracted him into his present attitude.

Our former correspondence was forthwith renewed, with the most hearty expressions of mutual good-will, and as we had met so unexpectedly, we agreed to dine together that very day at the tavern. My friend Quin, being luckily unengaged, obliged us with his company; and, truly, this was the most happy day I have passed these twenty years. You and I, Lewis, having been always together, never tasted friendship in this high goût, contracted from long absence. I cannot express the half of what I felt at this casual meeting of three or four companions, who had been so long separated, and so roughly treated by the storms of life. It was a renovation of youth; a kind of resuscitation of the dead, that realized those interesting dreams, in which we sometimes retrieve our ancient friends from the grave. Perhaps my enjoyment was not the less pleasing for being mixed with a strain of melancholy, produced by the remembrance of past scenes, that conjured up the ideas of some endearing connexions, which the hand of Death has actually dissolved.

The spirits and good humour of the company seemed to triumph over the wreck of their constitutions. They had even philosophy enough to joke upon their own calamities; such is the power of friendship, the sovereign cordial of life—I afterwards found, however, that they were not without their moments, and even hours, of disquiet. Each of them apart, in succeeding conferences, expatiated upon his own particular grievances; and they were all male-contents at bottom—Over and above their personal disasters, they thought themselves unfortunate in the lottery of life. Balderick complained, that all the recompence he had received for his long and hard service, was the half-pay of a rear-admiral. The colonel was mortified to see himself over-topped by upstart generals, some of whom he had once commanded; and, being a man of a liberal turn, could ill put up with a moderate annuity, for which he had sold his commission. As for the baronet, having run himself considerably in debt, on a contested election, he has been obliged to relinquish his seat in parliament, and his seat in the country at the same time, and put his estate to nurse; but his chagrin, which is the effect of his own misconduct, does not affect me half so much as that of the other two, who have acted honourable and distinguished parts on the great theatre, and are now reduced to lead a weary life in this stew-pan of idleness and insignificance. They have long left off using the waters, after having experienced their inefficacy. The diversions of the place they are not in a condition to enjoy. How then do they make shift to pass their time? In the forenoon, they crawl out to the Rooms or the coffeehouse, where they take a hand at whist, or descant upon the General Advertiser; and their evenings they murder in private parties, among peevish invalids, and insipid old women—This is the case with a good number of individuals, whom nature seems to have intended for better purposes.

About a dozen years ago, many decent families, restricted to small fortunes, besides those that came hither on the score of health, were tempted to settle at Bath, where they could then live comfortably, and even make a genteel appearance, at a small expence: but the madness of the times has made the place too hot for them, and they are now obliged to think of other migrations—Some have already fled to the mountains of Wales, and others have retired to Exeter. Thither, no doubt, they will be followed by the flood of

luxury and extravagance, which will drive them from place
to place to the very Land's End; and there, I suppose, they
will be obliged to ship themselves to some other country.
Bath is become a mere sink of profligacy and extortion.
Every article of house-keeping is raised to an enormous
price; a circumstance no longer to be wondered at, when
we know that every petty retainer of fortune piques himself upon keeping a table, and thinks it is for the honour
of his character to wink at the knavery of his servants, who
are in a confederacy with the market-people; and, of consequence, pay whatever they demand. Here is now a mush-
room of opulence, who pays a cook seventy guineas a week
for furnishing him with one meal a day. This portentous
frenzy is become so contagious, that the very rabble and
refuse of mankind are infected. I have known a negro-
driver, from Jamaica, pay over-night, to the master of one
of the rooms, sixty-five guineas for tea and coffee to the
company, and leave Bath next morning, in such obscurity,
that not one of his guests had the slightest idea of his person, or even made the least inquiry about his name. Incidents of this kind are frequent; and every day teems with
fresh absurdities, which are too gross to make a thinking
man merry——But I feel the spleen creeping on me
apace; and therefore will indulge you with a cessation,
that you may have no unnecessary cause to curse your correspondence with,

Dear Dick,

Yours ever,

MAT. BRAMBLE.

BATH, *May* 5.

To Miss Lœtitia Willis, at Gloucester

MY DEAR LETTY,

I wrote you at great length by the post, the twenty-
sixth of last month, to which I refer you for an account

of our proceedings at Bath; and I expect your answer with impatience. But, having this opportunity of a private hand, I send you two dozen of Bath rings; six of the best of which I desire you will keep for yourself, and distribute the rest among the young ladies, our common friends, as you shall think proper——I don't know how you will approve of the mottoes; some of them are not much to my own liking; but I was obliged to take such as I could find ready manufactured—I am vexed, that neither you nor I have received any further information of a certain person—Sure it cannot be wilful neglect!—O my dear Willis! I begin to be visited by strange fancies, and to have some melancholy doubts; which, however, it would be ungenerous to harbour without further inquiry—My uncle, who has made me a present of a very fine set of garnets, talks of treating us with a jaunt to London; which, you may imagine, will be highly agreeable; but I like Bath so well, that I hope he won't think of leaving it till the season is quite over; and yet, betwixt friends, something has happened to my aunt, which will probably shorten our stay in this place.

Yesterday, in the forenoon, she went by herself to a breakfasting in one of the rooms; and, in half an hour, returned in great agitation, having Chowder along with her in the chair. I believe some accident must have happened to that unlucky animal, which is the great source of all her troubles. Dear Letty! what a pity it is, that a woman of her years and discretion, should place her affection upon such an ugly, ill-conditioned cur, that snarls and snaps at every body. I asked John Thomas, the footman who attended her, what was the matter? and he did nothing but grin. A famous dog-doctor was sent for, and undertook to cure the patient, provided he might carry him home to his own house; but his mistress would not part with him out of her own sight——She ordered the cook to warm cloths, which she applied to his bowels, with her own hand. She gave up all thoughts of going to the ball in the evening; and when Sir Ulic came to drink tea, refused to be seen; so that he went away to look for another partner. My brother Jery whistles and dances. My uncle sometimes shrugs up his shoulders, and sometimes bursts out a-laughing. My aunt sobs and scolds by turns; and her woman, Win. Jenkins, stares and wonders with a foolish face of curiosity; and, for my part, I am as curious as she, but ashamed to ask questions.

Perhaps time will discover the mystery; for if it was any thing that happened in the Rooms, it cannot be long concealed—All I know is, that last night at supper, miss Bramble spoke very disdainfully of Sir Ulic Mackilligut, and asked her brother if he intended to keep us sweltering all the summer at Bath? 'No, sister Tabitha (said he, with an arch smile) we shall retreat before the Dog-days begin; though I make no doubt, that with a little temperance and discretion, our constitutions might be kept cool enough all the year, even at Bath.' As I don't know the meaning of this insinuation, I won't pretend to make any remarks upon it at present; hereafter, perhaps, I may be able to explain it more to your satisfaction——In the mean time, I beg you will be punctual in your correspondence, and continue to love your ever faithful

LYDIA MELFORD.

BATH, *May* 6.

To Sir Watkin Phillips, of Jesus college, Oxon.

So then Mrs. Blackerby's affair has proved a false alarm, and I have saved my money? I wish, however, her declaration had not been so premature; for though my being thought capable of making her a mother, might have given me some credit, the reputation of an intrigue with such a cracked pitcher does me no honour at all——In my last I

told you I had hopes of seeing Quin, in his hours of elevation at the tavern which is the temple of mirth and good
fellowship; where he, as priest of Comus, utters the inspira-
tions of wit and humour——I have had that satisfaction.
I have dined with his club at the Three Tuns, and had the
honour to sit him out. At half an hour past eight in the
evening, he was carried home with six good bottles of
claret under his belt; and it being then Friday, he gave
orders that he should not be disturbed till Sunday at noon
——You must not imagine that this dose had any other
effect upon his conversation, but that of making it more
extravagantly entertaining—He had lost the use of his
limbs, indeed, several hours before we parted, but he retained
all his other faculties in perfection; and as he gave vent to
every whimsical idea as it rose, I was really astonished at
the brilliancy of his thoughts, and the force of his expression. Quin is a real voluptuary in the articles of eating and
drinking; and so confirmed an epicure, in the common acceptation of the term, that he cannot put up with ordinary
fare. This is a point of such importance with him, that
he always takes upon himself the charge of catering; and a
man admitted to his mess, is always sure of eating delicate
victuals, and drinking excellent wine—He owns himself
addicted to the delights of the stomach, and often jokes
upon his own sensuality; but there is nothing selfish in
this appetite——He finds that good chear unites good company, exhilerates the spirits, opens the heart, banishes all
restraint from conversation, and promotes the happiest purposes of social life.—But Mr. James Quin is not a subject
to be discussed in the compass of one letter; I shall therefore, at present, leave him to his repose, and call another of
a very different complexion.

You desire to have further acquaintance with the person
of our aunt, and promise yourself much entertainment from
her connexion with Sir Ulic Mackilligut: but in this hope
you are baulked already; that connexion is dissolved. The

Irish baronet is an old hound, that, finding her carrion, has quitted the scent.—I have already told you, that Mrs. Tabitha Bramble is a maiden of forty-five. In her person, she is tall, raw-boned, aukward, flat-chested, and stooping; her complexion is sallow and freckled; her eyes are not grey, but greenish, like those of a cat, and generally inflamed; her hair is of a sandy, or rather dusty hue; her forehead low; her nose long, sharp, and, towards the extremity, always red in cool weather; her lips skinny, her mouth extensive, her teeth straggling and loose, of various colours and conformation; and her long neck shrivelled into a thousand wrinkles—In her temper, she is proud, stiff, vain, imperious, prying, malicious, greedy, and uncharitable. In all likelihood, her natural austerity has been soured by disappointment in love; for her long celibacy is by no means owing to her dislike of matrimony: on the contrary, she has left no stone unturned to avoid the reproachful epithet of old maid.

Before I was born, she had gone such lengths in the way of flirting with a recruiting officer, that her reputation was a little singed. She afterwards made advances to the curate of the parish, who dropped some distant hints about the next presentation to the living, which was in her brother's gift; but finding that was already promised to another, he flew off at a tangent; and Mrs. Tabby, in revenge, found means to deprive him of his cure. Her next lover was lieu-tenant of a man of war, a relation of the family, who did not understand the refinements of the passion, and expressed no aversion to grapple with cousin Tabby in the way of marriage; but before matters could be properly adjusted, he went out on a cruise, and was killed in an engagement with a French frigate. Our aunt, though baffled so often, did not yet despair—She layed all her snares for Dr. Lewis, who is the *fidus Achates* of my uncle. She even fell sick upon the occasion, and prevailed with Matt to interpose in her behalf with his friend; but the Doctor, being a shy cock, would not be caught with chaff, and flatly rejected the proposal: so that Mrs. Tabitha was content to exert her patience once more, after having endeavoured in vain to effect a rupture betwixt the two friends; and now she thinks proper to be very civil to Lewis, who is become necessary to her in the way of his profession.

These, however, are not the only efforts she has made towards a nearer conjunction with our sex. Her fortune was originally no more than a thousand pounds; but she gained an accession of five hundred by the death of a sister, and the lieutenant left her three hundred in his will. These sums she has more than doubled, by living free of all expence, in her brother's house; and dealing in cheese and Welsh flannel, the produce of his flocks and dairy. At present her capital is increased to about four thousand pounds; and her avarice seems to grow every day more and more rapacious: but even this is not so intolerable as the perverseness of her nature, which keeps the whole family in disquiet and uproar. She is one of those geniuses who find some diabolical enjoyment in being dreaded and detested by their fellow-creatures.

I once told my uncle, I was surprised that a man of his disposition could bear such a domestic plague, when it could be so easily removed—The remark made him sore, because it seemed to tax him with want of resolution— Wrinkling up his nose, and drawing down his eye-brows, 'A young fellow (said he) when he first thrusts his snout into the world, is apt to be surprised at many things which a man of experience knows to be ordinary and unavoidable —This precious aunt of yours is become insensibly a part of my constitution—Damn her! She's a *noli me tangere* in my flesh, which I cannot bear to be touched or tampered with.' I made no reply; but shifted the conversation. He really has an affection for this original; which maintains its ground in defiance of common sense, and in despite of that contempt which he must certainly feel for her character and understanding. Nay, I am convinced, that she has likewise a most virulent attachment to his person; though her love never shews itself but in the shape of discontent; and she persists in tormenting him out of pure tenderness— The only object within doors upon which she bestows any marks of affection, in the usual stile, is her dog Chowder; a filthy cur from Newfoundland, which she had in a present from the wife of a skipper in Swansey—One would imagine she had distinguished this beast with her favour on account of his ugliness and ill-nature, if it was not, indeed, an instinctive sympathy, between his disposition and her own. Certain it is she caresses him without ceasing; and even harrasses the family in the service of this cursed animal, which, indeed, has proved the proximate cause of her breach with Sir Ulic Mackilligut.

You must know, she yesterday wanted to steal a march of poor Liddy, and went to breakfast in the Room without any other companion than her dog, in expectation of meeting with the Baronet, who had agreed to dance with her in the evening—Chowder no sooner made his appearance in the Room, than the Master of the Ceremonies, incensed at his presumption, ran up to drive him away, and threatened him with his foot; but the other seemed to despise his authority, and displaying a formidable case of long, white, sharp teeth, kept the puny monarch at bay—While he stood under some trepidation, fronting his antagonist, and bawling to the waiter, Sir Ulic Mackilligut came to his assistance; and seeming ignorant of the connexion between this intruder and his mistress, gave the former such a kick in the jaws, as sent him howling to the door——Mrs. Tabitha, incensed at this outrage, ran after him, squalling in a tone equally disagreeable; while the Baronet followed her on one side, making apologies for his mistake; and Derrick on the other, making remonstrances upon the rules and regulations of the place.

Far from being satisfied with the Knight's excuses, she

aid she was sure he was no gentleman; and when the Master of the Ceremonies offered to hand her into the chair, she rapped him over the knuckles with her fan. My uncle's footman being still at the door, she and Chowder got into the same vehicle, and were carried off amidst the jokes of the chairmen and other populace——I had been riding out on Clerkendown, and happened to enter just as the *fracas* was over—The Baronet, coming up to me with an affected air of chagrin, recounted the adventure; at which I laughed heartily, and then his countenance cleared up. 'My dear soul (said he) when I saw a sort of a wild baist, snarling with open mouth at the Master of the Ceremonies, like the red cow going to devour Tom Thumb, I could do no less than go to the assistance of the little man; but I never dreamt the baist was one of Mrs. Bramble's attendants—— O! if I had, he might have made his breakfast upon Derrick and welcome—But you know, my dear friend, how natural it is for us Irishmen to blunder, and to take the wrong sow by the ear—However, I will confess judgment, and cry her mercy; and it is to be hoped, a penitent sinner may be for given.' I told him, that as the offence was not involuntary of his side, it was to be hoped he would not find her implacable.

But, in truth, all this concern was dissembled. In his approaches of gallantry to Mrs. Tabitha, he had been misled by a mistake of at least six thousand pounds, in the calculation of her fortune; and in this particular he was just undeceived. He, therefore, seized the first opportunity of incurring her displeasure decently, in such a manner as would certainly annihilate the correspondence; and he could not have taken a more effectual method, than that of beating her dog. When he presented himself at our door, to pay his respects to the offended fair, he was refused admittance, and given to understand that he should never find her at home for the future. She was not so inaccessible to Derrick, who came to demand satisfaction for the insult she had offered to him, even in the verge of his own court. She knew it was convenient to be well with the Master of the Ceremonies, while she continued to frequent the Rooms; and, having heard he was a poet, began to be afraid of making her appearance in a ballad or lampoon—She therefore made excuses for what she had done, imputing it to the flutter of her spirits; and subscribed handsomely for his poems: so that he was perfectly appeased, and overwhelmed her with a profusion of compliment. He even solicited a reconciliation with Chowder; which, however, the latter declined; and he declared, that if he could find a precedent in the annals of the Bath, which he would carefully examine for that purpose, her favourite should be admitted to the next public breakfasting—But, I believe, she will not expose herself or him to the risque of a second disgrace—Who will supply the place of Mackilligut in her affections, I cannot foresee; but nothing in the shape of man can come amiss. Though she is a violent church-woman, of the most intolerant zeal, I believe in my conscience she would have no objection, at present, to treat on the score of matrimony with an Anabaptist, Quaker, or Jew; and even ratify the treaty at the expence of her own conversion. But, perhaps, I think too hardly of this kinswoman; who, I must own, is very little beholden to the good opinion of

Yours,

J. MELFORD.

BATH, *May* 6.

To Dr. Lewis

You ask me, why I don't take the air a-horseback, during this fine weather?—In which of the avenues of this paradise would you have me take that exercise? Shall I commit myself to the high-roads of London or Bristol, to be stifled with dust, or pressed to death in the midst of post-chaises, flying-machines, waggons, and coal-horses; besides the troops of fine gentlemen that take to the high-way, to shew their horsemanship; and the coaches of fine ladies, who go thither to shew their equipages? Shall I attempt the Downs, and fatigue myself to death in climbing up an eternal ascent, without any hopes of reaching the summit? Know then, I have made divers desperate leaps at those upper regions; but always fell backward into this vapour-pit, exhausted and dispirited by those ineffectual efforts; and here we poor vale-tudinarians pant and struggle, like so many Chinese gudgeons, gasping in the bottom of a punch-bowl. By Heaven, it is a kind of enchantment! If I do not speedily break the spell, and escape, I may chance to give up the ghost in this nauseous stew of corruption—It was but two nights ago, that I had like to have made my public exit, at a minute's warning. One of my greatest weaknesses is that of suffering myself to be over-ruled by the opinion of people, whose judgment I despise—I own, with shame and confusion of face, that importunity of any kind I cannot resist. This want of courage and constancy is an original flaw in my nature, which you must have often observed with compassion, if not with contempt. I am afraid some of our boasted virtues may be traced up to this defect.——

Without further preamble, I was persuaded to go to a ball, on purpose to see Liddy dance a minuet with a young petulant jackanapes, the only son of a wealthy undertaker from London, whose mother lodges in our neighbourhood, and has contracted an acquaintance with Tabby. I sat a couple of long hours, half stifled, in the midst of a noisome crowd; and could not help wondering that so many hundreds of those that rank as rational creatures, could find entertainment in seeing a succession of insipid animals, describing the same dull figure for a whole evening, on an area, not much bigger than a taylor's shop-board. If there had been any beauty, grace, activity, magnificent dress, or variety of any kind, howsoever absurd, to engage the atten-

tion, and amuse the fancy, I should not have been surprised;
but there was no such object: it was a tiresome repetition of
the same languid, frivolous scene, performed by actors that
seemed to sleep in all their motions—The continual swim-
ming of these phantoms before my eyes, gave me a swim-
ming of the head; which was also affected by the fouled
air, circulating through such a number of rotten human
bellows——I therefore retreated towards the door, and
stood in the passage to the next room, talking to my friend
Quin; when an end being put to the minuets, the benches
were removed to make way for the country-dances; and
the multitude rising at once, the whole atmosphere was
put in commotion. Then, all of a sudden, came rushing
upon me an Egyptian gale, so impregnated with pestilential
vapours, that my nerves were overpowered, and I dropt
senseless upon the floor.

You may easily conceive what a clamour and confusion
this accident must have produced, in such an assembly—I
soon recovered, however, and found myself in an easy
chair, supported by my own people—Sister Tabby, in her
great tenderness, had put me to the torture, squeezing my
hand under her arm, and stuffing my nose with spirit of
hartshorn, till the whole inside was excoriated. I no sooner
got home, than I sent for Doctor Ch——, who assured me
I needed not be alarmed, for my swooning was entirely
occasioned by an accidental impression of fetid effluvia upon
nerves of uncommon sensibility. I know not how other people's nerves are constructed; but one would imagine they
must be made of very coarse materials, to stand the shock
of such a horrid assault. It was, indeed, *a compound of
villainous smells*, in which the most violent stinks, and the
most powerful perfumes, contended for the mastery. Imagine to yourself a high exalted essence of mingled odours,
arising from putrid gums, imposthumated lungs, sour flat-
ulencies, rank arm-pits, sweating feet, running sores and
issues, plaisters, ointments, and embrocations, hungary-water,

spirit of lavender, assa fœtida drops, musk, hartshorn, and sal volatile; besides a thousand frowzy steams, which I could not analyse. Such, O Dick! is the fragrant æther we breathe in the polite assemblies of Bath—Such is the atmosphere I have exchanged for the pure, elastic, animating air of the Welsh mountains——*O Rus, quando te aspiciam!*—I wonder what the devil possessed me—

But few words are best: I have taken my resolution—You may well suppose I don't intend to entertain the company with a second exhibition—I have promised, in an evil hour, to proceed to London, and that promise shall be performed; but my stay in the metropolis shall be brief. I have, for the benefit of my health, projected an expedition to the North, which, I hope, will afford some agreeable pastime. I have never travelled farther that way than Scarborough; and, I think, it is a reproach upon me, as a British freeholder, to have lived so long without making an excursion to the other side of the Tweed. Besides, I have some relations settled in Yorkshire, to whom it may not be improper to introduce my nephew and his sister—At present, I have nothing to add, but that Tabby is happily disentangled from the Irish Baronet; and that I will not fail to make you acquainted, from time to time, with the sequel of our adventures: a mark of consideration, which, perhaps, you would willingly dispence with in

Your humble servant,

M. BRAMBLE.

BATH, *May* 8.

To Sir Watkin Phillips, of Jesus college, Oxon.

DEAR PHILLIPS,

A few days ago we were terribly alarmed by my uncle's fainting at the ball—He has been ever since cursing his own folly, for going thither at the request of an impertinent woman. He declares, he will sooner visit a house infected with the plague, than trust himself in such a nauseous spital for the future, for he swears the accident was occasioned by the stench of the crowd; and that he would never desire a stronger proof of our being made of very gross materials, than our having withstood the annoyance, by which he was so much discomposed. For my part, I am very thankful for the coarseness of my organs, being in no danger of ever falling a sacrifice to the delicacy of my nose. Mr. Bramble is extravagantly delicate in all his sensations, both of soul and body. I was informed by Dr. Lewis, that he once fought a duel with an officer of the horse-guards, for turning aside to the Park-wall, on a necessary occasion, when he was passing with a lady under his protection. His blood rises at every instance of insolence and cruelty, even where he himself is no way concerned; and ingratitude makes his teeth chatter. On the other hand, the recital of a generous, humane, or grateful action, never fails to draw from him tears of approbation, which he is often greatly distressed to conceal.

Yesterday, one Paunceford gave tea, on particular invitation.—This man, after having been long buffetted by adversity, went abroad; and Fortune, resolved to make him amends for her former coyness, set him all at once up to the very ears in affluence. He has now emerged from obscurity, and blazes out in all the tinsel of the times. I don't find that he is charged with any practices that the law deems dishonest, or that his wealth has made him arrogant and inaccessible; on the contrary, he takes great pains to appear affable and gracious. But, they say, he is remarkable for shrinking from his former friendships, which were generally too plain and home-spun to appear amidst his present brilliant connexions; and that he seems uneasy at sight of some old benefactors, whom a man of honour would take pleasure to acknowledge—Be that as it may, he had so effectually engaged the company at Bath, that when I went with my uncle to the coffeehouse in the evening, there was not a soul in the room but one person, seemingly in years, who sat by the fire, reading one of the papers. Mr. Bramble, taking his station close by him, 'There is such a crowd and confusion of chairs in the passage to Simpson's (said he) that we could hardly get along——I wish those minions of fortune would fall upon more laudable ways of spending their money.—I suppose, Sir, you like this kind of entertainment as little as I do?' 'I cannot say I have any great relish for such entertainments,' answered the other, without taking his eyes off the paper——'Mr. Serle (resumed my uncle) I beg pardon for interrupting you; but I can't resist the curiosity I have to know if you received a card on this occasion?'

The man seemed surprised at this address, and made some pause, as doubtful what answer he should make. 'I know my curiosity is impertinent (added my uncle) but I have a particular reason for asking the favour.' 'If that be the case (replied Mr. Serle) I shall gratify you without hesitation, by owning that I have had no card. But, give me leave, Sir, to ask in my turn, what reason you think I have to expect such an invitation from the gentleman who gives tea?' 'I have my own reasons (cried Mr. Bramble, with some emotion) and am convinced, more than ever, that this Paunceford is a contemptible fellow.' 'Sir (said the other, laying down the paper) I have not the honour to know you; but your discourse is a little mysterious, and seems to require some explanation. The person you are pleased to treat so cavalierly, is a gentleman of some consequence in the community; and, for aught you know, I may also have my particular reasons for defending his character'——'If I was not convinced of the contrary (observed the other) I should not have gone so far'—'Let me tell you, Sir (said the stranger, raising his voice) you have gone too far, in hazarding such reflections'——

Here he was interrupted by my uncle; who asked peevishly, if he was Don Quixote enough, at this time of day, to throw down his gauntlet as champion for a man who had treated him with such ungrateful neglect. 'For my part (added he) I shall never quarrel with you again upon this subject; and what I have said now, has been suggested as much by my regard for you, as by my contempt of him'———

Mr. Serle, then pulling off his spectacles, eyed uncle very earnestly, saying, in a mitigated tone, 'Surely I am much obliged———Ah, Mr. Bramble; I now recollect your features, though I have not seen you these many years.' 'We might have been less strangers to one another (answered the squire) if our correspondence had not been interrupted, in consequence of a misunderstanding, occasioned by this very———, but no matter—Mr. Serle, I esteem your character; and my friendship, such as it is, you may freely command.' 'The offer is too agreeable to be declined; (said he) I embrace it very cordially; and, as the first fruits of it, request that you will change this subject, which, with me, is a matter of peculiar delicacy.'

My uncle owned he was in the right, and the discourse took a more general turn. Mr. Serle passed the evening with us at our lodgings; and appeared to be intelligent, and even entertaining; but his disposition was rather of a melancholy hue. My uncle says he is a man of uncommon parts, and unquestioned probity: that his fortune, which was originally small, has been greatly hurt by a romantic spirit of generosity which he has often displayed, even at the expence of his discretion, in favour of worthless individuals ———That he had rescued Paunceford from the lowest distress, when he was bankrupt, both in means and reputation—That he had espoused his interests with a degree of enthusiasm, broke with several friends, and even drawn his sword against my uncle, who had particular reasons for questioning the moral character of the said Paunceford: that, without Serle's countenance and assistance, the other never could have embraced the opportunity, which has raised him to this pinnacle of wealth: that Paunceford, in the first transports of his success, had written, from abroad, letters to different correspondents, owning his obligations to Mr. Serle, in the warmest terms of acknowledgement, and declared he considered himself only as a factor for the occasions of his best friend: that, without doubt, he had made declarations of the same nature to his benefactor himself, though this last was always silent and reserved on the subject; but for some years, those tropes and figures of rhetoric had been disused; that, upon his return to England, he had been lavish in his caresses to Mr. Serle, invited him to his house, and pressed him to make it his own: that he had overwhelmed him with general professions, and affected to express the warmest regard for him, in company of their common acquaintance; so that every body believed his gratitude was as liberal as his fortune; and some went so far as to congratulate Mr. Serle on both.

All this time Paunceford carefully and artfully avoided particular discussions with his old patron, who had too much spirit to drop the most distant hint of balancing the account of obligation: that, nevertheless, a man of his feelings could not but resent this shocking return for all his kindness: and, therefore, he withdrew himself from the connexion, without coming to the least explanation, or speaking a syllable on the subject to any living soul; so that now their correspondence is reduced to a slight salute with the hat, when they chance to meet in any public place; an accident that rarely happens, for their walks lie different ways. Mr. Paunceford lives in a palace, feeds upon dainties, is arrayed in sumptuous apparel, appears in all the pomp of equipage, and passes his time among the nobles of the land. Serle lodges in Stall-street, up two pair of stairs backwards, walks a-foot in a Bath-rug, eats for twelve shillings a-week, and drinks water as a preservative against the gout and gravel ——Mark the vicissitude. Paunceford once resided in a garret; where he subsisted upon sheep's trotters and cow-heel, from which commons he was translated to the table of Serle, that ever abounded with good-chear; until want of economy and retention reduced him to a slender annuity in his decline of years, that scarce affords the bare necessaries of life——Paunceford, however, does him the honour to speak of him still, with uncommon regard; and to declare what pleasure it would give him to contribute in any shape to his convenience: 'But you know (he never fails to add) he's a shy kind of a man——And then such a perfect philosopher, that he looks upon all superfluities with the most sovereign contempt.'

Having given you this sketch of squire Paunceford, I need not make any comment on his character, but leave it at the mercy of your own reflection; from which I dare say, it will meet with as little quarter as it has found with

Yours always,

J. MELFORD.

BATH, *May* 10.

To Mrs. Mary Jones, at Brambleton-hall

DEAR MOLLY,

We are all upon the ving—Hey for London, girl!—Fecks! we have been long enough here; for we're all turned tipsy turvy——Mistress has excarded Sir Ulic for kicking of Chowder; and I have sent O Frizzle away, with a flea in his ear—I've shewn him how little I minded his tinsy and his long tail—A fellor, who would think for to go, for to offer, to take up with a dirty trollop under my nose——I ketched him in the very fect, coming out of the house-maids garret.—But I have gi'en the dirty slut a siserary. O Molly! the sarvants at Bath are devils in garnet—They lite the candle at both ends—Here's nothing but ginketting, and wasting, and thieving and tricking, and trigging; and then they are never content—They won't suffer the squire and mistress to stay any longer; because they have been already above three weeks in the house; and they look for a couple of ginneys a-piece at our going away; and this is a parquisite they expect every month in the season; being as how no family has a right to stay longer than four weeks in the same lodgings; and so the cuck swears she will pin the dish-clout to mistress's tail; and the house-maid vows, she'll put cowitch in master's bed, if so be he don't discamp without furder ado——I don't blame them for making the most of their market, in the way of vails and parquisites; and I defy the devil to say I am a tail-carrier, or ever brought a poor sarvant into trouble————But then they oft to have some conscience, in vronging those that be sarvants like themselves ——For you must no, Molly, I missed three-quarters of blond lace, and a remnant of muslin, and my silver thimble; which was the gift of true love; they were all in my work-basket, that I left upon the table in the sarvants-hall, when mistresses bell rung; but if they had been under lock and kay, 'twould have been all the same; for there are double keys to all the locks in Bath; and they say as how the very teeth an't safe in your head, if you sleep with your mouth open—And so says I to myself, *them things could not go without hands; and so I'll watch their waters:* and so I did with a vitness; for then it was I found Bett consarned with O Frizzle. And as the cuck had thrown her slush at me, because I had taken part with Chowder, when he sit with the turnspit, I resolved to make a clear kitchen, and throw some of her fat into the fire. I ketched the chare-woman going out with her load in the morning, before she thought I was up, and brought her to mistress with her whole cargo—Marry, what do'st think she had got in the name of God? Her buckets were foaming full of our best bear, and her lap was stuffed with a cold tongue, part of a buttock of beef, half a turkey, and a swinging lump of butter, and the matter of ten mould kandles, that had scarce ever been lit. The cuck brazened it out, and said it was her rite to rummage the pantry; and she was ready for to go before the mare: that he had been her potticary many years, and would never think of hurting a poor sarvant, for giving away the scraps of the kitchen——I went another way to work with madam Betty, because she had been saucy, and called me skandelus names; and said O Frizzle couldn't abide me, and twenty other odorous falsehoods. I got a varrant from the mare, and her box being sarched by the constable, my things came out sure enuff; besides a full pound of vax candles, and a nite-cap of mistress, that I could sware to on my cruperal oaf—O! then madam Mopstick came upon her merry bones; and as the squire wouldn't hare of a pursecution, she scaped a skewering: but the longest day she has to live, she'll remember your

Humble sarvant,
W. Jenkins.

Bath, *May* 15.

If the hind should come again, before we be gone, pray send me the shift and apron, with the vite gallow manky shoes; which you'll find in my pillowber—Sarvice to Saul.——

To Sir Watkin Phillips, Bart. of Jesus college, Oxon.

You are in the right, dear Phillips; I don't expect regular answers to every letter—I know a college-life is too circumscribed to afford materials for such quick returns of communication. For my part, I am continually shifting the scene, and surrounded with new objects; some of which are striking enough. I shall therefore conclude my journal for your amusement; and, though, in all appearance, it will not treat of very important or interesting particulars, it may prove, perhaps, not altogether uninstructive and unenter-

taining. The music and entertainments of Bath are over
for this season; and all our gay birds of passage have taken
their flight to Bristol-well, Tunbridge, Brighthelmstone,
Scarborough, Harrowgate, &c. Not a soul is seen in this
place, but a few broken-winded parsons, waddling like so
many crows along the North Parade. There is always a
great shew of the clergy at Bath: none of your thin, puny,
yellow, hectic figures, exhausted with abstinence, and hard
study, labouring under the *morbi eruditorum*, but great
overgrown dignitaries and rectors, with rubicund noses and
gouty ancles, or broad bloated faces, dragging along great
swag bellies; the emblems of sloth and indigestion.

Now we are upon the subject of parsons, I must tell
you a ludicrous adventure, which was achieved the other
day by Tom Eastgate, whom you may remember on the
foundation of Queen's. He had been very assiduous to pin
himself upon George Prankley, who was a gentleman-com-
moner of Christ-church; knowing the said Prankley was
heir to a considerable estate, and would have the advowson
of a good living, the incumbent of which was very old
and infirm, he studied his passions, and flattered them so
effectually, as to become his companion and counsellor; and,
at last, obtained of him a promise of the presentation, when
the living should fall. Prankley, on his uncle's death, quitted Oxford, and made his first appearance in the fashionable
world at London; from whence he came lately to Bath,
where he has been exhibiting himself among the bucks and
gamsters of the place. Eastgate followed him hither; but
he should not have quitted him for a moment, at his first
emerging into life. He ought to have known he was a
fantastic, foolish, fickle fellow, who would forget his col-
lege-attachments the moment they ceased appealing to his
senses. Tom met with a cold reception from his old friend;
he proposed to offer himself a candidate at the next general
and was, moreover, informed, that he had promised the living to another man, who had a vote in the county, where

election. He now remembered nothing of Eastgate, but the freedoms he had used to take with him, while Tom had quietly stood his butt, with an eye to the benefice; and those freedoms he began to repeat in common-place sarcasms on his person and his cloth, which he uttered in the public coffeehouse, for the entertainment of the company. But he was egregiously mistaken in giving his own wit credit for that tameness of Eastgate, which had been entirely owing to prudential considerations. These being now removed, he retorted his repartee with interest, and found no great difficulty in turning the laugh upon the aggressor; who, losing his temper, called him names, and asked, *If he knew whom he talked to?* After much altercation, Prankley, shaking his cane, bid him hold his tongue, otherwise he would dust his cassock for him. 'I have no pretensions to such a valet (said Tom) but if you should do me that office, and overheat yourself, I have here a good oaken towel at your service.'

Prankley was equally incensed and confounded at this reply. After a moment's pause, he took him aside towards the window; and, pointing to the clump of firs, on Clerkendown, asked in a whisper, if he had spirit enough to meet him there, with a case of pistols, at six o'clock to-morrow morning. Eastgate answered in the affirmative; and, with a steady countenance, assured him, he would not fail to give him the rendezvous at the hour he mentioned. So saying, he retired; and the challenger stayed some time in manifest agitation. In the morning, Eastgate, who knew his man, and had taken his resolution, went to Prankley's lodgings, and roused him by five o'clock.

The squire, in all probability, cursed his punctuality in his heart, but he affected to talk big; and having prepared his artillery over-night, they crossed the water at the end of the South Parade. In their progress up the hill, Prankley often eyed the parson, in hopes of perceiving some reluctance in his countenance; but as no such marks appeared, he attempted to intimidate him by word of mouth. 'If these flints do their office (said he) I'll do thy business in a few minutes.' 'I desire you will do your best (replied the other); for my part, I come not here to trifle. Our lives are in the hands of God; and one of us already totters on the brink of eternity'——This remark seemed to make some impression upon the squire, who changed countenance, and with a faultering accent observed, 'That it ill became a clergyman to be concerned in quarrels and bloodshed'—— 'Your insolence to me (said Eastgate) I should have bore with patience, had not you cast the most infamous reflections upon my order, the honour of which I think myself in duty bound to maintain, even at the expence of my heart's blood; and surely it can be no crime to put out of the world a profligate wretch, without any sense of principle, morality, or religion'————'Thou may'st take away my life (cried Prankley, in great perturbation) but don't go to murder my character.——What! has't got no conscience?' 'My conscience is perfectly quiet (replied the other); and now, Sir, we are upon the spot—Take your ground as near as you please; prime your pistol; and the Lord, of his infinite mercy, have compassion upon your miserable soul!'

This ejaculation he pronounced in a loud solemn tone, with his hat off, and his eyes lifted up; then drawing a large horse-pistol, he presented, and put himself in a posture of action. Prankley took his distance, and endeavoured to prime, but his hand shook with such violence, that he found this operation impracticable.——His antagonist, seeing how it was with him, offered his assistance, and advanced for that purpose; when the poor squire, exceedingly alarmed at what he had heard and seen, desired the action might be deferred till next day, as he had not settled his affairs. 'I ha'n't made my will (said he); my sisters are not provided for; and I just now recollect an old promise, which my conscience tells me I ought to perform—I'll first convince thee, that I'm not a wretch without principle, and then thou shalt have an opportunity to take my life, which thou seem'st to thirst after so eagerly.'

Eastgate understood the hint; and told him, that one day should break no squares; adding, 'God forbid that I should be the means of hindering you from acting the part of an honest man, and a dutiful brother.'——By virtue of this cessation, they returned peaceably together. Prankley forthwith made out the presentation of the living, and delivered it to Eastgate, telling him at the same time, he had now settled his affairs, and was ready to attend him to the Fir-grove; but Tom declared he could not think of lifting his hand against the life of so great a benefactor—He did more: when they next met at the coffeehouse, he asked pardon of Mr. Prankley, if in his passion he had said any thing to give him offence; and the squire was so gracious as to forgive him with a cordial shake of the hand, declaring, that he did not like to be at variance with an old college companion—Next day, however, he left Bath abruptly; and then Eastgate told me all these particulars, not a little pleased with the effects of his own sagacity, by which he has secured a living worth 160*l. per annum.*

Of my uncle, I have nothing at present to say; but that we set out to-morrow for London *en famille.* He and the ladies, with the maid and Chowder in a coach; I and the man-servant a-horseback. The particulars of our journey you shall have in my next, provided no accident happens to prevent.

Yours ever,
J. MELFORD.

BATH, *May* 17.

To Dr. Lewis

DEAR DICK,

I shall to-morrow set out for London, where I have bespoke lodgings, at Mrs. Norton's in Golden-square. Although I am no admirer of Bath, I shall leave it with regret; because I must part with some old friends, whom, in all probability, I shall never see again. In the course of c)ffeehouse conversation, I had often heard very extraordinary encomiums passed on the performances of Mr. T——, a gentleman residing in this place, who paints landscapes for his amusement. As I have no great confidence in the taste and judgment of coffeehouse connoisseurs, and never received much pleasure from this branch of the art, those general praises made no impression at all on my curiosity; but, at the request of a particular friend, I went yesterday to see the pieces, which had been so warmly commended—I must own I am no judge of painting, though very fond of pictures. I don't imagine that my senses would play me so false, as to betray me into admiration of any thing that was very bad; but, true it is, I have often overlooked capital beauties, in pieces of extraordinary merit.—If I am not totally devoid of taste, however, this young gentleman of Bath is the best landscape-painter now living: I was struck with his performances in such a manner, as I had never been by painting before. His trees not only have a richness of foliage and warmth of colouring, which delights the view; but also a certain magnificence in the disposition and spirit in the expression, which I cannot describe. His management of the *chiaro oscuro,* or light and shadow, especially gleams of sunshine, is altogether wonderful, both in the contrivance and execution; and he is so happy in his perspective, and marking his distances at sea, by a progressive series of ships, vessels, capes, and promontories, that I could not help thinking, I had a distant view of thirty leagues upon the back-ground of the picture. If there is any taste for ingenuity left in a degenerate age, fast sinking into barbarism, this artist, I apprehend, will make a capital figure, as soon as his works are known.

Two days ago, I was favoured with a visit by Mr. Fitz owen; who, with great formality, solicited my vote and interest at the general election. I ought not to have been shocked at the confidence of this man; though it was remarkable, considering what had passed between him and me on a former occasion——These visits are mere matter of form, which a candidate makes to every elector; even to those who, he knows, are engaged in the interest of his competitor, lest he should expose himself to the imputation of pride, at a time when it is expected he should appear humble. Indeed, I know nothing so abject as the behaviour of a man canvassing for a seat in parliament——This mean prostration (to borough-electors, especially) has, I imagine, contributed in a great measure to raise that spirit of insolence among the vulgar; which, like the devil, will be found very difficult to lay. Be that as it may, I was in some confusion at the effrontery of Fitz owen; but I soon recollected myself, and told him, I had not yet determined for whom I should give my vote, nor whether I should give it for any.—— The truth is, I look upon both candidates in the same light; and should think myself a traitor to the constitution of my country, if I voted for either. If every elector would bring the same consideration home to his conscience, we should not have such reason to exclaim against the venality of p——ts. But we are all a pack of venal and corrupted rascals; so lost to all sense of honesty, and all tenderness of character, that, in a little time, I am fully persuaded, nothing will be infamous but virtue and public-spirit.

G. H——, who is really an enthusiast in patriotism, and represented the capital in several successive parliaments, de-clared to me t'other day, with the tears in his eyes, that he had lived above thirty years in the city of London, and dealt in the way of commerce with all the citizens of note in their turns; but that, as he should answer to God, he had never, in the whole course of his life, found above three or four whom he could call thoroughly honest: a declaration which was rather mortifying than surprising to me; who have found so few men of worth in the course of my acquaintance, that they serve only as exceptions; which, in the grammarian's phrase, confirm and prove a general canon——I know you will say, G. H——saw imperfectly through the mist of prejudice, and I am rankled by the spleen—Perhaps, you are partly in the right; for I have perceived that my opinion of mankind, like mercury in the thermometer, rises and falls according to the variations of the weather.

Pray settle accompts with Barnes; take what money of mine is in his hands, and give him acquaintance. If you think Davis has stock or credit enough to do justice to the farm, give him a discharge for the rent that is due: this will animate his industry; for I know that nothing is so discouraging to a farmer as the thoughts of being in arrears with his landlord. He becomes dispirited, and neglects his labour; and so the farm goes to wreck. Tabby has been clamouring for some days about the lamb's skin, which Williams, the hind, begged of me, when he was last at Bath. Prithee take it back, paying the fellow the full value of it, that I may have some peace in my own house; and let him keep his own counsel, if he means to keep his place—O! I shall never presume to despise or censure any poor man, for suffering himself to be henpecked; conscious how I myself am obliged to truckle to a domestic demon; even though (blessed be God) she is not yoked with me for life, in the matrimonial waggon—She has quarrelled with the servants of the house about vails; and such intolerable scolding ensued on both sides, that I have been fain to appease the cook and chamber-maid by stealth. Can't you find some poor gentleman of Wales, to take this precious commodity off the hands of

yours,

MATT. BRAMBLE.

BATH, *May* 19.

To Dr. Lewis

DOCTER LEWS,

Give me leaf to tell you, methinks you mought employ your talons better, than to encourage servants to pillage their masters—I find by Gwyllim, that Villiams has got my skin; for which he is an impotent rascal. He has not only got my skin, but, moreover, my butter-milk to fatten his pigs; and, I suppose, the next thing he gets, will be my pad to carry his daughter to church and fair: Roger gets this, and Roger gets that; but I'd have you to know, I won't be rogered at this rate by any ragmatical fellow in the kingdom—And I am surprised, docter Lews, you would offer to put my affairs in composition with the refuge and skim of the hearth. I have toiled and moyled to a good purpuss, for the advantage of Matt's family, if I can't safe as much owl as will make me an under petticoat. As for the butter-milk, ne'er a pig in the parish shall thrust his snout in it, with my good-will. There's a famous physician at the Hot Well, that prescribes it to his patience, when the case is consumptive; and the Scots and Irish have begun to drink it already, in such quantities, that there is not a drop left for the hogs in the whole neighbourhood of Bristol. I'll have our butter-milk barrelled up, and sent twice a-week to Aberginny, where it may be sold for a half-penny the quart; and so Roger may carry his pigs to another market—I hope, Docter, you will not go to put any more such phims in my brother's head, to the prejudice of my pockat; but rather give me some raisins (which hitherto you have not done) to subscribe myself

your humble servant,

TAB. BRAMBLE.

BATH, *May* 19.

To Sir Watkin Phillips, of Jesus college, Oxon.

DEAR PHILLIPS,

Without waiting for your answer to my last, I proceed to give you an account of our journey to London, which has not been wholly barren of adventure. Tuesday last the squire took his place in a hired coach and four, accompanied by his sister and mine, and Mrs. Tabby's maid, Winifrid Jenkins, whose province it was to support Chowder on a cushion in her lap. I could scarce refrain from laughing when I looked into the vehicle, and saw that animal sitting opposite to my uncle, like any other passenger. The squire, ashamed of his situation, blushed to the eyes: and, calling to the postilions to drive on, pulled the glass up in my face. I, and his servant, John Thomas, attended them on horseback.

Nothing worth mentioning occurred, till we arrived on the edge of Marlborough Downs. There one of the four horses fell, in going down hill at a round trot; and the postilion behind, endeavouring to stop the carriage, pulled it on one side into a deep rut, where it was fairly overturned. I had rode on about two hundred yards before, but, hearing a loud scream, galloped back and dismounted, to give what assistance was in my power. When I looked into the coach, I could see nothing distinctly, but the nether end of Jenkins, who was kicking her heels and squalling, with great vociferation. All of a sudden, my uncle thrust up his bare pate, and bolted through the window, as nimble as a grasshopper, having made use of poor Win's posteriors as a step to rise in his ascent—The man (who had likewise quitted his horse) dragged this forlorn damsel, more dead than alive, through the same opening. Then Mr. Bramble, pulling the door off its hinges with a jerk, laid hold on Liddy's arm, and brought her to the light; very much frighted, but little hurt. It fell to my share to deliver our aunt Tabitha, who had lost her cap in the struggle, and being rather more than half frantic, with rage and terror, was no bad representation of one of the sister Furies that guard the gates of hell——She expressed no sort of concern for her brother, who ran about in the cold, without his periwig, and worked with the most astonishing agility, in helping to disentangle the horses from the carriage: but she cried, in a tone of distraction, 'Chowder! Chowder! my dear Chowder! my poor Chowder is certainly killed!'

This was not the case——Chowder, after having tore my uncle's leg in the confusion of the fall, had retreated under the seat, and from thence the footman drew him by the neck; for which good office, he bit his fingers to the bone. The fellow, who is naturally surly, was so provoked at this assault, that he saluted his ribs with a hearty kick, exclaiming, 'Damn the nasty son of a bitch, and them he belongs to!' A benediction, which was by no means lost upon the implacable virago his mistress——Her brother, however, prevailed upon her to retire into a peasant's house, near the scene of action, where his head and hers were covered, and poor Jenkins had a fit——Our next care was to apply some sticking plaister to the wound in his leg, which exhibited the impression of Chowder's teeth; but he never opened his lips against the delinquent——Mrs. Tabby, alarmed at this scene, 'You say nothing, Matt (cried she); but I know your mind—I know the spite you have to that poor unfortunate animal! I know you intend to take his life away!' 'You are mistaken, upon my honour! (replied the squire, with a sarcastic smile) I should be incapable of harbouring any such cruel design against an object so amiable and inoffensive; even if he had not the happiness to be your favourite.'

John Thomas was not so delicate. The fellow, whether really alarmed for his life, or instigated by the desire of revenge, came in, and bluntly demanded, that the dog should be put to death; on the supposition, that if ever he should run mad hereafter, he, who had been bit by him, would be infected—My uncle calmly argued upon the absurdity of his opinion, observing, that he himself was in the same predicament, and would certainly take the precaution he proposed, if he was not sure he ran no risque of infection. Nevertheless, Thomas continued obstinate; and, at length declared, that if the dog was not shot immediately, he himself would be his executioner——This declaration opened the flood-gates of Tabby's eloquence, which would have shamed the first-rate oratress of Billingsgate. The footman retorted in the same stile; and the squire dismissed him from his service, after having prevented me from giving him a good horse-whipping for his insolence.

The coach being adjusted, another difficulty occurred—Mrs. Tabitha absolutely refused to enter it again, unless another driver could be found to take the place of the postilion; who, she affirmed, had overturned the carriage from malice aforethought—After much dispute, the man resigned his place to a shabby country fellow, who undertook to go as far as Marlborough, where they could be better provided; and at that place we arrived about one o'clock, without farther impediment. Mrs. Bramble, however, found new matter of offence; which, indeed, she has a particular genius for extracting at will from almost every incident in life. We had scarce entered the room at Marlborough, where we stayed to dine, when she exhibited a formal complaint against the poor fellow who had superseded the postilion. She said he was such a beggarly rascal that he had ne'er a shirt to his back, and had the impudence to shock her sight by shewing his bare posteriors, for which act of indelicacy he deserved to be set in the stocks. Mrs. Winifred Jenkins confirmed the assertion, with respect to his nakedness, observing, at the same time, that he had a skin as fair as alabaster.

'This is a heinous offence, indeed (cried my uncle) let us hear what the fellow has to say in his own vindication.'

He was accordingly summoned, and made his appearance, which was equally queer and pathetic. He seemed to be about twenty years of age, of a middling size, with bandy legs, stooping shoulders, high forehead, sandy locks, pinking eyes, flat nose, and long chin—but his complexion was of a sickly yellow; his looks denoted famine, and the rags that he wore could hardly conceal what decency requires to be covered——My uncle, having surveyed him attentively, said, with an ironical expression in his countenance. 'An't you ashamed, fellow, to ride postilion without a shirt to cover your backside from the view of the ladies in the coach?' 'Yes, I am, an please your noble honour (answered the man) but necessity has no law, as the saying is——And more than that, it was an accident——My breeches cracked behind, after I had got into the saddle'——'You're an impudent varlet (cried Mrs. Tabby) for presuming to ride before persons of fashion without a shirt'——'I am so, an please your worthy ladyship (said he) but I am a poor Wiltshire lad—I ha'n't a shirt in the world, that I can call my own, nor a rag of clothes, an please your ladyship, but what you see—I have no friend nor relation upon earth to help me out——I have had the fever and ague these six months, and spent all I had in the world upon doctors, and to keep soul and body together; and, saving your ladyship's good presence, I han't broke bread these four and twenty hours.'

Mrs. Bramble, turning from him, said, she had never seen such a filthy tatterdemalion, and bid him begone; observing, that he would fill the room full of vermin—Her brother darted a significant glance at her, as she retired with Liddy into another apartment, and then asked the man if he was known to any person in Marlborough?—When he answered, that the landlord of the inn had known him from his infancy; mine host was immediately called, and being interrogated on the subject, declared that the young fellow's name was Humphry Clinker. That he had been a love begotten babe, brought up in the work-house, and put out apprentice by the parish to a country black-smith, who died before the boy's time was out: that he had for some time worked under his ostler, as a helper and extra postilion, till he was taken ill of the ague, which disabled him from getting his bread: that, having sold or pawned every thing he had in the world for his cure and subsistence, he became so miserable and shabby, that he disgraced the stable, and was dismissed; but that he never heard any thing to the prejudice of his character in other respects. 'So that the fellow being sick and destitute (said my uncle) you turned him out to die in the streets.' 'I pay the poor's rate (replied the other) and I have no right to maintain idle vagrants, either in sickness or health; besides, such a miserable object would have brought a discredit upon my house.'

'You perceive (said the squire, turning to me) our landlord is a Christian of bowels—Who shall presume to censure the morals of the age, when the very publicans exhibit such examples of humanity?——Hark ye, Clinker, you are a most notorious offender——You stand convicted of sickness, hunger, wretchedness, and want—But, as it does not belong to me to punish criminals, I will only take upon me the task of giving you a word of advice—Get a shirt with all convenient dispatch, that your nakedness may not henceforward give offence to travelling gentlewomen, especially maidens in years.'

So saying, he put a guinea into the hand of the poor fellow, who stood staring at him in silence, with his mouth wide open, till the landlord pushed him out of the room.

In the afternoon, as our aunt stept into the coach, she observed, with some marks of satisfaction, that the postilion, who rode next to her, was not a shabby wretch like the ragamuffin who had drove them into Marlborough. Indeed, the difference was very conspicuous: this was a smart fellow, with a narrow brimmed hat, with gold cording, a cut bob, a decent blue jacket, leather-breeches, and a clean linen shirt, puffed above the waist-band. When we arrived at the Castle on Spin-hill, where we lay, this new postilion was remarkably assiduous in bringing in the loose parcels; and, at length, displayed the individual countenance of Humphry Clinker, who had metamorphosed himself in this manner, by relieving from pawn part of his own clothes, with the money he had received from Mr. Bramble.

Howsoever pleased the rest of the company were with such a favourable change in the appearance of this poor creature it soured on the stomach of Mrs. Tabby, who had not yet digested the affront of his naked skin——She tossed her nose in disdain, saying, she supposed her brother had taken him into favour, because he had insulted her with his obscenity: that a fool and his money were soon parted; but that if Matt intended to take the fellow with him to London, she would not go a foot further that way——My uncle said nothing with his tongue, though his looks were sufficiently expressive; and next morning Clinker did not appear, so that we proceeded without further altercation to Salt-hill, where we proposed to dine—There, the first person that came to the side of the coach, and began to adjust the foot-board, was no other than Humphry Clinker—When I handed out Mrs. Bramble, she eyed him with a furious look, and passed into the house—My uncle was embarrassed, and asked him peevishly, what had brought him hither? The fellow said, his honour had been so good to him, that he had not the heart to part with him; that he would follow him to the world's end, and serve him all the days of his life, without fee or reward.

Mr. Bramble did not know whether to chide or laugh at this declaration——He foresaw much contradiction on the side of Tabby; and on the other hand, he could not but be pleased with the gratitude of Clinker, as well as with the simplicity of his character—'Suppose I was inclined to take you into my service (said he) what are your qualifications?

what are you good for?' 'An please your honour (answered this original) I can read and write, and do the business of the stable indifferent well—I can dress a horse, and shoe him, and bleed and rowel him; and, as for the practice of sow-gelding, I won't turn my back on e'er a he in the county of Wilts——Then I can make hog's puddings and hob-nails, mend kettles and tin sauce-pans.'—Here uncle burst out a-laughing; and inquired what other accomplishments he was master of—'I know something of single-stick, and psalmody (proceeded Clinker) I can play upon the Jew's-harp, sing Black-ey'd Susan, Arthur-o'Bradley, and divers other songs; I can dance a Welsh jig, and Nancy Dawson; wrestle a fall with any lad of my inches, when I'm in heart; and, under correction, I can find a hare when your honour wants a bit of game.' 'Foregad! thou art a complete fellow (cried my uncle, still laughing) I have a good mind to take thee into my family——Prithee, go and try if thou can'st make peace with my sister—Thou ha'st given her much offence by shewing her thy naked tail.'

Clinker accordingly followed us into the room, cap in hand, where, addressing himself to Mrs. Tabitha, 'May it please your ladyship's worship (cried he) to pardon and forgive my offences, and, with God's assistance, I shall take care that my tail shall never rise up in judgment against me, to offend your ladyship again——Do, pray, good, sweet, beautiful lady, take compassion on a poor sinner—God bless your noble countenance; I am sure you are too handsome and generous to bear malice—I will serve you on my bended knees, by night and by day, by land and by water; and all for the love and pleasure of serving such an excellent lady.'

This compliment and humiliation had some effect upon Tabby; but she made no reply; and Clinker, taking silence for consent, gave his attendance at dinner. The fellow's natural aukwardness and the flutter of his spirits were productive of repeated blunders in the course of his attendance

—At length, he spilt part of a custard upon her right shoulder; and, starting back, trod upon Chowder, who set up a dismal howl——Poor Humphry was so disconcerted at this double mistake, that he dropt the china dish, which broke into a thousand pieces; then, falling down upon his knees, remained in that posture gaping, with a most ludicrous aspect of distress——Mrs. Bramble flew to the dog, and, snatching him in her arms, presented him to her brother saying, 'This is all a concerted scheme against this unfortunate animal, whose only crime is its regard for me—Here it is, kill it at once, and then you'll be satisfied.'

Clinker, hearing these words, and taking them in the literal acceptation, got up in some hurry, and seizing a knife from the side-board, cried, 'Not here, an please your ladyship—It will daub the room—Give him to me, and I'll carry him to the ditch by the roadside'——To this proposal he received no other answer, than a hearty box on the ear, that made him stagger to the other side of the room. 'What! (said she to her brother) am I to be affronted by every mangy hound that you pick up on the highway? I insist upon your sending this rascalion about his business immediately' ——'For God's sake, sister, compose yourself (said my uncle) and consider that the poor fellow is innocent of any intention to give you offence'—'Innocent as the babe unborn' (cried Humphry). 'I see it plainly (exclaimed this implacable maiden) he acts by your direction; and you are resolved to support him in his impudence—This is a bad return for all the services I have done you; for nursing you in your sickness, managing your family, and keeping you from ruining yourself by your own imprudence——But now you shall part with that rascal or me, upon the spot, without farther loss of time; and the world shall see whether you have more regard for your own flesh and blood, or for a beggarly foundling taken from the dunghill.'

Mr. Bramble's eyes began to glisten, and his teeth to

chatter. 'If stated fairly (said he, raising his voice) the question is, whether I have spirit to shake off an intolerable yoke, by one effort of resolution, or meanness enough to do an act of cruelty and injustice, to gratify the rancour of a capricious woman——Heark ye, Mrs. Tabitha Bramble, I will now propose an alternative in my turn—Either discard your four-footed favourite, or give me leave to bid you eternally adieu—For I am determined that he and I shall live no longer under the same roof; and now *to dinner with what appetite you may*'——Thunderstruck at this declaration, she sat down in a corner; and, after a pause of some minutes. 'Sure I don't understand you, Matt! (said she)' 'And yet I spoke in plain English'——answered the squire, with a peremptory look. 'Sir, (resumed this virago, effectually humbled) it is your prerogative to command, and my duty to obey. I can't dispose of the dog in this place; but if you'll allow him to go in the coach to London, I give you my word, he shall never trouble you again.'

Her brother, entirely disarmed by this mild reply, declared, she could ask him nothing in reason that he would refuse; adding, 'I hope, sister, you have never found me deficient in natural affection.' Mrs. Tabitha immediately rose, and, throwing her arms about his neck, kissed him on the cheek: he returned her embrace with great emotion. Liddy sobbed, Win. Jenkins cackled, Chowder capered, and Clinker skipped about, rubbing his hands for joy of this reconciliation.

Concord being thus restored, we finished our meal with comfort; and in the evening arrived at London, without having met with any other adventure. My aunt seems to be much mended by the hint she received from her brother. She has been graciously pleased to remove her displeasure from Clinker, who is now retained as a footman; and in a day or two will make his appearance in a new suit of livery; but as he is little acquainted with London, we have taken an occasional valet, whom I intend hereafter to hire as my own

servant. We lodge in Golden-square, at the house of one
Mrs. Norton, a decent sort of a woman, who takes great
pains to make us all easy. My uncle proposes to make a circuit
of all the remarkable scenes of this metropolis, for the entertainment of his pupils; but as both you and I are already
acquainted with most of those he will visit, and with some
others he little dreams of, I shall only communicate what
will be in some measure new to your observation. Remember
me to our Jesuitical friends, and believe me ever,

Dear Knight,

yours affectionately,

J. MELFORD.

LONDON, *May* 24.

To Dr. Lewis

DEAR DOCTOR,
    London is literally new to me; new in its streets,
houses, and even in its situation; as the Irishman said, 'London is now gone out of town.' What I left open fields,
producing hay and corn, I now find covered with streets
and squares, and palaces, and churches. I am credibly informed, that in the space of seven years, eleven thousand
new houses have been built in one quarter of Westminster,
exclusive of what is daily added to other parts of this
unwieldy metropolis. Pimlico and Knightsbridge are now
almost joined to Chelsea and Kensington; and if this infatuation continues for half a century, I suppose the whole
county of Middlesex will be covered with brick.
    It must be allowed, indeed, for the credit of the present
age, that London and Westminster are much better paved
and lighted than they were formerly. The new streets are
spacious, regular, and airy; and the houses generally convenient. The bridge at Blackfriars is a noble monument of
taste and public-spirit.——I wonder how they stumbled

upon a work of such magnificence and utility. But, not-withstanding these improvements, the capital is become an overgrown monster; which, like a dropsical head, will in time leave the body and extremities without nourishment and support. The absurdity will appear in its full force, when we consider that one sixth part of the natives of this whole extensive kingdom is crowded within the bills of mortality. What wonder that our villages are depopulated, and our farms in want of day-labourers? The abolition of small farms is but one cause of the decrease of population. Indeed, the incredible increase of horses and black cattle, to answer the purposes of luxury, requires a prodigious quantity of hay and grass, which are raised and managed without much labour; but a number of hands will always be wanted for the different branches of agriculture, whether the farms be large or small. The tide of luxury has swept all the inhabitants from the open country——The poorest squire, as well as the richest peer, must have his house in town, and make a figure with an extraordinary number of domestics. The plough-boys, cow-herds, and lower hinds are debauched and seduced by the appearance and discourse of those coxcombs in livery, when they make their summer excursions. They desert their dirt and drudgery, and swarm up to London, in hopes of getting into service, where they can live luxuriously and wear fine clothes, without being obliged to work; for idleness is natural to man——Great numbers of these, being disappointed in their expectation, become thieves and sharpers; and London being an immense wilderness, in which there is neither watch nor ward of any signification, nor any order or police, affords them lurking-places as well as prey.

There are many causes that contribute to the daily increase of this enormous mass; but they may be all resolved into the grand source of luxury and corruption——About five and twenty years ago, very few, even of the most opulent citizens of London, kept any equipage, or even any servants in livery. Their tables produced nothing but plain boiled and roasted, with a bottle of port and a tankard of beer. At present, every trader in any degree of credit, every broker and attorney, maintains a couple of footmen, a coachman, and postilion. He has his town-house, and his country-house, his coach, and his post-chaise. His wife and daughters appear in the richest stuffs, bespangled with diamonds. They frequent the court, the opera, the theatre, and the masquerade. They hold assemblies at their own houses; they make sumptuous entertainments, and treat with the richest wines of Bordeaux, Burgundy, and Champagne. The substantial tradesman, who wont to pass his evenings at the ale-house for fourpence half-penny, now spends three shillings at the tavern, while his wife keeps card-tables at home; she must likewise have fine clothes, her chaise, or pad, with country lodgings, and go three times a week to public diversions. Every clerk, apprentice, and even waiter of tavern or coffeehouse, maintains a gelding by himself, or in partnership, and assumes the air and apparel of a petit maitre—— The gayest places of public entertainment are filled with fashionable figures; which, upon inquiry, will be found to be journeymen taylors, serving-men, and abigails, disguised like their betters.

In short, there is no distinction or subordination left—— The different departments of life are jumbled together —The hod-carrier, the low mechanic, the tapster, the publican, the shop-keeper, the pettifogger, the citizen, and courtier, *all tread upon the kibes of one another:* actuated by the demons of profligacy and licentiousness, they are seen every where rambling, riding, rolling, rushing, justling, mixing, bouncing, cracking, and crashing in one vile ferment of stupidity and corruption—All is tumult and hurry; one would imagine they were impelled by some disorder of the brain, that will not suffer them to be at rest. The foot-passengers run along as if they were pursued by bailiffs. The porters and chairmen trot with their burthens. People, who keep their own equipages, drive through the streets at full speed. Even citizens, physicians, and apothecaries, glide in their chariots like lightning. The hackney-coachmen make their horses smoke, and the pavement shakes under them; and I have actually seen a waggon pass through Piccadilly at the hand-gallop. In a word, the whole nation seems to be running out of their wits.

The diversions of the times are not ill suited to the genius of this incongruous monster, called *the public*. Give it noise, confusion, glare, and glitter; it has no idea of elegance and propriety—What are the amusements of Ranelagh? One half of the company are following at the other's tails, in an eternal circle; like so many blind asses in an olive-mill, where they can neither discourse, distinguish, nor be distinguished; while the other half are drinking hot water, under the denomination of tea, till nine or ten o'clock at night, to keep them awake for the rest of the evening. As for the orchestra, the vocal music especially, it is well for the performers that they cannot be heard distinctly. Vauxhall is a composition of baubles, overcharged with paltry ornaments, ill conceived, and poorly executed; without any unity of design, or propriety of disposition. It is an unnatural assembly of objects, fantastically illuminated in broken masses; seemingly contrived to dazzle the eyes and divert the imagination of the vulgar—Here a wooden lion, there a stone statue; in one place, a range of things like coffeehouse boxes, covered a-top; in another, a parcel of alehouse benches; in a third, a puppet-show representation of a tin cascade; in a fourth, a gloomy cave of a circular form, like a sepulchral vault half lighted; in a fifth, a scanty flip of grass-plat, that would not afford pasture sufficient for an ass's colt. The walks, which nature seems to have intended for solitude, shade, and silence, are filled with crowds of noisy people, sucking up the nocturnal rheums of an aguish climate; and through these gay scenes, a few lamps glimmer like so many farthing candles.

When I see a number of well dressed people, of both sexes, sitting on the covered benches, exposed to the eyes of the mob; and, which is worse, to the cold, raw, night-air, devouring sliced beef, and swilling port, and punch, and cyder, I can't help compassionating their temerity; while I despise their want of taste and decorum; but, when they course along those damp and gloomy walks, or crowd together upon the wet gravel, without any other cover than the cope of Heaven, listening to a song, which one half of them cannot possibly hear, how can I help supposing they are actually possessed by a spirit, more absurd and pernicious than any thing we meet with in the precincts of Bedlam? In all probability, the proprietors of this, and other public gardens of inferior note, in the skirts of the metropolis, are, in some shape, connected with the faculty of physic, and the company of undertakers; for, considering that eagerness in the pursuit of what is called pleasure, which now predominates through every rank and denomination of life, I am persuaded that more gouts, rheumatisms, catarrhs, and consumptions are caught in these nocturnal pastimes, *sub dio,* than from all the risques and accidents to which a life of toil and danger is exposed.

These, and other observations, which I have made in this excursion, will shorten my stay at London, and send me back with a double relish to my solitude and mountains; but I shall return by a different route from that which brought me to town. I have seen some old friends, who constantly resided in this virtuous metropolis, but they are so changed in manners and disposition, that we hardly know or care for one another—In our journey from Bath, my sister Tabby provoked me into a transport of passion; during which, like a man who has drank himself pot-valiant, I talked to her in such a stile of authority and resolution, as produced a most blessed effect. She and her dog have been remarkably quiet and orderly ever since this expostulation. How long this agreeable calm will last, Heaven above knows—I flatter myself, the exercise of travelling has been of service to my health; a circumstance which encourages me to proceed in my projected expedition to the North. But I must, in the mean time, for the benefit and amusement of my pupils, explore the depths of this chaos; this misshapen and monstrous capital, without head or tail, members or proportion.

Thomas was so insolent to my sister on the road, that I was obliged to turn him off abruptly, betwixt Chippenham and Marlborough, where our coach was overturned. The fellow was always sullen and selfish; but, if he should return to the country, you may give him a character for honesty and sobriety; and, provided he behaves with proper respect to the family, let him have a couple of guineas in the name of

Yours always,
MATT. BRAMBLE.

LONDON, *May* 29.

To Miss Lætitia Willis, at Gloucester

MY DEAR LETTY,

Inexpressible was the pleasure I received from yours of the 25th, which was last night put into my hands by Mrs. Brentford, the millener, from Gloucester———I rejoice to hear that my worthy governess is in good health, and, still more, that she no longer retains any displeasure towards her poor Liddy. I am sorry you have lost the society of the agreeable Miss Vaughan; but, I hope, you won't have cause much longer to regret the departure of your school companions, as I make no doubt but your parents will, in a little time, bring you into the world, where you are so well qualified to make a distinguished figure. When that is the case, I flatter myself you and I shall meet again, and be happy together; and even improve the friendship which we contracted in our tender years———This at

least I can promise—It shall not be for the want of my
utmost endeavours, if our intimacy does not continue
for life.

About five days ago we arrived in London, after an easy
journey from Bath; during which, however, we were
overturned, and met with some other little incidents, which,
had like to have occasioned a misunderstanding betwixt my
uncle and aunt; but now, thank God, they are happily
reconciled: we live in harmony together, and every day
make parties to see the wonders of this vast metropolis,
which, however, I cannot pretend to describe; for I have
not as yet seen one hundredth part of its curiosities, and
I am quite in a maze of admiration.

The cities of London and Westminster are spread out
into an incredible extent. The streets, squares, rows, lanes,
and alleys, are innumerable. Palaces, public buildings, and
churches rise in every quarter; and, among these last, St.
Paul's appears with the most astonishing pre-eminence. They
say it is not so large as St. Peter's at Rome; but, for my
own part, I can have no idea of any earthly temple more
grand and magnificent.

But even these superb objects are not so striking as the
crowds of people that swarm in the streets. I at first
imagined that some great assembly was just dismissed, and
wanted to stand aside till the multitude should pass; but
this human tide continues to flow, without interruption or
abatement, from morn till night. Then there is such an infinity of gay equipages, coaches, chariots, chaises, and other
carriages, continually rolling and shifting before your eyes,
that one's head grows giddy looking at them; and the
imagination is quite confounded with splendour and variety.
Nor is the prospect by water less grand and astonishing than
that by land: you see three stupendous bridges, joining the
opposite banks of a broad, deep, and rapid river; so vast, so
stately, so elegant, that they seem to be the work of the
giants; betwixt them, the whole surface of the Thames is

covered with small vessels, barges, boats, and wherries, passing to and fro; and below the three bridges, such a prodigious forest of masts, for miles together, that you would think all the ships in the universe were here assembled. All that you read of wealth and grandeur in the Arabian Nights' Entertainment, and the Persian Tales, concerning Bagdad, Diarbekir, Damascus, Ispahan, and Samarkand, is here realized.

Ranelagh looks like the inchanted palace of a genie, adorned with the most exquisite performances of painting, carving, and gilding, enlightened with a thousand golden lamps, that emulate the noon-day sun; crowded with the great, the rich, the gay, the happy, and the fair; glittering with cloth of gold and silver, lace, embroidery, and precious stones. While these exulting sons and daughters of felicity tread this round of pleasure, or regale in different parties, and separate lodges, with fine imperial tea and other delicious refreshments, their ears are entertained with the most ravishing delights of music, both instrumental and vocal. There I heard the famous Tenducci, a thing from Italy— It looks for all the world like a man, though they say it is not. The voice, to be sure, is neither man's nor woman's; but it is more melodious than either; and it warbled so divinely, that, while I listened, I really thought myself in paradise.

At nine o'clock, in a charming moonlight evening, we embarked at Ranelagh for Vauxhall, in a wherry so light and slender that we looked like so many fairies sailing in a nut-shell. My uncle, being apprehensive of catching cold upon the water, went round in the coach, and my aunt would have accompanied him, but he would not suffer me to go by water if she went by land; and therefore she favoured us with her company, as she perceived I had a curiosity to make this agreeable voyage——After all, the vessel was sufficiently loaded; for, besides the waterman, there was my brother Jery, and a friend of his, one Mr.

Barton, a country gentleman, of a good fortune, who had
dined at our house——The pleasure of this little excursion
was, however, damped by my being sadly frighted at our
landing; where there was a terrible confusion of wherries,
and a crowd of people bawling, and swearing, and quar-
relling: nay, a parcel of ugly-looking fellows came running
into the water, and laid hold of our boat with great violence,
to pull it a-shore; nor would they quit their hold till my
brother struck one of them over the head with his cane. But
this flutter was fully recompensed by the pleasures of Vauxhall; which I no sooner entered, than I was dazzled and
confounded with the variety of beauties that rushed all at
once upon my eye. Image to yourself, my dear Letty, a
spacious garden, part laid out in delightful walks, bounded
with high hedges and trees, and paved with gravel; part
exhibiting a wonderful assemblage of the most picturesque
and striking objects, pavilions, lodges, groves, grottoes,
lawns, temples and cascades; porticoes, colonades, and rotun-
das; adorned with pillars, statues, and painting; the whole
illuminated with an infinite number of lamps, disposed in
different figures of suns, stars, and constellations; the place
crowded with the gayest company, ranging through those
blissful shades, or supping in different lodges on cold colla-
tions, enlivened with mirth, freedom, and good humour,
and animated by an excellent band of music. Among the
vocal performers I had the happiness to hear the celebrated
Mrs. ————, whose voice was loud and so shrill, that it
made my head ake through excess of pleasure.

In about half an hour after we arrived we were joined
by my uncle, who did not seem to relish the place. People
of experience and infirmity, my dear Letty, see with very
different eyes from those that such as you and I make use
of——Our evening's entertainment was interrupted by an
unlucky accident. In one of the remotest walks we were
surprised with a sudden shower, that set the whole company
a-running, and drove us in heaps, one upon another, into

the rotunda; where my uncle, finding himself wet, began to be very peevish and urgent to be gone. My brother went to look for the coach, and found it with much difficulty; but as it could not hold us all, Mr. Barton stayed behind. It was some time before the carriage could be brought up to the gate, in the confusion, notwithstanding the utmost endeavours of our new footman, Humphry Clinker, who lost his scratch periwig, and got a broken head in the scuffle. The moment we were seated, my aunt pulled off my uncle's shoes, and carefully wrapped his poor feet in her capuchin; then she gave him a mouth-ful of cordial, which she always keeps in her pocket, and his clothes were shifted as soon as we arrived at lodgings; so that, blessed be God, he escaped a severe cold, of which he was in great terror.

As for Mr. Barton, I must tell you in confidence, he was a little particular; but, perhaps, I mistake his complaisance; and I wish I may, for his sake—You know the condition of my poor heart: which, in spite of hard usage—And yet I ought not to complain: nor will I, till farther information.

Besides Ranelagh and Vauxhall, I have been at Mrs. Cornelys' assembly, which, for the rooms, the company, the dresses, and decorations, surpasses all description; but as I have no great turn for card playing, I have not yet entered thoroughly into the spirit of the place: indeed I am still such a country hoyden, that I could hardly find patience to be put in a condition to appear, yet, as I was not above six hours under the hands of the hair-dresser, who stuffed my head with as much black wool as would have made a quilted petticoat; and, after all, it was the smallest head in the assembly, except my aunt's—She, to be sure, was so particular with her rumpt gown and petticoat, her scanty curls, her lappet-head, deep triple ruffles, and high stays, that every body looked at her with surprise: some whispered, and some tittered; and lady Griskin, by whom we were introduced, flatly told her, she was twenty good years behind the fashion.

Lady Griskin is a person of fashion, to whom we have the honour to be related. She keeps a small rout at her own house, never exceeding ten or a dozen card-tables, but these are frequented by the best company in town—She has been so obliging as to introduce my aunt and me to some of her particular friends of quality, who treat us with the most familiar good-humour: we have once dined with her, and she takes the trouble to direct us in all our motions. I am so happy as to have gained her good-will to such a degree, that she sometimes adjusts my cap with her own hands; and she has given me a kind invitation to stay with her all the winter. This, however, has been cruelly declined by my uncle who seems to be (I know not how) prejudiced against the good lady; for, whenever my aunt happens to speak in her com-mendation, I observe that he makes wry faces, though he says nothing——Perhaps, indeed, these grimaces may be the effect of pain arising from the gout and rheumatism, with which he is sadly distressed——To me, however, he is always good-natured and generous, even beyond my wish. Since we came hither, he has made me a present of a suit of clothes, with trimmings and laces, which cost more money than I shall mention; and Jery, at his desire, has given me my mother's diamond drops, which are ordered to be set a-new; so that it won't be his fault if I do not glitter among the stars of the fourth or fifth magnitude. I wish my weak head may not grow giddy in the midst of all this gallantry and dissipation; though, as yet, I can safely de-clare, I could gladly give up all these tumultuous pleasures, for country solitude, and a happy retreat with those we love; among whom, my dear Willis will always possess the first place in the breast of her

Ever affectionate,

LYDIA MELFORD.

LONDON, *May* 31.

To Sir Watkin Phillips, of Jesus college, Oxon.

DEAR PHILLIPS,

I send you this letter, franked by our old friend **Bar-ton**; who is as much altered as it was possible for a man of his kidney to be—Instead of the careless, indolent sloven we knew at Oxford, I found him a busy talkative politician; a petit-maître in his dress, and a ceremonious courtier in his manners. He has not gall enough in his constitution to be enflamed with the rancour of party, so as to deal in scurrilous invectives; but, since he obtained a place, he is become a warm partizan of the ministry, and sees every thing through such an exaggerating medium, as to me, who am happily of no party, is altogether incomprehensible—Without all doubt, the fumes of faction not only disturb the faculty of reason, but also pervert the organs of sense; and I would lay a hundred guineas to ten, that if Barton on one side, and the most conscientious patriot in the opposition on the other, were to draw, upon honour, the picture of the k—— or m——, you and I, who are still uninfected, and unbiassed, would find both painters equally distant from the truth. One thing, however, must be allowed for the honour of Barton, he never breaks out into illiberal abuse, far less endeavours, by infamous calumnies, to blast the moral character of any individual on the other side.

Ever since we came hither, he has been remarkably assiduous in his attention to our family; an attention, which, in a man of his indolence and avocations, I should have thought altogether odd, and even unnatural, had not I perceived that my sister Liddy had made some impression upon his heart. I cannot say that I have any objection to his trying his fortune in this pursuit: if an opulent estate and a great flock of good-nature are sufficient qualifications in a husband, to render the marriage-state happy for life, she may be happy with Barton; but, I imagine, there is something else required to engage and secure the affection of a woman of sense and delicacy: something which nature has denied our friend——Liddy seems to be of the same opinion. When he addresses himself to her in discourse, she seems to listen with reluctance, and industriously avoids all particular communication; but in proportion to her coyness, our aunt is coming. Mrs. Tabitha goes more than half way to meet his advances; she mistakes, or affects to mistake, the meaning of his courtesy, which is rather formal and fulsome; she returns his compliments with hyperbolical interest, she persecutes him with her civilities at table, she appeals to him for ever in conversation, she sighs, and flirts, and ogles, and by her hideous affectation and impertinence, drives the poor courtier to the very extremity of his complaisance; in short, she seems to have undertaken the siege of Barton's heart, and carries on her approaches in such a desperate manner, that I don't know whether he will not be obliged to capitulate. In the mean time, his aversion to this inamorata struggling with his acquired affability, and his natural fear of giving offence, throws him into a kind of distress which is extremely ridiculous.

Two days ago, he persuaded my uncle and me to accompany him to St. James's, where he undertook to make us acquainted with the persons of all the great men in the kingdom; and, indeed, there was a great assemblage of distinguished characters, for it was a high festival at court. Our conductor performed his promise with great punctuality. He pointed out almost every individual of both sexes, and generally introduced them to our notice, with a flourish of panegyrick——Seeing the king approach, 'There comes (said he) the most amiable sovereign that ever swayed the sceptre of England; the *deliciæ humani generis*; Augustus, in patronizing merit; Titus Vespasian in generosity; Trajan in beneficence; and Marcus Aurelius in philosophy.' 'A very honest kind-hearted gentleman (added my uncle) he's too good for the times. A king of England should have a spice of the devil in his composition.' Barton, then turning to the

duke of C—, proceeded,—'You know the duke, that illustrious hero, who trode rebellion under his feet, and secured
us in possession of every thing we ought to hold dear, as
Englishmen and Christians. Mark what an eye, how penetrating, yet pacific! what dignity in his mien! what humanity
in his aspect——Even malice must own, that he is one of
the greatest officers in Christendom.' 'I think he is (said Mr.
Bramble) but who are these young gentlemen that stand
beside him?' 'Those! (cried our friend) those are his royal
nephews; the princes of the blood. Sweet young princes! the
sacred pledges of the Protestant line; so spirited, so sensible,
so princely'——'Yes; very sensible! very spirited! (said
my uncle, interrupting him) but see the queen! ha, there's
the queen!——There's the queen! let me see—Let me
see——Where are my glasses? ha! there's meaning in that
eye——There's sentiment—There's expression—Well, Mr.
Barton, what figure do you call next?' The next person he
pointed out, was the favourite *yearl;* who stood solitary by
one of the windows—'Behold yon northern star (said he)
shorn of his beams'——'What! the Caledonian luminary,
that lately blazed so bright in our hemisphere! methinks, at
present, it glimmers through a fog; like Saturn without his
ring, bleak, and dim, and distant——Ha, there's the other
great phenomenon, the grand pensionary, that weathercock
of patriotism that veers about in every point of the political
compass, and still feels the wind of popularity in his tail.
He too, like a portentous comet, has risen again above the
court-horizon; but how long he will continue to ascend, it
is not easy to foretell, considering his great eccentricity—
Who are those two satellites that attend his motions?' When
Barton told him their names, 'To their characters (said
Mr. Bramble) I am no stranger. One of them, without a
drop of red blood in his veins, has a cold intoxicating vapour
in his head; and rancour enough in his heart to inoculate
and affect a whole nation. The other is (I hear) intended
for a share in the ad———n, and the pensionary vouches

for his being duly qualified—The only instance I ever heard of his sagacity, was his deserting his former patron, when he found him declining in power, and in disgrace with the people. Without principle, talent, or intelligence, he is ungracious as a hog, greedy as a vulture, and thievish as a jackdaw; but, it must be owned, he is no hypocrite. He pretends to no virtue, and takes no pains to disguise his character—His ministry will be attended with one advantage, no man will be disappointed by his breach of promise, as no mortal ever trusted to his word. I wonder how lord —— first discovered this happy genius, and for what purpose lord —— has now adopted him: but one would think, that as amber has a power to attract dirt, and straws, and chaff, a minister is endued with the same kind of faculty, to *lick up every knave and blockhead in his way*'—His eulogium was interrupted by the arrival of the old duke of N——; who, squeezing into the circle with a busy face of importance, thrust his head into every countenance, as if he had been in search of somebody, to whom he wanted to impart something of great consequence—My uncle, who had been formerly known to him, bowed as he passed; and the duke seeing himself saluted so respectfully by a well-dressed person, was not slow in returning the courtesy—He even came up, and, taking him cordially by the hand, 'My dear friend, Mr. A—— (said he) I am rejoiced to see you —How long have you been come from abroad?—How did you leave our good friends the Dutch? The king of Prussia don't think of another war, ah?——He's a great king! a great conqueror! a very great conqueror! Your Alexanders and Hannibals were nothing at all to him, sir——Corporals! drummers! dross! mere trash——Damned trash, heh?'—His grace being by this time out of breath, my uncle took the opportunity to tell him he had not been out of England, that his name was Bramble, and that he had the honour to sit in the last parliament but one of the late king, as representative for the borough of Dymkymraig.

'Odso! (cried the duke) I remember you perfectly well, my dear Mr. Bramble——You was always a good and loyal subject——a stanch friend to administration——I made your brother an Irish bishop'—'Pardon me, my lord (said the squire) I once had a brother, but he was a captain in the army'——'Ha? (said his grace) he was so—He was, indeed! But who was the Bishop then! Bishop Blackberry ——Sure it was bishop Blackberry—Perhaps some relation of yours'———'Very likely, my lord (replied my uncle); the Blackberry is the fruit of the Bramble—But, I believe, the bishop is not a berry of our bush'——'No more he is— No more he is, ha, ha, ha! (exclaimed the duke) there you gave me a scratch, good Mr. Bramble, ha, ha, ha!—Well, I shall be glad to see you at Lincoln's-inn-fields—You know the way——Times are altered. Though I have lost the power, I retain the inclination—Your very humble servant, good Mr. Blackberry'———So saying, he shoved to another corner of the room. 'What a fine old gentleman (cried Mr. Barton) what spirits! what a memory!—He never forgets an old friend.' 'He does me too much honour (observed our squire) to rank me among the number—Whilst I sat in parliament, I never voted with the ministry but three times, when my conscience told me they were in the right: however, if he still keeps levee, I will carry my nephew thither, that he may see, and learn to avoid the scene; for, I think, an English gentleman never appears to such disadvantage, as at the levee of a minister—Of his grace I shall say nothing at present, but that for thirty years he was the constant and common butt of ridicule and execration. He was generally laughed at as an ape in politics, whose office and influence served only to render his folly the more notorious; and the opposition cursed him, as the indefatigable drudge of a first-mover, who was justly stiled and stigmatized as the father of corruption: but this ridiculous ape, this venal drudge, no sooner lost the places he was so ill qualified to fill, and unfurled the banners of faction, than he was metamorphosed into a pattern of public virtue; the very people who reviled him before, now extolled him to the skies, as a wise, experienced statesman, chief pillar of the Protestant succession, and corner stone of English liberty. I should be glad to know how Mr. Barton reconciles these contradictions, without obliging us to resign all title to the privilege of common sense.' 'My dear sir (answered Barton) I don't pretend to justify the extravagations of the multitude; who, I suppose, were as wild in their former censure, as in their present praise: but I shall be very glad to attend you on Thursday next to his grace's levee; where, I'm afraid, we shall not be crowded with company; for, you know, there's a wide difference between his present office of president of the council, and his former post of first lord commissioner of the treasury.'

This communicative friend having announced all the remarkable characters of both sexes, that appeared at court, we resolved to adjourn, and retired. At the foot of the stair-case, there was a crowd of laqueys and chairmen, and in the midst of them stood Humphry Clinker, exalted upon a stool, with his hat in one hand, and a paper in the other, in the act of holding forth to the people——Before we could inquire into the meaning of this exhibition, he perceived his master, thrust the paper into his pocket, descended from his elevation, bolted through the crowd, and brought up the carriage to the gate.

My uncle said nothing till we were seated, when, after having looked at me earnestly for some time, he burst out a-laughing, and asked if I knew upon what subject Clinker was holding forth to the mob——'If (said he) the fellow is turned mountebank, I must turn him out of my service, otherwise he'll make Merry Andrews of us all'——I observed, that, in all probability, he had studied medicine under his master, who was a farrier.

At dinner, the squire asked him, if he had ever practised physic? 'Yes, an please your honour (said he) among brute beasts; but I never meddle with rational creatures.' 'I know not whether you rank in that class the audience you was haranguing in the court at St. James's, but I should be glad to know what kind of powders you was distributing; and whether you had a good sale'——'Sale, sir! (cried Clinker) I hope I shall never be base enough to sell for gold and silver, what freely comes of God's grace. I distributed nothing, an like your honour, but a word of advice to my fellows in servitude and sin.' 'Advice! concerning what?' 'Concerning profane swearing, an please your honour; so horrid and shocking, that it made my hair stand on end.' 'Nay, if thou can'st cure them of that disease, I shall think thee a wonderful doctor indeed'——'Why not cure them, my good master? the hearts of those poor people are not so stubborn as your honour seems to think—Make them first sensible that you have nothing in view but their good, then they will listen with patience, and easily be convinced of the sin and folly of a practice that affords neither profit nor pleasure' ——At this remark, our uncle changed colour, and looked round the company, conscious that his *own withers were not altogether unwrung*. 'But, Clinker (said he) if you should have eloquence enough to persuade the vulgar to resign those tropes and figures of rhetoric, there will be little or nothing left to distinguish their conversation from that of their betters.' 'But then your honour knows, their conversation will be void of offence; and, at the day of judgment, there will be no distinction of persons.'

Humphry going down stairs to fetch up a bottle of wine, my uncle congratulated his sister upon having such a reformer in the family; when Mrs. Tabitha declared, he was a sober civilized fellow; very respectful, and very industrious; and, she believed, a good Christian into the bargain. One would think, Clinker must really have some very extraordinary talent, to ingratiate himself in this manner with a virago of her character, so fortified against him with prejudice and resentment; but the truth is, since the adventure of Salt-hill, Mrs. Tabby seems to be entirely changed. She has left off scolding the servants, an exercise which was grown habitual, and even seemed necessary to her constitution; and is become so indifferent to Chowder, as to part with him in a present to lady Griskin, who proposes to bring the breed of him into fashion. Her ladyship is the widow of Sir Timothy Griskin, a distant relation of our family. She enjoys a jointure of five hundred pounds a-year, and makes shift to spend three times that sum. Her character before marriage was a little equivocal; but at present she lives in the *bon ton,* keeps card-tables, gives private suppers to select friends, and is visited by persons of the first fashion—She has been remarkably civil to us all, and cultivates my uncle with the most particular regard; but the more she strokes him, the more his bristles seem to rise—To her compliments he makes very laconic and dry returns—T'other day, she sent us a pottle of fine strawberries, which he did not receive without signs of disgust, muttering from the Æneid, *timeo Danaos et Dona ferentes.* She has twice called for Liddy, of a forenoon, to take an airing in the coach; but Mrs. Tabby was always so alert (I suppose by his direction) that she never could have the niece without her aunt's company—I have endeavoured to sound Square-toes on this subject; but he carefully avoids all explanation.

I have now, dear Phillips, filled a whole sheet; and if you have read it to an end, I dare say, you are as tired as

Your humble servant,

J. MELFORD.

LONDON, *June* 2.

To Dr. Lewis

Yes, Doctor, I have seen the British Museum; which is a noble collection, and even stupendous, if we consider it was made by a private man, a physician who was obliged to make his own fortune at the same time: but great as the collection is, it would appear more striking if it was arranged in one spacious saloon, instead of being divided into different apartments, which it does not entirely fill—I could wish the series of medals was connected, and the whole of the animal, vegetable, and mineral kingdoms completed, by adding to each, at the public expence, those articles that are wanting. It would likewise be a great improvement, with respect to the library, if the deficiencies were made up, by purchasing all the books of character that are not to be found already in the collection—They might be classed in centuries, according to the dates of their publication, and catalogues printed of them and the manuscripts, for the information of those that want to consult, or compile from such authorities. I could also wish, for the honour of the nation, that there was a complete apparatus for a course of mathematics, mechanics, and experimental philosophy; and a good salary settled upon an able professor, who should give regular lectures on these subjects.

But this is all idle speculation, which will never be reduced to practice—Considering the temper of the times, it is a wonder to see any institution whatsoever established for the benefit of the public. The spirit of party is risen to a kind of phrenzy, unknown to former ages, or rather degenerated to a total extinction of honesty and candour—You know I have observed, for some time, that the public papers are become the infamous vehicles of the most cruel and perfidious defamation: every rancorous knave——every desperate incendiary, that can afford to spend half a crown or three shilling, may skulk behind the press of a newsmonger, and have a stab at the first character in the kingdom, without running the least hazard of detection or punishment.

I have made acquaintance with a Mr. Barton, whom Jery knew at Oxford; a good sort of a man, though most ridiculously warped in his political principles; but his partiality is the less offensive, as it never appears in the stile of

scurrility and abuse. He is a member of parliament, and a
retainer to the court; and his whole conversation turns upon
the virtues and perfections of the ministers, who are his
patrons. T'other day, when he was bedaubing one of those
worthies, with the most fulsome praise, I told him I had
seen the same nobleman characterised very differently, in
one of the daily-papers; indeed, so stigmatized, that if one
half of what was said of him was true, he must be not
only unfit to rule, but even unfit to live: that those impeach-
ments had been repeated again and again, with the addition
of fresh matter; and that as he had taken no steps towards
his own vindication, I began to think there was some foundation for the charge. 'And pray, Sir, (said Mr. Barton)
what steps would you have him take?—Suppose he should
prosecute the publisher, who screens the anonymous accuser,
and bring him to the pillory for a libel; this is so far from
being counted a punishment, *in terrorem*, that it will probably make his fortune. The multitude immediately take him
into their protection, as a martyr to the cause of defamation,
which they have always espoused——They pay his fine,
they contribute to the increase of his stock, his shop is
crowded with customers, and the sale of his paper rises in
proportion to the scandal it contains. All this time the
prosecutor is inveighed against as a tyrant and oppressor, for
having chosen to proceed by the way of information, which
is deemed a grievance; but if he lays an action for damages,
he must prove the damage, and I leave you to judge, whether
a gentleman's character may not be brought into contempt,
and all his views in life blasted by calumny, without his
being able to specify the particulars of the damage he has
sustained.

'This spirit of defamation is a kind of heresy, that thrives
under persecution. *The liberty of the press* is a term of
great efficacy; and like that of *the Protestant religion*, has
often served the purposes of sedition—A minister, therefore, must arm himself with patience, and bear those attacks

without repining—Whatever mischief they may do in other respects they certainly contribute, in one particular, to the advantages of government; for those defamatory articles have multiplied papers in such a manner, and augmented their sale to such a degree, that the duty upon stamps and advertisements has made a very considerable addition to the revenue.' Certain it is, a gentleman's honour is a very delicate subject to be handled by a jury, composed of men, who cannot be supposed remarkable either for sentiment or impartiality—In such a case, indeed, the defendant is tried, not only by his peers, but also by his party; and I really think, that of all patriots, he is the most resolute who exposes himself to such detraction, for the sake of his country—If, from the ignorance or partiality of juries, a gentleman can have no redress from law, for being defamed in a pamphlet or newspaper, I know but one other method of proceeding against the publisher, which is attended with some risque, but has been practised successfully, more than once, in my remembrance—A regiment of horse was represented, in one of the news-papers, as having misbehaved at Dettingen; a captain of that regiment broke the publisher's bones, telling him, at the same time, if he went to law, he should certainly have the like salutation from every officer of the corps. Governor —— took the same satisfaction on the ribs of an author, who traduced him by name in a periodical paper—I know a low fellow of the same class, who, being turned out of Venice for his impudence and scurrility, retired to Lugano, a town of the Grisons (a free people, God wot) where he found a printing press, from whence he squirted his filth at some respectable characters in the republic, which he had been obliged to abandon. Some of these, finding him out of the reach of legal chastisement, employed certain useful instruments, such as may be found in all countries, to give him the bastinado; which, being repeated more than once, effectually stopt the current of his abuse.

As for the liberty of the press, like every other privilege,

.t must be restrained within certain bounds; for if it is carried to a branch of law, religion, and charity, it becomes one of the greatest evils that ever annoyed the community. If the lowest ruffian may stab your good name with impunity in England, will you be so uncandid as to exclaim against Italy for the practice of common assassination? To what purpose is our property secured, if our moral character is left defenceless? People thus baited, grow desperate; and the despair of being able to preserve one's character, untainted by such vermin, produces a total neglect of fame; so that one of the chief incitements to the practice of virtue is effectually destroyed.

Mr. Barton's last consideration, respecting the stamp-duty, is equally wise and laudable with another maxim which has been long adopted by our financiers, namely, to connive at drunkenness, riot, and dissipation, because they inhance the receipt of the excise; not reflecting, that in providing this temporary convenience, they are destroying the morals, health, and industry of the people——Notwithstanding my contempt for those who flatter a minister, I think there is something still more despicable in flattering a mob. When I see a man of birth, education, and fortune, put himself on a level with the dregs of the people, mingle with low mechanics, feed with them at the same board, and drink with them in the same cup, flatter their prejudices, harangue in praise of their virtues, expose themselves to the belchings of their beer, the fumes of their tobacco, the grossness of their familiarity, and the impertinence of their conversation, I cannot help despising him, as a man guilty of the vilest prostitution, in order to effect a purpose equally selfish and illiberal.

I should renounce politics the more willingly, if I could find other topics of conversation discussed with more modesty and candour; but the dæmon of party seems to have usurped every department of life. Even the world of literature and taste is divided into the most virulent factions, which revile, decry, and traduce the works of one another. Yesterday, I went to return an afternoon's visit to a gentleman of my acquaintance, at whose house I found one of the authors of the present age, who has written with some success— As I had read one or two of his performances, which gave me pleasure, I was glad of this opportunity to know his person; but his discourse and deportment destroyed all the impressions which his writings had made in his favour. He took upon him to decide dogmatically upon every subject, without deigning to shew the least cause for his differing from the general opinions of mankind, as if it had been our duty to acquiesce in the *ipse dixit* of this new Pythagoras. He rejudged the characters of all the principal authors, who had died within a century of the present time; and, in this revision, paid no sort of regard to the reputation they had acquired——Milton was harsh and prosaic; Dryden, languid and verbose; Butler and Swift without humour; Congreve, without wit; and Pope destitute of any sort of poetical merit—As for his cotemporaries, he could not bear to hear one of them mentioned with any degree of applause— They were all dunces, pedants, plagiaries, quacks, and impostors; and you could not name a single performance, but what was tame, stupid, and insipid. It must be owned, that this writer had nothing to charge his conscience with, on the side of flattery; for I understand, he was never known to praise one line that was written, even by those with whom he lived on terms of good fellowship. This arrogance and presumption, in depreciating authors, for whose reputation the company may be interested, is such an insult upon the understanding, as I could not bear without wincing.

I desired to know his reasons for decrying some works, which had afforded me uncommon pleasure; and, as demonstration did not seem to be his talent, I dissented from his opinion with great freedom. Having been spoiled by the deference and humility of his hearers, he did not bear contradiction with much temper; and the dispute might have

grown warm, had it not been interrupted by the entrance of
a rival bard, at whose appearance he always quits the place
——They are of different cabals, and have been at open
war these twenty years——If the other was dogmatical,
this genius was declamatory: he did not discourse, but harangue: and his orations were equally tedious and turgid. He
too pronounces *ex cathedra* upon the characters of his cotemporaries; and though he scruples not to deal out praise,
even lavishly, to the lowest reptile in Grub-street, who will
either flatter him in private, or mount the public rostrum
as his panegyrist, he damns all the other writers of the age,
with the utmost insolence and rancour—One is a blunderbuss, as being a native of Ireland; another, a half-starved
louse of literature, from the banks of the Tweed; a third,
an ass, because he enjoys a pension from the government;
a fourth, the very angel of dulness, because he succeeded in
a species of writing in which this Aristarchus had failed; a
fifth, who presumed to make strictures upon one of his
performances, he holds as a bug in criticism, whose stench
is more offensive than his sting—In short, except himself
and his myrmidons, there is not a man of genius or learning
in the three kingdoms. As for the success of those, who
have written without the pale of this confederacy, he im-
putes it entirely to want of taste in the public; not considering, that to the approbation of that very tasteless public,
he himself owes all the consequence he has in life.

Those originals are not fit for conversation. If they
would maintain the advantage they have gained by their
writing, they should never appear but upon paper—For my
part, I am shocked to find a man have sublime ideas in his
head, and nothing but illiberal sentiments in his heart—
The human soul will be generally found most defective in
the article of candour—I am inclined to think, no mind
was ever wholly exempt from envy; which, perhaps, may
have been implanted, as an instinct essential to our nature,

I am afraid we sometimes palliate this vice, under the spacious name of emulation. I have known a person remarkably generous, humane, moderate, and apparently self-denying, who could not hear even a friend commended, without betraying marks of uneasiness; as if that commendation had implied an odious comparison to his prejudice, and every wreath of praise added to the other's character, was a garland plucked from his own temples. This is a malignant species of jealousy, of which I stand acquitted in my own conscience——Whether it is a vice, or an infirmity, I leave you to inquire.

There is another point, which I would much rather see determined; whether the world was always as contemptible, as it appears to me at present?—If the morals of mankind have not contracted an extraordinary degree of depravity, within these thirty years, then must I be infected with the common vice of old men, *difficilis, querulus, laudator temporis acti;* or, which is more probable, the impetuous pursuits and avocations of youth have formerly hindered me from observing those rotten parts of human nature, which now appear so offensively to my observation.

We have been at court, and 'change, and every where; and every where we find food for spleen, and subject for ridicule—My new servant, Humphry Clinker, turns out a great original: and Tabby is a changed creature——She has parted with Chowder; and does nothing but smile, like Malvolio in the play——I'll be hanged if she is not acting a part which is not natural to her disposition, for some purpose which I have not yet discovered.

With respect to the character of mankind, my curiosity is quite satisfied: I have done with the science of men, and must now endeavour to amuse myself with the novelty of things. I am, at present, by a violent effort of the mind, forced from my natural bias; but this power ceasing to act, I shall return to my solitude with redoubled velocity. Every thing I see, and hear, and feel, in this great reservoir of folly, knavery, and sophistication, contributes to inhance the value of a country life, in the sentiments of

Yours always,

MATT. BRAMBLE.

LONDON, *June* 2.

To Mrs. *Mary Jones, at Brambleton-hall*

DEAR MARY JONES,

Lady Griskin's botler, Mr. Crumb, having got squire Barton to frank me a kiver, I would not neglect to let you know how it is with me, and the rest of the family.

I could not rite by John Thomas, for because he went away in a huff, at a minute's warning. He and Chowder could not agree, and so they fitt upon the road, and Chowder bitt his thumb, and he swore he would do him a mischief, and he spoke saucy to mistress, whereby the squire turned him off in gudgeon; and by God's providence we picked up another footman, called Umphry Klinker; a good sole as ever broke bread; which shews that a scalded cat may prove a good mouser, and a hound be staunch, thof he has got narro hare on his buttocks; but the proudest nose may be bro't to the grinestone, by sickness and misfortunes.

O Molly! what shall I say of London? All the towns that ever I beheld in my born-days, are no more than Welsh barrows and crumlecks to this wonderful sitty! Even Bath itself is but a sillitch, in the naam of God——One would think there's no end of the streets, but the land's end. Then there's such a power of people, going hurry skurry! Such a racket of coxes! Such a noise, and haliballoo! So many strange sites to be seen! O gracious! my poor Welsh brain has been spinning like a top ever since I came hither! And I have seen the Park, and the paleass of Saint Gimses, and the king's and the queen's magisterial pursing, and the sweet young princes, and the hillyfents, and pye bald ass, and all the rest of the royal family.

Last week I went with mistress to the Tower, to see the

crowns and wild beastis; and there was a monstracious lion, with teeth half a quarter long; and a gentleman bid me not go near him, if I wasn't a maid; being as how he would roar, and tear, and play the dickens——Now I had no mind to go near him; for I cannot abide such dangerous honey-mils, not I——but, mistress would go; and the beast kept such a roaring and bouncing, that I tho't he would have broke his cage and devoured us all; and the gentleman tittered forsooth; but I'll go to death upon it, I will, that my lady is as good a firchin, as the child unborn; and, there-fore, either the gentleman told a fib, or the lion oft to be set in the stocks for bearing false witness again his neigh-bour; for the commandment sayeth, *Thou shalt not bear false witness against thy neighbour.*

I was afterwards of a party at Sadler's-wells, where I saw such tumbling and dancing upon ropes and wires, that I was frightened and ready to go into a fit——tho't it was all inchantment; and, believing myself bewitched, began for to cry——You knows as how the witches in Wales fly upon broom-sticks: but here was flying without any broom-stick, or thing in the varsal world, and firing of pistols in the air, and blowing of trumpets, and swinging, and rolling of wheel-barrows upon a wire (God bless us!) no thicker than a sewing-thread; that, to be sure, they must deal with the devil!——A fine gentleman, with a pig's-tail, and a golden sord by his side, came to comfit me, and offered for to treat me with a pint of wind; but I would not stay; and so, in going through the dark passage, he began to shew his cloven futt, and went for to be rude: my fellow-sarvant, Umphry Klinker, bid him be sivil, and he gave the young man a dowse in the chops; but, I fackins, Mr. Klinker wa'n't long in his debt——with a good oaken sapling he dusted his doublet, for all his golden cheese toaster; and, fipping me under his arm, carried me huom, I nose not how, being I was in such a flustration—But, thank God! I'm now vaned from all such vanities; for what are all those rarities and vagaries to the glory that shall be revealed hereafter? O Molly! let not your poor heart be puffed up with vanity.

I had almost forgot to tell you, that I have had my hair cut and pippered, and singed, and bolstered, and buckled, in the newest fashion, by a French freezer—*Parley vow Francey—Vee madmansell——*I now carries my head hither than arrow private gentlewoman of Vales. Last night, coming huom from the meeting, I was taken by lamp-light for an iminent poulterer's daughter, a great beauty—But as I was saying, this is all vanity and vexation of spirit—The pleasures of London are no better than sower whey and stale cyder, when compared to the joys of the new Gerusalem.

Dear Mary Jones! An please God when I return, I'll bring you a new cap, with a turkey-shell coom, and a pyehouse sermon, that was preached in the Tabernacle; and I pray of all love, you will mind your vriting and your spilling; for, craving your pardon, Molly, it made me suet to disseyffer your last scrabble, which was delivered by the hind at Bath—O, voman! voman! if thou had'st but the least consumption of what pleasure we scullers have, when we can cunster the crabbidst buck off hand, and spell the ethnitch vords without lucking at the primmer. As for Mr. Klinker, he is qualified to be a clerk to a parish—But I'll say no more—Remember me to Saul—poor sole! it goes to my hart to think she don't yet know her letters—But all in God's good time—It shall go hard, but I will bring her the A B C in gingerbread; and that, you nose, will be learning to her taste.

Mistress says, we are going a long gurney to the North; but go where we will, I shall ever be,

> Dear Mary Jones,
> yours with true infection
> WIN. JENKINS

LONDON, *June* 3.

To Sir Watkin Phillips, of Jesus college, Oxon.

DEAR WAT,

I mentioned in my last, my uncle's design of going to
the duke of N————'s levee; which design has been executed accordingly. His grace has been so long accustomed
to this kind of homage, that though the place he now fills
does not imply the tenth part of the influence, which he
exerted in his former office, he has given his friends to
understand, that they cannot oblige him in any thing more,
than in contributing to support the shadow of that power,
which he no longer retains in substance; and therefore he
has still public days, on which they appear at his levee.

My uncle and I went thither with Mr. Barton, who,
being one of the duke's adherents, undertook to be our
introducer—The room was pretty well filled with people,
in a great variety of dress; but there was no more than
one gown and cassock, though I was told his grace had,
while he was minister, preferred almost every individual
that now filled the bench of bishops in the house of lords;
but in all probability, the gratitude of the clergy is like
their charity, which shuns the light—Mr. Barton was immediately accosted by a person well stricken in years, tall,
and raw-boned, with a hook-nose, and an arch leer, that
indicated, at least, as much cunning as sagacity. Our conductor saluted him, by the name of captain C————, and
afterwards informed us he was a man of shrewd parts,
whom the government occasionally employed in secret services—But I have had the history of him more at large, from
another quarter————He had been, many years ago, concerned in fraudulent practices, as a merchant, in France;
and being convicted of some of them, was sent to the gal-
lies, from whence he was delivered by the interest of the
late duke of Ormond, to whom he had recommended himself in letter, as his name-sake and relation—He was, in

the sequel, employed by our ministry as a spy; and in the war of 1740, traversed all Spain, as well as France, in the disguise of a capuchin, at the extreme hazard of his life, in as much as the court of Madrid had actually got scent of him, and given orders to apprehend him at St. Sebastian's, from whence he had fortunately retired but a few hours before the order arrived. This and other hair-breadth 'scapes he pleaded so effectually as a merit with the English ministry, that they allowed him a comfortable pension, which he now enjoys in his old age—He has still access to all the ministers, and is said to be consulted by them on many subjects, as a man of uncommon understanding and great experience—He is, in fact, a fellow of some parts, and invincible assurance; and, in his discourse, he assumes such an air of self-sufficiency, as may very well impose upon some of the shallow politicians, who now labour at the helm of administration. But, if he is not belied, this is not the only imposture of which he is guilty———They say, he is at bottom not only a Roman-catholic, but really a priest; and while he pretends to disclose to our state-pilots all the springs that move the cabinet of Versailles, he is actually picking up intelligence for the service of the French minister———Be that as it may, captain C—— entered into conversation with us in the most familiar manner, and treated the duke's character without any ceremony—'This wise-acre (said he) is still a-bed; and, I think, the best thing he can do, is to sleep on till Christmas; for, when he gets up, he does nothing but expose his own folly.—Since Grenville was turned out, there has been no minister in this nation worth the meal that whitened his peri-wig—They are so ignorant, they scarce know a crab from a cauliflower; and then they are such dunces, that there's no making them comprehend the plainest proposition———In the beginning of the war, this poor half-witted creature told me, in a great fright, that thirty thousand French had marched from Acadie to Cape Breton———Where did they find transports?

(said I) "Transports! (cried he) I tell you they marched by land"——By land to the island of Cape Breton? "What! is Cape Breton an island?" Certainly. "Ha! are you sure of that?" When I pointed it out in the map, he examined it earnestly with his spectacles; then, taking me in his arms, "My dear C——! (cried he) you always bring us good news—Egad! I'll go directly, and tell the king that Cape Breton is an island."

He seemed disposed to entertain us with more anecdotes of this nature, at the expence of his grace, when he was interrupted by the arrival of the Algerine ambassador; a venerable Turk, with a long white beard, attended by his dragoman, or interpreter, and another officer of his household, who had got no stockings to his legs——Captain C—— immediately spoke with an air of authority to a servant in waiting, bidding him go and tell the duke to rise, as there was a great deal of company come, and, among others, the ambassador from Algiers——Then, turning to us, 'This poor Turk (said he) notwithstanding his grey beard, is a green-horn——He has been several years resident in London, and still is ignorant of our political revolutions. This visit is intended for the prime minister of England; but you'll see how this wise duke will receive it as a mark of attachment to his own person'——Certain it is, the duke seemed eager to acknowledge the compliment ——A door opened, he suddenly bolted out; with a shaving-cloth under his chin, his face frothed up to the eyes with soap lather; and running up to the ambassador, grinned hideous in his face—'My dear Mahomet! (said he) God love your long beard, I hope the dey will make you a horse-tail at the next promotion, ha, ha, ha!——Have but a moment's patience, and I'll send you in a twinkling,'—— So saying, he retired into his den, leaving the Turk in some confusion. After a short pause, however, he said something to his interpreter, the meaning of which I had great curiosity to know, as he turned up his eyes while he spoke, expressing astonishment, mixed with devotion——We were gratified by means of the communicative captain C——, who conversed with the dragoman, as an old acquaintance. Ibrahim, the ambassador, who had mistaken his grace for the minister's fool, was no sooner undeceived by the interpreter, than he exclaimed to this effect——'Holy prophet! I don't wonder that this nation prospers, seeing it is governed by the counsel of idiots; a series of men, whom all good mussulmen revere as the organs of immediate inspiration!' Ibrahim was favoured with a particular audience of short duration; after which the duke conducted him to the door, and then returned to diffuse his gracious looks among the crowd of his worshippers.

As Mr. Barton advanced to present me to his grace, it was my fortune to attract his notice, before I was announced——He forthwith met me more than half way, and, seizing me by the hand, 'My dear Sir Francis! (cried he) this is so kind——I vow to Gad! I am so obliged——Such attention to a poor broken minister——Well——Pray when does your excellency set sail?——For God's sake have a care of your health, and eat stewed prunes in the passage——Next to your own precious health, pray, my dear excellency, take care of the Five Nations——Our good friends the Five Nations——The Toryrories, the Maccolmacks, the Out-o'-theways, the Crickets, and the Kickshaws——Let 'em have plenty of blankets, and stinkubus, and wampum; and your excellency won't fail to scour the kettle, and boil the chain, and bury the tree, and plant the hatchet——Ha, ha, ha!' When he had uttered this rhapsody, with his usual precipitation, Mr. Barton gave him to understand, that I was neither Sir Francis, nor St. Francis, but simply Mr. Melford, nephew to Mr. Bramble; who, stepping forward, made his bow at the same time. 'Odso! no more it is Sir Francis——(said this wise statesman) Mr. Melford, I'm glad to see you—— I sent you an engineer to fortify your dock——Mr. Bramble ——your servant, Mr. Bramble——How d'ye, good Mr. Bramble? Your nephew is a pretty young fellow—Faith and troth, a very pretty fellow!—His father is my old friend— How does he hold it? Still troubled with that damned disorder, ha?' 'No, my lord (replied my uncle), all his troubles are over—He has been dead these fifteen years.' 'Dead! how—Yes faith! now I remember: he is dead sure enough —Well, and how—does the young gentleman stand for Haverford West? or—a—what d'ye—My dear Mr. Milfordhaven, I'll do you all the service in my power—I hope I have some credit left'——My uncle then gave him to understand, that I was still a minor; and that we had no intention to trouble him at present, for any favour whatsoever—'I came hither with my nephew (added he) to pay our respects to your grace; and I may venture to say, that his views and mine are at least as disinterested as those of any individual in this assembly.' 'My dear Mr. Brambleberry! you do me infinite honour—I shall always rejoice to see you and your hopeful nephew, Mr. Milfordhaven— My credit, such as it is, you may command—I wish we had more friends of your kidney.'

Then, turning to captain C——, 'Ha, C——! (said he) what news, C——? How does the world wag? ha!' 'The world wags much after the old fashion, my lord (answered the captain): the politicians of London and Westminster have begun again to wag their tongues against your grace; and your short-lived popularity wags like a feather, which the next puff of antiministerial calumny will blow away'—'A pack of rascals (cried the duke)—Tories, Jacobites, rebels; one half of them would wag their heels at Tyburn, if they had their deserts'——So saying, he wheeled about; and going round the levee, spoke to every individual, with the most courteous familiarity; but he scarce ever opened his mouth without making some blunder, in relation to the person or business of the party with whom he conversed; so that he really looked like a comedian, hired to burlesque the character of a minister—At length, a person of a very prepossessing appearance coming in, his grace ran up, and, hugging him in his arms, with the appellation of 'My dear Ch——s!' led him forthwith into the inner apartment, or *Sanctum Sanctorum* of this political temple. 'That (said captain C——) is my friend C—— T——, almost the only man of parts who has any concern in the present administration—Indeed, he would have no concern at all in the matter, if the ministry did not find it absolutely necessary to make use of his talents upon some particular occasions—As for the common business of the nation, it is carried on in a constant routine by the clerks of the different offices, otherwise the wheels of government would be wholly stopt amidst the abrupt succession of ministers, every one more ignorant than his predecessor—— I am thinking what a fine hovel we should be in, if all the clerks of the treasury, the secretaries, of the war-office, and the admiralty, should take it in their heads to throw up their places in imitation of the great pensioner—But, to return to C—— T——; he certainly knows more than all the ministry and all the opposition, if their heads were laid together, and talks like an angel on a vast variety of subjects—He would really be a great man, if he had any consistency or stability of character—Then, it must be owned, he wants courage, otherwise he would never allow himself to be cowed by the great political bully, for whose understanding he has justly a very great contempt. I have seen him as much afraid of that overbearing Hector, as ever schoolboy was of his pedagogue; and yet this Hector, I shrewdly suspect, is no more than a craven at bottom—Besides this defect, C—— has another, which he is at too little pains to hide—There's no faith to be given to his assertions, and no trust to be put in his promises—However, to give the devil his due, he's very good-natured; and even friendly, when close urged in the way of solicitation—As for principle, that's out of the question—In a word, he is a wit and an orator, extremely entertaining, and he shines very often at the expence even of those ministers to whom he is a retainer—This is a mark of great imprudence, by which he has made them all his enemies, whatever face they may put upon the matter; and sooner or later he'll have cause to wish he had been able to keep his own counsel—I have several times cautioned him on this subject; but 'tis all preaching to the desert—His vanity runs away with his discretion'————I could not help thinking the captain himself might have been the better for some hints of the same nature—His panegyric, excluding principle and veracity, puts me in mind of a contest I once over-heard, in the way of altercation, betwixt two apple-women in Spring-garden ————One of those viragos having hinted something to the prejudice of the other's moral character, her antagonist, setting her hands in her sides, replied—'Speak out, hussy—I scorn your malice—I own I'm both a whore and a thief; and what more have you to say?—Damn you, what more have you to say? baiting that, which all the world knows, I challenge you to say black is the white of my eye.'—We did not wait for Mr. T—'s coming forth; but after captain C—— had characterised all the originals in waiting, we adjourned to a coffeehouse, where we had buttered muffins and tea to breakfast, the said captain still favouring us with his company————Nay, my uncle was so diverted with his anecdotes, that he asked him to dinner, and treated him with a fine turbot, to which he did ample justice————That same evening I spent at the tavern with some friends, one of whom let me into C—'s character, which Mr. Bramble no sooner understood, than he expressed some concern for the connexion he had made, and resolved to disengage himself from it without ceremony.

We are become members of the Society for the Encouragement of the Arts, and have assisted at some of their deliberations, which were conducted with equal spirit and sagacity—My uncle is extremely fond of the institution, which will certainly be productive of great advantages to the public, if, from its democratical form, it does not degenerate into cabal and corruption—You are already acquainted with his aversion to the influence of the multitude, which, he affirms, is incompatible with excellence, and subversive of order—Indeed his detestation of the mob has been heightened by fear, ever since he fainted in the room at Bath; and this apprehension has prevented him from going to the Little Theatre in the Hay-market, and other places of entertainment, to which, however, I have had the honour to attend the ladies.

It grates old Square-toes to reflect, that it is not in his power to enjoy even the most elegant diversions of the capital, without the participation of the vulgar; for they now thrust themselves into all assemblies, from a ridotto at St. James's, to a hop at Rotherhithe.

I have lately seen our old acquaintance Dick Ivy, who we imagined had died of dram-drinking; but he is lately emerged from the Fleet, by means of a pamphlet which he wrote and published against the government with some success. The sale of this performance enabled him to appear in clean linen, and he is now going about soliciting subscriptions for his Poems; but his breeches are not yet in the most decent order.

Dick certainly deserves some countenance for his intrepidity and perseverance—It is not in the power of disappointment, nor even of damnation, to drive him to despair—After some unsuccessful essays in the way of poetry, he commenced brandy-merchant, and I believe his whole stock ran out through his own bowels; then he consorted with a milk-woman, who kept a cellar in Petty France: but he could not make his quarters good; he was dislodged and driven up stairs into the kennel by a corporal in the second regiment of foot-guards—He was afterwards the laureat of Blackfriars, from whence there was a natural transition to the fleet.—As he had formerly miscarried in panegyric, he now turned his thoughts to satire, and really seems to have some talent for abuse. If he can hold out till the meeting of the parliament, and be prepared for another charge, in all probability Dick will mount the pillory, or obtain a pension, in either of which events his fortune will be made—— Mean while he has acquired some degree of consideration with the respectable writers of the age; and as I have subscribed for his works, he did me the favour t'other night to introduce me to a society of those geniuses; but I found them exceedingly formal and reserved—They seemed afraid and jealous of one another, and sat in a state of mutual repulsion, like so many particles of vapour, each surrounded by its own electrified atmosphere. Dick, who has more vivacity than judgment, tried more than once to enliven the conversation; sometimes making an effort at wit, sometimes letting off a pun, and sometimes discharging a conundrum; nay, at length he started a dispute upon the hackneyed comparison betwixt blank verse and rhyme, and the professors opened with great clamour; but, instead of keeping to the subject, they launched out into tedious dissertations on the poetry of the ancients; and one of them, who had been a school-master, displayed his whole knowledge of prosody, gleaned from Disputer and Ruddiman. At last, I ventured to say, I did not see how the subject in question could be at all elucidated by the practice of the ancients, who certainly had neither blank verse nor rhyme in their poems, which were measured by feet, whereas ours are reckoned by the number of syllables—This remark seemed to give umbrage to the pedant, who forthwith involved himself in a cloud of Greek and Latin quotations, which nobody attempted to dispel—A confused hum of insipid observations and comments ensued; and, upon the whole, I never passed a duller evening in my life—Yet, without all doubt, some of them were men of learning, wit, and ingenuity. As they are afraid of making free with one another, they should bring each his butt, or whet-stone, along with him, for the entertainment of the company—My uncle says, he never

desires to meet with more than one wit at a time———One
wit, like a knuckle of ham in soup, gives a zest and flavour
to the dish; but more than one serves only to spoil the
pottage———And now I'm afraid I have given you an unconscionable mess, without any flavour at all; for which, I
suppose, you will bestow your benedictions upon

Your friend,
and servant
J. MELFORD.

LONDON, *June* 5.

To Dr. Lewis

DEAR LEWIS,
    Your fable of the monkey and the pig, is what the
Italians call *ben trovata:* but I shall not repeat it to my
apothecary, who is a proud Scotchman, very thin skinned,
and, for aught I know, may have his degree in his pocket
—A right Scotchman has always two strings to his
bow, and is *in utrumque paratus*—Certain it is, I have not
'scaped a scouring; but, I believe, by means of that scouring,
I have 'scaped something worse, perhaps a tedious fit of the
gout or rheumatism; for my appetite began to flag, and
I had certain croakings in the bowels, which boded me
no good———Nay, I am not yet quite free of these remem-
brances, which warn me to be gone from this centre of
infection———
    What temptation can a man of my turn and tempera-
ment have, to live in a place where every corner teems
with fresh objects of detestation and disgust? What kind
of taste and organs must those people have, who really
prefer the adulterate enjoyments of the town to the genuine
pleasures of a country retreat? Most people, I know, are
originally seduced by vanity, ambition, and childish curiosity; which cannot be gratified, but in the *busy haunts of*

men: but, in the course of this gratification, their very organs of sense are perverted, and they become habitually lost to every relish of what is genuine and excellent in its own nature.

Shall I state the difference between my town grievances, and my country comforts? At Brambleton-hall, I have elbow-room within doors, and breathe a clear, elastic, salutary air——I enjoy refreshing sleep, which is never disturbed by horrid noise, nor interrupted, but in a-morning, by the sweet twitter of the martlet at my window—I drink the virgin lymph, pure and chrystalline as it gushes from the rock, or the sparkling beveridge, home-brewed from malt of my own making; or I indulge with cyder, which my own orchard affords; or with claret of the best growth, imported for my own use, by a correspondent on whose integrity I can depend; my bread is sweet and nourishing, made from my own wheat, ground in my own mill, and baked in my own oven; my table is, on a great measure, furnished from my own ground; my five-year old mutton, fed on the fragrant herbage of the mountains, that might vie with venison in juice and flavour; my delicious veal, fattened with nothing but the mother's milk, that fills the dish with gravy; my poultry from the barn-door, that never knew confinement, but when they were at roost; my rabbits panting from the warren; my game fresh from the moors; my trout and salmon struggling from the stream; oysters from their native banks; and herrings, with other sea-fish, I can eat in four hours after they are taken— My sallads, roots, and pot-herbs, my own garden yields in plenty and perfection; the produce of the natural soil, prepared by moderate cultivation. The same soil affords all the different fruits which England may call her own, so that my dessert is every day fresh-gathered from the tree; my dairy flows with nectarious tides of milk and cream, from whence we derive abundance of excellent butter, curds, and cheese; and the refuse fattens my pigs, that are destined for hams and bacon—I go to bed betimes, and rise with the sun—I make shift to pass the hours without weariness or regret, and am not destitute of amusements within doors, when the weather will not permit me to go abroad—I read, and chat, and play at billiards, cards, or back-gammon—Without doors, I superintend my farm, and execute plans of improvement, the effects of which I enjoy with unspeakable delight—Nor do I take less pleasure in seeing my tenants thrive under my auspices, and the poor live comfortably by the employment which I provide—You know I have one or two sensible friends, to whom I can open all my heart; a blessing which, perhaps, I might have sought in vain among the crowded scenes of life: there are a few others of more humble parts, whom I esteem for their integrity; and their conversation I find inoffensive, though not very entertaining. Finally, I live in the midst of honest men, and trusty dependants, who, I flatter myself, have a disinterested attachment to my person——You, yourself, my dear Doctor, can vouch for the truth of these assertions.

Now, mark the contrast at London—I am pent up in frowzy lodgings, where there is not room enough to swing a cat; and I breathe the streams of endless putrefaction; and these would, undoubtedly, produce a pestilence, if they were not qualified by the gross acid of sea-coal, which is itself a pernicious nuisance to lungs of any delicacy of texture: but even this boasted corrector cannot prevent those languid, sallow looks, that distinguish the inhabitants of London from those ruddy swains that lead a country-life——I go to bed after midnight, jaded and restless from the dissipations of the day—I start every hour from my sleep, at the horrid noise of the watchmen bawling the hour through every street, and thundering at every door; a set of useless fellows, who serve no other purpose but that of disturbing the repose of the inhabitants; and by five o'clock I start out of bed, in consequence of the still more dreadful alarm made by the country carts, and noisy rustics bellowing green pease under my window. If I would drink water, I must quaff the maukish contents of an open aqueduct, exposed to all manner of defilement; or swallow that which comes from the river Thames, impregnated with all the filth of London and Westminster——Human excrement is the least offensive part of the concrete, which is composed of all the drugs, minerals, and poisons, used in mechanics and manufacture, enriched with the putrefying carcasses of beasts and men; and mixed with the scourings of all the wash-tubs, kennels, and common sewers, within the bills of mortality.

This is the agreeable potation, extolled by the Londoners, as the finest water in the universe—As to the intoxicating potion, sold for wine, it is a vile, unpalatable, and pernicious sophistication, balderdashed with cyder, corn-spirit, and the juice of sloes. In an action at law, laid against a carman for having staved a cask of port, it appeared from the evidence of the cooper, that there were not above five gallons of real wine in the whole pipe, which held above a hundred, and even that had been brewed and adulterated by the merchant at Oporto. The bread I eat in London, is a deleterious paste, mixed up with chalk, alum, and bone-ashes; insipid to the taste, and destructive to the constitution. The good people are not ignorant of this adulteration; but they prefer it to wholesome bread, because it is whiter than the meal of corn: thus they sacrifice their taste and their health, and the lives of their tender infants, to a most absurd gratification of a mis-judging eye; and the miller, or the baker, is obliged to poison them and their families, in order to live by his profession. The same monstrous depravity appears in their veal, which is bleached by repeated bleedings, and other villainous arts, till there is not a drop of juice left in the body, and the poor animal is paralytic before he dies; so void of all taste, nourishment, and savour, that a man might dine as comfortably on a white fricassee of kid-skin gloves; or chip hats from Leghorn.

As they have discharged the natural colour from their bread, their butchers-meat, and poultry, their cutlets, ragouts, fricassees and sauces of all kinds; so they insist upon having the complexion of their pot-herbs mended, even at the hazard of their lives. Perhaps, you will hardly believe they can be so mad as to boil their greens with brass half-pence in order to improve their colour; and yet nothing is more true—Indeed, without this improvement in the colour, they have no personal merit. They are produced in an artificial soil, and taste of nothing but the dunghills, from whence they spring. My cabbage, cauliflower, and 'sparagus in the country, are as much superior in flavour to those that are sold in Covent-garden, as my heath-mutton is to that of St. James's-market; which in fact, is neither lamb nor mutton, but something betwixt the two, gorged in the rank fens of Lincoln and Essex, pale, coarse, and frowzy—As for the pork, it is an abominable carnivorous animal, fed with horse-flesh and distillers' grains; and the poultry is all rotten, in consequence of a fever, occasioned by the infamous practice of sewing up the gut, that they may be the sooner fattened in coops, in consequence of this cruel retention.

Of the fish, I need say nothing in this hot weather, but that it comes sixty, seventy, fourscore, and a hundred miles by land-carriage; a circumstance sufficient without any comment, to turn a Dutchman's stomach, even if his nose was not saluted in every alley with the sweet flavour of *fresh* mackarel, selling by retail—This is not the season for oysters; nevertheless, it may not be amiss to mention, that the right Colchester are kept in slime-pits, occasionally overflowed by the sea; and that the green colour, so much admired by the voluptuaries of this metropolis, is occasioned by the vitriolic scum, which rises on the surface of the stagnant and stinking water—Our rabbits are bred and fed in the poulterer's cellar, where they have neither air nor exercise, consequently they must be firm in flesh, and delicious in flavour; and there is no game to be had for love or money.

It must be owned, the Covent-garden affords some good fruit; which, however, is always engrossed by a few individuals of over-grown fortune, at an exorbitant price; so that little else than the refuse of the market falls to the share of the community; and that is distributed by such filthy hands, as I cannot look at without loathing. It was but yesterday that I saw a dirty barrow-bunter in the street, cleaning her dusty fruit with her own spittle; and, who knows but some fine lady of St. James's parish might admit into her delicate mouth those very cherries, which had been rolled and moistened between the filthy, and, perhaps, ulcerated chops of a St. Giles's huckster—I need not dwell upon the pallid, contaminated mash, which they call strawberries; soiled and tossed by greasy paws through twenty baskets crusted with dirt; and then presented with the worst milk, thickened with the worst flour, into a bad likeness of cream: but the milk itself should not pass unanalysed, the produce of faded cabbage-leaves and sour draff, lowered with hot water, frothed with bruised snails, carried through the streets in open pails, exposed to foul rinsings, discharged from doors and windows, spittle, snot, and tobacco-quids from foot passengers, overflowings from mud carts, spatterings from coach wheels, dirt and trash chucked into it by roguish boys for the joke's sake, the spewings of infants, who have slabbered in the tin-measure, which is thrown back in that condition among the milk, for the benefit of the next customer; and, finally the vermin that drops from the rags of the nasty drab that vends this precious mixture, under the respectable denomination of milk-maid.

I shall conclude this catalogue of London dainties, with that table-beer, guiltless of hops and malt, vapid and nauseous; much fitter to facilitate the operation of a vomit, than to quench thirst and promote digestion; the tallowy rancid mass, called butter, manufactured with candle-grease and kitchen stuff; and their fresh eggs, imported from France and Scotland.——Now, all these enormities might be remedied with a very little attention to the article of police, or civil regulation; but the wise patriots of London have taken it into their heads, that all regulation is inconsistent with liberty; and that every man ought to live in his own way, without restraint——Nay, as there is not sense enough left among them, to be discomposed by the nuisance I have mentioned, they may, for aught I care, wallow in the mire of their own pollution.

A companionable man will, undoubtedly, put up with many inconveniences for the sake of enjoying agreeable society. A facetious friend of mine used to say, the wine could not be bad, where the company was agreeable; a maxim which, however, ought to be taken *cum grano salis:* but what is the society of London, that I should be tempted, for its sake, to mortify my senses, and compound with such uncleanness as my soul abhors? All the people I see, are too much engrossed by schemes of interest or ambition, to have any room left for sentiment or friendship——Even in some of my old acquaintance, those schemes and pursuits have obliterated all traces of our former connexion—— Conversation is reduced to party disputes, and illiberal alter-cation—Social commerce, to formal visits and card-playing —If you pick up a diverting original by accident, it may be dangerous to amuse yourself with his oddities——He is generally a tartar at bottom; a sharper, a spy, or a lunatic. Every person you deal with endeavours to over-reach you in the way of business; you are preyed upon by idle mendi-cants, who beg in the phrase of borrowing, and live upon the spoils of the stranger——Your tradesmen are without conscience, your friends without affection, and your de-pendents without fidelity.———

My letter would swell into a treatise, were I to particularize every cause of offence that fills up the measure of my aversion to this, and every other crowded city—Thank Heaven! I am not so far sucked into the vortex, but that I can disengage myself without any great effort of philosophy—From this wild uproar of knavery, folly, and impertinence, I shall fly with double relish to the serenity of retirement, the cordial effusions of unreserved friendship, the hospitality and protection of the rural gods; in a word, the *jucunda oblivia vitæ*, which Horace himself had not taste enough to enjoy.—

I have agreed for a good travelling-coach and four, at a guinea a day, for three months certain; and next week we intend to begin our journey to the North; hoping still to be with you by the latter end of October——I shall continue to write from every stage where we make any considerable halt, as often as anything occurs, which I think can afford you the least amusement. In the mean time, I must beg you will superintend the œconomy of Barns, with respect to my hay and corn harvests; assured that my ground produces nothing but what you may freely call your own——On any other terms I should be ashamed to subscribe myself

your unvariable friend,

MATT. BRAMBLE.

LONDON, *June* 8.

To Sir Watkin Phillips, Bart. of Jesus college, Oxon.

DEAR PHILLIPS,

In my last, I mentioned my having spent an evening with a society of authors, who seemed to be jealous and afraid of one another. My uncle was not at all surprised to hear me say I was disappointed in their conversation. 'A man may be very entertaining and instructive upon paper, (said he) and exceedingly dull in common discourse.

I have observed, that those who shine most in private company, are but secondary stars in the constellation of genius—
A small stock of ideas is more easily managed, and sooner
displayed, than a great quantity crowded together. There
is very seldom any thing extraordinary in the appearance
and address of a good writer; whereas a dull author generally distinguishes himself by some oddity or extravagance.
For this reason, I fancy, that an assembly of Grubs must
be very diverting.'

My curiosity being excited by this hint, I consulted my
friend Dick Ivy, who undertook to gratify it the very
next day, which was Sunday last.—He carried me to dine
with S———, whom you and I have long known by his
writings.—He lives in the skirts of the town, and every
Sunday his house is opened to all unfortunate brothers of the
quill, whom he treats with beef, pudding, and potatoes, port,
punch, and Calvert's entire butt beer.—He has fixed upon
the first day of the week for the exercise of his hospitality,
because some of his guests could not enjoy it on any other,
for reasons that I need not explain. I was civilly received
in a plain, yet decent habitation, which opened backwards
into a very pleasant garden, kept in excellent order; and,
indeed, I saw none of the outward signs of authorship,
either in the house or the landlord, who is one of those
few writers of the age that stand upon their own foundation, without patronage, and above dependence. If there
was nothing characteristic in the entertainer, the company
made ample amends for his want of singularity.

At two in the afternoon, I found myself one of ten mess-
mates seated at table; and, I question, if the whole kingdom could produce such another assemblage of originals.
Among their peculiarities, I do not mention those of dress,
which may be purely accidental. What struck me were
oddities originally produced by affectation, and afterwards
confirmed by habit. One of them wore spectacles at dinner,
and another his hat flapped; though (as Ivy told me) the

first was noted for having a seaman's eye, when a bailiff
was in the wind; and the other was never known to labour
under any weakness or defect of vision, except about five
years ago, when he was complimented with a couple of
black eyes by a player, with whom he had quarrelled in
his drink. A third wore a laced stocking, and made use of
crutches, because, once in his life, he had been laid up with
a broken leg, though no man could leap over a stick with
more agility. A fourth had contracted such an antipathy
to the country, that he insisted upon sitting with his back
towards the window that looked into the garden, and when
a dish of cauliflower was set upon the table, he snuffed
up volatile salts to keep him from fainting; yet this
delicate person was the son of a cottager, born under a
hedge, and had many years run wild among asses on a
common. A fifth affected distraction—When spoke to, he
always answered from the purpose—sometimes he suddenly started up, and rapped out a dreadful oath—sometimes he burst out a-laughing—then he folded his arms,
and sighed—and then, he hissed like fifty serpents.

At first I really thought he was mad, and, as he sat
near me, began to be under some apprehensions for my
own safety, when our landlord, perceiving me alarmed,
assured me aloud that I had nothing to fear. 'The gentleman (said he) is trying to act a part for which he is by
no means qualified—if he had all the inclination in the
world, it is not in his power to be mad. His spirits are too
flat to be kindled into frenzy.' ''Tis no bad p-p-puff,
how-ow-ever (observed a person in a tarnished laced coat):
aff-ffected m-madness w-will p-pass for w-wit w-with
nine-ninet-teen out of t-twenty.'—'And affected stuttering
for humour: replied our landlord, tho', God knows, there
is an affinity betwixt them.' It seems, this wag, after having
made some abortive attempts in plain speaking, had recourse
to this defect, by means of which he frequently extorted
the laugh of the company, without the least expence of

genius; and that imperfection, which he had at first coun-
terfeited, was now become so habitual, that he could not
lay it aside.

A certain winking genius, who wore yellow gloves at
dinner, had, on his first introduction, taken such offence
at S——, because he looked and talked, and ate and drank
like any other man, that he spoke contemptuously of his
understanding ever after, and never would repeat his visit,
until he had exhibited the following proof of his caprice.
Wat Wyvil, the poet, having made some unsuccessful advances towards an intimacy with S——, at last gave him
to understand, by a third person, that he had written a poem
in his praise, and a satire against his person; that if he
would admit him to his house, the first should be immediately sent to press; but that if he persisted in declining his
friendship, he would publish his satire without delay. S——
replied, that he looked upon Wyvil's panegyrick, as in effect,
a species of infamy, and would resent it accordingly with
a good cudgel; but if he published the satire, he might
deserve his compassion, and had nothing to fear from his
revenge. Wyvil having considered the alternative, resolved
to mortify S—— by printing the panegyrick, for which he
received a sound drubbing. Then he swore the peace against
the aggressor, who, in order to avoid a prosecution at law,
admitted him to his good graces. It was the singularity in
S——'s conduct on this occasion, that reconciled him to
the yellow-gloved philosopher, who owned he had some
genius, and from that period cultivated his acquaintance.

Curious to know upon what subjects the several talents
of my fellow-guests were employed, I applied to my communicative friend Dick Ivy, who gave me to understand,
that most of them were, or had been, understrappers, or
journeymen, to more creditable authors, for whom they
translated, collated, and compiled, in the business of book-
making; and that all of them had, at different times,
laboured in the service of our landlord, though they had

now set up for themselves in various departments of literature. Not only their talents, but also their nations and dialects were so various, that our conversation resembled the confusion of tongues at Babel. We had the Irish brogue, the Scotch accent, and foreign idiom, twanged off by the most discordant vociferation; for, as they all spoke together, no man had any chance to be heard, unless he could bawl louder than his fellows. It must be owned, however, there was nothing pedantic in their discourse; they carefully avoided all learned disquisitions, and endeavoured to be facetious; nor did their endeavours always miscarry ————some droll repartee passed, and much laughter was excited; and if any individual lost his temper so far as to transgress the bounds of decorum, he was effectually checked by the master of the feast, who exerted a sort of paternal authority over this irritable tribe.

The most learned philosopher of the whole collection, who had been expelled the university for atheism, has made great progress in a refutation of lord Bolingbroke's metaphysical works, which is said to be equally ingenious and orthodox; but, in the mean time, he has been presented to the grand jury as a public nuisance, for having blasphemed in an ale-house on the Lord's day. The Scotchman gives lectures on the pronunciation of the English language, which he is now publishing by subscription.

The Irishman is a political writer, and goes by the name of my Lord Potatoe. He wrote a pamphlet in vindication of a minister, hoping his zeal would be rewarded with some place or pension; but, finding himself neglected in that quarter, he whispered about, that the pamphlet was written by the minister himself, and he published an answer to his own production. In this, he addressed the author under the title of *your lordship* with such solemnity, that the public swallowed the deceit, and bought up the whole impression. The wise politicians of the metropolis declared they were both masterly performances, and chuckled over the flimsy

reveries of an ignorant garretteer, as the profound specu-
lations of a veteran statesman, acquainted with all the
secrets of the cabinet. The imposture was detected in the
sequel, and our Hibernian pamphleteer retains no part of
his assumed importance, but the bare title of *my lord*, and
the upper part of the table at the potatoe-ordinary in Shoe-
lane.

Opposite to me sat a Piedmontese, who had obliged the
public with a humourous satire, intituled, *The Ballance of
the English Poets*, a performance which evinced the great
modesty and taste of the author, and, in particular, his
intimacy with the elegancies of the English language. The
sage, who laboured under the αγ𝛇οφβία, or *horror of green
fields*, had just finished a treatise on practical agriculture,
though, in fact, he had never seen corn growing in his
life, and was so ignorant of grain, that our entertainer, in
the face of the whole company, made him own, that a
plate of hominy was the best rice pudding he had ever eat.

The stutterer had almost finished his travels through
Europe and part of Asia, without ever budging beyond the
liberties of the King's Bench, except in term-time, with
a tipstaff for his companion; and as for little Tim Cropdale, the most facetious member of the whole society, he
had happily wound up the catastrophe of a virgin tragedy,
from the exhibition of which he promised himself a large
fund of profit and reputation. Tim had made shift to live
many years by writing novels, at the rate of five pounds a
volume; but that branch of business is now engrossed by
female authors, who publish merely for the propagation of
virtue, with so much ease and spirit, and delicacy, and knowledge of the human heart, and all in the serene tranquillity
of high life, that the reader is not only inchanted by their
genius, but reformed by their morality.

After dinner, we adjourned into the garden, where, I
observed, Mr. S—— gave a short separate audience to
every individual in a small remote filbert walk, from

whence most of them dropt off one after another, without further ceremony; but they were replaced by fresh recruits of the same clan, who came to make an afternoon's visit; and, among others, a spruce bookseller, called Birkin, who rode his own gelding, and made his appearance in a pair of new jemmy boots, with massy spurs of plate. It was not without reason, that this midwife of the Muses used exercise a-horseback, for he was too fat to walk a-foot, and he underwent some sarcasms from Tim Cropdale, on his unwieldy size and inaptitude for motion. Birkin, who took umbrage at this poor author's petulance in presuming to joke upon a man so much richer than himself, told him, he was not so unwieldy but that he could move the Marshalsea court for a writ, and even overtake him with it, if he did not very speedily come and settle accounts with him, respecting the expence of publishing his last ode to the king of Prussia, of which he had sold but three, and one of them was to Whitfield the methodist. Tim affected to receive this intimation with good humour, saying, he expected in a post or two, from Potsdam, a poem of thanks from his Prussian majesty, who knew very well how to pay poets in their own coin; but, in the mean time, he proposed, that Mr. Birkin and he should run three times round the garden for a bowl of punch, to be drank at Ashley's in the evening, and he would run boots against stockings. The bookseller, who valued himself upon his mettle, was persuaded to accept the challenge, and he forthwith resigned his boots to Cropdale, who, when he had put them on, was no bad representation of captain Pistol in the play.

Every thing being adjusted, they started together with great impetuosity, and, in the second round, Birkin had clearly the advantage, *larding the lean earth as he puff'd along*. Cropdale had no mind to contest the victory further; but, in a twinkling, disappeared through the back-door of the garden, which opened into a private lane, that had com-

munication with the high road.——The spectators immediately
began to hollow, 'Stole away!' and Birkin set off in pursuit
of him with great eagerness; but he had not advanced
twenty yards in the lane, when a thorn running into his
foot, sent him hopping back into the garden, roaring with
pain, and swearing with vexation. When he was delivered
from this annoyance by the Scotchman, who had been bred
to surgery, he looked about him wildly, exclaiming, 'Sure,
the fellow won't be such a rogue as to run clear away
with my boots!' Our landlord, having reconnoitered the
shoes he had left, which, indeed, hardly deserved that name,
'Pray, (said he) Mr. Birkin, wa'n't your boots made of calf
skin?' 'Calf-skin or cow-skin (replied the other) I'll find
a slip of sheep-skin that will do his business——I lost twenty
pounds by his farce which you persuaded me to buy——I am
out of pocket five pounds by his damn'd ode; and now this
pair of boots, bran new, cost me thirty shillings, as per
receipt——But this affair of the boots is felony——transporta-
tion.——I'll have the dog indicted at the Old Bailey——I
will, Mr. S——. I will be reveng'd, even though I should
lose my debt in consequence of his conviction.'

Mr. S—— said nothing at present, but accommodated
him with a pair of shoes; then ordered his servant to rub
him down, and comfort him with a glass of rum-punch,
which seemed, in a great measure, to cool the rage of his
indignation. 'After all (said our landlord) this is no more
than a *humbug* in the way of wit, though it deserves a more
respectable epithet, when considered as an effort of invention. Tim, being (I suppose) out of credit with the cord-
wainer, fell upon this ingenious expedient to supply the
want of shoes, knowing that Mr. Birkin, who loves humour,
would himself relish the joke upon a little recollection.
Cropdale literally lives by his wit, which he has exercised
upon all his friends in their turns. He once borrowed my
poney for five or six days to go to Salisbury, and sold him
in Smithfield at his return. This was a joke of such a serious

nature, that, in the first transports of my passion, I had some thoughts of prosecuting him for horse-stealing; and even when my resentment had in some measure subsided, as he industriously avoided me, I vowed, I would take satisfaction on his ribs with the first opportunity. One day, seeing him at some distance in the street, coming towards me, I began to prepare my cane for action, and walked in the shadow of a porter, that he might not perceive me soon enough to make his escape; but, in the very instant I had lifted up the instrument of correction, I found Tim Cropdale metamorphosed into a miserable blind wretch, feeling his way with a long stick from post to post, and rolling about two bald unlighted orbs instead of eyes. I was exceedingly shocked at having so narrowly escaped the concern and disgrace that would have attended such a misapplication of vengeance: but, next day, Tim prevailed upon a friend of mine to come and solicit my forgiveness, and offer his note, payable in six weeks, for the price of the poney.——This gentleman gave me to understand, that the blind man was no other than Cropdale, who having seen me advancing, and guessing my intent, had immediately converted himself into the object aforesaid——I was so diverted at the ingenuity of the evasion, that I agreed to pardon his offence, refusing his note, however, that I might keep a prosecution for felony hanging over his head, as a security for his future good behaviour——But Timothy would by no means trust himself in my hands till the note was accepted——then he made his appearance at my door as a blind beggar, and imposed in such a manner upon my man, who had been his old acquaintance and pot-companion, that the fellow threw the door in his face, and even threatened to give him the bastinado. Hearing a noise in the hall, I went thither, and immediately recollecting the figure I had passed in the street, accosted him by his own name, to the unspeakable astonishment of the footman.'

Birkin declared he loved a joke as well as another; but asked if any of the company could tell where Mr. Cropdale lodged, that he might send him a proposal about restitution, before the boots should be made away with. 'I would willingly give him a pair of new shoes, (said he) and half a guinea into the bargain, for the boots, which fitted me like a glove; and I shan't be able to get the fellows of them till the good weather for riding is over.' The stuttering wit declared, that the only secret which Cropdale ever kept, was the place of his lodgings; but he believed, that, during the heats of summer, he commonly took his repose upon a bulk, or indulged himself, in fresco, with one of the kennel-nymphs, under the portico of St. Martin's church. 'Pox on him! (cried the bookseller) he might as well have taken my whip and spurs—In that case, he might have been tempted to steal another horse, and then he would have rid to the devil of course.'

After coffee, I took my leave of Mr. S——, with proper acknowledgments of his civility, and was extremely well pleased with the entertainment of the day, though not yet satisfied, with respect to the nature of this connexion, betwixt a man of character in the literary world, and a parcel of authorlings, who, in all probability, would never be able to acquire any degree of reputation by their labours. On this head I interrogated my conductor, Dick Ivy, who answered me to this effect—'One would imagine S—— had some view to his own interest, in giving countenance and assistance to those people, whom he knows to be bad men, as well as bad writers; but, if he has any such view, he will find himself disappointed; for if he is so vain as to imagine he can make them subservient to his schemes of profit or ambition, they are cunning enough to make him their property in the mean time. There is not one of the company you have seen to-day (myself excepted) who does not owe him particular obligations——One of them he bailed out of a spunging-house, and afterwards paid the debt—another he translated into his family, and clothed, when he was turned out half naked from jail in consequence of an act for the relief of insolvent debtors—a third, who was reduced to a woollen night cap, and lived upon sheeps trotters, up three pair of stairs backward in Butcher-row, he took into present pay and free quarters, and enabled him to appear as a gentleman, without having the fear of sheriff's officers before his eyes. Those who are in distress he supplies with money when he has it, and with his credit when he is out of cash. When they want business, he either finds employment for them in his own service, or recommends them to booksellers to execute some project he has formed for their subsistence. They are always welcome to his table (which though plain is plentiful) and to his good offices as far as they will go, and when they see occasion, they make use of his name with the most petulant familiarity; nay, they do not even scruple to arrogate to themselves the merit of some of his performances, and have been known to sell their own lucubrations as the produce of his brain. The Scotchman you saw at dinner once personated him at an ale-house in West-Smithfield and, in the character of S———, had his head broke by a cow-keeper, for having spoke disrespectfully of the Christian religion; but he took the law of him in his own person, and the assailant was fain to give him ten pounds to withdraw his action.'

I observed, that all this appearance of liberality on the side of Mr. S—— was easily accounted for, on the supposition that they flattered him in private, and engaged his adversaries in public; and yet I was astonished, when I recollected that I often had seen this writer virulently abused in papers, poems, and pamphlets, and not a pen was drawn in his defence—'But you will be more astonished (said he) when I assure you, those very guests whom you saw at his table to-day, were the authors of great part of that abuse; and he himself is well aware of their particular favours, for they are all eager to detect and betray one another.' 'But this is doing the devil's work for nothing (cried I). What should induce them to revile their bene-factor without provocation?' 'Envy (answered Dick) is the general incitement; but they are galled by an additional scourge of provocation. S—— directs a literary journal, in which their productions are necessarily brought to trial; and though many of them have been treated with such lenity and favour as they little deserved, yet the slightest censure, such as, perhaps, could not be avoided with any pretensions to candour and impartiality, has rankled in the hearts of those authors to such a degree, that they have taken immediate vengeance on the critic in anonymous libels, letters, and lampoons. Indeed, all the writers of the age, good, bad, and indifferent, from the moment he as-sumed this office, became his enemies, either professed or in petto, except those of his friends who knew they had nothing to fear from his strictures; and he must be a wiser man than me who can tell what advantage or satisfac-tion he derives from having brought such a nest of hornets about his ears.'

I owned, that was a point which might deserve considera-tion; but still I expressed a desire to know his real motives for continuing his friendship to a set of rascals equally un-grateful and insignificant.—He said, he did not pretend to assign any reasonable motive; that, if the truth must be told, the man was, in point of conduct, a most incorrigible fool; that, though he pretended to have a knack at hitting off characters, he blundered strangely in the distribution of his favours, which were generally bestowed on the most undeserving of those who had recourse to his assistance; that, indeed, this preference was not so much owing to want of discernment as to want of resolution, for he had not fortitude enough to resist the importunity even of the most worthless; and, as he did not know the value of money, there was very little merit in parting with it so easily; that his pride was gratified in seeing himself courted by such a number of literary dependents; that, probably, he delighted in hearing them expose and traduce one another; and, finally, from their information, he became acquainted with all the transactions of Grub-street, which he had some thoughts of compiling for the entertainment of the public.

I could not help suspecting, from Dick's discourse, that he had some particular grudge against S——, upon whose conduct he had put the worst construction it would bear; and, by dint of cross-examination, I found he was not at all satisfied with the character which had been given in the Review of his last performance, though it had been treated civilly in consequence of the author's application to the critic. By all accounts, S—— is not without weakness and caprice; but he is certainly good-humoured and civilized; nor do I find that there is any thing overbearing, cruel, or implacable in his disposition.

I have dwelt so long upon authors, that you will perhaps suspect I intend to enroll myself among the fraternity; but, if I were actually qualified for the profession, it is at best but a desperate resource against starving, as it affords no provision for old age and infirmity. Salmon, at the age of fourscore, is now in a garret, compiling matter, at a guinea a sheet, for a modern historian, who, in point of age, might be his grand-child; and Psalmonazar, after having drudged half a century in the literary mill, in all the simplicity and abstinence of an Asiatic, subsists upon the charity of a few booksellers, just sufficient to keep him from the parish,—I think Guy, who was himself a bookseller, ought to have appropriated one wing or ward of his hospital to the use of decayed authors; though indeed, there is neither hospital, college, nor work-house, within the bills of mortality, large enough to contain the poor of this society, composed, as it is, from the refuse of every other profession.

I know not whether you will find any amusement in

this account of an odd race of mortals, whose constitution
had, I own, greatly interested the curiosity of

Yours,

J. MELFORD.

LONDON, *June* 10.

To Miss Lœtitia Willis, at Gloucester

MY DEAR LETTY,

There is something on my spirits, which I should not
venture to communicate by the post, but having the opportunity of Mrs. Brentwood's return, I seize it eagerly,
to disburthen my poor heart, which is oppressed with fear
and vexation.—O Letty! what a miserable situation it is,
to be without a friend to whom one can apply for counsel
and consolation in distress! I hinted in my last, that one Mr.
Barton had been very particular in his civilities: I can no
longer mistake his meaning—he has formally professed
himself my admirer; and, after a thousand assiduities, perceiving I made but a cold return to his addresses, he had
recourse to the mediation of lady Griskin, who has acted
the part of a very warm advocate in his behalf:——but, my
dear Willis, her ladyship over acts her part—she not only
expatiates on the ample fortune, the great connexions, and
the unblemished character of Mr. Barton, but she takes
the trouble to catechise me; and, two days ago, peremp-
torily told me, that a girl of my age could not possibly resist
so many considerations, if her heart was not pre-engaged.

This insinuation threw me into such a flutter, that she
could not but observe my disorder; and, presuming upon the
discovery, insisted upon my making her the confidante of
my passion. But, although I had not such command of
myself as to conceal the emotion of my heart, I am not
such a child as to disclose its secret to a person who would
certainly use them to its prejudice. I told her, it was no

wonder if I was out of countenance at her introducing a subject of conversation so unsuitable to my years and inexperience; that I believed Mr. Barton was a very worthy gentleman, and I was much obliged to him for his good opinion; but the affections were involuntary, and mine, in particular, had as yet made no concessions in his favour. She shook her head with an air of distrust that made me tremble; and observed, that if my affections were free, they would submit to the decision of prudence, especially when enforced by the authority of those who had a right to direct my conduct. This remark implied a design to interest my uncle or my aunt, perhaps my brother, in behalf of Mr. Barton's passion; and I am sadly afraid that my aunt is already gained over. Yesterday in the forenoon, he had been walking with us in the Park, and stopping in our return at a toy-shop, he presented her with a very fine snuff-box, and me with a gold etuis, which I resolutely refused, till she commanded me to accept it on pain of her displeasure: nevertheless, being still unsatisfied with respect to the propriety of receiving this toy, I signified my doubts to my brother, who said he would consult my uncle on the subject, and seemed to think Mr. Barton had been rather premature in his presents.

What will be the result of this consultation, Heaven knows; but I am afraid it will produce an explanation with Mr. Barton, who will, no doubt, avow his passion, and solicit their consent to a connexion which my soul abhors; for, my dearest Letty, it is not in my power to love Mr. Barton, even if my heart was untouched by any other tenderness. Not that there is any thing disagreeable about his person, but there is a total want of that nameless charm which captivates and controuls the inchanted spirit—at least, he appears to me to have this defect; but if he had all the engaging qualifications which a man can possess, they would be excited in vain against that constancy, which, I flatter myself, is the characteristic of my nature. No, my dear Willis, I may be involved in fresh troubles, and I believe I shall, from the importunities of this gentleman and the violence of my relations; but my heart is incapable of change.

You know I put no faith in dreams; and yet I have been much disturbed by one that visited me last night.——I thought I was in a church, where a certain person, whom you know, was on the point of being married to my aunt; that the clergyman was Mr. Barton, and that poor forlorn I, stood weeping in a corner, half naked, and without shoes or stockings.——Now, I know there is nothing so childish as to be moved by those vain illusions; but, nevertheless, in spite of all my reason, this hath made a strong impression upon my mind, which begins to be very gloomy. Indeed, I have another more substantial cause of affliction——I have some religious scruples, my dear friend, which lie heavy on my conscience.——I was persuaded to go to the Tabernacle, where I heard a discourse that affected me deeply.——I have prayed fervently to be enlightened, but as yet I am not sensible of these inward motions, those operations of grace, which are the signs of a regenerated spirit; and therefore I begin to be in terrible apprehensions about the state of my poor soul. Some of our family have had very uncommon accessions, particularly my aunt and Mrs. Jenkins, who sometimes speak as if they were really inspired; so that I am not like to want for either exhortation or example, to purify my thoughts, and recall them from the vanities of this world, which, indeed, I would willingly resign, if it was in my power; but to make this sacrifice, I must be enabled by such assistance from above as hath not yet been indulged to

Your unfortunate friend,

LYDIA MELFORD.

June 10.

To Sir Watkin Phillips, of Jesus college, Oxon.

DEAR PHILLIPS,

The moment I received your letter, I began to execute your commission—With the assistance of mine host at the Bull and Gate, I discovered the place to which your fugitive valet had retreated, and taxed him with his dishonesty—The fellow was in manifest confusion at sight of me, but he denied the charge with great confidence, till I told him, that if he would give up the watch, which was a family piece, he might keep the money and the clothes, and go to the devil his own way, at his leisure; but if he rejected this proposal, I would deliver him forthwith to the constable, whom I had provided for that purpose, and he would carry him before the justice without further delay. After some hesitation, he desired to speak with me in the next room, where he produced the watch, with all its appendages, and I have delivered it to our landlord, to be sent you by the first safe conveyance——So much for business.

I shall grow vain, upon your saying you find entertainment in my letters; barren, as they certainly are, of incident and importance, because your amusement must arise, not from the matter, but from the manner, which you know is all my own—Animated, therefore, by the approbation of a person, whose nice taste and consummate judgment I can no longer doubt, I will chearfully proceed with our memoirs—As it is determined we shall set out next week for Yorkshire, I went to-day in the forenoon with my uncle to see a carriage, belonging to a coach-maker in our neighbourhood—Turning down a narrow lane, behind Long-acre, we perceived a crowd of people standing at a door; which, it seems, opened into a kind of a methodist meeting, and were informed, that a footman was then holding forth to the congregation within. Curious to see this phœnomenon, we squeezed into the place with much difficulty; and who should this preacher be, but the identical Humphry Clinker. He had finished his sermon, and given out a psalm, the first stave of which he sung with peculiar graces——But if we were astonished to see Clinker in the pulpit we were altogether confounded at finding all the females of our family among the audience—There was lady Griskin, Mrs. Tabitha Bramble, Mrs. Winifred Jenkins, my sister Liddy, and Mr. Barton, and all of them joined in the psalmody, with strong marks of devotion.

I could hardly keep my gravity on this ludicrous occasion; but old Square-toes was differently affected—The first thing that struck him, was the presumption of his lacquey, whom he commanded to come down, with such an air of authority as Humphry did not think proper to disregard. He descended immediately, and all the people were in commotion. Barton looked exceedingly sheepish, lady Griskin flirted her fan, Mrs. Tabby groaned in spirit, Liddy changed countenance, Mrs. Jenkins sobbed as if her heart was breaking— My uncle, with a sneer, asked pardon of the ladies, for having interrupted their devotion, saying, he had particular business with the preacher, whom he ordered to call a hackney-coach. This being immediately brought up to the end of the lane, he handed Liddy into it, and my aunt and I following him, we drove home, without taking any further notice of the rest of the company, who still remained in silent astonishment.

Mr. Bramble, perceiving Liddy in great trepidation, assumed a milder aspect, bidding her be under no concern, for he was not at all displeased at any thing she had done— 'I have no objection (said he) to your being religiously inclined; but I don't think my servant is a proper ghostly director for a devotee of your sex and character—if, in fact (as I rather believe) your aunt is not the sole conductress of this machine'——Mrs. Tabitha made no answer, but threw up the whites of her eyes, as if in the act of ejaculation

—Poor Liddy, said, she had no right to the title of a devotee; that she thought there was no harm in hearing a pious discourse, even if it came from a footman, especially as her aunt was present; but that if she had erred from ignorance, she hoped he would excuse it, as she could not bear the thoughts of living under his displeasure. The old gentleman, pressing her hand with a tender smile, said she was a good girl, and that he did not believe her capable of doing any thing that could give him the least umbrage or disgust.

When we arrived at our lodgings, he commanded Mr. Clinker to attend him up stairs, and spoke to him in these words——'Since you are called upon by the spirit to preach and to teach, it is high time to lay aside the livery of an earthly master; and for my part, I am unworthy to have an apostle in my service—' 'I hope (said Humphry) I have not failed in my duty to your honour—I should be a vile wretch if I did, considering the misery from which your charity and compassion relieved me—but having an inward admonition of the spirit——' 'An admonition of the devil—(cried the squire, in a passion) What admonition, you blockhead?—What right has such a fellow as you to set up for a reformer?' 'Begging your honour's pardon (replied Clinker) may not the new light of God's grace shine upon the poor and the ignorant in their humility, as well as upon the wealthy, and the philosopher in all his pride of human learning?' 'What you imagine to be the new light of grace (said his master) I take to be a deceitful vapour, glimmering through a crack in your upper story—In a word, Mr. Clinker, I will have no light in my family but what pays the king's taxes, unless it be the light of reason, which you don't pretend to follow.'

'Ah, sir! (cried Humphry) the light of reason, is no more in comparison to the light I mean, than a farthing candle to the sun at noon—' 'Very true, (said uncle) the one will serve to shew you your way, and the other to dazzle and confound your weak brain—Heark-ye, Clinker, you are either an hypocritical knave, or a wrong-headed enthusiast; and in either case, unfit for my service——If you are a quack in sanctity and devotion, you will find it an easy matter to impose upon silly women, and others of crazed understanding, who will contribute lavishly for your support——If you are really seduced by the reveries of a disturbed imagination, the sooner you lose your senses entirely, the better for yourself and the community. In that case, some charitable person might provide you with a dark room and clean straw in Bedlam, where it would not be in your power to infect others with your fanaticism; whereas, if you have just reflection enough left to maintain the character of a chosen vessel in the meetings of the godly, you and your hearers will be misled by a Will-o'-the-wisp, from one error into another, till you are plunged into religious frenzy; and then, perhaps, you will hang yourself in despair——' 'Which the Lord of his infinite mercy forbid! (exclaimed the affrighted Clinker) It is very possible I may be under the temptation of the devil, who wants to wreck me on the rocks of spiritual pride——Your honour says, I am either a knave or a madman; now, as I'll assure your honour, I am no knave, it follows that I must be mad; therefore, I beseech your honour, upon my knees, to take my case into consideration, that means may be used for my recovery——'

The 'squire could not help smiling at the poor fellow's simplicity, and promised to take care of him, provided he would mind the business of his place, without running after the new light of methodism: but Mrs. Tabitha took offence at his humility, which she interpreted into poorness of spirit and worldly mindedness——She upbraided him with the want of courage to suffer for conscience sake——She observed, that if he should lose his place for bearing testimony to the truth, Providence would not fail to find him another, perhaps more advantageous; and, declaring that it could not be very agreeable to live in a family where an inquisition was established, retired to another room in great agitation.

My uncle followed her with a significant look, then, turning to the preacher, 'You hear what my sister says—If you cannot live with me upon such terms as I have prescribed, the vineyard of methodism lies before you, and she seems very well disposed to reward your labour—' 'I would not willingly give offence to any soul upon earth (answered Humphry); her ladyship has been very good to me, ever since we came to London; and surely she has a heart turned for religious exercises; and both she and lady Griskin sing psalms and hymns like two cherubims——But, at the same time, I'm bound to love and obey your honour—It becometh not such a poor ignorant fellow as me, to hold dispute with gentlemen of rank and learning—As for the matter of knowledge, I am no more than a beast in comparison of your honour; therefore I submit; and, with God's grace, I will follow you to the world's end, if you don't think me too far gone to be out of confinement—'

His master promised to keep him for some time longer on trial; then desired to know in what manner lady Griskin and Mr. Barton came to join their religious society, he told him, that her ladyship was the person who first carried my aunt and sister to the Tabernacle, whither he attended them, and had his devotion kindled by Mr. W——'s preaching: that he was confirmed in this new way, by the preacher's sermons, which he had bought and studied with great attention: that his discourse and prayers had brought over Mrs. Jenkins and the house-maid to the same way of thinking; but as for Mr. Barton, he had never seen him at service before this day, when he came in company with lady Griskin——Humphry, moreover, owned that he had been encouraged to mount the rostrum, by the example and success of a weaver, who was much followed as a powerful minister: that on his first trial he found himself under such strong impulsions, as made him believe he was certainly moved by the spirit; and that he had assisted in lady Griskin's, and several private houses, at exercises of devotion.

Mr. Bramble was no sooner informed, that her ladyship had acted as the primum mobile of this confederacy, than he concluded she had only made use of Clinker as a tool, subservient to the execution of some design, to the true secret of which he was an utter stranger—He observed, that her ladyship's brain was a perfect mill for projects; and that she and Tabby had certainly engaged in some secret treaty, the nature of which he could not comprehend. I told him I thought it was no difficult matter to perceive the drift of Mrs. Tabitha, which was to ensnare the heart of Barton, and that in all likelihood my lady Griskin acted as her auxiliary: that this supposition would account for their endeavours to convert him to methodism; an event which would occasion a connexion of souls that might be easily improved into a matrimonial union.

My uncle seemed to be much diverted by the thoughts of this scheme's succeeding; but I gave him to understand, that Barton was pre-engaged: that he had the day before made a present of an etuis to Liddy, which her aunt had obliged her to receive, with a view, no doubt, to countenance her own accepting of a snuff-box at the same time; that my sister having made me acquainted with this incident, I had desired an explanation of Mr. Barton, who declared his intentions were honourable, and expressed his hope that I would have no objections to his alliance; that I had thanked him for the honour he intended our family; but told him, it would be necessary to consult her uncle and aunt, who were her guardians; and their approbation being obtained, I could have no objection to his proposal; though I was persuaded that no violence would be offered to my sister's inclinations, in a transaction that so nearly interested the happiness of her future life: that he had assured me, he should never think of availing himself of a guardian's authority, unless he could render his addresses agreeable to the young lady herself; and that he would immediately demand permission of Mr. and Mrs. Bramble, to make Liddy a tender of his hand and fortune.

The squire was not insensible to the advantages of such a match, and declared he would promote it with all his influence; but when I took notice that there seemed to be an aversion on the side of Liddy, he said he would sound her on the subject; and if her reluctance was such as would not be easily overcome, he would civilly decline the proposal of Mr. Barton; for he thought that, in the choice of a husband a young woman ought not to sacrifice the feelings of her heart for any consideration upon earth—'Liddy is not so desperate (said he) as to worship fortune at such an expence.' I take it for granted, this whole affair will end in smoke; though there seems to be a storm brewing in the quarter of Mrs. Tabby, who sat with all the sullen dignity of silence at dinner, seemingly pregnant with complaint and expostulation. As she had certainly marked Barton for her own prey, she cannot possibly favour his suit to Liddy; and therefore I expect something extraordinary will attend his declaring himself my sister's admirer. This declaration will certainly be made in form, as soon as the lover can pick up resolution enough to stand the brunt of Mrs. Tabby's disappointment; for he is, without doubt, aware of her designs upon his person——The particulars of the *denouement* you shall know in due season: mean while I am

Always yours,

J. MELFORD.

LONDON, *June* 10.

To Dr. Lewis

DEAR LEWIS,

The deceitful calm was of short duration. I am plunged again in a sea of vexation, and the complaints in my stomach and bowels are returned; so that I suppose I shall be disabled from prosecuting the excursion I had planned—What the devil had I to do, to come a plague hunting with a leash of females in my train? Yesterday my precious sister (who, by the bye, has been for some time a professed methodist) came into my apartment, attended by Mr. Barton, and desired an audience with a very stately air—'Brother, (said she) this gentleman has something to propose, which I flatter myself will be the more acceptable, as it will rid you of a troublesome companion.' Then Mr. Barton proceeded to this effect—'I am, indeed, extremely ambitious of being allied to your family, Mr. Bramble, and I hope you will see no cause to interpose your authority.' 'As for authority, (said Tabby, interrupting him with some warmth) I know of none that he has a right to use on this occasion——If I pay him the compliment of making him acquainted with the step I intend to take, it is all he can expect in reason—This is as much as I believe he would do by me, if he intended to change his own situation in life —In a word, brother, I am so sensible of Mr. Barton's extraordinary merit, that I have been prevailed upon to alter my resolution of living a single life, and to put my happiness in his hands, by vesting him with a legal title to my person and fortune, such as they are. The business at present, is to have the writings drawn; and I shall be obliged to you, if you will recommend a lawyer to me for that purpose—'

You may guess what an effect this overture had upon me; who, from the information of my nephew, expected that Barton was to make a formal declaration of his passion for Liddy; I could not help gazing in silent astonishment, alternately at Tabby, and her supposed admirer, who last hung his head in the most awkward confusion for a few minutes, and then retired on pretence of being suddenly seized with a vertigo——Mrs. Tabitha affected much concern, and would have had him make use of a bed in the house; but he insisted upon going home, that he might have recourse of some drops, which he kept for such emergencies, and his innamorata acquiesced—In the mean time I was exceedingly puzzled at this adventure (though I suspected the truth) and did not know in what manner to demean myself towards Mrs. Tabitha, when Jery came in and told me, he had just seen Mr. Barton alight from his chariot at lady Griskin's door—This incident seemed to threaten a visit from her ladyship, with which we were honoured accordingly, in less than half an hour—'I find (said she) there has been a match of cross purposes among you good folks; and I'm come to set you to rights—' So saying, she presented me with the following billet——

    'DEAR SIR,

     'I no sooner recollected myself from the extreme confusion I was thrown into, by that unlucky mistake of your sister, that I thought it my duty to assure you, that my devoirs to Mrs. Bramble never exceeded the bounds of ordinary civility; and that my heart is unalterably fixed upon Miss Liddy Melford, as I had the honour to declare to her brother, when he questioned me upon that subject—Lady Griskin has been so good as to charge herself, not only with the delivery of this note, but also with the task of undeceiving Mrs. Bramble, for whom I have the most profound respect and veneration, though my affection being otherwise engaged is no longer in the power of
                'Sir,
      'Your very humble servant,
                   'RALPH BARTON.'

Having cast my eyes over this billet, I told her ladyship, that I would no longer retard the friendly office she had undertaken: and I and Jery forthwith retired into another room. There we soon perceived the conversation grow very warm betwixt the two ladies; and, at length, could distinctly hear certain terms of altercation, which we could no longer delay interrupting, with any regard to decorum.

When we entered the scene of contention, we found Liddy
had joined the disputants, and stood trembling betwixt them,
as if she had been afraid they would have proceeded to
something more practical than words————Lady Griskin's
face was like the full moon in a storm of wind, glaring,
fiery, and portentuous; while Tabby looked grim and
ghastly, with an aspect breathing discord and dismay.——Our
appearance put a stop to their mutual revilings; but her
ladyship turning to me, 'Cousin (said she) I can't help
saying I have met with a very ungrateful return from this
lady, for the pains I have taken to serve her family——' 'My
family is much obliged to your ladyship (cried Tabby, with
a kind of hysterical giggle); but we have no right to the
good offices of such an honourable go-between.' 'But, for
all that, good Mrs. Tabitha Bramble (resumed the other),
I shall be content with the reflection, That virtue is its own
reward; and it shall not be my fault, if you continue to
make yourself ridiculous—Mr. Bramble, who has no little
interest of his own to serve, will, no doubt, contribute all
in his power to promote a match betwixt Mr. Barton and
his niece, which will be equally honourable and advantageous; and, I dare say, Miss Liddy herself will have no
objection to a measure so well calculated to make her happy
in life————' 'I beg your ladyship's pardon (exclaimed Liddy,
with great vivacity) I have nothing but misery to expect
from such a measure; and I hope my guardians will have
too much compassion, to barter my peace of mind for any
consideration of interest or fortune——' 'Upon my word,
Miss Liddy! (said she) you have profited by the example
of your good aunt—I comprehend your meaning, and will
explain it when I have a proper opportunity————In the
mean time, I shall take my leave————Madam, your most
obedient, and devoted humble servant,' said she, advancing
close up to my sister, and curtsying so low, that I thought
she intended to squat herself down on the floor————This
salutation Tabby returned with equal solemnity; and the

expression of the two faces, while they continued in this attitude, would be no bad subject for a pencil like that of the incomparable Hogarth, if any such should ever appear again, in these times of dullness and degeneracy.

Jery accompanied her ladyship to her house, that he might have an opportunity to restore the etuis to Barton, and advise him to give up his suit, which was so disagreeable to his sister, against whom, however, he returned much irritated—Lady Griskin had assured him that Liddy's heart was pre-occupied; and immediately the idea of Wilson recurring to his imagination, his family-pride took the alarm —He denounced vengeance against the adventurer, and was disposed to be very peremptory with his sister; but I desired he would suppress his resentment, until I should have talked with her in private.

The poor girl, when I earnestly pressed her on this head, owned with a flood of tears, that Wilson had actually come to the Hot Well at Bristol, and even introduced himself into our lodgings as a Jew pedlar; but that nothing had passed betwixt them, further than her begging him to withdraw immediately, if he had any regard for her peace of mind: that he had disappeared accordingly, after having attempted to prevail upon my sister's maid, to deliver a letter; which, however, she refused to receive, though she had consented to carry a message, importing that he was a gentleman of a good family; and that, in a very little time, he would avow his passion in that character—She confessed, that although he had not kept his word in this particular, he was not yet altogether indifferent to her affection; but solemnly promised, she would never carry on any correspondence with him, or any other admirer, for the future, without the privity and approbation of her brother and me.

By this declaration, she made her own peace with Jery; but the hot-headed boy is more than ever incensed against Wilson, whom he now considers as an impostor, that harbours some infamous design upon the honour of his family

——As for Barton, he was not a little mortified to find his present returned, and his addresses so unfavourably received; but he is not a man to be deeply affected by such disappointments; and I know not whether he is not as well pleased with being discarded by Liddy, as he would have been with a permission to prosecute his pretensions, at the risque of being every day exposed to the revenge or machinations of Tabby, who is not to be slighted with impunity —I had not much time to moralize on these occurrences; for the house was visited by a constable and his gang, with a warrant from justice Buzzard, to search the box of Humphry Clinker, my footman, who was just apprehended as a highwayman—This incident threw the whole family into confusion. My sister scolded the constable for presuming to enter the lodgings of a gentleman on such an errand, without having first asked, and obtained permission; her maid was frightened into fits, and Liddy shed tears of compassion for the unfortunate Clinker, in whose box, however, nothing was found to confirm the suspicion of robbery.

For my own part, I made no doubt of the fellow's being mistaken for some other person, and I went directly to the justice, in order to procure his discharge; but there I found the matter much more serious than I expected—Poor Clinker stood trembling at the bar, surrounded by thief-takers; and at a little distance, a thick, squat fellow, a postilion, his accuser, who had seized him on the street, and swore positively to his person, that the said Clinker had, on the 15th day of March last, on Blackheath, robbed a gentleman in a post-chaise, which he (the postilion) drove—This deposition was sufficient to justify his commitment; and he was sent accordingly to Clerkenwell prison, whither Jery accompanied him in the coach, in order to recommend him properly to the keeper, that he may want for no convenience which the place affords.

The spectators, who assembled to see this highwayman, were sagacious enough to discern something very villainous in his aspect; which (begging their pardon) is the very picture of simplicity; and the justice himself put a very unfavourable construction upon some of his answers, which, he said, favoured of the ambiguity and equivocation of an old offender; but, in my opinion, it would have been more just and humane to impute them to the confusion into which we may suppose a poor country lad to be thrown on such an occasion. I am still persuaded he is innocent; and, in this persuasion, I can do no less than use my utmost endeavours that he may not be oppressed—I shall, to-morrow, send my nephew to wait on the gentleman who was robbed, and beg he will have the humanity to go and see the prisoner; that, in case he should find him quite different from the person of the highwayman, he may bear testimony in his behalf— Howsoever it may fare with Clinker, this cursed affair will be to me productive of intolerable chagrin—I have already caught a dreadful cold, by rushing into the open air from the justice's parlour, where I had been stewing in the crowd; and though I should not be laid up with the gout, as I believe I shall, I must stay at London for some weeks, till this poor devil comes to his trial at Rochester; so that, in all probability, my northern expedition is blown up.

If you can find any thing in your philosophical budget, to console me in the midst of these distresses and apprehensions, pray let it be communicated to

your unfortunate friend,

MATT. BRAMBLE.

LONDON, *June* 12.

To Sir Watkin Phillips, of Jesus college, Oxon.

DEAR WAT,

The farce is finished, and another piece of a graver cast brought upon the stage.——Our aunt made a desperate attack upon Barton, who had no other way of saving himself, but by leaving her in possession of the field, and avowing his pretensions to Liddy, by whom he has been rejected in his turn.——Lady Griskin acted as his advocate and agent on this occasion, with such zeal as embroiled her with Mrs. Tabitha, and a high scene of altercation passed betwixt these two religionists, which might have come to action, had not my uncle interposed. They are however reconciled, in consequence of an event which hath involved us all in trouble and disquiet. You must know, the poor preacher, Humphry Clinker, is now exercising his ministry among the felons in Clerkenwell prison.——A postilion having sworn a robbery against him, no bail could be taken, and he was committed to jail, notwithstanding all the remonstrances and interest my uncle could make in his behalf.

All things considered, the poor fellow cannot possibly be guilty, and yet, I believe, he runs some risque of being hanged.——Upon his examination, he answered with such hesitation and reserve, as persuaded most of the people, who crowded the place, that he was really a knave, and the justice's remarks confirmed their opinion. Exclusive of my uncle and myself, there was only one person who seemed inclined to favour the culprit.——He was a young man, well dressed, and, from the manner in which he cross-examined the evidence, we took it for granted, that he was a student in one of the inns of court.——He freely checked the justice for some uncharitable inferences he made to the prejudice of the prisoner, and even ventured to dispute with his worship on certain points of law.

My uncle, provoked at the unconnected and dubious answers of Clinker, who seemed in danger of falling a sacrifice to his own simplicity, exclaimed, 'In the name of God, if you are innocent, say so.' 'No (cried he) God forbid that I should call myself innocent, while my conscience is burthened with sin.' 'What then, you did commit this robbery?' resumed his master. 'No, sure (said he) blessed be the Lord, I'm free of that guilt.'

Here the justice interposed, observing, that the man seemed inclined to make a discovery by turning king's evidence, and desired the clerk to take his confession; upon which Humphry declared, that he looked upon confession to be a popish fraud, invented by the whore of Babylon. The Templar affirmed, that the poor fellow was *non compos;* and exhorted the justice to discharge him as a lunatic. ——'You know very well (added he) that the robbery in question was not committed by the prisoner.'

The thief-takers grinned at one another; and Mr. Justice Buzzard replied with great emotion, 'Mr. Martin, I desire you will mind your own business; I shall convince you one of these days that I understand mine.' In short, there was no remedy; the mittimus was made out, and poor Clinker sent to prison in a hackney-coach, guarded by the constable, and accompanied by your humble servant. By the way, I was not a little surprised to hear this retainer to justice bid the prisoner to keep up his spirits, for that he did not at all doubt but that he would get off for a few weeks confinement—He said, his worship knew very well that Clinker was innocent of the fact, and that the real highwayman who robbed the chaise, was no other than that very individual Mr. Martin, who had pleaded so strenuously for honest Humphry.

Confounded at this information, I asked, 'Why then is he suffered to go about at his liberty, and this poor innocent fellow treated as a malefactor?' 'We have exact intelligence of all Mr. Martin's transactions; (said he) but as yet there is not evidence sufficient for his conviction; and as for this young man, the justice could do no less than commit him, as the postilion swore point-blank to his identity.' 'So if this rascally postilion should persist in the falsity to which he is sworn (said I) this innocent lad may be brought to the gallows.'

The constable observed, that he would have time enough to prepare for his trial, and might prove an *alibi;* or, perhaps, Martin might be apprehended and convicted for another fact; in which case, he might be prevailed upon to take this affair upon himself; or, finally, if these chances should fail, and the evidence stand good against Clinker, the jury might recommend him to mercy, in consideration of his youth, especially if this should appear to be the first fact of which he had been guilty.

Humphry owned, he could not pretend to recollect where he had been on the day when the robbery was committed, much less prove a circumstance of that kind so far back as six months, though he knew he had been sick of the fever and ague, which, however, did not prevent him from going about—then, turning up his eyes, he ejaculated, 'The Lord's will be done! if it be my fate to suffer, I hope I shall not disgrace the faith of which, though unworthy, I make profession.'

When I expressed my surprize that the accuser should persist in charging Clinker, without taking the least notice of the real robber who stood before him, and to whom, indeed, Humphry bore not the smallest resemblance; the constable (who was himself a thief-taker) gave me to understand, that Mr. Martin was the best qualified for business of all the gentlemen on the road he had ever known; that he had always acted on his own bottom, without partner or correspondent, and never went to work but when he was cool and sober; that his courage and presence of mind never failed him; that his address was genteel, and his behaviour void of all cruelty and insolence; that he never encumbered himself with watches or trinkets, nor even with bank-notes, but always dealt for ready money, and that in the current coin of the kingdom; and that he could disguise himself and his horse in such a manner, that, after the action, it was impossible to recognize either the one or the other—'This great man (said he) has reigned paramount in all the roads within fifty miles of London above fifteen months, and has done more business in that time, than all the rest of the profession put together; for those who pass through his hands are so delicately dealt with, that they have no desire to give him the least disturbance; but for all that, his race is almost run—he is now fluttering about justice, like a moth about a candle—there are so many lime-twigs laid in his way, that I'll bett a cool hundred, he swings before Christmas.'

Shall I own to you, that this portrait, drawn by a ruffian, heightened by what I myself had observed in his deportment, has interested me warmly in the fate of poor Martin, whom nature seems to have intended for a useful and honourable member of that community upon which he now preys for subsistence? It seems, he lived some time as a clerk to a timber-merchant, whose daughter Martin having privately married, was discarded, and his wife turned out of doors. She did not long survive her marriage; and Martin, turning fortune-hunter, could not supply his occasions any other way, than by taking to the road, in which he has travelled hitherto with uncommon success.—He pays his respects regularly to Mr. Justice Buzzard, the thief-catcher-general of this metropolis, and sometimes they smoke a pipe together very lovingly, when the conversation generally turns upon the nature of evidence.—The justice has given him fair warning to take care of himself, and he has received his caution in good part.—Hitherto he has baffled all the vigilance, art, and activity of Buzzard and his emissaries, with such conduct as would have done honour to the genius of a Cæsar or a Turenne; but he has one weakness, which has proved fatal to all the heroes of his tribe, namely, an indiscreet devotion to the fair sex, and, in all probability, he will be attacked on this defenceless quarter.

Be that as it may, I saw the body of poor Clinker consigned to the gaoler of Clerkenwell, to whose indulgence I recommended him so effectually, that he received him in the most hospitable manner, though there was a necessity for equipping him with a suit of irons, in which he made a very

rueful appearance. The poor creature seemed as much affected by my uncle's kindness, as by his own misfortune.
When I assured him, that nothing should be left undone
for procuring his enlargement, and making his confinement
easy in the mean time, he fell down on his knees, and kissing
my hand, which he bathed with his tears, 'O 'squire! (cried
he, sobbing) what shall I say?—I can't—no, I can't speak
—my poor heart is bursting with gratitude to you and my
dear—dear—generous—noble benefactor.'

I protest, the scene became so pathetic, that I was fain to
force myself away, and returned to my uncle, who sent me
in the afternoon with a compliment to one Mr. Mead, the
person who had been robbed on Black-heath. As I did not
find him at home, I left a message, in consequence of which
he called at our lodgings this morning, and very humanely
agreed to visit the prisoner. By this time, lady Griskin had
come to make her formal compliments of condolance to
Mrs. Tabitha, on this domestic calamity; and that prudent
maiden, whose passion was now cooled, thought proper to
receive her ladyship so civilly, that a reconciliation immediately ensued. These two ladies resolved to comfort the
poor prisoner in their own persons, and Mr. Mead and I
'squired them to Clerkenwell, my uncle being detained at
home by some slight complaints in his stomach and bowels.

The turnkey, who received us at Clerkenwell, looked
remarkably sullen; and when we enquired for Clinker, 'I
don't care, if the devil had him; (said he) here has been
nothing but canting and praying since the fellow entered
the place.—Rabbit him! the tap will be ruined—we han't
sold a cask of beer, nor a dozen of wine, since he paid his
garnish—the gentlemen get drunk with nothing but your
damned religion.——For my part, I believe as how your
man deals with the devil.—Two or three as bold hearts as
ever took the air upon Hounslow, have been blubbering all
night; and if the fellow an't speedily removed by Habeas
Corpus, or otherwise, I'll be damn'd if there's a grain of

true spirit left within these walls—we shan't have a soul to do credit to the place, or make his exit like a true-born Englishman—damn my eyes! there will be nothing but snivelling in the cart—we shall all die like so many psalm-singing weavers.'

In short, we found that Humphry was, at that very instant, haranguing the felons in the chapel; and that the gaoler's wife and daughter, together with my aunt's woman, Win Jenkins, and our house-maid, were among the audience, which we immediately joined. I never saw any thing so strongly picturesque as this congregation of felons clanking their chains, in the midst of whom stood orator Clinker, expatiating in a transport of fervor, on the torments of hell, denounced in scripture against evil-doers, comprehending murderers, robbers, thieves, and whore-mongers. The variety of attention exhibited in the faces of those ragamuffins, formed a groupe that would not have disgraced the pencil of a Raphael. In one, it denoted admiration; in another, doubt; in a third, disdain; in a fourth, contempt; in a fifth, terror; in a sixth, derision; and in a seventh, indignation.— As for Mrs. Winifred Jenkins, she was in tears, overwhelmed with sorrow; but whether for her own sins, or the misfortune of Clinker, I cannot pretend to say. The other females seemed to listen with a mixture of wonder and devotion. The gaoler's wife declared he was a saint in trouble, saying, she wished from her heart there was such another good soul, like him, in every gaol in England.

Mr. Mead, having earnestly surveyed the preacher, declared his appearance was so different from that of the person who robbed him on Black-heath, that he could freely make oath he was not the man: but Humphry himself was by this time pretty well rid of all apprehensions of being hanged; for he had been the night before solemnly tried and acquitted by his fellow prisoners, some of whom he had already converted to methodism. He now made proper acknowledgements for the honour of our visit, and was permitted to kiss the hands of the ladies, who assured him, he might depend upon their friendship and protection. Lady Griskin, in her great zeal, exhorted his fellow-prisoners to profit by the precious opportunity of having such a saint in bonds among them, and turn over a new leaf for the benefit of their poor souls; and, that her admonition might have the greater effect, she reinforced it with her bounty.

While she and Mrs. Tabby returned in the coach with the two maid-servants, I waited on Mr. Mead to the house of justice Buzzard, who, having heard his declaration, said his oath could be of no use at present, but that he would be a material evidence for the prisoner at his trial; so that there seems to be no remedy but patience for poor Clinker; and, indeed, the same virtue, or medicine, will be necessary for us all, the squire in particular, who had set his heart upon his excursion to the northward.

While we were visiting honest Humphry in Clerkenwell prison, my uncle received a much more extraordinary visit at his own lodgings. Mr. Martin, of whom I have made such honourable mention, desired permission to pay him his respects, and was admitted accordingly. He told him, that having observed him, at Mr. Buzzard's, a good deal disturbed by what had happened to his servant, he had come to assure him he had nothing to apprehend for Clinker's life; for, if it was possible that any jury could find him guilty upon such evidence, he, Martin himself, would produce in court a person, whose deposition would bring him off clear as the sun at noon.—Sure, the fellow would not be so romantic as to take the robbery upon himself!—He said, the postilion was an infamous fellow, who had been a dabbler in the same profession, and saved his life at the Old Bailey by impeaching his companions; that being now reduced to great poverty, he had made this desperate push, to swear away the life of an innocent man, in hopes of having the reward upon his conviction; but that he would find himself miserably disappointed, for the justice and his myrmidons were determined to admit of no interloper in this branch of business; and that he did not at all doubt but that they would find matter enough to shop the evidence himself before the next gaol-delivery. He affirmed, that all these circumstances were well known to the justice; and that his severity to Clinker was no other than a hint to his master to make him a present in private, as an acknowledgment of his candour and humanity.

This hint, however, was so unpalatable to Mr. Bramble, that he declared, with great warmth, he would rather confine himself for life to London, which he detested, than be at liberty to leave it to-morrow, in consequence of encouraging corruption in a magistrate. Hearing, however, how favourable Mr. Mead's report had been for the prisoner, he is resolved to take the advice of counsel in what manner to proceed for his immediate enlargement. I make no doubt, but that in a day or two this troublesome business may be discussed; and in this hope we are preparing for our journey. If our endeavours do not miscarry, we shall have taken the field before you hear again from

Yours,

J. Melford.

London, *June* 11.

To Dr. Lewis

Thank Heaven! dear Lewis, the clouds are dispersed, and I have now the clearest prospect of my summer campaign, which, I hope, I shall be able to begin to-morrow. I took the advice of counsel with respect to the case of Clinker, in whose favour a lucky incident has intervened. The fellow who accused him, has had his own battery turned upon himself.—Two days ago he was apprehended for a robbery on the highway, and committed, on the evidence of an accomplice. Clinker, having moved for a writ of *habeas cor-*

pus, was brought before the lord chief justice, who, in consequence of an affidavit of the gentleman who had been robbed, importing that the said Clinker was not the person who stopped him on the highway, as well as in consideration of the postilion's character and present circumstances, was pleased to order, that my servant should be admitted to bail, and he has been discharged accordingly, to the unspeakable satisfaction of our whole family, to which he has recommended himself in an extraordinary manner, not only by his obliging deportment, but by his talents of preaching, praying, and singing psalms, which he has exercised with such effect, that even Tabby respects him as a chosen vessel. If there was any thing like affectation or hypocrisy in this excess of religion, I would not keep him in my service; but, so far as I can observe, the fellow's character is downright simplicity, warmed with a kind of enthusiasm, which renders him very susceptible of gratitude and attachment to his benefactors.

As he is an excellent horseman, and understands farriery, I have bought a stout gelding for his use, that he may attend us on the road, and have an eye to our cattle, in case the coachman should not mind his business. My nephew, who is to ride his own saddle-horse, has taken, upon trial, a servant just come from abroad with his former master, Sir William Strollop, who vouches for his honesty. The fellow, whose name is Dutton, seems to be a petit maitre.——He has got a smattering of French, bows, and grins, and shrugs, and takes snuff *a la mode de France,* but values himself chiefly upon his skill and dexterity in hair-dressing.——If I am not much deceived by appearance, he is, in all respects, the very contrast of Humphry Clinker.

My sister has made up matters with lady Griskin; though, I must own, I should not have been sorry to see that connexion entirely destroyed: but Tabby is not of a disposition to forgive Barton, who, I understand, is gone to his seat in Berkshire for the summer season. I cannot help suspecting, that in the treaty of peace, which has been lately ratified betwixt those two females, it is stipulated, that her ladyship shall use her best endeavours to provide an agreeable helpmate for our sister Tabitha, who seems to be quite desperate in her matrimonial designs. Perhaps, the match-maker is to have a valuable consideration in the way of brokerage, which she will most certainly deserve, if she can find any man in his senses, who will yoke with Mrs. Bramble from motives of affection or interest.

I find my spirits and my health affect each other reciprocally—that is to say, every thing that discomposes my mind, produces a correspondent disorder in my body; and my bodily complaints are remarkably mitigated by those considerations that dissipate the clouds of mental chagrin.—The imprisonment of Clinker brought on those symptoms which I mentioned in my last, and now they are vanished at his discharge.—It must be owned, indeed, I took some of the tincture of ginseng, prepared according to your prescription, and found it exceedingly grateful to the stomach; but the pain and sickness continued to return, after short intervals, till the anxiety of my mind was entirely removed, and then I found myself perfectly at ease. We have had fair weather these ten days, to the astonishment of the Londoners, who think it portentous. If you enjoy the same indulgence in Wales, I hope Barns has got my hay made, and safe cocked by this time. As we shall be in motion for some weeks, I cannot expect to hear from you as usual; but I shall continue to write from every place at which we make any halt, that you may know our track, in case it should be necessary to communicate any thing to

Your assured friend,

MATT. BRAMBLE.

LONDON, *June* 14.

To Mrs. Mary Jones, at Brambleton-hall, &c.

DEAR MARY,

Having the occasion of my cousin Jenkins of Aberga'ny, I send you, as a token, a turkey-shell comb, a kiple of
yards of green ribbon, and a sarment upon the nothingness
of good works, which was preached in the Tabernacle; and
you will also receive a horn-buck for Saul, whereby she may
learn her letters; for I'm much consarned about the state
of her poor sole—and what are all the pursuits of this life
to the consarns of that immortal part?—What is life but a
veil of affliction? O Mary! the whole family have been in
such a constipation!—Mr. Clinker has been in trouble, but
the gates of hell have not been able to prevail again him.
——His virtue is like poor gould, seven times tried in the
fire. He was tuck up for a rubbery, and had before gustass
Busshard, who made his mittamouse; and the pore youth
was sent to prison upon the false oaf of a willian, that
wanted to sware his life away for the looker of cain.

The squire did all in his power, but could not prevent
his being put in chains, and confined among common manu-
factors, where he stood like an innocent sheep in the midst
of wolves and tygers.—Lord knows what mought have happened to this pyehouse young man, if master had not applied
to Apias Korkus, who lives with the ould bailiff, and is, they
say, five hundred years old, (God bless us!) and a congeror:
but, if he be, sure I am he don't deal with the devil, otherwise he wouldn't have sought out Mr. Clinker, as he did,
in spite of stone walls, iron bolts, and double locks, that
flew open at his command; for Ould Scratch has not a
greater enemy upon hearth than Mr. Clinker, who is, indeed, a very powerfull labourer in the Lord's vineyard. I
do no more than yuse the words of my good lady, who has
got the infectual calling; and, I trust, that even myself,
though unworthy, shall find grease to be excepted.——
Miss Liddy has been touch'd to the quick, but is a little

timorsome: howsomever, I make no doubt, but she, and all of us, will be brought, by the endeavours of Mr. Clinker, to produce blessed fruit of generation and repentance.———As for master and the young squire, they have as yet had narro glimpse of the new light.———I doubt as how their harts are hardened by worldly wisdom, which, as the pyebill saith, is foolishness in the sight of God.

O Mary Jones, pray without seizing for grease to prepare you for the operations of this wonderful instrument, which, I hope, will be exorcised this winter upon you and others at Brambleton-hall.———To-morrow, we are to set out in a cox and four for Yorkshire; and, I believe, we shall travel that way far, and far, and farther than I can tell; but I shan't go so far as to forget my friends; and Mary Jones will always be remembred as one of them by her

humble sarvant,

WIN. JENKINS.

LONDON, *June* 14.

To Mrs. Gwyllim, house-keeper at Brambleton-hall

MRS. GWYLLIM,

I can't help thinking it very strange, that I never had an answer to the letter I wrote you some weeks ago from Bath, concerning the sour bear, the gander, and the maids eating butter, which I won't allow to be waisted.———We are now going upon a long journey to the north, whereby I desire you will redouble your care and circumflexion, that the family may be well managed in our absence; for, you know, you must render account, not only to your earthly master, but also to him that is above; and if you are found a good and faithful sarvant, great will be your reward in haven. I hope there will be twenty stun of cheese ready for market by the time I get huom, and as much owl spun, as will make half a dozen pair of blankets; and that the savings of the butter-milk will fetch me a good penny before Martinmass, as the two pigs are to be fed for baking with bitchmast and acrons.

I wrote to doctor Lewis for the same porpuss, but he never had the good manners to take the least notice of my letter; for which reason, I shall never favour him with another, though he beshits me on his bended knees. You will do well to keep a watchful eye over the hind Villiams, who is one of his amissories, and, I believe, no better than he should be at bottom. God forbid that I should lack christian charity; but charity begins at huom, and sure nothing can be a more charitable work than to rid the family of such vermine. I do suppose, that the brindled cow has been had to the parson's bull, that old Moll has had another litter of pigs, and that Dick is become a mighty mouser. Pray order every thing for the best, and be frugal, and keep the maids to their labour.—If I had a private opportunity, I would send them some hymns to sing instead of profane ballads; but, as I can't, they and you must be contented with the prayers of

Your assured friend,

T. BRAMBLE.

LONDON, *June* 14.

To Sir Watkin Phillips, Bart. of Jesus college, Oxon.

DEAR PHILLIPS,

The very day after I wrote my last, Clinker was set at liberty—As Martin had foretold, the accuser was himself committed for a robbery, upon unquestionable evidence. He had been for some time in the snares of the thief-taking society; who, resenting his presumption in attempting to incroach upon their monopoly of impeachment, had him taken up and committed to Newgate, on the deposition of an accomplice, who has been admitted as evidence for the king. The postilion being upon record as an old offender, the chief justice made no scruple of admitting Clinker to bail, when he perused the affidavit of Mr. Mead, importing that the said Clinker was not the person that robbed him on Blackheath; and honest Humphry was discharged.—When he came home, he expressed great eagerness to pay his respects to his master, and here his elocution failed him, but his silence was pathetic; he fell down at his feet and embraced his knees, shedding a flood of tears, which my uncle did not see without emotion—He took snuff in some confusion; and, putting his hand in his pocket, gave him his blessing in something more substantial than words—'Clinker, (said he) I am so well convinced, both of your honesty and courage, that I am resolved to make you my life-guard-man on the highway.'

He was accordingly provided with a case of pistols, and a carbine to be flung a-cross his shoulders; and every other preparation being made, we set out last Thursday, at seven in the morning; my uncle, with the three women in the coach; Humphry, well mounted on a black gelding bought for his use; myself a-horseback, attended by my new valet, Mr. Dutton, an exceeding cox-comb, fresh from his travels, whom I have taken upon trial—The fellow wears a soli-taire, uses paint, and takes rappee with all the grimace of a French marquis. At present, however, he is in a riding-dress, jack-boots, leather breeches, a scarlet waistcoat, with gold binding, a laced hat, a hanger, a French posting-whip in his hand, and his hair *en queue*.

Before we had gone nine miles, my horse lost one of his shoes; so that I was obliged to stop at Barnet to have an-other, while the coach proceeded at an easy pace over the common. About a mile short of Hatfield, the postilions, stopping the carriage, gave notice to Clinker that there were two suspicious fellows a-horseback, at the end of a lane, who semed waiting to attack the coach. Humphry forthwith apprised my uncle, declaring he would stand by him to the

last drop of his blood; and unflinging his carbine, prepared
for action. The squire had pistols in the pockets of the coach,
and resolved to make use of them directly; but he was effectually prevented by his female companions, who flung themselves about his neck, and screamed in concert—At that
instant, who should come up at a hand-gallop, but Martin,
the highway-man, who, advancing to the coach, begged the
ladies would compose themselves for a moment; then, desiring Clinker to follow him to the charge, he pulled a pistol
out of his bosom, and they rode up together to give battle
to the rogues, who, having fired at a great distance, fled
a-cross the common. They were in pursuit of the fugitives
when I came up, not a little alarmed at the shrieks in the
coach, where I found my uncle in a violent rage, without
his periwig, struggling to disentangle himself from Tabby
and the other two, and swearing with great vociferation.
Before I had time to interpose, Martin and Clinker returned
from the pursuit, and the former payed his compliments with
great politeness, giving us to understand, that the fellows
had scampered off, and that he believed they were a couple
of raw 'prentices from London. He commended Clinker
for his courage, and said, if we would give him leave, he
would have the honour to accompany us as far as Stevenage,
where he had some business.

The squire, having recollected and adjusted himself, was
the first to laugh at his own situation: but it was not without
difficulty, that Tabby's arms could be untwisted from his
neck, Liddy's teeth chattered, and Jenkins was threatened
with a fit as usual. I had communicated to my uncle the
character of Martin, as it was described by the constable,
and he was much struck with its singularity—He could not
suppose the fellow had any design on our company, which
was so numerous and well armed; he therefore thanked him,
for the service he had just done them, said he would be glad
of his company, and asked him to dine with us at Hatfield.
This invitation might not have been agreeable to the ladies,

had they known the real profession of our guest, but this was a secret to all, except my uncle and myself—Mrs. Tabitha, however, would by no means consent to proceed with a case of loaded pistols in the coach, and they were forthwith discharged in complaisance to her and the rest of the women.

Being gratified in this particular, she became remarkably good-humoured, and at dinner behaved in the most affable manner to Mr. Martin, with whose polite address and agreeable conversation she seemed to be much taken. After dinner, the landlord accosting me in the yard, asked with a significant look, if the gentleman that rode the sorrel belonged to our company?—I understood his meaning, but answered *no;* that he had come up with us on the common, and helped us to drive away two fellows, that looked like highwaymen—He nodded three times distinctly, as much as to say, he knows his cue. Then he inquired, if one of those men was mounted on a bay mare, and the other on a chestnut gelding with a white streak down his forehead? and being answered in the affirmative, he assured me they had robbed three post-chaises this very morning—I inquired, in my turn, if Mr. Martin was of his acquaintance; and, nodding thrice again, he answered, that *he had seen the gentleman.*

Before we left Hatfield, my uncle, fixing his eyes on Martin with such expression as is more easily conceived than described, asked, if he often travelled that road? and he replied with a look which denoted his understanding the question, that he very seldom did business in that part of the country. In a word, this adventurer favoured us with his company to the neighbourhood of Stevenage, where he took his leave of the coach and me, in very polite terms, and turned off upon a cross-road, that led to a village on the left—At supper, Mrs. Tabby was very full in the praise of Mr. Martin's good-sense and good-breeding, and seemed to regret that she had not a further opportunity to make some experiment upon his affection. In the morning, my

uncle was not a little surprised to receive, from the waiter,
a billet couched in these words—

'SIR,
    'I could easily perceive from your looks, when I had
the honour to converse with you at Hatfield, that my character is not unknown to you; and, I dare say you won't think
it strange, that I should be glad to change my present way
of life, for any other honest occupation, let it be ever so
humble, that will afford me bread in moderation, and sleep
in safety—Perhaps you may think I flatter, when I say, that
from the moment I was witness to your generous concern
in the cause of your servant, I conceived a particular esteem
and veneration for your person; and yet what I say is true.
I should think myself happy, if I could be admitted into
your protection and service, as house-steward, clerk, butler,
or bailiff, for either of which places I think myself tolerably well qualified; and, sure I am, I should not be found
deficient in gratitude and fidelity—At the same time, I am
very sensible how much you must deviate from the common
maxims of discretion, even in putting my professions to the
trial; but I don't look upon you as a person that thinks in
the ordinary stile; and the delicacy of my situation, will,
I know, justify this address to a heart warmed with beneficence and compassion—Understanding you are going pretty
far north, I shall take an opportunity to throw myself in
your way again, before you reach the borders of Scotland;
and, I hope, by that time, you will have taken into consideration, the truly distressful case of,
                            'honoured sir,
                                ' your very humble,
                                    'and devoted servant,
                                        'EDWARD MARTIN.'

    The squire, having perused this letter, put it into my
hand, without saying a syllable; and when I had read it,

we looked at each other in silence. From a certain sparkling in his eyes, I discovered there was more in his heart, than he cared to express with his tongue, in favour of poor Martin; and this was precisely my own feeling, which he did not fail to discern, by the same means of communication—'What shall we do (said he) to save this poor sinner from the gallows, and make him a useful member of the commonwealth; and yet the proverb says, Save a thief from the gallows, and he'll cut your throat.' I told him I really believed Martin was capable of giving the proverb the lie; and that I should heartily concur in any step he might take in favour of his solicitation. We mutually resolved to deliberate upon the subject, and, in the mean time, proceeded on our journey. The roads, having been broken up by the heavy rains in the spring, were so rough, that although we travelled very slowly, the jolting occasioned such pain to my uncle, that he was become exceedingly peevish when we arrived at this place, which lies about eight miles from the post-road, between Wetherby and Boroughbridge.

Harrigate-water, so celebrated for its efficacy in the scurvy and other distempers, is supplied from a copious spring, in the hollow of a wild common, round which, a good many houses have been built for the convenience of the drinkers, though few of them are inhabited. Most of the company lodge at some distance, in five separate inns, situated in different parts of the commons, from whence they go every morning to the well, in their own carriages. The lodgers of each inn form a distinct society, that eat together; and there is a commodious public room, where they breakfast in disabille, at separate tables, from eight o'clock till eleven, as they chance or chuse to come in—Here also they drink tea in the afternoon, and play at cards or dance in the evening. One custom, however, prevails, which I look upon as a solecism in politeness—The ladies treat with tea in their turns; and even girls of sixteen are not exempted from this shameful imposition——There is a public ball by subscription every night at one of the houses, to which all the company from the others are admitted by tickets; and, indeed, Harrigate treads upon the heels of Bath, in the articles of gaiety and dissipation—with this difference, however, that here we are more sociable and familiar. One of the inns is already full up to the very garrets, having no less than fifty lodgers, and as many servants. Our family does not exceed thirty-six; and I should be sorry to see the number augmented, as our accommodations won't admit of much increase.

At present, the company is more agreeable than one could expect from an accidental assemblage of persons, who are utter strangers to one another—There seems to be a general disposition among us to maintain good-fellowship, and promote the purposes of humanity, in favour of those who come hither on the score of health. I see several faces which we left at Bath, although the majority are of the Northern counties, and many come from Scotland for the benefit of these waters—In such a variety, there must be some originals, among whom Mrs. Tabitha Bramble is not the most inconsiderable—No place where there is such an intercourse between the sexes, can be disagreeable to a lady of her views and temperament—She has had some warm disputes at table, with a lame parson from Northumberland, on the new birth, and the insignificance of moral virtue; and her arguments have been reinforced by an old Scotch lawyer, in a tye periwig, who, though he has lost his teeth, and the use of his limbs, can still wag his tongue with great volubility. He has paid her such fulsome compliments, upon her piety and learning, as seem to have won her heart; and she, in her turn, treats him with such attention as indicates a design upon his person, but, by all accounts, he is too much of a fox to be inveigled into any snare that she can lay for his affection.

We do not propose to stay long at Harrigate, though, at present, it is our headquarters, from whence we shall make some excursions, to visit two or three of our rich relations.

who are settled in this county.———Pray, remember me to all our friends of Jesus, and allow me to be still

Yours affectionately,

J. MELFORD.

HARRIGATE, *June* 23.

To Dr. Lewis

DEAR DOCTOR,

Considering the tax we pay for turnpikes, the roads of this country constitute a most intolerable grievance. Between Newark and Weatherby, I have suffered more from jolting and swinging than ever I felt in the whole course of my life, although the carriage is remarkably commodious and well hung, and the postilions were very careful in driving. I am now safely housed at the New Inn, at Harrigate, whither I came to satisfy my curiosity, rather than with any view of advantage to my health; and, truly, after having considered all the parts and particulars of the place, I cannot account for the concourse of people one finds here, upon any other principle but that of caprice, which seems to be the character of our nation.

Harrigate is a wild common, bare and bleak, without tree or shrub, or the least signs of cultivation; and the people who come to drink the water, are crowded together in paltry inns, where the few tolerable rooms are monopolized by the friends and favourites of the house, and all the rest of the lodgers are obliged to put up with dirty holes, where there is neither space, air, nor convenience. My apartment is about ten feet square; and when the folding bed is down, there is just room sufficient to pass between it and the fire. One might expect, indeed, that there would be no occasion for a fire at Midsummer; but here the climate is so backward, that an ash tree, which our landlord has planted before my window, is just beginning to put forth its leaves; and I am fain to have my bed warmed every night.

As for the water, which is said to have effected so many surprising cures, I have drank it once, and the first draught has cured me of all desire to repeat the medicine.—Some people say it smells of rotten eggs, and others compare it to the scourings of a foul gun.—It is generally supposed to be strongly impregnated with sulphur; and Dr. Shaw, in his book upon mineral water, says, he has seen flakes of sulphur floating in the well—*Pace tanti viri;* I, for my part, have never observed any thing like sulphur, either in or about the well, neither do I find that any brimstone has ever been extracted from the water. As for the smell, if I may be allowed to judge from my own organs, it is exactly that of bilge-water; and the saline taste of it seems to declare that it is nothing else than salt water putrified in the bowels of the earth. I was obliged to hold my nose with one hand, while I advanced the glass to my mouth with the other; and after I had made shift to swallow it, my stomach could hardly retain what it had received.—The only effects it produced were sickness, griping, and insurmountable disgust.—I can hardly mention it without puking.—The world is strangely misled by the affectation of singularity. I cannot help suspecting, that this water owes its reputation in a great measure to its being so strikingly offensive.—On the same kind of analogy, a German doctor has introduced hemlock and other poisons, as specifics, into the *materia medica.*—I am persuaded, that all the cures ascribed to the Harrigate water, would have been as efficaciously, and infinitely more agreeably performed, by the internal and external use of sea-water. Sure I am, this last is much less nauseous to the taste and smell, and much more gentle in its operation as a purge, as well as more extensive in its medical qualities.

Two days ago we went across the country to visit squire Burdock, who married a first cousin of my father, an heiress, who brought him an estate of a thousand a-year. This gentleman is a declared opponent of the ministry in parliament; and having an opulent fortune, piques himself upon

living in the country, and maintaining *old English hospitality*
—By the bye, this is a phrase very much used by the English
themselves both in words and writing; but I never heard
of it out of the island, except by way of irony and sarcasm.
What the hospitality of our fore-fathers has been I should
be glad to see recorded, rather in the memoirs of strangers
who have visited our country, and were the proper objects
and judges of such hospitality, than in the discourse and
lucubrations of the modern English, who seem to describe
it from theory and conjecture. Certain it is, we are generally looked upon by foreigners, as a people totally destitute
of this virtue; and I never was in any country abroad,
where I did not meet with persons of distinction, who complained of having been inhospitably used in Great Britain.
A gentleman of France, Italy, or Germany, who has
entertained and lodged an Englishman at his house, when he
afterwards meets with his guest at London, is asked to dinner
at the Saracen's-head, the Turk's-head, the Boar's-head,
or the Bear, eats raw beef and butter, drinks execrable port,
and is allowed to pay his share of the reckoning.

But to return from this digression, which my feeling for
the honour of my country obliged me to make——our
Yorkshire cousin has been a mighty fox-hunter *before the
Lord;* but now he is too fat and unwieldy to leap ditches
and five-bar gates; nevertheless, he still keeps a pack of
hounds, which are well exercised; and his huntsman every
night entertains him with the adventures of the day's chace,
which he recites in a tone and terms that are extremely curious and significant. In the mean time, his broad brawn is
scratched by one of his grooms.——This fellow, it seems,
having no inclination to curry any beast out of the stable,
was at great pains to scollop his nails in such a manner that
the blood followed at every stroke.—He was in hopes that he
would be dismissed from this disagreeable office, but the
event turned out contrary to his expectation.—His master
declared he was the best scratcher in the family; and now

he will not suffer any other servant to draw a nail upon his carcase.

The squire's lady is very proud, without being stiff or inaccessible.——She receives even her inferiors in point of fortune with a kind of arrogant civility; but then she thinks she has a right to treat them with the most ungracious freedoms of speech, and never fails to let them know she is sensible of her own superior affluence—In a word, she speaks well of no living soul, and has not one single friend in the world. Her husband hates her mortally; but, although the brute is sometimes so very powerful in him that he will have his own way, he generally truckles to her dominion, and dreads, like a school-boy, the lash of her tongue. On the other hand, she is afraid of provoking him too far, lest he should make some desperate effort to shake off her yoke.—— She, therefore, acquiesces in the proofs he daily gives of his attachment to the liberty of an English freeholder, by saying and doing, at his own table, whatever gratifies the brutality of his disposition, or contributes to the ease of his person. The house, though large, is neither elegant nor comfortable.—It looks like a great inn, crowded with travellers, who dine at the landlord's ordinary, where there is a great profusion of victuals and drink, but mine host seems to be misplaced; and I would rather dine upon filberts with a hermit, than feed up venison with a hog. The footmen might be aptly compared to the waiters of a tavern, if they were more serviceable and less rapacious; but they are generally insolent and inattentive, and so greedy, that, I think, I can dine better, and for less expence, at the Star and Garter in Pall mall, than at our cousin's castle in Yorkshire. The 'squire is not only accommodated with a wife, but he is also blessed with an only son, about two and twenty, just returned from Italy, a complete fidler and *dillettante;* and he slips no opportunity of manifesting the most perfect contempt for his own father.

When we arrived, there was a family of foreigners at

the house, on a visit to this virtuoso, with whom they had
been acquainted at the Spa; it was the count de Melville,
with his lady, on their way to Scotland. Mr. Burdock had
met with an accident, in consequence of which both the
count and I would have retired but the young gentleman and
his mother insisted upon our staying dinner; and their serenity seemed to be so little ruffled by what had happened,
that we complied with their invitation. The 'squire had been
brought home over night in his post-chaise, so terribly be-
laboured about the pate, that he seemed to be in a state of
stupefaction, and had ever since remained speechless. A country apothecary, called Grieve, who lived in a neighbouring
village, having been called to his assistance, had let him
blood, and applied a poultice to his head, declaring, that he
had no fever, nor any other bad symptom but the loss of
speech, if he really had lost that faculty. But the young
'squire said this practitioner was an *ignor antaccio*, that there
was a fracture in the *cranium*, and that there was a necessity
for having him trepanned without loss of time. His mother,
espousing this opinion, had sent an express to York for a
surgeon to perform the operation, and he was already come
with his 'prentice and instruments. Having examined the
patient's head, he began to prepare his dressings; though
Grieve still retained his first opinion that there was no fracture, and was the more confirmed in it as the 'squire had
passed the night in profound sleep, uninterrupted by any
catching or convulsion. The York surgeon said he could not
tell whether there was a fracture, until he should take off
the scalp; but, at any rate, the operation might be of service
in giving vent to any blood that might be extravasated, either
above or below the *dura mater*. The lady and her son were
clear for trying the experiment; and Grieve was dismissed
with some marks of contempt, which, perhaps, he owed to
the plainness of his appearance. He seemed to be about the
middle age, wore his own black hair without any sort of
dressing; by his garb, one would have taken him for a

quaker, but he had none of the stiffness of that sect, on the contrary he was very submissive, respectful, and remarkably taciturn.

Leaving the ladies in an apartment by themselves we adjourned to the patient's chamber where the dressings and instruments were displayed in order upon a pewter dish. The operator, laying aside his coat and periwig, equipped himself with a night-cap, apron, and sleeves, while his 'prentice and footman, seizing the 'squire's head, began to place it in a proper posture.——But mark what followed.—The patient, bolting upright in the bed, collared each of these assistants with the grasp of Hercules, exclaiming, in a bellowing tone, 'I ha'n't lived so long in Yorkshire to be trepanned by such vermin as you'; and leaping on the floor, put on his breeches quietly, to the astonishment of us all. The Surgeon still insisted upon the operation, alleging it was now plain that the brain was injured, and desiring the servants put him into bed again; but nobody would venture to execute his orders, or even to interpose: when the 'squire turned him and his assistants out of doors, and threw his apparatus out at the window. Having thus asserted his prerogative, and put on his cloaths with the help of a valet, the count, with my nephew and me, were introduced by his son, and received with his usual stile of rustic civility; then turning to signor Macaroni, with a sarcastic grin, 'I tell thee what, Dick, (said he) a man's scull is not to be bored every time his head is broken; and I'll convince thee and thy mother, that I know as many tricks as e'er an old fox in the West Riding.'

We afterwards understood he had quarrelled at a public house with an exciseman, whom he challenged to a bout at single stick, in which he had been worsted; and that the shame of this defeat had tied up his tongue. As for madam, she had shewn no concern for his disaster, and now heard of his recovery without emotion—She had taken some little notice of my sister and niece, though rather with a view to indulge her own petulance, than out of any sentiment of regard to our family.——She said Liddy was a fright, and ordered her woman to adjust her head before dinner; but she would not meddle with Tabby, whose spirit, she soon perceived, was not to be irritated with impunity. At table, she acknowledged me so far as to say she had heard of my father; though she hinted, that he had disobliged her family by making a poor match in Wales. She was disagreeably familiar in her enquiries about our circumstances; and asked, if I intended to bring up my nephew to the law. I told her, that, as he had an independent fortune, he should follow no profession but that of a country gentleman; and that I was not without hopes of procuring for him a seat in parliament——, 'Pray, cousin (said she) what may his fortune be?' When I answered, that, with what I should be able to give him, he would have better than two thousand a year, she replied, with a disdainful toss of her head, that it would be impossible for him to preserve his independence on such a paltry provision.

Not a little nettled at his arrogant remark, I told her, I had the honour to sit in parliament with her father, when he had little more than half that income; and I believed there was not a more independent and incorruptible member in the house. 'Ay; but times are changed (cried the 'squire) ——Country gentlemen now-a-days live after another fashion.——My table alone stands me in a cool thousand a quarter, though I raise my own stock, import my own liquors, and have every thing at the first hand.——True it is, I keep open house, and receive all comers, for the honour of Old England.' 'If that be the case, (said I) 'tis a wonder you can maintain it at so small an expence; but every private gentleman is not expected to keep a *caravansera* for the accommodation of travellers; indeed, if every individual lived in the same stile, you would not have such a number of guests at your table, of consequence your hospitality would not shine so bright for the glory of the West Riding.' The young 'squire, tickled by this ironical observation, exclaimed, '*O che burla!*'—his mother eyed me in silence with a supercilious air; and the father of the feast, taking a bumper of October, 'My service to you, cousin Bramble, (said he) I have always heard there was something keen and biting in the air of the Welch mountains.'

I was much pleased with the count de Melville, who is sensible, easy, and polite; and the countess is the most amiable woman I ever beheld. In the afternoon they took leave of their entertainers, and the young gentleman, mounting his horse, undertook to conduct their coach through the park, while one of their servants rode round to give notice to the rest, whom they had left at a public house on the road. The moment their backs were turned, the censorious dæmon took possession of our Yorkshire landlady and our sister Tabitha——The former observed, that the countess was a good sort of a body, but totally ignorant of good breeding, consequently aukward in her address. The squire said, he did not pretend to the breeding of any thing but colts; but that the jade would be very handsome, if she was a little more in flesh. 'Handsome! (cried Tabby) she has indeed a pair of black eyes without any meaning; but then there is not a good feature in her face.' 'I know not what you call good features in Wales (replied our landlord); but they'll pass in Yorkshire.' Then turning to Liddy, he added, 'What say you, my pretty Redstreak?—what is your opinion of the countess?' 'I think, (cried Liddy, with great emotion) she's an angel.' Tabby chid her for talking with such freedom in company; and the lady of the house said, in a contemptuous tone, she supposed miss had been brought up at some country boarding-school.

Our conversation was suddenly interrupted by the young gentleman, who galloped into the yard all aghast, exclaiming, that the coach was attacked by a great number of highwaymen. My nephew and I rushed out, found his own and his servant's horse ready saddled in the stable, with pistols in the caps——We mounted instantly, ordering Clinker and

Dutton to follow with all possible expedition; but notwithstanding all the speed we could make, the action was over
before we arrived, and the count with his lady, safe lodged
at the house of Grieve, who had signalized himself in a
very remarkable manner on this occasion. At the turning of
a lane, that led to the village where the count's servants remained, a couple of robbers a-horseback suddenly appeared,
with their pistols advanced: one kept the coachman in awe,
and the other demanded the count's money, while the young
squire went off at full speed, without ever casting a look
behind. The count desiring the thief to withdraw his pistol,
as the lady was in great terror, delivered his purse without
making the least resistance; but not satisfied with this booty,
which was pretty considerable, the rascal insisted upon rifling
her of her ear-rings and necklace, and the countess screamed
with affright. Her husband, exasperated at the violence with
which she was threatened, wrested the pistol out of the
fellow's hand, and turning it upon him, snapped it in his
face; but the robber knowing there was no charge in it,
drew another from his bosom, and in all probability would
have killed him on the spot, had not his life been saved by
a wonderful interposition. Grieve, the apothecary, chancing
to pass that very instant, ran up to the coach, and with a
crab-stick, which was all the weapon he had, brought the
fellow to the ground with the first blow; then seizing his
pistol, presented it to his colleague, who fired his piece at
random, and fled without further opposition. The other was
secured by the assistance of the count and the coachman;
and his legs being tied under the belly of his own horse,
Grieve conducted him to the village, whither also the carriage proceeded. It was with great difficulty the countess
could be kept from swooning; but at last she was happily
conveyed to the house of the apothecary, who went into the
shop to prepare some drops for her, while his wife and
daughter administered to her in another apartment.

I found the count standing in the kitchen with the parson

of the parish, and expressing much impatience to see his protector, whom as yet he had scarce found time to thank for the essential service he had done him and the countess.—— The daughter passing at the same time with a glass of water, monsieur de Melville could not help taking notice of her figure, which was strikingly engaging.—'Ay, (said the parson) she is the prettiest girl, and the best girl in all my parish: and if I could give my son an estate of ten thousand a year, he should have my consent to lay it at her feet. If Mr. Grieve had been as solicitous about getting money, as he has been in performing all the duties of a primitive Christian, Fy would not have hung so long upon his hands.' 'What is her name?' said I. 'Sixteen years ago (answered the vicar) I christened her by the names of Seraphina Melvilia.' 'Ha? what! how! (cried the count eagerly) sure, you said Seraphina Melvilia.' 'I did (said he); Mr. Grieve told me those were the names of two noble persons abroad, to whom he had been obliged for more than life.'

The count, without speaking another syllable, rushed into the parlour, crying, 'This is your god-daughter, my dear.' Mrs. Grieve, then seizing the countess by the hand, exclaimed with great agitation, 'O madam!—O sir!—I am— I am your poor Elinor.——This is my Seraphina Melvilia ——O child! these are the count and countess of Melville, the generous—the glorious benefactors of thy once unhappy parents.'

The countess rising from her seat threw her arms about the neck of the amiable Seraphina, and clasped her to her breast with great tenderness, while she herself was embraced by the weeping mother. This moving scene was completed by the entrance of Grieve himself, who falling on his knees before the count, 'Behold (said he) a penitent, who at length can look upon his patron without shrinking.' 'Ah, Ferdinand! (cried he, raising and folding him in his arms) the playfellow of my infancy—the companion of my youth!

——Is it to you then I am indebted for my life?' 'Heaven has heard my prayer, (said the other) and given me an opportunity to prove myself not altogether unworthy of your clemency and protection.' He then kissed the hand of the countess, while monsieur de Melville saluted his wife and lovely daughter, and all of us were greatly affected by this pathetic recognition.

In a word, Grieve was no other than Ferdinand count Fathom, whose adventures were printed many years ago. Being a sincere convert to virtue; he had changed his name, that he might elude the enquiries of the count, whose generous allowance he determined to forego, that he might have no dependence but upon his own industry and moderation. He had accordingly settled in this village as a practitioner in surgery and physic, and for some years wrestled with all the miseries of indigence, which, however, he and his wife had borne with the most exemplary resignation. At length, by dint of unwearied attention to the duties of his profession, which he exercised with equal humanity and success, he had acquired a tolerable share of business among the farmers and common people, which enabled him to live in a decent manner. He had been scarce ever seen to smile; was unaffectedly pious; and all the time he could spare from the avocations of his employment, he spent in educating his daughter, and in studying for his own improvement.—In short, the adventurer Fathom was, under the name of Grieve, universally respected among the commonalty of this district, as a prodigy of learning and virtue. These particulars I learned from the vicar, when we quitted the room, that they might be under no restraint in their mutual effusions. I make no doubt that Grieve will be pressed to leave off business, and re-unite himself to the count's family; and as the countess seemed extremely fond of his daughter, she will, in all probability, insist upon Seraphina's accompanying her to Scotland.

Having paid our compliments to these noble persons, we

returned to the 'squire's, where we expected an invitation to pass the night, which was wet and raw; but it seems, 'squire Burdock's hospitality reached not so far for the honour of Yorkshire; we therefore departed in the evening, and lay at an inn, where I caught cold.

In hope of riding it down before it could take fast hold on my constitution, I resolved to visit another relation, one Mr. Pimpernel, who lived about a dozen miles from the place where we lodged. Pimpernel being the youngest of four sons, was bred an attorney at Furnival's inn; but all his elder brothers dying, he got himself called to the bar for the honour of his family, and soon after this preferment, succeeded to his father's estate which was very considerable. He carried home with him all the knavish chicanery of the lowest pettifogger, together with a wife whom he had purchased of a drayman for twenty pounds; and he soon found means to obtain a *dedimus* as an acting justice of peace. He is not only a sordid miser in his disposition, but his avarice is mingled with a spirit of despotism, which is truly diabolical.——He is a brutal husband, an unnatural parent, a harsh master, an oppressive landlord, a litigious neighbour, and a partial magistrate——Friends he has none; and in point of hospitality and good breeding, our cousin Burdock is a prince in comparison of this ungracious miscreant, whose house is the lively representation of a gaol. Our reception was suitable to the character I have sketched. Had it depended upon the wife, we should have been kindly treated.——She is really a good sort of a woman, in spite of her low original, and well respected in the country; but she has not interest enough in her own house to command a draught of table beer, far less to bestow any kind of education on her children, who run about, like ragged colts, in a state of nature.——Pox on him! he is such a dirty fellow, that I have not patience to prosecute the subject.

By that time we reached Harrigate, I began to be visited by certain rheumatic symptoms. The Scotch lawyer, Mr.

Micklewhimmen, recommended a hot bath of these waters
so earnestly, that I was overpersuaded to try the experiment.
—He had used it often with success and always stayed an
hour in the bath, which was a tub filled with Harrigate
water, heated for the purpose. If I could hardly bear the
smell of a single tumbler when cold, you may guess how
my nose was regaled by the streams arising from a hot bath
of the same fluid. At night, I was conducted into a dark
hole on the ground floor, where the tub smoaked and stunk
like the pot of Acheron, in one corner, and in another stood
a dirty bed provided with thick blankets, in which I was to
sweat after coming out of the bath. My heart seemed to
die within me when I entered this dismal bagnio, and found
my brain assaulted by such insufferable effluvia. I cursed
Micklewhimmen for not considering that my organs were
formed on this side of the Tweed; but being ashamed to
recoil upon the threshold, I submitted to the process.

After having endured all but real suffocation for above
a quarter of an hour in the tub, I was moved to the bed
and wrapped in blankets.—There I lay a full hour panting
with intolerable heat; but not the least moisture appearing
on my skin, I was carried to my own chamber, and passed
the night without closing an eye, in such a flutter of spirits
as rendered me the most miserable wretch in being. I should
certainly have run distracted, if the rarefaction of my blood,
occasioned by that Stygian bath, had not burst the vessels,
and produced a violent hæmorrhage, which, though dreadful
and alarming, removed the horrible disquiet.—I lost two
pounds of blood, and more, on this occasion; and find
myself still weak and languid; but, I believe, a little exercise will forward my recovery, and therefore I am resolved
to set out to-morrow for York, in my way to Scarborough,
where I propose to brace up my fibres by sea-bathing, which,
I know, is one of your favourite specificks. There is, however, one disease, for which you have found as yet no spe-
cific, and that is old age, of which this tedious unconnected

epistle is an infallible symptom: *what, therefore, cannot be cured, must be endured,* by you, as well as by

Yours,

MATT. BRAMBLE.

HARRIGATE, *June* 26.

To Sir Watkin Phillips, Bart. of Jesus college, Oxon.

DEAR KNIGHT,

The manner of living at Harrigate was so agreeable to my disposition, that I left the place with some regret—Our aunt Tabby would have probably made some objection to our departing so soon, had not an accident embroiled her with Mr. Micklewhimmen, the Scotch advocate, on whose heart she had been practising, from the second day after our arrival—That original, though seemingly precluded from the use of his limbs, had turned his genius to good account—In short, by dint of groaning, and whining, he had excited the compassion of the company so effectually, that an old lady, who occupied the very best apartment in the house, gave it up for his ease and convenience. When his man led him into the Long Room, all the females were immediately in commotion.—One set an elbow-chair; another shook up the cushion; a third brought a stool; and a fourth a pillow, for the accommodation of his feet—Two ladies (of whom Tabby was always one) supported him into the dining-room, and placed him properly at the table; and his taste was indulged with a succession of delicacies, culled by their fair hands. All this attention he repaid with a profusion of compliments and benedictions, which were not the less agreeable for being delivered in the Scottish dialect. As for Mrs. Tabitha, his respects were particularly addressed to her, and he did not fail to mingle them with religious reflections, touching free grace, knowing her bias to methodism, which he also professed upon a calvinistical model.

For my part, I could not help thinking this lawyer was not such an invalid as he pretended to be. I observed he ate very heartily three times a day; and though his bottle was marked *stomachic tincture,* he had recourse to it so often, and seemed to swallow it with such peculiar relish, that I suspected it was not compounded in the apothecary's shop, or the chemist's laboratory. One day, while he was earnest in discourse with Mrs. Tabitha, and his servant had gone out on some occasion or other, I dexterously exchanged the labels, and situation of his bottle and mine; and having tasted his tincture, found it was excellent claret. I forthwith handed it about me to some of my neighbours, and it was quite emptied before Mr. Micklewhimmen had occasion to repeat his draught. At length, turning about, he took hold of my bottle, instead of his own, and, filling a large glass, drank to the health of Mrs. Tabitha—It had scarce touched his lips, when he perceived the change which had been put upon him, and was at first a little out of countenance—He seemed to retire within himself, in order to deliberate, and in half a minute his resolution was taken; addressing himself to our quarter, 'I give the gentleman credit for his wit (said he); it was a gude practical joke; but sometimes *hi joci in seria ducunt mala*—I hope for his own sake he has na drank all the liccor; for it was a vara poorful infusion of jallap in Bourdeaux wine; at its possable he may ha ta'en sic a dose as will produce a terrible catastrophe in his ain booels—'

By far the greater part of the contents had fallen to the share of a young clothier from Leeds, who had come to make a figure at Harrigate, and was, in effect a great coxcomb in his way. It was with a view to laugh at his fellow-guests, as well as to mortify the lawyer, that he had emptied the bottle, when it came to his turn, and he had laughed accordingly: but now his mirth gave way to his apprehension—He began to spit, to make wry faces, and writhe himself into various contorsions—'Damn the stuff! (cried he) I thought it had a villainous twang—pah! He that would cozen a Scot, mun get oope betimes, and take Old Scratch for his counsellor—' 'In troth, mester what d'ye ca'um, (replied the lawyer) your wit has run you into a filthy puddle—I'm truly consarned for your waeful case— The best advice I can give you, in sic a delemma, is to send an express to Rippon for doctor Waugh, without delay, and, in the mean time, swallow all the oil and butter you can find in the hoose, to defend your poor stomach and intastines from the villication of the particles of the jallap, which is vara violent, even when taken in moderation.'

The poor clothier's torments had already begun: he retired, roaring with pain, to his own chamber; the oil was swallowed, and the doctor sent for; but before he arrived, the miserable patient had made such discharges upwards and downwards, that nothing remained to give him further offence; and this double evacuation, was produced by imagination alone; for what he had drank was genuine wine of Bourdeaux, which the lawyer had brought from Scotland for his own private use. The clothier, finding the joke turn out so expensive and disagreeable, quitted the house next morning, leaving the triumph to Micklewhimmen, who enjoyed it internally without any outward signs of exultation —on the contrary, he affected to pity the young man for what he had suffered; and acquired fresh credit from this shew of moderation.

It was about the middle of the night, which succeeded this adventure, that the vent of the kitchen chimney being foul, the soot took fire, and the alarm was given in a dreadful manner—Every body leaped naked out of bed, and in a minute the whole house was filled with cries and confusion —There was two stairs in the house, and to these we naturally ran; but they were both so blocked up, by the people pressing one upon another, that it seemed impossible

to pass, without throwing down and trampling upon the
women. In the midst of this anarchy, Mr. Micklewhimmen,
with a leathern portmanteau on his back, came running as
nimble as a buck along the passage; and Tabby in her under-
petticoat, endeavouring to hook him under the arm, that
she might escape through his protection, he very fairly
pushed her down, crying, 'Na, na, gude faith, charity begins
at hame!' Without paying the least respect to the shrieks
and intreaties of his female friends, he charged through the
midst of the crowd, overturning every thing that opposed
him; and actually fought his way to the bottom of the
stair-case—By this time Clinker had found a ladder, by
which he entered the window of my uncle's chamber, where
our family was assembled, and proposed that we should
make our exit successively by that conveyance. The 'squire
exhorted his sister to begin the descent; but, before she
could resolve, her woman, Mrs. Winifred Jenkins, in a
transport of terror, threw herself out at the window upon
the ladder, while Humphry dropped upon the ground, that
he might receive her in her descent———This maiden
was just as she had started out of bed, the moon shone very
bright, and a fresh breeze of wind blowing, none of Mrs.
Winifred's beauties could possibly escape the view of the
fortunate Clinker, whose heart was not able to withstand
the united force of so many charms; at least I am much
mistaken, if he has not been her humble slave from that
moment—He received her in his arms, and, giving her his
coat to protect her from the weather, ascended again with
admirable dexterity.

At that instant, the landlord of the house called out with
an audible voice, that the fire was extinguished, and the
ladies had nothing further to fear: this was a welcome note
to the audience, and produced an immediate effect; the
shrieking ceased, and a confused sound of expostulation
ensued. I conducted Mrs. Tabitha and my sister to their
own chamber, where Liddy fainted away; but was soon

brought to herself. Then I went to offer my services to the
other ladies, who might want assistance—They were all
scudding through the passage to their several apartments;
and as the thoroughfair was lighted by two lamps, I had
a pretty good observation of them in their transit; but as
most of them were naked to the smock, and all their heads
shrowded in huge night-caps, I could not distinguish one
face from another, though I recognized some of their
voices—These were generally plaintive; some wept, some
scolded, and some prayed—I lifted up one poor old gentlewoman, who had been overturned and sore bruised by a
multitude of feet; and this was also the case with the lame
person from Northumberland, whom Micklewhimmen had
in his passage overthrown, though not with impunity, for
the cripple, in falling, gave him such a good pelt on the
head with his crutch, that the blood followed.

As for this lawyer, he waited below till the hurly burly
was over, and then stole softly to his own chamber, from
whence he did not venture to make a second sally till eleven
in the forenoon, when he was led into the Public Room by
his own servant and another assistant, groaning most woefully, with a bloody napkin round his head. But things were
greatly altered—The selfish brutality of his behaviour on
the stairs had steeled their hearts against all his arts and
address——Not a soul offered to accommodate him with
a chair, cushion, or footstool; so that he was obliged to sit
down on a hard wooden bench—In that position, he looked
around with a rueful aspect, and, bowing very low, said in
a whining tone, 'Your most humble servant, ladies—Fire
is a dreadful calamity—' 'Fire purifies gold, and it tries
friendship,' cried Mrs. Tabitha, bridling. 'Yea, madam (replied Micklewhimmen); and it trieth discretion also—' 'If
discretion consists in forsaking a friend in adversity, you are
eminently possessed of that virtue' (resumed our aunt).——
'Na, madam, (rejoined the advocate) well I wot, I cannot
claim any merit from the mode of my retreat—Ye'll please

to observe, ladies, there are twa independent principles that actuate our nature—One is instinct, which we have in common with the brute creation, and the other is reason—Noo, in certain great emergencies, when the faculty of reason is suspended, instinct taks the lead, and when this predominates, having no affinity with reason, it pays no sort of regard to its connections; it only operates for the preservation of the individual, and that by the most expeditious and effectual means; therefore, begging your pardon, ladies, I'm no accountable in *foro conscientiœ*, for what I did, while under the influence of this irresistible pooer.'

Here my uncle interposing, 'I should be glad to know, (said he) whether it was instinct that prompted you to retreat with bag and baggage; for, I think, you had a portmanteau on your shoulder—' The lawyer answered, without hesitation, 'Gif I might tell my mind freely, withoot incuring the suspicion of presumption, I should think it was something superior to either reason or instinct which suggested that measure, and this on a twafald accoont: in the first place, the portmanteau contained the writings of a worthy nobleman's estate; and their being burnt would have occasioned a loss that could not be repaired; secondly, my good angel seems to have laid the portmanteau on my shoulders, by way of defence, to sustain the violence of a most inhuman blow, from the crutch of a reverend clergyman, which, even in spite of that medium, hath wounded me sorely, even unto the pericranium.' 'By your own doctrine, (cried the parson, who chanced to be present) I am not accountable for the blow, which was the effect of instinct.' 'I crave your pardon, reverend sir, (said the other) instinct never acts but for the preservation of the individual; but your preservation was out of the case——you had already received the damage, and therefore the blow must be imputed to revenge, which is a sinful passion, that ill becomes any Christian, especially a protestant divine; and let me tell you, most reverend doctor, gin I had a mind to plea, the law would hauld my libel relevant.' 'Why, the damage is pretty equal on both sides (cried the parson); your head is broke, and my crutch is snapt in the middle—Now, if you will repair the one, I will be at the expence of curing the other.'

This sally raised the laugh against Micklewhimmen, who began to look grave; when my uncle, in order to change the discourse, observed, that instinct had been very kind to him in another respect; for it had restored to him the use of his limbs, which, in his exit, he had moved with surprising agility.——He replied, that it was the nature of fear to brace up the nerves; and mentioned some surprising feats of strength and activity performed by persons under the impulse of terror; but he complained, that in his own particular, the effects had ceased when the cause was taken away—The 'squire said, he would lay a tea-drinking on his head, that he should dance a Scotch measure, without making a false step; and the advocate grinning, called for the piper —A fidler being at hand, this original started up, with his bloody napkin over his black tye-periwig, and acquitted himself in such a manner as excited the mirth of the whole company; but he could not regain the good graces of Mrs. Tabby, who did not understand the principle of instinct; and the lawyer did not think it worth his while to proceed to further demonstration.

From Harrigate, we came hither, by the way of York, and here we shall tarry some days, as my uncle and Tabitha are both resolved to make use of the waters. Scarborough, though a paltry town, is romantic from its situation along a cliff that overhangs the sea. The harbour is formed by a small elbow of land that runs out as a natural mole, directly opposite to the town; and on that side is the castle, which stands very high, of considerable extent, and, before the invention of gun-powder, was counted impregnable. At the other end of Scarborough are two public rooms for the use of the company, who resort to this place in the summer, to drink the waters and bathe in the sea; and the diversions are pretty much on the same footing here as at Bath. The Spa is a little way beyond the town, on this side, under a cliff, within a few paces of the sea, and thither the drinkers go every morning in dishabille; but the descent is by a great number of steps, which invalids find very inconvenient. Betwixt the well and the harbour, the bathing machines are ranged along the beach, with all their proper utensils and attendants——You have never seen one of these machines —Image to yourself a small, snug, wooden chamber, fixed upon a wheel-carriage, having a door at each end, and on each side a little window above, a bench below—The bather, ascending into this apartment by wooden steps, shuts himself in, and begins to undress, while the attendant yokes a horse to the end next the sea, and draws the carriage forwards, till the surface of the water is on a level with the floor of the dressing-room, then he moves and fixes the horse to the other end——The person within being stripped, opens the door to the sea-ward, where he finds the guide ready, and plunges headlong into the water——After having bathed, he re-ascends into the apartment, by the steps which had been shifted for that purpose, and puts on his clothes at his leisure, while the carriage is drawn back again upon the dry land; so that he has nothing further to do, but to open the door, and come down as he went up—Should he be so weak or ill as to require a servant to put off and on his clothes, there is room enough in the apartment for half a dozen people. The guides who attend the ladies in the water, are of their own sex, and they and the female bathers have a dress of flannel for the sea; nay, they are provided with other conveniences for the support of decorum. A certain number of the machines are fitted with tilts, that project from the sea-ward ends of them, so as to screen the bathers from the view of all persons whatsoever—The beach is admirably adapted for this practice, the descent being gently gradual, and the sand soft as velvet; but then the machines can be used only at a certain time of the tide, which varies every day; so that sometimes the bathers are obliged to rise very early in the morning——For my part, I love swim-ming as an exercise, and can enjoy it at all times of the tide, without the formality of an apparatus—You and I have often plunged together into the Isis; but the sea is a much more noble bath, for health as well as pleasure. You cannot conceive what a flow of spirits it gives, and how it braces every sinew of the human frame. Were I to enu-merate half the diseases which are every day cured by sea-bathing, you might justly say you had received a treatise, instead of a letter, from

your affectionate friend
and servant,
J. MELFORD.

To Dr. Lewis

I have not found all the benefit I expected at Scarbor-ough, where I have been these eight days—From Harrigate we came hither by the way of York, where we stayed only one day to visit the Castle, the Minster and the Assembly-room. The first, which was heretofore a fortress, is now converted to a prison, and is the best, in all respects, I ever saw, at home or abroad—It stands in a high situation, ex-tremely well ventilated; and has a spacious area within the walls, for the health and convenience of all the prison-ers, except those whom it is necessary to secure in close confinement——Even these last have all the comforts that the nature of their situation can admit. Here the assizes are held, in a range of buildings erected for that purpose.

As for the Minster, I know not how to distinguish it, except by its great size and the height of its spire, from those other antient churches in different parts of the kingdom, which used to be called monuments of Gothic architecture; but it is now agreed, that this stile is Saracen rather than

Gothic; and, I suppose, it was first imported into England from Spain, great part of which was under the dominion of the Moors. Those British architects who adopted this stile, don't seem to have considered the propriety of their adoption. The climate of the country, possessed by the Moors or Saracens, both in Africa and Spain, was so exceedingly hot and dry, that those who built places of worship for the multitude, employed their talents in contriving edifices that should be cool; and, for this purpose, nothing could be better adopted than those buildings; vast, narrow, dark, and lofty, impervious to the sun-beams, and having little communication with the scorched external atmosphere; but ever affording a refreshing coolness, like subterranean cellars in the heats of summer, or natural caverns in the bowels of huge mountains. But nothing could be more preposterous, than to imitate such a mode of architecture in a country like England, where the climate is cold, and the air eternally loaded with vapours; and where, of consequence, the builder's intention should be to keep the people dry and warm—For my part, I never entered the Abbey church at Bath but once, and the moment I stept over the threshold, I found myself chilled to the very marrow of my bones—When we consider, that in our churches, in general, we breathe a gross stagnated air, surcharged with damps from vaults, tombs, and charnel-houses, may we not term them so many magazines of rheums, created for the benefit of the medical faculty? and safely aver, that more bodies are lost, than souls saved, by going to church, in the winter especially, which may be said to engross eight months in the year. I should be glad to know, what offence it would give to tender consciences, if the house of God was made more comfortable, or less dangerous to the health of valetudinarians; and whether it would not be an encouragement to piety, as well as the salvation of many lives, if the place of worship was well floored, wainscotted, warmed, and ventilated, and its area kept sacred from the pollution of the dead. The practice of burying in churches was the effect of ignorant superstition, influenced by knavish priests, who pretended that the devil could have no power over the defunct if he was interred in holy ground; and this, indeed, is the only reason that can be given for consecrating all cemeteries, even at this day.

The external appearance of an old cathedral cannot be but displeasing to the eye of every man, who has any idea of propriety or proportion, even though he may be ignorant of architecture as a science; and the long slender spire puts one in mind of a criminal impaled, with a sharp stake rising up through his shoulder—These towers, or steeples, were likewise borrowed from the Mahometans; who, having no bells, used such minarets for the purpose of calling the people to prayers—They may be of further use, however, for making observations and signals; but I would vote for their being distinct from the body of the church, because they serve only to make the pile more barbarous, or Saracencial.

There is nothing of this Arabic architecture in the Assembly Room, which seems to me to have been built upon a design of Palladio, and might be converted into an elegant place of worship; but it is indifferently contrived for that sort of idolatry, which is performed in it at present: the grandeur of the fane gives a diminutive effect to the little painted divinities that are adorned in it, and the company, on a ball-night, must look like an assembly of fantastic fairies, revelling by moon-light among the cloumns of a Grecian temple.

Scarborough seems to be falling off, in point of reputation——All these places (Bath excepted) have their vogue, and then the fashion changes—I am persuaded, there are fifty spaws in England as efficacious and salutary as that of Scarborough, though they have not yet risen to fame; and, perhaps, never will, unless some medical encomiast should find an interest in displaying their virtues to the public view

——Be that as it may, recourse will always be had to this place for the convenience of sea bathing, while this practice prevails; but it were to be wished, they would make the beach more accessible to invalids.

I have here met with my old acquaintance, H——t, whom you have often heard me mention as one of the most original characters upon earth——I first knew him at Venice, and afterwards saw him in different parts of Italy, where he was well known by the nick-name of Cavallo Bianco, from his appearing always mounted on a pale horse, like Death in the Revelations. You must remember the account I once gave you of a curious dispute he had at Constantinople, with a couple of Turks, in defence of the Christian religion; a dispute from which he acquired the epithet of Demonstrator—The truth is, H—— owns no religion but that of nature; but, on this occasion, he was stimulated to shew his parts, for the honour of his country—Some years ago, being in the Campidoglio at Rome, he made up to the bust of Jupiter, and, bowing very low, exclaimed in the Italian language, 'I hope, sir, if ever you get your head above water again, you will remember that I paid my respects to you in your adversity.' This sally was reported to the cardinal Camerlengo, and by him laid before pope Benedict XIV, who could not help laughing at the extravagance of the address, and said to the cardinal, 'Those English heretics think they have a right to go to the devil in their own way.'

Indeed H—— was the only Englishman I ever knew, who had resolution enough to live in his own way, in the midst of foreigners; for, neither in dress, diet, customs, or conversation, did he deviate one tittle from the manner in which he had been brought up. About twelve years ago, he began a Giro or circuit, which he thus performed—At Naples, where he fixed his head-quarters, he embarked for Marseilles, from whence he travelled with a Voiturin to

Antibes—There he took his passage to Genoa and Lerici; from which last place he proceeded, by the way of Cambratina, to Pisa and Florence—After having halted some time in this metropolis, he set out with a Vetturino for Rome, where he reposed himself a few weeks, and then continued his route for Naples, in order to wait for the next opportunity of embarkation—After having twelve times described this circle, he lately flew off at a tangent to visit some trees at his country-house in England, which he had planted above twenty years ago, after the plan of the double colonnade in the piazza of St. Peter's at Rome——He came hither to Scarborough, to pay his respects to his noble friend and former pupil, the M— of G——, and, forgetting that he is now turned of seventy, sacrificed so liberally to Bacchus, that next day he was seized with a fit of the apoplexy, which has a little impaired his memory; but he retains all the oddity of his character in perfection, and is going back to Italy, by the way of Geneva, that he may have a conference with his friend Voltaire, about giving the last blow to the Christian superstition—He intends to take shipping here for Holland or Hamburgh; for it is a matter of great indifference to him at what part of the continent he first lands.

When he was going abroad the last time, he took his passage in a ship bound for Leghorn, and his baggage was actually embarked. In going down the river by water, he was by mistake put on board of another vessel under sail; and, upon inquiry understood she was bound to Petersburgh——'Petersburgh,—Petersburgh—(said he) I don't care if I go along with you.' He forthwith struck a bargain with the captain; bought a couple of shirts of the mate, and was safe conveyed to the court of Muscovy, from whence he travelled by land to receive his baggage at Leghorn.——He is now more likely than ever to execute a whim of the same nature; and I will hold any wager, that as he cannot be supposed to live much longer, according to the course of nature, his exit will be as odd as his life has been extravagant.[1]

But, to return from one humourist to another, you must know I have received benefit, both from the chalybeate and the sea, and would have used them longer, had not a most ridiculous adventure, by making me the town-talk, obliged me to leave the place; for I can't bear the thoughts of affording a spectacle to the multitude——Yesterday morning, at six o'clock, I went down to the bathing-place, attended by my servant Clinker, who waited on the beach as usual—The wind blowing from the north, and the weather being hazy, the water proved so chill, that when I rose from my first plunge, I could not help sobbing and bawling out, from the effects of the cold. Clinker, who heard me cry, and saw me indistinctly a good way without the guide, buffetting the waves, took it for granted I was drowning, and rushing into the sea, clothes and all, overturned the guide in his hurry to save his master. I had swam out a few strokes, when hearing a noise, I turned about and saw Clinker, already up to his neck, advancing towards me, with all the wildness of terror in his aspect—Afraid he would get out of his depth, I made haste to meet him, when, all of a sudden, he seized me by one ear, dragged me bellowing with pain upon the dry beach, to the astonishment of all the people, men, and women, and children there assembled.

[1] This gentleman crossed the sea to France, visited and conferred with Mr. de Voltaire at Fernay, resumed his old circuit at Genoa, and died in 1767, at the house of Vanini in Florence. Being taken with a suppression of urine, he resolved, in imitation of Pomponius Atticus, to take himself off by abstinence; and this resolution he executed like an ancient Roman. He saw company to the last, cracked his jokes, conversed freely, and entertained his guests with music. On the third day of his fast, he found himself entirely freed of his complaint; but refused taking sustenance. He said the most disagreeable part of the voyage was past, and he should be a cursed fool indeed, to put about ship, when he was just entering the harbour. In these sentiments he persisted, without any marks of affectation, and thus finished his course with such ease and serenity, as would have done honour to the firmest Stoic of antiquity.

I was so exasperated by the pain of my ear, and the disgrace of being exposed in such an attitude, that, in the first transport I struck him down; then, running back into the sea, took shelter in the machine where my clothes had been deposited. I soon recollected myself so far as to do justice to the poor fellow, who, in great simplicity of heart, had acted from motives of fidelity and affection——Opening the door of the machine, which was immediately drawn on shore, I saw him standing by the wheel, dropping like a waterwork, and trembling from head to foot; partly from cold, and partly from the dread of having offended his master——I made my acknowledgments for the blow he had received, assured him I was not angry, and insisted upon his going home immediately, to shift his clothes; a command which he could hardly find in his heart to execute, so well disposed was he to furnish the mob with further entertainment at my expence. Clinker's intention was laudable without all doubt, but, nevertheless, I am a sufferer by his simplicity——I have had a burning heat, and a strange buzzing noise in that ear, ever since it was so roughly treated; and I cannot walk the street without being pointed at, as the monster that was hauled naked a-shore upon the beach—— Well, I affirm that folly is often more provoking than knavery, aye and more mischievous too; and whether a man had not better choose a sensible rogue, than an honest simpleton for his servant, is no matter of doubt with

yours,
MATT. BRAMBLE.

SCARBOROUGH, *July* 4.

To Sir Watkin Phillips, Bart. of Jesus college, Oxon.

DEAR WAT,

We made a precipitate retreat from Scarborough, owing to the excessive delicacy of our 'squire, who cannot bear the thoughts of being *prætereuntium digito monstratus.*

One morning, while he was bathing in the sea, his man Clinker took it in his head that his master was in danger of drowning; and, in this conceit, plunging into the water, he lugged him out naked on the beach, and almost pulled off his ear in the operation. You may guess how this atchievement was relished by Mr. Bramble, who is impatient, irascible, and has the most extravagant ideas of decency and decorum in the œconomy of his own person—In the first ebullition of his choler, he knocked Clinker down with his fist; but he afterwards made him amends for his outrage, and, in order to avoid further notice of the people, among whom this incident had made him remarkable, he resolved to leave Scarborough next day.

We set out accordingly over the moors, by the way of Whitby, and began our journey betimes, in hopes of reaching Stockton that night; but in this hope we were disappointed—In the afternoon, crossing a deep gutter, made by a torrent, the coach was so hard strained, that one of the irons, which connect the frame, snapt, and the leather sling on the same side, cracked in the middle—The shock was so great, that my sister Liddy struck her head against Mrs. Tabitha's nose with such violence that the blood flowed; and Win Jenkins was darted through a small window, in that part of the carriage next the horses, where she stuck like a bawd in the pillory, till she was released by the hand of Mr. Bramble. We were eight miles distant from any place where we could be supplied with chaises, and it was impossible to proceed with the coach, until the damage should be repaired—In this dilemma, we discovered a blacksmith's forge on the edge of a small common, about half a mile from the scene of our disaster, and thither the postilions made shift to draw the carriage slowly, while the company walked a-foot; but we found the black-smith had been dead some days; and his wife, who had been lately delivered, was deprived of her senses, under the care of a nurse, hired by the parish. We were exceedingly mortified at this disappointment, which, however, was surmounted by the help of Humphry Clinker, who is a surprising compound of genius and simplicity. Finding the tools of the defunct, together with some coals in the smithy, he unscrewed the damaged iron in a twinkling, and, kindling a fire, united the broken pieces with equal dexterity and dispatch—While he was at work upon this operation, the poor woman in the straw, struck with the well-known sound of the hammer and anvil, started up, and, notwithstanding all the nurse's efforts, came running into the smithy, where, throwing her arms about Clinker's neck, 'Ah, Jacob! (cried she) how could you leave me in such a condition?'

This incident was too pathetic to occasion mirth——it brought tears into the eyes of all present. The poor widow was put to bed again; and we did not leave the village without doing something for her benefit—Even Tabitha's charity was awakened on this occasion. As for the tender-hearted Humphry Clinker, he hammered the iron and wept at the same time—But his ingenuity was not confined to his own province of farrier and blacksmith—It was necessary to join the leather sling, which had been broke; and this service he likewise performed, by means of a broken awl, which he new-pointed and ground, a little hemp, which he spun into lingels, and a few tacks which he made for the purpose— Upon the whole, we were in a condition to proceed in little more than an hour; but even this delay obliged us to pass the night at Gisborough—Next day we crossed the Tees at Stockton, which is a neat agreeable town; and there we resolved to dine, with purpose to lie at Durham.

Whom should we meet in the yard, when we alighted, but Martin the adventurer? Having handed out the ladies, and conducted them into an apartment, where he payed his compliments to Mrs. Tabby, with his usual address, he begged leave to speak to my uncle in another room; and there, in some confusion, he made an apology for having taken the liberty to trouble him with a letter at Stevenage. He expressed his hope, that Mr. Bramble had bestowed some consideration on his unhappy case, and repeated his desire of being taken into his service.

My uncle, calling me into the room, told him, that we were both very well inclined to rescue him from a way of life that was equally dangerous and dishonourable; and that he should have no scruples in trusting to his gratitude and fidelity, if he had any employment for him, which he thought would suit his qualifications and his circumstances; but that all the departments he had mentioned in his letter, were filled up by persons of whose conduct he had no reason to complain; of consequence he could not, without injustice, deprive any one of them of his bread—Nevertheless, he declared himself ready to assist him in any feasible project, either with his purse or credit.

Martin seemed deeply touched at this declaration—The tear started in his eye, while he said, in a faultering accent—'Worthy sir—your generosity oppresses me—I never dreamed of troubling you for any pecuniary assistance—indeed I have no occasion—I have been so lucky at billiards and betting in different places, at Buxton, Harrigate, Scarborough, and Newcastle races, that my stock in ready-money amounts to three hundred pounds, which I would willingly employ, in prosecuting some honest scheme of life; but my friend, justice Buzzard, has set so many springs for my life, that I am under the necessity of either retiring immediately to a remote part of the country, where I can enjoy the protection of some generous patron, or of quitting the kingdom altogether—It is upon this alternative that I now beg leave to ask your advice—I have had information of all your route, since I had the honour to see you at Stevenage; and, supposing you would come this way from Scarborough, I came hither last night from Darlington, to pay you my respects.'

'It would be no difficult matter to provide you with an

asylum in the country (replied my uncle); but a life of
indolence and obscurity would not suit with your active and
enterprizing disposition—I would therefore advise you to
try your fortune in the East Indies—I will give you a letter
to a friend in London, who will recommend you to the
direction, for a commission in the company's service; and if
that cannot be obtained, you will at least be received as a
volunteer—in which case, you may pay for your passage,
and I shall undertake to procure you such credentials, that
you will not be long without a commission.'

Martin embraced the proposal with great eagerness; it
was therefore resolved, that he should sell his horse, and
take a passage by sea for London, to execute the project
without delay—In the mean time he accompanied us to
Durham, where we took up our quarters for the night—
Here, being furnished with letters from my uncle, he took
his leave of us, with strong symptoms of gratitude and attachment, and set out for Sunderland, in order to embark
in the first collier, bound for the river Thames. He had not
been gone half an hour, when we were joined by another
character, which promised something extraordinary—A tall,
meagre figure, answering, with his horse, the description of
Don Quixote mounted on Rozinante, appeared in the twilight at the inn door, while my aunt and Liddy stood at a
window in the dining-room—He wore a coat, the cloth of
which had once been scarlet, trimmed with Brandenburgs,
now totally deprived of their metal, and he had holster-caps
and housing of the same stuff and same antiquity. Perceiving ladies at the window above, he endeavoured to dismount
with the most graceful air he could assume; but the ostler
neglecting to hold the stirrup when he wheeled off his right
foot, and stood with his whole weight on the other, the girth
unfortunately gave way, the saddle turned, down came the
cavalier to the ground, and his hat and perriwig falling off,
displayed a head-piece of various colours, patched and plais-
tered in a woeful condition—The ladies, at the window

above, shrieked with affright, on the supposition that the stranger had received some notable damages in his fall; but the greatest injury he had sustained arose from the dishonour of his descent, aggravated by the disgrace of exposing the condition of his cranium; for certain plebeians that were about the door, laughed aloud, in the belief that the captain had got either a scald head, or a broken head, both equally opprobrious.

He forthwith leaped up in a fury, and snatching one of his pistols, threatened to put the ostler to death, when another squall from the women checked his resentment. He then bowed to the window, while he kissed the butt-end of his pistol, which he replaced; adjusted his wig in great confusion, and led his horse into the stable—By this time I had come to the door, and could not help gazing at the strange figure that presented itself to my view—He would have measured above six feet in height had he stood upright; but he stooped very much; was very narrow in the shoulders, and very thick in the calves of his legs, which were cased in black spatterdashes—As for his thighs, they were long and slender, like those of a grasshopper; his face was, at least, half a yard in length, brown and shrivelled, with projecting cheek-bones, little grey eyes on the greenish hue, a large hook-nose, a pointed chin, a mouth from ear to ear, very ill furnished with teeth, and a high, narrow fore-head, well furrowed with wrinkles. His horse was exactly in the stile of its rider; a resurrection of dry bones which (as we afterwards learned) he valued exceedingly, as the only present he had ever received in his life.

Having seen this favourite steed properly accommodated in the stable, he sent up his compliments to the ladies, begging permission to thank them in person for the marks of concern they had shewn at his disaster in the court yard— As the 'squire said they could not decently decline his visit, he was shewn up stairs, and paid his respects in the Scotch dialect, with much formality——'Leddies, (said he) perhaps ye may be scandaleezed at the appearance my heed made, when it was uncovered by accident; but I can assure you, the condition you saw it in, is neither the effects of disease, nor of drunkenness: but an honest scar received in the service of my country.' He then gave us to understand, that having been wounded at Ticonderoga, in America, a party of Indians rifled him, scalped him, broke his scull with the blow of a tomahawk, and left him for dead on the field of battle; but that being afterwards found with signs of life, he had been cured in the French hospital, though the loss of substance could not be repaired; so that the scull was left naked in several places, and these he covered with patches.

There is no hold by which an Englishman is sooner taken than that of compassion—We were immediately interested in behalf of this veteran—Even Tabby's heart was melted; but our pity was warmed with indignation, when we learned, that in the course of two sanguinary wars, he had been wounded, maimed, mutilated, taken, and enslaved, without ever having attained a higher rank than that of lieutenant— My uncle's eyes gleamed, and his nether lip quivered, while he exclaimed, 'I vow to God, sir, your case is a reproach to the service—The injustice you have met with is so fla-grant————' 'I must crave your pardon, sir, (cried the other, interrupting him) I complain of no injustice—I pur-chased an ensigncy thirty years ago; and, in the course of service rose to be a lieutenant, according to my seniority—' 'But in such a length of time, (resumed the 'squire) you must have seen a great many young officers put over your head—' 'Nevertheless, (said he) I have no cause to murmur —They bought their preferment with their money—I had no money to carry to market—that was my misfortune; but no body was to blame—' 'What! no friend to advance a sum of money?' (said Mr. Bramble) 'Perhaps, I might have borrowed money for the purchase of a company (an-swered the other); but that loan must have been refunded;

and I did not chuse to incumber myself with a debt of a thousand pounds, to be payed from an income of ten shillings a-day.' 'So you have spent the best part of your life, (cried Mr. Bramble) your youth, your blood, and your constitution, amidst the dangers, the difficulties, the horrors and hardships of a war, for the consideration of three or four shillings a-day—a consideration—' 'Sir, (replied the Scot, with great warmth) you are the man that does me injustice, if you say or think I have been actuated by any such paltry consideration————I am a gentleman; and entered the service as other gentlemen do, with such hopes and sentiments as honourable ambition inspires—If I have not been lucky in the lottery of life, so neither do I think myself unfortunate—I owe to no man a farthing; I can always command a clean shirt, a mutton-chop, and a truss of straw; and when I die, I shall leave effects sufficient to defray the expence of my burial.'

My uncle assured him, he had no intention to give him the least offence, by the observations he had made; but, on the contrary, spoke from a sentiment of friendly regard to his interest—The lieutenant thanked him with a stiffness of civility, which nettled our old gentleman, who perceived that his moderation was all affected; for, whatsoever his tongue might declare, his whole appearance denoted dissatisfaction————In short, without pretending to judge of his military merit, I think I may affirm, that this Caledonian is a self-conceited pedant, aukward, rude, and disputacious—He has had the benefit of a school-education, seems to have read a good number of books, his memory is tenacious, and he pretends to speak several different languages; but he is so addicted to wrangling, that he will cavil at the clearest truths, and, in the pride of argumentation, attempt to reconcile contradictions————Whether his address and qualifications are really of that stamp which is agreeable to the taste of our aunt, Mrs. Tabitha, or that indefatigable maiden is determined to shoot at every sort of game, certain it is she has begun to practice upon the heart of the lieutenant, who favoured us with his company to supper.

I have many other things to say of this man of war, which I shall communicate in a post or two; mean while, it is but reasonable that you should be indulged with some respite from those weary lucubrations of

Yours,
J. MELFORD.

NEWCASTLE UPON TYNE,
   July 10.

To Sir Watkin Phillips, Bart. of Jesus college, Oxon.

DEAR PHILLIPS,
   In my last I treated you with a high flavoured dish, in the character of the Scotch lieutenant, and I must present him once more for your entertainment. It was our fortune to feed upon him the best part of three days; and I do not doubt that he will start again in our way before we shall have finished our northern excursion. The day after our meeting with him at Durham proved so tempestuous that we did not choose to proceed on our journey; and my uncle persuaded him to stay till the weather should clear up, giving him, at the same time, a general invitation to our mess. The man has certainly gathered a whole budget of shrewd observations, but he brings them forth in such an ungracious manner as would be extremely disgusting, if it was not marked by that characteristic oddity which never fails to attract the attention——He and Mr. Bramble discoursed, and even disputed, on different subjects in war, policy, the belles lettres, law, and metaphysics; and sometimes they were warmed into such altercation as seemed to threaten an abrupt dissolution of their society; but Mr. Bramble set a guard over his own irascibility, the more vigilantly as the officer was his guest; and when, in spite of all his efforts, he began

to wax warm, the other prudently cooled in the same proportion.

Mrs. Tabitha chancing to accost her brother by the familiar diminutive of Matt, 'Pray, sir, (said the lieutenant) 'is your name Matthias?' You must know it is one of our uncle's foibles to be ashamed of his name Matthew, because it is puritanical; and this question chagrined him so much, that he answered, 'No, by G—d!' in a very abrupt tone of displeasure.—The Scot took umbrage at the manner of his reply, and bristling up, 'If I had known (said he) that you did not care to tell your name, I should not have asked the question—The leddy called you Matt, and I naturally thought it was Matthias:———perhaps, it may be Methuselah, or Metrodorus, or Metellus, or Mathutinus, or Malthinnus, or Matamorus, or———' 'No, (cried my uncle laughing) it is neither of those, captain:—my name is Matthew Bramble, at your service.—The truth is, I have a foolish pique at the name of Matthew, because it favours of those canting hypocrites, who, in Cromwell's time, christened all their children by names taken from the scripture.'—'A foolish pique indeed, (cried Mrs. Tabby) and even sinful, to fall out with your name because it is taken from holy writ.—I would have you to know, you was called after great-uncle Matthew ap Madoc ap Meredith, esquire, of Llanwysthin, in Montgomeryshire, justice of the *quorum*, and *crusty ruttleorum*, a gentleman of great worth and property, descended in a strait line, by the female side, from Llewellyn, prince of Wales.'

This genealogical anecdote seemed to make some impression upon the North-Briton, who bowed very low to the descendants of Llewellyn, and observed that he himself had the honour of a scriptural nomination. The lady expressing a desire of knowing his address, he said, he designed himself Lieutenant Obadiah Lismahago; and in order to assist her memory, he presented her with a slip of paper inscribed with these three words, which she repeated with great emphasis, declaring, it was one of the most noble and sonorous names she had ever heard. He observed that Obadiah was an adventitious appellation, derived from his great-grandfather, who had been one of the original covenanters; but Lismahago was the family surname, taken from a place in Scotland so called. He likewise dropped some hints about the antiquity of his pedigree, adding, with a smile of self-denial, *Sed genus et proavos, et quœ non fecimus ipsi, vix ea nostra voco*, which quotation he explained in deference to the ladies; and Mrs. Tabitha did not fail to compliment him on his modesty in waving the merit of his ancestry, adding, that it was the less necessary to him, as he had such a considerable fund of his own. She now began to glew herself to his favour with the grossest adulation.——She expatiated upon the antiquity and virtues of the Scottish nation, upon their valour, probity, learning, and politeness.——She even descended to encomiums on his own personal address, his gallantry, good sense, and erudition.——She appealed to her brother, whether the captain was not the very image of our cousin governor Griffith.——She discovered a surprising eagerness to know the particulars of his life, and asked a thousand questions concerning his atchievements in war; all which Mr. Lismahago answered with a sort of jesuitical reserve, affecting a reluctance to satisfy her curiosity on a subject that concerned his own exploits.

By dint of her interrogations, however, we learned, that he and ensign Murphy had made their escape from the French hospital at Montreal, and taken to the woods, in hope of reaching some English settlement; but mistaking their route, they fell in with a party of Miamis, who carried them away in captivity. The intention of these Indians was to give one of them as an adopted son to a venerable sachem, who had lost his own in the course of the war, and to sacrifice the other according to the custom of the country. Murphy, as being the younger and handsomer of the two, was designed to fill the place of the deceased, not only as the son of the sachem, but as the spouse of a beautiful squaw, to whom his predecessor had been betrothed; but in passing through the different whigwhams or villages of the Miamis, poor Murphy was so mangled by the women and children, who have the privilege of torturing all prisoners in their passage, that, by the time they arrived at the place of the sachem's residence, he was rendered altogether unfit for the purposes of marriage: it was determined therefore, in the assembly of the warriors, that ensign Murphy should be brought to the stake, and that the lady should be given to lieutenant Lismahago, who had likewise received his share of torments, though they had not produced emasculation.——A joint of one finger had been cut, or rather sawed off with a rusty knife; one of his great toes was crushed into a mash betwixt two stones; some of his teeth were drawn, or dug out with a crooked nail; splintered reeds had been thrust up his nostrils and other tender parts; and the calves of his legs had been blown up with mines of gunpowder dug in the flesh with the sharp point of the tomahawk.

The Indians themselves allowed that Murphy died with great heroism, singing, as his death song, the *Drimmendoo*, in concert with Mr. Lismahago, who was present at the solemnity. After the warriors and the matrons had made a hearty meal upon the muscular flesh which they pared from the victim, and had applied a great variety of tortures, which he bore without flinching, an old lady, with a sharp knife, scooped out one of his eyes, and put a burning coal in the socket. The pain of this operation was so exquisite that he could not help bellowing, upon which the audience raised a shout of exultation, and one of the warriors stealing behind him, gave him the *coup de grace* with a hatchet.

Lismahago's bride, the squaw Squinkinacoosta, distinguished herself on this occasion.——She shewed a great superiority of genius in the tortures which she contrived and executed with her own hands.——She vied with the stoutest warrior in eating the flesh of the sacrifice; and after all the other females were fuddled with dram-drinking, she was not so intoxicated but that she was able to play the game of the platter with the conjuring sachem, and afterwards go through the ceremony of her own wedding, which was consummated that same evening. The captain had lived very happily with this accomplished squaw for two years, during which she bore him a son, who is now the representative of his mother's tribe; but, at length, to his unspeakable grief, she had died of a fever, occasioned by eating too much raw bear, which they had killed in a hunting excursion.

By this time, Mr. Lismahago was elected sachem, acknowledged first warrior of the Badger tribe, and dignified with the name or epithet of Occacanastaogarora, which signifies *nimble as a weasel;* but all these advantages and honours he was obliged to resign, in consequence of being exchanged for the orator of the community, who had been taken prisoner by the Indians that were in alliance with the English. At the peace, he had sold out upon half pay, and was returned to Britain, with a view to pass the rest of his life in his own country, where he hoped to find some retreat where his slender finances would afford him a decent subsistance. Such are the out-lines of Mr. Lismahago's history, to which Tabitha *did seriously incline her ear;*—indeed, she seemed to be taken with the same charms that captivated the heart of Desdemona, who loved the Moor *for the dangers he had past.*

The description of poor Murphy's sufferings, which threw my sister Liddy into a swoon, extracted some sighs from the breast of Mrs. Tabby: when she understood he had been rendered unfit for marriage, she began to spit, and ejaculated, 'Jesus, what cruel barbarians!' and she made wry faces at the lady's nuptial repast; but she was eagerly curious to know the particulars of her marriage-dress; whether she wore high-breasted stays or bodice, a robe of silk or velvet, and laces of Mechlin or minionette——she supposed, as they were connected with the French, she used *rouge*, and had her hair dressed in the Parisian fashion. The captain would have declined giving a catagorical explanation of all these particulars, observing, in general, that the Indians were too tenacious of their own customs to adopt the modes of any nation whatsoever: he said, moreover, that neither the simplicity of their manners nor the commerce of their country, would admit of those articles of luxury which are deemed magnificence in Europe; and that they were too virtuous and sensible to encourage the introduction of any fashion which might help to render them corrupt and effeminate.

These observations served only to inflame her desire of knowing the particulars about which she had enquired; and, with all his evasion, he could not help discovering the following circumstances—that his princess had neither shoes, stockings, shift, nor any kind of linen—that her bridal dress consisted of a petticoat of red bays, and a fringed blanket, fastened about her shoulders with a copper skewer; but of ornaments she had great plenty.—Her hair was curiously plaited, and interwoven with bobbins of human bone—one eye-lid was painted green, and the other yellow; the cheeks were blue, the lips white, the teeth red, and there was a black list drawn down the middle of the forehead as far as the tip of the nose—a couple of gaudy parrot's feathers were stuck through the division of the nostrils—there was a blue stone set in the chin—her ear-rings consisted of two pieces of hickery, of the size and shape of drum-sticks—her arms and legs were adorned with bracelets of wampum—her breast glittered with numerous strings of glass beads—she wore a curious pouch, or pocket of woven grass, elegantly painted with various colours——about her neck was hung the fresh scalp of a Mohawk warrior, whom her deceased lover had lately slain in battle——and, finally, she was anointed from head to foot with bear's grease, which sent forth a most agreeable odour.

One would imagine that these paraphernalia would not have been much admired by a modern fine lady; but Mrs. Tabitha was resolved to approve of all the captain's connexions.——She wished, indeed, the squaw had been better provided with linen; but she owned there was much taste and fancy in her ornaments; she made no doubt, therefore, that madam Squinkinacoosta was a young lady of good sense and rare accomplishments, and a good christian at bottom. Then she asked whether his consort had been high-church or low-church, presbyterian or anabaptist, or had been favoured with any glimmering of the new light of the gospel? When he confessed that she and her whole nation were utter strangers to the christian faith, she gazed at him with signs of astonishment, and Humphry Clinker, who chanced to be in the room, uttered a hollow groan.

After some pause, 'In the name of God, captain Lismahago, (cried she) what religion do they profess?' 'As to religion, madam, (answered the lieutenant) it is among those Indians a matter of great simplicity—they never heard of any *Alliance between Church and State*.—They, in general, worship two contending principles; one the Fountain of all Good, the other the source of all evil.—The common people there, as in other countries, run into the absurdities of superstition; but sensible men pay adoration to a Supreme Being, who created and sustains the universe.' 'O! what pity, (exclaimed the pious Tabby) that some holy man has not been inspired to go and convert these poor heathens!'

The lieutenant told her, that while he resided among them, two French missionaries arrived, in order to convert them to the catholic religion; but when they talked of mysteries and revelations, which they could neither explain nor authenticate, and called in the evidence of miracles which they believed upon hearsay; when they taught that the Supreme Creator of Heaven and Earth had allowed his only Son, his own equal in power and glory, to enter the bowels of a woman, to be born as a human creature, to be

insulted, flagellated, and even executed as a malefactor;
when they pretended to create God himself, to swallow,
digest, revive, and multiply him *ad infinitum*, by the help
of a little flour and water, the Indians were shocked at the
impiety of their presumption.—They were examined by the
assembly of the sachems who desired them to prove the
divinity of their mission by some miracle.—They answered,
that it was not in their power.———'If you were really sent
by Heaven for our conversion, (said one of the sachems)
you would certainly have some supernatural endowments,
at least you would have the gift of tongues, in order to
explain your doctrine to the different nations among which
you are employed; but you are so ignorant of our language,
that you cannot express yourselves even on the most trifling
subjects.'

In a word, the assembly were convinced of their being
cheats, and even suspected them of being spies:—they ordered them a bag of Indian corn a-piece, and appointed a
guide to conduct them to the frontiers; but the missionaries
having more zeal than discretion, refused to quit the vineyard.——They persisted in saying mass, in preaching, bap-
tizing, and squabbling with the conjurers, or priests of the
country, till they had thrown the whole community into
confusion.—Then the assembly proceeded to try them as
impious impostors, who represented the Almighty as a
trifling, weak, capricious being, and pretended to make, un-
make, and reproduce him at pleasure; they were, therefore,
convicted of blasphemy and sedition, and condemned to the
stake, where they died singing *Salve regina*, in a rapture of
joy, for the crown of martyrdom which they had thus
obtained.

In the course of this conversation, lieutenant Lismahago
dropt some hints by which it appeared he himself was a
free-thinker. Our aunt seemed to be startled at certain
sarcasms he threw out against the creed of saint Athanasius
—He dwelt much upon the words, *reason, philosophy*, and

HUMPHRY CLINKER   235

contradiction in terms—he bid defiance to the eternity of
hell-fire; and even threw such squibs at the immortality of
the soul, as singed a little the whiskers of Mrs. Tabitha's
faith; for, by this time she began to look upon Lismahago
as a prodigy of learning and sagacity.——In short, he could
be no longer insensible to the advances she made towards
his affection; and although there was something repulsive
in his nature, he overcame it so far as to make some return
to her civilities.—Perhaps, he thought it would be no bad
scheme, in a superannuated lieutenant on half-pay, to effect
a conjunction with an old maid, who, in all probability, had
fortune enough to keep him easy and comfortable in the
fag-end of his days.—An ogling correspondence forthwith
commenced between this amiable pair of originals—He began to sweeten the natural acidity of his discourse with the
treacle of compliment and commendation——He from
time to time offered her snuff, of which he himself took
great quantities, and even made her a present of a purse
of silk grass, woven by the hands of the amiable Squinkinacoosta, who had used it as a shot-pouch in her hunting-
expeditions.

From Doncaster northwards, all the windows of all the
inns are scrawled with doggerel rhimes, in abuse of the
Scotch nation; and what surprised me very much, I did not
perceive one line written in the way of recrimination—
Curious to hear what Lismahago would say on this subject,
I pointed out to him a very scurrilous epigram against his
countrymen, which was engraved on one of the windows
of the parlour where we sat.——He read it with the most
starched composure; and when I asked his opinion of the
poetry, 'It is vara terse and vara poignant; (said he) but
with the help of a wat dish-clout, it might be rendered more
clear and parspicuous.—I marvel much that some modern
wit has not published a collection of these essays under the
title of the *Glazier's Triumph over Sawney the Scot*——
I'm persuaded it would be a vara agreeable offering to the

patriots of London and Westminster.' When I expressed
some surprize that the natives of Scotland, who travel this
way, had not broke all the windows upon the road, 'With
submission, (replied the lieutenant) that were but shallow
policy—it would only serve to make the satire more cutting
and severe; and I think it is much better to let it stand in
the window, than have it presented in the reckoning.'

My uncle's jaws began to quiver with indignation.———
He said, the scribblers of such infamous stuff deserved to
be scourged at the cart's tail for disgracing their country
with such monuments of malice and stupidity.—'These
vermin (said he) do not consider, that they are affording
their fellow subjects, whom they abuse, continual matter
of self-gratulation, as well as the means of executing the
most manly vengeance that can be taken for such low,
illiberal attacks. For my part, I admire the philosophic forbearance of the Scots, as much as I despise the insolence of
those wretched libellers, which is akin to the arrogance of
the village cock, who never crows but upon his own dunghill.' The captain, with an affectation of candour, observed,
that men of illiberal minds were produced in every soil;
that in supposing those were the sentiments of the English
in general, he should pay too great a compliment to his own
country, which was not of consequence enough to attract
the envy of such a flourishing and powerful people.

Mrs. Tabby broke forth again in praise of his moderation, and declared that Scotland was the soil which produced
every virtue under heaven.—When Lismahago took his
leave for the night, she asked her brother if the captain
was not the prettiest gentleman he had ever seen; and
whether there was not something wonderfully engaging in
his aspect?—Mr. Bramble having eyed her sometime in
silence, 'Sister, (said he) the lieutenant is, for aught I know,
an honest man and a good officer—he has a considerable
share of understanding, and a title to more encouragement
than he seems to have met with in life; but I cannot, with

a safe conscience, affirm, that he is the prettiest gentleman
I ever saw; neither can I descern any engaging charm in
his countenance, which, I vow to Gad, is, on the contrary,
very hard-favoured and forbidding.'

I have endeavoured to ingratiate myself with this North-
Briton, who is really a curiosity; but he has been very shy
of my conversation ever since I laughed at his asserting that
the English tongue was spoke with more propriety at Edinburgh than at London. Looking at me with a double squeeze
of souring in his aspect, 'If the old definition be true, (said
he) that risibility is the distinguishing characteristic of a
rational creature, the English are the most distinguished for
rationality of any people I ever knew.' I owned, that the
English were easily struck with any thing that appeared
ludicrous, and apt to laugh accordingly; but it did not follow, that, because they were more given to laughter, they
had more rationality than their neighbours: I said, such an
inference would be an injury to the Scots, who were by
no means defective in rationality, though generally supposed
little subject to the impressions of humour.

The captain answered, that this supposition must have
been deduced either from their conversation or their compositions, of which the English could not possibly judge
with precision, as they did not understand the dialect used
by the Scots in common discourse, as well as in their works
of humour. When I desired to know what those works of
humour were, he mentioned a considerable number of
pieces, which he insisted were equal in point of humour to
any thing extant in any language dead or living——He, in
particular, recommended a collection of detached poems,
in two small volumes, intituled, *The Ever-Green*, and the
works of Allan Ramsay, which I intend to previde myself
with at Edinburgh.——He observed, that a North-Briton is
seen to a disadvantage in an English company, because he
speaks in a dialect that they can't relish, and in a phrase-
ology which they don't understand.——He therefore finds

himself under a restraint, which is a great enemy to wit and humour.——These are faculties which never appear in full lustre, but when the mind is perfectly at ease, and, as an excellent writer says, enjoys *her elbow-room.*

He proceeded to explain his assertion that the English language was spoken with greater propriety at Edinburgh than in London.——He said, what we generally called the Scottish dialect was, in fact, true, genuine old English, with a mixture of some French terms and idioms, adopted in a long intercourse betwixt the French and Scotch nations; that the modern English, from affectation and false refinement, had weakened, and even corrupted their language, by throwing out the guttural sounds, altering the pronunciation and the quantity, and disusing many words and terms of great significance. In consequence of these innovations, the works of our best poets, such as Chaucer, Spenser, and even Shakespeare, were become, in many parts, unintelligible to the natives of South Britain, whereas the Scots, who retain the antient language, understand them without the help of a glossary. 'For instance, (said he) how have your commentators been puzzled by the following expression in the *Tempest——He's gentle and not fearful:* as if it was a paralogism to say, that being *gentle*, he must of course be *courageous:* but the truth is, one of the original meanings, if not the sole meaning, of that word was, *noble, high-minded*; and to this day, a Scotch woman, in the situation of the young lady in the *Tempest*, would express herself nearly in the same terms——Don't provoke him; for being gentle, that is, *high-spirited*, he won't tamely bear an insult. Spenser, in the very first stanza of his *Fai y Queen*, says,

A *gentle* knight was pricking on the plain;

which knight, far from being *tame* and fearful, was so stout that

Nothing did he dread, but ever was ydrad.

To prove that we had impaired the energy of our language by false refinement, he mentioned the following words, which, though widely different in signification, are pronounced exactly in the same manner—*wright, write, right, rite*; but among the Scots, these words are as different in pronunciation, as they are in meaning and orthography; and this is the case with many others which he mentioned by way of illustration.——He, moreover, took notice, that we had (for what reason he could never learn) altered the sound of our vowels from that which is retained by all the nations in Europe; an alteration which rendered the language extremely difficult to foreigners, and made it almost impracticable to lay down general rules for orthography and pronunciation. Besides, the vowels were no longer simple sounds in the mouth of an Englishman, who pronounced both *i* and *u* as diphthongs. Finally, he affirmed, that we mumbled our speech with our lips and teeth, and ran the words together without pause or distinction, in such a manner, that a foreigner, though he understood English tolerably well, was often obliged to have recourse to a Scotchman to explain what a native of England had said in his own language.

The truth of this remark was confirmed by Mr. Bramble from his own experience; but he accounted for it on another principle.—He said, the same observation would hold in all languages; that a Swiss talking French was more easily understood than a Parisian, by a foreigner who had not made himself master of the language; because every language had its peculiar recitative, and it would always require more pains, attention, and practice, to acquire both the words and the music, than to learn the words only; and yet no body would deny, that the one was imperfect without the other: he therefore apprehended, that the Scotchman and the Swiss were better understood by learners, because they spoke the words only, without the music, which they could not rehearse. One would imagine this check might have damped the North-Briton; but it served only to agitate his humour for disputation.——He said, if every nation had its own recitative or music, the Scots had theirs, and the Scotchman who had not yet acquired the cadence of the English, would naturally use his own in speaking their language; therefore, if he was better understood than the native, his recitative must be more intelligible than that of the English; of consequence, the dialect of the Scots had an advantage over that of their fellow-subjects, and this was another strong presumption that the modern English had corrupted their language in the article of pronunciation.

The lieutenant was, by this time, become so polemical, that every time he opened his mouth out flew a paradox, which he maintained with all the enthusiasm of altercation; but all his paradoxes favoured strong of a partiality for his own country. He undertook to prove that poverty was a blessing to a nation; that *oatmeal* was preferable to *wheat-flour;* and that the worship of Cloacina, in temples which admitted both sexes, and every rank of votaries promiscuously, was a filthy species of idolatry that outraged every idea of delicacy and decorum. I did not so much wonder at his broaching these doctrines, as at the arguments, equally whimsical and ingenious, which he adduced in support of them.

In fine, lieutenant Lismahago is a curiosity which I have not yet sufficiently perused; and therefore I shall be sorry when we lose his company, though, God knows, there is nothing very amiable in his manner or disposition.—As he goes directly to the south-west division of Scotland, and we proceed in the road to Berwick, we shall part to-morrow at a place called Feltonbridge; and, I dare say, this separation will be very grievous to our aunt Mrs. Tabitha, unless she has received some flattering assurance of his meeting her again. If I fail in my purpose of entertaining you with these unimportant occurrences, they will at least serve as exercises of patience, for which you are indebted to

Yours always,

J. MELFORD.

MORPETH, *July* 13.

To Dr. Lewis

DEAR DOCTOR,

I have now reached the northern extremity of England, and see, close to my chamber-window, the Tweed gliding through the arches of that bridge which connects this suburb to the town of Berwick.——Yorkshire you have seen, and therefore I shall say nothing of that opulent province. The city of Durham appears like a confused heap of stones and brick, accumulated so as to cover a mountain, round which a river winds its brawling course. The streets are generally narrow, dark, and unpleasant, and many of them almost impassible in consequence of their declivity. The cathedral is a huge gloomy pile; but the clergy are well lodged.——The bishop lives in a princely manner—the golden prebends keep plentiful tables—and, I am told, there is some good sociable company in the place; but the country, when viewed from the top of Gateshead-Fell, which extends to Newcastle, exhibits the highest scene of cultivation that ever I beheld. As for Newcastle, it lies mostly in a bottom, on the banks of the Tyne, and makes an appearance still more disagreeable than that of Durham; but it is rendered populous and rich by industry and commerce; and the country lying on both sides the river, above the town, yields a delightful prospect of agriculture and plantation. Morpeth and Alnwick are neat, pretty towns, and this last is famous for the castle which has belonged so many ages to the noble house of Piercy, earls of Northumberland.——It is, doubtless, a large edifice, containing a great number of apartments, and stands in a commanding situation; but the strength of it seems to have consisted not so much in its site, or the manner in which it is fortified, as in the valour of its defendants.

Our adventures since we left Scarborough, are scarce worth reciting; and yet I must make you acquainted with my sister Tabby's progress in husband-hunting, after her disappointments at Bath and London. She had actually begun to practise upon a certain adventurer, who was in fact a highwayman by profession; but he had been used to snares much more dangerous than any she could lay, and escaped accordingly.—Then she opened her batteries upon an old weather-beaten Scotch lieutenant, called Lismahago, who joined us at Durham, and is, I think, one of the most singular personages I ever encountered—His manner is as harsh as his countenance; but his peculiar turn of thinking, and his pack of knowledge made up of the remnants of rarities, rendered his conversation desirable, in spite of his pedantry and ungracious address.—I have often met with a crab-apple in a hedge, which I have been tempted to eat for its flavour, even while I was disgusted by its austerity. The spirit of contradiction is naturally so strong in Lismahago, that I believe in my conscience he has rummaged, and read, and studied with indefatigable attention, in order to qualify himself to refuse established maxims, and thus raise trophies for the gratification of polemical pride.—Such is the asperity of his self-conceit, that he will not even acquiesce in a transient compliment made to his own individual in particular, or to his country in general.

When I observed, that he must have read a vast number of books to be able to discourse on such a variety of subjects, he declared he had read little or nothing, and asked how he should find books among the woods of America, where he had spent the greatest part of his life. My nephew remarking that the Scots in general were famous for their learning, he denied the imputation, and defied him to prove it from their works—'The Scots (said he) have a slight tincture of letters, with which they make a parade among people who are more illiterate than themselves; but they may be said to float on the surface of science, and they have made very small advances in the useful arts.' 'At least, (cried Tabby) all the world allows that the Scots behaved gloriously in fighting and conquering the savages of America.' 'I can assure you, madam, you have been misinformed; (replied the lieutenant) in that continent the Scots did nothing more than their duty, nor was there one corps in his majesty's service, that distinguished it self more than another.—Those who affected to extol the Scots for superior merit, were no friends to that nation.'

Though he himself made free with his countrymen, he would not suffer any other person to glance a sarcasm at them with impunity. One of the company chancing to mention lord B——'s inglorious peace, the lieutenant immediately took up the cudgels in his lordship's favour, and argued very strenuously to prove that it was the most honourable and advantageous peace that England had ever made since the foundation of the monarchy.—Nay, between friends, he offered such reasons on this subject, that I was really confounded, if not convinced.—He would not allow that the Scots abounded above their proportion in the army and navy of Great-Britain, or that the English had any reason to say his countrymen had met with extraordinary encouragement in the service.—'When a South and North-Briton (said he) are competitors for a place or commission, which is in the disposal of an English minister or an English general, it would be absurd to suppose that the preference will not be given to the native of England, who has so many advantages over his rival.—First and foremost, he has in his favour that laudable partiality, which, Mr. Addison says, never fails to cleave to the heart of an Englishman; secondly, he has more powerful connexions, and a greater share of parliamentary interest, by which those contests are generally decided; and lastly, he has a greater command of money to smooth the way to his success. For my own part, (said he) I know no Scotch officer, who has risen in the army above the rank of a subaltern, without purchasing every degree of preferment either with money or recruits; but I know many gentlemen of that country, who, for want of money and interest, have grown grey in the rank of lieu-tenants; whereas very few instances of this ill-fortune are to be found among the natives of South-Britain.—Not that I would insinuate that my countrymen have the least reason to complain.—Preferment in the service, like success in any other branch of traffic, will naturally favour those who have the greatest stock of cash and credit, merit and capacity being supposed equal on all sides.'

But the most hardy of all this original's positions were these:—That commerce would, sooner or later, prove the ruin of every nation, where it flourishes to any extent—that the parliament was the rotten part of the British constitu-tion—that the liberty of the press was a national evil—and that the boasted institution of juries, as managed in England, was productive of shameful perjury and flagrant injustice. He observed, that traffick was an enemy to all the liberal passions of the soul, founded on the thirst of lucre, a sordid disposition to take advantage of the necessities of our fellow creatures.——He affirmed, the nature of commerce was such, that it could not be fixed or perpetuated, but, having flowed to a certain height, would immediately begin to ebb, and so continue till the channels should be left almost dry; but there was no instance of the tide's rising a second time to any considerable influx in the same nation. Mean while the sudden affluence occasioned by trade, forced open all the sluices of luxury and overflowed the land with every species of profligacy and corruption; a total pravity of man-ners would ensue, and this must be attended with bank-ruptcy and ruin. He observed of the parliament, that the practice of buying boroughs, and canvassing for votes, was an avowed system of venality, already established on the ruins of principle, integrity, faith, and good order, in consequence of which the elected and the elector, and, in short, the whole body of the people, were equally and universally contaminated and corrupted. He affirmed, that of a parliament thus constituted, the crown would always have influence enough to secure a great majority in its dependence, from the great number of posts, places, and pensions it had to bestow; that such a parliament would (as it had already done) lengthen the term of its sitting and authority, whenever the prince should think it for his interest to continue the representatives; for, without doubt, they had the same right to protect their authority *ad infinitum*, as they had to extend it from three to seven years.———With a parliament, therefore, dependent upon the crown, devoted to the prince, and supported by a standing army, garbled and modelled for the purpose, any king of England may, and probably some ambitious sovereign will, totally overthrow all the bulwarks of the constitution; for it is not to be supposed that a prince of a high spirit will tamely submit to be thwarted in all his measures, abused and insulted by a populace of unbridled ferocity, when he has it in his power to crush all opposition under his feet with the concurrence of the legislature. He said, he should always consider the liberty of the press as a national evil, while it enabled the vilest reptile to soil the lustre of the most shining merit, and furnished the most infamous incendiary with the means of disturbing the peace and destroying the good order of the community. He owned, however, that, under due restrictions, it would be a valuable privilege; but affirmed, that at present there was no law in England sufficient to restrain it within proper bounds.

With respect to juries, he expressed himself to this effect ———Juries are generally composed of illiterate plebeians, apt to be mistaken, easily misled, and open to sinister influence; for if either of the parties to be tried, can gain over one of the twelve jurors, he has secured the verdict in his favour; the juryman thus brought over will, in despight of all evidence and conviction, generally hold out till his fellows are fatigued, and harrassed, and starved into concurrence; in which case the verdict is unjust, and the jurors are all perjured: but cases will often occur, when the jurors are really divided in opinion, and each side is convinced in opposition to the other; but no verdict will be received, unless they are unanimous, and they are all bound, not only in conscience, but by oath, to judge and declare according to their conviction.——What then will be the consequence?——They must either starve in company, or one side must sacrifice their conscience to their convenience, and join in a verdict which they believe to be false. This absurdity is avoided in Sweden, where a bare majority is sufficient; and in Scotland, where two thirds of the jury are required to concur in the verdict.

You must not imagine that all these deductions were made on his part, without contradictions on mine.—No—the truth is, I found myself piqued in point of honour, at his pretending to be so much wiser than his neighbours.—I questioned all his assertions, started innumerable objections, argued and wrangled with uncommon perseverance, and grew very warm, and even violent, in the debate.—Sometimes he was puzzled, and once or twice, I think, fairly refuted; but from those falls he rose again, like Antæus, with redoubled vigour, till at length I was tired, exhausted, and really did not know how to proceed, when luckily he dropped a hint, by which he discovered he had been bred to the law; a confession which enabled me to retire from the dispute with a good grace, as it could not be supposed that a man like me, who had been bred to nothing, should be able to cope with a veteran in his own profession. I believe, however, that I shall for some time continue to chew the cud of reflection upon many observations which this original discharged.

Whether our sister Tabby was really struck with his conversation, or is resolved to throw at every thing she meets in the shape of a man, till she can fasten the matrimonial noose, certain it is, she has taken desperate strides towards the affection of Lismahago, who cannot be said to have met her half way, though he does not seem altogether insensible to her civilities.——She insinuated more than once how happy we should be to have his company through that part of Scotland which we proposed to visit, till at length he plainly told us, that his road was totally different from that which we intended to take; that, for his part, his company would be of very little service to us in our progress, as he was utterly unacquainted with the country, which he had left in his early youth, consequently, he could neither direct us in our enquiries, nor introduce us to any family of distinction. He said, he was stimulated by an irresistible impulse to revisit the *paternus lar*, or *patria domus*, though he expected little satisfaction, inasmuch as he understood that his nephew, the present possessor, was but ill qualified to support the honour of the family.——He assured us, however, as we design to return by the west road, that he will watch our motions, and endeavour to pay his respects to us at Dumfries.——Accordingly he took his leave of us at a place half way betwixt Morpeth and Alnwick, and pranced away in great state, mounted on a tall, meagre, raw-boned, shambling grey gelding, without e'er a tooth in his head, the very counter-part of the rider; and, indeed, the appearance of the two was so picturesque, that I would give twenty guineas to have them tolerably presented on canvas.

Northumberland is a fine county, extending to the Tweed, which is a pleasant pastoral stream; but you will be surprised when I tell you that the English side of that river is neither so well cultivated nor so populous as the other.—— The farms are thinly scattered, the lands uninclosed, and scarce a gentleman's seat is to be seen in some miles from

the Tweed; whereas the Scots are advanced in crowds to
the very brink of the river, so that you may reckon above
thirty good houses, in the compass of a few miles, belonging to proprietors whose ancestors had fortified castles in
the same situations, a circumstance that shews what dangerous neighbours the Scots must have formerly been to the
northern counties of England.

Our domestic œconomy continues on the old footing.
——My sister Tabby still adheres to methodism, and had
the benefit of a sermon at Wesley's meeting in Newcastle;
but I believe the passion of love has in some measure abated
the fervour of devotion both in her and her woman, Mrs.
Jenkins, about whose good graces there has been a violent
contest betwixt my nephew's valet, Mr. Dutton, and my
man, Humphry Clinker.——Jery has been obliged to interpose his authority to keep the peace; and to him I have left
the discussion of that important affair, which had like to
have kindled the flames of discord in the family of

yours always,

MATT. BRAMBLE.

TWEEDMOUTH, *July* 15.

To Sir Watkin Phillips, Bart. of Oxon.

DEAR WAT,

In my two last you had so much of Lismahago, that I
suppose you are glad he is gone off the stage for the present.
—I must now descend to domestic occurrences.—Love, it
seems, is resolved to assert his dominion over all the females
of our family.——After having practised upon poor Liddy's heart, and played strange vagaries with our aunt Mrs.
Tabitha, he began to run riot in the affections of her woman,
Mrs. Winifred Jenkins, whom I have had occasion to mention more than once in the course of our memoirs. Nature
intended Jenkins for something very different from the

character of her mistress; yet custom and habit have effected a wonderful resemblance betwixt them in many particulars. Win, to be sure, is much younger and more agreeable in her person; she is likewise tender-hearted and benevolent, qualities for which her mistress is by no means remarkable, no more than she is for being of a timorous disposition, and much subject to fits of the mother, which are the infirmities of Win's constitution: but then she seems to have adopted Mrs. Tabby's manner with her cast cloaths.——She dresses and endeavours to look like her mistress, although her own looks are much more engaging.——She enters into her scheme of œconomy, learns her phrases, repeats her remarks, imitates her stile in scolding the inferior servants, and finally, subscribes implicitly to her system of devotion.—— This, indeed, she found the more agreeable, as it was in a great measure introduced and confirmed by the ministry of Clinker, with whose personal merit she seems to have been struck ever since he exhibited the pattern of his naked skin at Marlborough.

Nevertheless, though Humphry had this double hank upon her inclinations, and exerted all his power to maintain the conquest he had made, he found it impossible to guard it on the side of vanity, where poor Win was as frail as any female in the kingdom. In short, my rascal Dutton professed himself her admirer, and, by dint of his outlandish qualifications, threw his rival Clinker out of the saddle of her heart. Humphry may be compared to an English pudding, composed of good wholesome flour and suet, and Dutton to a syllabub or iced froth, which, though agreeable to the taste, has nothing solid or substantial. The traitor not only dazzled her with his second-hand finery, but he fawned, and flattered, and cringed—he taught her to take rappee, and presented her with a snuff-box of *papier mâché*—he supplied her with a powder for her teeth—he mended her complexion, and he dressed her hair in the Paris fashion—he undertook to be her French master and her dancing-master, as well as friseur, and thus imperceptibly wound himself into her good graces. Clinker perceived the progress he had made, and repined in secret.—He attempted to open her eyes in the way of exhortation, and finding it produced no effect had recourse to prayer. At Newcastle, while he attended Mrs. Tabby to the methodist meeting, his rival accompanied Mrs. Jenkins to the play. He was dressed in a silk coat, made at Paris for his former master, with a tawdry waistcoat of tarnished brocade; he wore his hair in a great bag with a huge solitaire, and a long sword dangled from his thigh. The lady was all of a flutter with faded lutestring, washed gauze, and ribbons three times refreshed; but she was most remarkable for the frisure of her head, which rose, like a pyramid, seven inches above the scalp, and her face was primed and patched from the chin up to the eyes; nay, the gallant himself had spared neither red nor white in improving the nature of his own complexion. In this attire, they walked together through the high street to the theatre, and as they passed for players ready dressed for acting, they reached it unmolested; but as it was still light when they returned, and by that time the people had got information of their real character and condition, they hissed and hooted all the way, and Mrs. Jenkins was all bespattered with dir*, as well as insulted with the opprobrious name of *painted Jezabel,* so that her fright and mortification threw her into an hysteric fit the moment she came home.

Clinker was so incensed at Dutton, whom he considered as the cause of her disgrace, that he upbraided him severely for having turned the poor young woman's brain. The other affected to treat him with contempt, and mistaking his forbearance for want of courage, threatened to horse-whip him into good manners. Humphry then came to me, humbly begging I would give him leave to chastise my servant for his insolence—'He has challenged me to fight him at sword's point (said he); but I might as well challenge him to make a horse-shoe, or a plough iron; for I know no more of the one than he does of the other.——Besides, it doth not become servants to use those weapons, or to claim the privilege of gentlemen to kill one another when they fall out; moreover, I would not have his blood upon my conscience for ten thousand times the profit or satisfaction I should get by his death; but if your honour won't be angry, I'll engage to gee 'en a good drubbing, that, may hap, will do 'en service, and I'll take care it shall do 'en no harm.' I said, I had no objection to what he proposed, provided he could manage matters so as not to be found the aggressor, in case Dutton should prosecute him for an assault and battery.

Thus licensed, he retired; and that same evening easily provoked his rival to strike the first blow, which Clinker returned with such interest that he was obliged to call for quarter, declaring, at the same time, that he would exact severe and bloody satisfaction the moment we should pass the border, when he could run him through the body without fear of the consequence.——This scene passed in presence of lieutenant Lismahago, who encouraged Clinker to hazard a thrust of cold iron with his antagonist. 'Cold iron (cried Humphry) I shall never use against the life of any human creature; but I am so far from being afraid of his cold iron, that I shall use nothing in my defence but a good cudgel, which shall always be at his service.' In the mean time, the fair cause of this contest, Mrs. Winifred Jenkins, seemed overwhelmed with affliction, and Mr. Clinker acted much on the reserve, though he did not presume to find fault with her conduct.

The dispute between the two rivals was soon brought to a very unexpected issue. Among our fellow-lodgers at Berwick, was a couple from London, bound to Edinburgh, on the voyage of matrimony. The female was the daughter and heiress of a pawn-broker deceased, who had given her guardians the slip, and put herself under the tuition of a tall Hibernian, who had conducted her thus far in quest of a clergyman to unite them in marriage, without the formalities required by the law of England. I know not how the lover had behaved on the road, so as to decline in the favour of his inamorata; but, in all probability, Dutton perceived a coldness on her side, which encouraged him to whisper, it was a pity she should have cast her affections upon a taylor, which he affirmed the Irishman to be. This discovery completed her disgust, of which my man taking the advantage, began to recommend himself to her good graces, and the smooth-tongued rascal found no difficulty to insinuate himself into the place of her heart, from which the other had been discarded—Their resolution was immediately taken. In the morning, before day, while poor Teague lay snoring a-bed, his indefatigable rival ordered a post-chaise, and set out with the lady for Coldstream, a few miles up the Tweed, where there was a parson who dealt in this branch of commerce and there they were noosed, before the Irishman ever dreamt of the matter. But when he got up at six o'clock, and found the bird was flown, he made such a noise as alarmed the whole house. One of the first persons he encountered, was the postilion returned from Coldstream, where he had been witness to the marriage, and over and above an handsome gratuity, had received a bride's favour, which he now wore in his cap—When the forsaken lover understood they were actually married, and set out for London; and that Dutton had discovered to the lady, that he (the Hibernian) was a taylor, he had like to have run distracted. He tore the ribbon from the fellow's cap, and beat it about his ears. He swore he would pursue him to the gates of hell, and ordered a post-chaise and four to be got ready as soon as possible; but, recollecting that his finances would not admit of this way of travelling, he was obliged to countermand this order.

For my part, I knew nothing at all of what had happened, till the postilion brought me the keys of my trunk and portmanteau, which he had received from Dutton, who sent me his respects, hoping I would excuse him for his abrupt departure, as it was a step upon which his fortune depended—

Before I had time to make my uncle acquainted with this event, the Irishman burst into my chamber, without any introduction, exclaiming,—'By my soul, your sarvant has robbed me of five thousand pounds, and I'll have satisfaction, if I should be hanged to-morrow.—' When I asked him who he was, 'My name (said he) is Master Macloughlin—but it should be Leighlin Oneale, for I am come from Tir-Owen the Great; and so I am as good a gentleman as any in Ireland; and that rogue, your sarvant, said I was a taylor, which was as big a lie as if he had called me the pope —I'm a man of fortune, and have spent all I had; and so being in distress, Mr. Coshgrave, the fashioner in Shuffolk-street, tuck me out, and made me his own private secretary: by the same token, I was the last he bailed; for his friends obliged him to tie himself up, that he would bail no more above ten pounds; for why, because as how, he could not refuse any body that asked, and therefore in time would have robbed himself of his whole fortune, and, if he had lived long at that rate, must have died bankrupt very soon— and so I made my addresses to Miss Skinner, a young lady of five thousand pounds fortune, who agreed to take me for better nor worse; and, to be sure, this day would have put me in possession, if it had not been for that rogue, your sarvant, who came like a tief, and stole away my property, and made her believe I was a taylor; and that she was going to marry the ninth part of a man: but the devil burn my soul, if ever I catch him on the mountains of Tulloghobegly, if I don't shew him that I'm nine times as good a man as he, or e'er a bug of his country.'

When he had rung out his first alarm, I told him I was sorry he had allowed himself to be so jockied; but it was no business of mine; and that the fellow who robbed him of his bride, had likewise robbed me of my servant—'Didn't I tell you then (cried he) that Rogue was his true Christian name.—Oh, if I had but one fair trust with him upon the sod, I'd give him lave to brag all the rest of his life.'

My uncle hearing the noise, came in, and being informed of this adventure, began to comfort Mr. Oneale for the lady's elopement; observing that he seemed to have had a lucky escape, that it was better she should elope before, than after marriage—The Hibernian was of a very different opinion. He said, 'If he had been once married, she might have eloped as soon as she pleased; he would have taken care that she should not have carried her fortune along with her —Ah (said he) she's a Judas Iscariot, and has betrayed me with a kiss; and, like Judas, she carried the bag, and has not left me money enough to bear my expences back to London; and so I'm come to this pass, and the rogue that was the occasion of it has left you without a sarvant, you may put me in his place; and by Jasus, it is the best thing you can do.—' I begged to be excused, declaring I could put up with any inconvenience, rather than treat as a footman the descendant of Tir-Owen the Great. I advised him to return to his friend, Mr. Cosgrave, and take his passage from Newcastle by sea, towards which I made him a small present, and he retired, seemingly resigned to his evil fortune. I have taken upon trial a Scotchman, called Archy M'Alpin, an old soldier, whose last master, a colonel, lately died at Berwick. The fellow is old and withered; but he has been recommended to me for his fidelity, by Mrs. Humphreys, a very good sort of a woman, who keeps the inn at Tweedmouth, and is much respected by all the travellers on this road.

Clinker, without doubt, thinks himself happy in the removal of a dangerous rival, and he is too good a Christian, to repine at Dutton's success. Even Mrs. Jenkins will have reason to congratulate herself upon this event, when she cooly reflects upon the matter; for, howsoever she was forced from her poise for a season, by snares laid for her vanity, Humphry is certainly the north-star to which the needle of her affection would have pointed at the long run. At present, the same vanity is exceedingly mortified, upon finding herself abandoned by her new admirer, in favour of another inamorata. She received the news with a violent burst of laughter, which soon brought on a fit of crying; and this gave the finishing blow to the patience of her mistress, which had held out beyond all expectation. She now opened all those floodgates of reprehension, which had been shut so long. She not only reproached her with her levity and indiscretion, but attacked her on the score of religion, declaring roundly that she was in a state of apostacy and reprobation; and finally, threatened to send her a packing at this extremity of the kingdom. All the family interceded for poor Winifred, not even excepting her slighted swain, Mr. Clinker, who, on his knees, implored and obtained her pardon.

There was, however, another consideration that gave Mrs. Tabitha some disturbance. At Newcastle, the servants had been informed by some wag, that there was nothing to eat in Scotland, but *oat-meal* and *sheep's-heads*; and lieutenant Lismahago being consulted, what he said served rather to confirm than to refute the report. Our aunt being apprised of this circumstance, very gravely advised her brother to provide a sumpter horse with store of hams, tongues, bread, biscuit, and other articles for our subsistence, in the course of our peregrination, and Mr. Bramble as gravely replied, that he would take the hint into consideration: but finding no such provision was made, she now revived the proposal, observing that there was a tolerable market at Berwick, where we might be supplied; and that my man's horse would serve as a beast of burthen—The 'squire, shrugging his shoulders, eyed her askance with a look of ineffable contempt: and, after some pause, 'Sister, (said he) I can hardly persuade myself you are serious.' She was so little acquainted with the geography of the island, that she imagined we could not go to Scotland but by sea; and, after we had passed through the town of Berwick, when he told her we were upon Scottish ground, she could hardly believe the assertion—If the truth must be told, the South Britons in general are woefully ignorant in this particular. What, between want of curiosity, and traditional sarcasms, the effect of ancient animosity, the people at the other end of the island know as little of Scotland as of Japan.

If I had never been in Wales, I should have been more struck with the manifest difference in appearance betwixt the peasants and commonalty on different sides of the Tweed. The boors of Northumberland are lusty fellows, fresh complexioned, cleanly, and well cloathed; but the labourers in Scotland are generally lank, lean, hard-featured, sallow, soiled, and shabby, and their little pinched blue caps have a beggarly effect. The cattle are much in the same stile with their drivers, meagre, stunted, and ill equipt. When I talked to my uncle on this subject, he said, 'Though all the Scottish hinds would not bear to be compared with those of the rich counties of South Britain, they would stand very well in competition with the peasants of France, Italy, and Savoy —not to mention the mountaineers of Wales, and the redshanks of Ireland.'

We entered Scotland by a frightful moor of sixteen miles, which promises very little for the interior parts of the kingdom; but the prospect mended as we advanced. Passing through Dunbar, which is a neat little town, situated on the sea-side, we lay at a country inn, where our entertainment far exceeded our expectation; but for this we cannot give the Scots credit, as the landlord is a native of England. Yesterday we dined at Haddington, which has been a place of some consideration, but is now gone to decay; and in the evening arrived at this metropolis, of which I can say very little. It is very romantic, from its situation on the declivity of a hill, having a fortified castle at the top, and a royal palace at the bottom. The first thing that strikes the nose of a stranger, shall be nameless; but what first strikes the eye, is the unconscionable height of the houses, which generally rise to five, six, seven, and eight stories, and, in some places, (as I am assured) to twelve. This manner of building, attended with numberless inconveniences, must have been originally owing to want of room. Certain it is, the town seems to be full of people: but their looks, their language, and their customs, are so different from ours, that I can hardly believe myself in Great-Britain.

The inn at which we put up (if it may be so called) was so filthy and disagreeable in all respects, that my uncle began to fret, and his gouty symptoms to recur—Recollecting, however, that he had a letter of recommendation to one Mr. Mitchelson, a lawyer, he sent it by his servant, with a compliment, importing that we would wait upon him next day in person; but that gentleman visited us immediately, and insisted upon our going to his own house, until he could provide lodgings for our accommodation. We gladly accepted of his invitation, and repaired to his house, where we were treated with equal elegance and hospitality, to the utter confusion of our aunt, whose prejudices, though beginning to give way, were not yet entirely removed. To-day, by the assistance of our friend, we are settled in convenient lodgings, up four pair of stairs, in the High-street, the fourth story being, in this city, reckoned more genteel than the first. The air is, in all probability, the better; but it requires good lungs to breathe it at this distance above the surface of the earth.—While I do remain above it, whether higher or lower, provided I breathe at all,

I shall ever be,
dear Phillips, yours,
J. MELFORD

July 18.

To Dr. Lewis

DEAR LEWIS,

That part of Scotland contiguous to Berwick, nature seems to have intended as a barrier between two hostile nations. It is a brown desert of considerable extent, that produces nothing but heath and fern; and what rendered it the more dreary when we passed, there was a thick fog that hindered us from seeing above twenty yards from the carriage——My sister began to make wry faces, and use her smelling-bottle; Liddy looked blank, and Mrs. Jenkins dejected; but in a few hours these clouds were dissipated; the sea appeared upon our right, and on the left the mountains retired a little, leaving an agreeable plain betwixt them and the beach; but, what surprised us all, this plain, to the extent of several miles, was covered with as fine wheat as ever I saw in the most fertile parts of South Britain——This plentiful crop is raised in the open field, without any inclosure, or other manure than the *alga marina*, or sea-weed, which abounds on this coast; a circumstance which shews that the soil and climate are favourable; but that agriculture in this country is not yet brought to that perfection which it has attained in England. Inclosures would not only keep the grounds warm, and the several fields distinct, but would also protect the crop from the high winds, which are so frequent in this part of the island.

Dunbar is well situated for trade, and has a curious bason, where ships of small burthen may be perfectly secure; but there is little appearance of business in the place——From thence, all the way to Edinburgh, there is a continual succession of fine seats, belonging to noblemen and gentlemen; and as each is surrounded by its own parks and plantation, they produce a very pleasing effect in a country which lies otherwise open and exposed. At Dunbar there is a noble park, with a lodge, belonging to the Duke of Roxburgh, where Oliver Cromwell had his head-quarters, when Lesley, at the head of a Scotch army, took possession of the mountains in the neighbourhood, and hampered him in such a manner, that he would have been obliged to embark and get away by sea, had not the fanaticism of the enemy forfeited the advantage which they had obtained by their general's conduct——Their ministers, by exhortation, prayer, assurance, and prophecy, instigated them to go down and slay the Philistines in Gilgal, and they quitted their ground accordingly, notwithstanding all that Lesley could do to restrain the madness of their enthusiasm——When Oliver saw them in motion, he exclaimed, 'Praised be the Lord, he hath delivered them into the hands of his servant!' and ordered his troops to sing a psalm of thanksgiving, while they advanced in order to the plain, where the Scots were routed with great slaughter.

In the neighbourhood of Haddington, there is a gentleman's house, in the building of which, and the improvements about it, he is said to have expended forty thousand pounds: but I cannot say I was much pleased with either the architecture or the situation; though it has in front a pastoral stream, the banks of which are laid out in a very agreeable manner. I intended to pay my respects to Lord Elibank, whom I had the honour to know at London many years ago. He lives in this part of Lothian; but was gone to the North, on a visit——You have often heard me mention this nobleman, whom I have long revered for his humanity and universal intelligence, over and above the entertainment arising from the originality of his character—At Mussel-burgh, however, I had the good-fortune to drink tea with my old friend Mr. Cardonel; and at his house I met with Dr. C——, the parson of the parish, whose humour and conversation inflamed me with a desire of being better acquainted with his person—I am not at all surprised that these Scots make their way in every quarter of the globe.

This place is but four miles from Edinburgh, towards which we proceeded along the sea-shore, upon a firm bottom of smooth sand, which the tide had left uncovered in its retreat——Edinburgh, from this avenue, is not seen to much advantage—We had only an imperfect view of the Castle and upper parts of the town, which varied incessantly according to the inflexions of the road, and exhibited the appearance of detached spires and turrets, belonging to some magnificent edifice in ruins. The palace of Holyrood house stands on the left, as you enter the Canongate—This is a street continued from hence to the gate called Nether Bow, which is now taken away; so that there is no interruption for a long mile, from the bottom to the top of the hill on which the castle stands in a most imperial situation ——Considering its fine pavement, its width, and the lofty houses on each side, this would be undoubtedly one of the noblest streets in Europe, if an ugly mass of mean buildings, called the Lucken-Booths, had not thrust itself, by what accident I know not, into the middle of the way, like Middle-Row in Holborn. The city stands upon two hills, and the bottom between them; and, with all its defects, may very well pass for the capital of a moderate kingdom. —It is full of people, and continally resounds with the noise of coaches and other carriages, for luxury as well as commerce. As far as I can perceive, here is no want of provisions—The beef and mutton are as delicate here as in Wales; the sea affords plenty of good fish; the bread is remarkably fine; and the water is excellent, though I'm afraid not in sufficient quantity to answer all the purposes of cleanliness and convenience; articles in which, it must be allowed, our fellow-subjects are a little defective—The water is brought in leaden pipes from a mountain in the neighbourhood, to a cistern on the Castle-hill, from whence it is distributed to public conduits in different parts of the city—From these it is carried in barrels, on the backs of male and female porters, up two, three, four, five, six, seven, and eight pair of stairs, for the use of particular families—— Every story is a complete house, occupied by a separate family; and the stair being common to them all, is generally left in a very filthy condition; a man must tread with great circumspection to get safe housed with unpolluted shoes—Nothing can form a stronger contrast, than the difference betwixt the outside and inside of the door; for the good-women of this metropolis are remarkably nice in the ornaments and propriety of their apartments, as if they were resolved to transfer the imputation from the individual to the public. You are no stranger to their method of discharging all their impurities from their windows, at a certain hour of the night, as the custom is in Spain, Portugal, and some parts of France and Italy—A practice to which I can by no means be reconciled, for notwithstanding all the care that is taken by their scavengers to remove this nuisance every morning by break of day, enough still remains to offend the eyes, as well as other organs of those whom use has not hardened against all delicacy of sensation.

The inhabitants seem insensible to these impressions, and are apt to imagine the disgust that we avow is little better than affectation; but they ought to have some compassion for strangers, who have not been used to this kind of sufferance; and consider, whether it may not be worth while to take some pains to vindicate themselves from the reproach that, on this account, they bear among their neighbours. As to the surprising height of their houses, it is absurd in many respects; but in one particular light I cannot view it without horror; that is, the dreadful situation of all the families above, in case the common staircase should be rendered impassable by a fire in the lower stories—In order to prevent the shocking consequences that must attend such an accident, it would be a right measure to open doors of communication from one house to another, on every story, by which the people might fly from such a terrible visitation. In all parts of the world, we see the force of habit prevailing over all the dictates of convenience and sagacity——All the people of business at Edinburgh, and even the genteel company, may be seen standing in crowds every day, from one to two in the afternoon, in the open street, at a place where formerly stood a market-cross, which (by the bye) was a curious piece of Gothic architecture, still to be seen in lord Sommerville's garden in this neighbourhood—I say, the people stand in the open street from the force of custom, rather than move a few yards to an Exchange that stands empty on one side, or to the Parliament-close on the other, which is a noble square adorned with a fine equestrian statue of king Charles II.—The company thus assembled, are entertained with a variety of tunes, played upon a set of bells, fixed in a steeple hard by—As these bells are well-toned, and the musician, who has a salary from the city, for playing upon them with keys, is no bad performer, the entertainment is really agreeable, and very striking to the ears of a stranger.

The public inns of Edinburgh, are still worse than those of London; but by means of a worthy gentleman, to whom I was recommended, we have got decent lodgings in the house of a widow gentlewoman of the name of Lockhart; and here I shall stay until I have seen every thing that is remarkable in and about this capital. I now begin to feel the good effect of exercise——I eat like a farmer, sleep from mid-night till eight in the morning without interruption, and enjoy a constant tide of spirits, equally distant from inanition and excess; but whatever ebbs or flows my constitution may undergo, my heart will still declare that I am,

Dear Lewis,

Your affectionate friend and servant,

MATT. BRAMBLE.

EDR. *July* 18.

To Mrs. Mary Jones, at Brambleton-hall

DEAR MARY,

The 'squire has been so kind as to rap my bit of nonsense under the kiver of his own sheet—O, Mary Jones! Mary Jones! I have had trials and tremblulation. God help me! I have been a vixen and a griffin these many days—Sattin has had power to temp me in the shape of van Ditton, the young 'squire's wally de shamble; but by God's grease he did not purvail—I thoft as how, there was no arm in going to a play at Newcastle, with my hair dressed in the Parish fashion; and as for the trifle of paint, he said as how my complexion wanted rouch, and so I let him put it on with a little Spanish owl; but a mischievous mob of colliers, and such promiscous ribble rabble, that could bare no smut but their own, attacked us in the street, and called me *hoar* and *painted Issabel*, and splashed my close, and spoiled me a complete set of blond lace triple ruffles, not a pin the worse for the ware—They cost me seven good sillings, to lady Griskin's woman at London.

When I axed Mr. Clinker what they meant by calling me Issabel, he put the byebill into my hand, and I read of van Issabel a painted harlot, that vas thrown out of a vindore, and the dogs came and licked her blood—But I am no harlot; and, with God's blessing, no dog shall have my poor blood to lick: marry, Heaven forbid, amen! As for Ditton, after all his courting, and his compliment, he stole away an Irishman's bride, and took a French leave of me and his master; but I vally not his going a farting; but I have had hanger on his account—Mistress scoulded like mad; thof I have the comfit that all the family took my part, and even Mr. Clinker pleaded for me on his bended knee; thof, God he knows, he had raisins enuff to complain; but he's a good sole, abounding with Christian meekness, and one day will meet with his reward.

And now, dear Mary, we have got to Haddingborrough, among the Scots, who are civil enuff for our money, thof I don't speak their lingo—But they should not go for to impose upon foreigners; for the bills in their houses say, they have different *easements* to let; and behold there is nurro geaks in the whole kingdom, nor any thing for poor sarvants, but a barrel with a pair of tongs thrown a-cross; and all the chairs in the family are emptied into this here barrel once a-day; and at ten o'clock at night the whole cargo is flung out of a back windore that looks into some street or lane, and the maids calls *gardy loo* to the passengers which signifies *Lora have mercy upon you!* and this is done every night in every house in Haddingborrough; so you may guess, Mary Jones, what a sweet savour comes from such a number of profuming pans; but they say it is wholsome, and, truly, I believe it is; for being in the vapours, and thinking of Issabel and Mr. Clinker, I was going into a fit of astericks, when this fiff, saving your presence, took me by the nose so powerfully that I sneezed three times, and found myself wonderfully refreshed; and this to be sure is the raisin why there are no fits in Haddingborrough.

I was likewise made believe, that there was nothing to be had but *oat-meal* and *seeps-heads;* but if I hadn't been a fool, I mought have known there could be no *heads* without kerkasses——This very blessed day I dined upon a delicate leg of Velsh mutton and cully-flower; and as for the oat-meal, I leave that to the sarvants of the country, which are pore drudges, many of them without shoes or stockings— Mr. Clinker tells me here is a great call of the gospel; but I wish, I wish some of our family be not fallen off from the rite way—O, if I was given to tail-baring, I have my own secrets to discover——There has been a deal of huggling and flurtation betwixt mistress and an ould Scotch officer, called Kismycago. He looks for all the orld like the scare-crow that our gardener has set up to frite away the sparrows; and what will come of it, the Lord knows; but come what will, it shall never be said that I mentioned a syllabub of the matter—Remember me kindly to Saul and the kitten——I hope they got the horn-buck, and will put it to a good yuse, which is the constant prayer of

                    Dear Molly,
                        Your loving friend,
                              WIN. JENKINS.

ADDINGBOROUGH, *July* 18.

To Sir Watkin Phillips, Bart. of Jesus college, Oxon.

DEAR PHILLIPS,

If I stay much longer at Edinburgh, I shall be changed into a downright Caledonian—My uncle observes, that I have already acquired something of the country accent. The people here are so social and attentive in their civilities to strangers, that I am insensibly sucked into the channel of their manners and customs, although they are in fact much more different from ours than you can imagine—That difference, however, which struck me very much at my first arrival, I now hardly perceive, and my ear is perfectly reconciled to the Scotch accent, which I find even agreeable in the mouth of a pretty woman— It is a sort of Doric dialect, which gives an idea of amiable simplicity——You cannot imagine how we have been caressed and feasted in the *good town of Edinburgh,* of which we are become free denizens and guild brothers, by the special favour of the magistracy.

I had a whimsical commission from Bath, to a citizen of this metropolis—Quin, understanding our intention to visit Edinburgh, pulled out a guinea, and desired the favour I would drink it at a tavern, with a particular friend and bottle-companion of his, one Mr. R— C—, a lawyer of this city—I charged myself with the commission, and, taking the guinea, 'You see (said I) I have pocketed your bounty.' 'Yes (replied Quin, laughing); and a head-ake into the bargain, if you drink fair.' I made use of this introduction to Mr. C——, who received me with open arms, and gave me the rendezvous, according to the cartel. He had provided a company of jolly fellows, among whom I found myself extremely happy; and did Mr. C—— and Quin all the justice in my power; but, alas, I was no more than a tiro among a troop of veterans, who had compassion upon my youth and conveyed me home in the morning by what means I know not—Quin was mistaken, however, as to the head-ake; the claret was too good to treat me so roughly.

While Mr. Bramble holds conferences with the graver literati of the place, and our females are entertained at visits by the Scotch ladies, who are the best and kindest creatures upon earth, I pass my time among the bucks of Edinburgh; who, with a great share of spirit and vivacity, have a certain shrewdness and self-command that is not often found among their neighbours, in the high-day of youth and exultation———Not a hint escapes a Scotchman that can be interpreted into offence by any individual in the company; and national reflections are never heard—In this particular, I must own, we are both unjust and ungrateful to the Scots; for, as far as I am able to judge, they have a real esteem for the natives of South-Britain; and never mention our country, but with expressions of regard —Nevertheless, they are far from being servile imitators of our modes and fashionable vices. All their customs and regulations of public and private œconomy, of business and diversion, are in their own stile. This remarkably predominates in their looks, their dress and manner, their music, and even their cookery. Our 'squire declares, that he knows not another people upon earth, so strongly marked with a national character—Now we are upon the article of cookery, I must own, some of their dishes are savoury, and even delicate; but I am not yet Scotchman enough to relish their singed sheep's-head and haggice, which were provided at our request, one day at Mr. Mitchelson's, where we dined—The first put me in mind of the history of Congo, in which I had read of negroes' heads sold publickly in the markets; the last, being a mess of minced lights, livers, suet, oatmeal, onions, and pepper, inclosed in a sheep's stomach, had a very sudden effect upon mine, and the delicate Mrs. Tabby changed colour; when the cause of our disgust was instantaneously removed at the nod of our entertainer. The Scots, in general, are attached to this composition, with a sort of national fondness, as well as to their oat-meal bread; which is presented at every table, in thin triangular cakes, baked upon a plate of iron, called a girdle; and these, many of the natives, even in the higher ranks of life, prefer to wheaten-bread, which they have here in perfection—You know we used to vex poor Murray of Baliol-college, by asking, if there was really no fruit but turnips in Scotland?——Sure enough, I have seen turnips make their appearance, not as a desert, but by way of *hors d'œuvres*, or whets, as radishes are served up betwixt more substantial dishes in France and Italy; but it must be observed, that the turnips of this country are as much superior in sweetness, delicacy, and flavour, to those in England, as a musk-melon is to the stock of a common cabbage. They are small and conical, of a yellowish colour, with a very thin skin; and, over and above their agreeable taste, are valuable for their antiscorbutic quality—As to the fruit now in season, such as cherries, gooseberries, and currants, there is no want of them at Edinburgh; and in the gardens of some gentlemen, who live in the neighbourhood, there is now a very favourable appearance of apricots, peaches, nectarines, and even grapes: nay, I have seen a very fine shew of pineapples within a few miles of this metropolis. Indeed, we have no reason to be surprised at these particulars, when we consider how little difference there is, in fact, betwixt this climate and that of London.

All the remarkable places in the city and its avenues, for ten miles around, we have visited, much to our satisfaction. In the Castle are some royal apartments, where the sovereign occasionally resided; and here are carefully preserved the regalia of the kingdom, consisting of a crown, said to be of great value, a sceptre, and a sword of state, adorned with jewels—Of these symbols of sovereignty, the people are exceedingly jealous—A report being spread during the sitting of the union-parliament, that they were removed to London, such a tumult arose, that the lord commissioner would have been torn to pieces, if he had not produced them for the satisfaction of the populace.

The palace of Holyrood-house is an elegant piece of architecture, but sunk in an obscure, and, as I take it, unwholesome bottom, where one would imagine it had been placed on purpose to be concealed. The apartments are lofty, but unfurnished; and as for the pictures of the Scottish kings, from Fergus I. to king William, they are paultry daubings, mostly by the same hand, painted either from the imagination, or porters hired to sit for the purpose. All the diversions of London we enjoy at Edinburgh, in a small compass. Here is a well conducted concert, in which several gentlemen perform on different instruments—The Scots are all musicians—Every man you meet plays on the flute, the violin, or violoncello; and there is one nobleman, whose compositions are universally admired—Our company of actors is very tolerable; and a subscription is now on foot for building a new theatre; but their assemblies please me above all other public exhibitions.

We have been at the hunters' ball, where I was really astonished to see such a number of fine women—The English, who have never crossed the Tweed, imagine erroneously, that the Scotch ladies are not remarkable for personal attractions; but, I can declare with a safe conscience, I never saw so many handsome females together, as were assembled on this occasion. At the Leith races, the best company comes hither from the remoter provinces; so that, I suppose, we had all the beauty of the kingdom concentrated as it were into one focus; which was, indeed, so vehement, that my heart could hardly resist its power—Between friends, it has sustained some damage from the bright eyes of the charming Miss R—n, whom I had the honour to dance with at the ball—The countess of Melville attracted all eyes, and the admiration of all present—She was accompanied by the agreeable miss Grieve, who made many conquests; nor did my sister Liddy pass unnoticed in the

assembly—She is become a toast at Edinburgh, by the name
of the Fair Cambrian, and has already been the occasion
of much wine-shed; but the poor girl met with an accident
at the ball, which has given us great disturbance.

A young gentleman, the express image of that rascal
Wilson, went up to ask her to dance a minuet; and his sudden appearance shocked her so much, that she fainted away
—I call Wilson a rascal, because, if he had been really a
gentleman, with honorouble intentions, he would have, ere
now, appeared in his own character—I must own, my blood
boils with indignation when I think of that fellow's presumption; and Heaven confound me if I don't—-But I
won't be so womanish as to rail—Time will, perhaps, furnish occasion—Thank God, the cause of Liddy's disorder
remains a secret. The lady directress of the ball, thinking
she was overcome by the heat of the place, had her conveyed
to another room, where she soon recovered so well, as to
return and join in the country dances, in which the Scotch
lasses acquit themselves with such spirit and agility, as put
their partners to the height of their mettle—I believe our
aunt, Mrs. Tabitha, had entertained hopes of being able to
do some execution among the cavaliers at this assembly——
She had been several days in consultation with milliners and
mantua-makers, preparing for the occasion, at which she
made her appearance in a full suit of damask, so thick and
heavy, that the sight of it alone, at this season of the year,
was sufficient to draw drops of sweat from any man of
ordinary imagination—She danced one minuet with our
friend Mr. Mitchelson, who favoured her so far, in the
spirit of hospitality and politeness; and she was called out
a second time by the young laird of Ballymawhawple, who,
coming in by accident, could not readily find any other partner; but as the first was a married man, and the second
payed no particular homage to her charms, which were also
over-looked by the rest of the company, she became dissatis-
fied and censorious—At supper, she observed that the Scotch

gentlemen made a very good figure, when they were a little improved by travelling; and therefore it was pity they did not all take the benefit of going abroad——She said the women were aukward, masculine creatures; that, in dancing, they lifted their legs like so many colts; that they had no idea of graceful motion, and put on their clothes in a frightful manner; but if the truth must be told, Tabby herself was the most ridiculous figure, and the worst dressed of the whole assembly——The neglect of the male sex rendered her malcontent and peevish; she now found fault with every thing at Edinburgh, and teized her brother to leave the place, when she was suddenly reconciled to it on a religious consideration——There is a sect of fanaticks, who have separated themselves from the established kirk, under the name of Seceders——They acknowledge no earthly head of the church, reject lay-patronage, and maintain the methodist doctrines of the new birth, the new light, the efficacy of grace, the insufficiency of works, and the operation of the spirit. Mrs. Tabitha, attended by Humphry Clinker, was introduced to one of their conventicles, where they both received much edification; and she has had the good fortune to come acquainted with a pious Christian, called Mr. Moffat, who is very powerful in prayer, and often assists her in private exercises of devotion.

I never saw such a concourse of genteel company at any races in England, as appeared on the course of Leith——Hard by, in the fields called the Links, the citizens of Edinburgh divert themselves at a game called golf, in which they use a curious kind of bats, tipt with horn, and small elastic balls of leather, stuffed with feathers, rather less than tennis balls, but of a much harder consistence——This they strike with such force and dexterity from one hole to another, that they will fly to an incredible distance. Of this diversion the Scots are so fond, that when the weather will permit, you may see a multitude of all ranks, from the senator of justice to the lowest tradesman, mingled together in their shirts, and following the balls with the utmost eagerness—Among others, I was shewn one particular set of golfers, the youngest of whom was turned of fourscore——They were all gentlemen of independent fortunes, who had amused themselves with this pastime for the best part of a century, without having ever felt the least alarm from sickness or disgust; and they never went to bed, without having each the best part of a gallon of claret in his belly. Such uninterrupted exercise, co-operating with the keen air from the sea, must, without all doubt, keep the appetite always on edge, and steel the constitution against all the common attacks of distemper.

The Leith races gave occasion to another entertainment of a very singular nature—There is at Edinburgh a society or corporation of errand-boys, called cawdies, who ply in the streets at night with paper lanthorns, and are very serviceable in carrying messages—These fellows, though shabby in their appearance, and rudely familiar in their address, are wonderfully acute, and so noted for fidelity, that there is no instance of cawdy's having betrayed his trust— Such is their intelligence, that they know, not only every individual of the place, but also every stranger, by that time he has been four and twenty hours in Edinburgh; and no transaction, even the most private, can escape their notice— They are particularly famous for their dexterity in executing one of the functions of Mercury; though, for my own part, I never employed them in this department of business—Had I occasion for any service of this nature, my own man, Archy M'Alpine, is as well qualified as e'er a cawdie in Edinburgh; and I am much mistaken, if he has not been heretofore of their fraternity. Be that as it may, they resolved to give a dinner and a ball at Leith, to which they formally invited all the young noblemen and gentlemen that were at the races; and this invitation was reinforced by an assurance that all the celebrated ladies of pleasure would grace the entertainment with their company.

—I received a card on this occasion, and went thither with half a dozen of my acquaintance.—In a large hall the cloth was laid on a long range of tables joined together, and here the company seated themselves, to the number of about fourscore, lords, and lairds, and other gentlemen, courtezans and cawdies mingled together, as the slaves and their masters were in the time of the Saturnalia in ancient Rome. —The toastmaster, who sat at the upper end, was one Cawdie Fraser, a veteran pimp, distinguished for his humour and sagacity, well known and much respected in his profession by all the guests, male and female, that were here assembled.—He had bespoke the dinner and the wine: he had taken care that all his brethren should appear in decent apparel and clean linen; and he himself wore a periwig with three tails in honour of the festival.——I assure you the banquet was both elegant and plentiful, and seasoned with a thousand sallies, that promoted a general spirit of mirth and good humour.—After the desert, Mr. Fraser proposed the following toasts, which I don't pretend to explain.—'The best in Christendom.'—'Gibb's contract.'— 'The beggar's benison.'—'King and kirk.'—'Great Britain and Ireland.'——Then, filling a bumper, and turning to me, 'Meester Malford, (said he) may a' unkindness cease betwixt John Bull and his sister Moggy.'—The next person he singled out, was a nobleman who had been long abroad. ——'Ma lord, (cried Fraser) here is a bumper to a' those noblemen who have virtue enough to spend their rents in their ain countray.'—He afterwards addressed himself to a member of parliament in these words:—'Meester—I'm sure ye'll ha' nae objection to my drinking, disgrace and dule to ilka Scot, that sells his conscience and his vote.'—He discharged a third sarcasm at a person very gaily dressed, who had risen from small beginnings, and made a considerable fortune at play.—Filling his glass, and calling him by name, 'Lang life, (said he) to the wylie loon that gangs a-field with a toom poke at his lunzie, and comes hame

with a sackful of siller.'——All these toasts being received
with loud bursts of applause, Mr. Fraser called for pint
glasses, and filled his own to the brim: then standing up,
and all his brethren following his example, 'Ma lords and
gentlemen (cried he), here is a cup of thanks for the great
and undeserved honour you have done your poor errand-
boys this day.'—So saying, he and they drank off their glasses
in a trice, and quitting their seats, took their station each
behind one of the other guests;—exclaiming, 'Noo we're
your honours' cawdies again.'

The nobleman who had bore the first brunt of Mr.
Fraser's satire, objected to his abdication. He said, as the
company was assembled by invitation from the cawdies, he
expected they were to be entertained at their expense. 'By
no means, my lord, (cried Fraser) I wad na be guilty of
sic presumption for the wide warld—I never affronted a
gentleman since I was born; and sure at this age, I wonnot
offer an indignity to sic an houourable convention.' 'Well
(said his Lordship) as you have expended some wit, you
have a right to save your money. You have given me good
counsel, and I take it in good part. As you have voluntarily
quitted your seat, I will take your place with the leave of
the good company, and think myself happy to be hailed,
Father of the Feast.' He was forthwith elected into the
chair, and complimented in a bumper in his new character.

The claret continued to circulate without interruption,
till the glasses seemed to dance upon the table, and this,
perhaps, was a hint to the ladies to call for music—At eight
in the evening the ball began in another apartment: at midnight we went to supper; but it was broad day before I
found the way to my lodgings; and, no doubt, his Lordship
had a swinging bill to discharge.

In short, I have lived so riotously for some weeks, that
my uncle begins to be alarmed on the score of my constitution, and very seriously observes, that all his own infirmities
are owing to such excesses indulged in his youth—Mrs.

Tabitha says it would be more to the advantage of my soul as well as body, if, instead of frequenting these scenes of debauchery, I would accompany Mr. Moffat and her to hear a sermon of the reverend Mr. M'Corkindale.——— Clinker often exhorts me, with a groan, to take care of my precious health; and even Archy M'Alpine, when he happens to be overtaken, (which is oftener the case than I could wish) reads me a long lecture upon temperance and sobriety; and is so very wise and sententious, that, if I could provide him with a professor's chair, I would willingly give up the benefit of his admonitions and service together; for I was tutor-sick at alma mater.

I am not, however, so much engrossed by the gaieties of Edinburgh, but that I find time to make parties in the family way.——We have not only seen all the villas and villages within ten miles of the capital, but we have also crossed the Firth, which is an arm of the sea seven miles broad, that divides Lothian from the shire, or, as the Scots call it, the *kingdom of Fife*. There is a number of large open sea-boats that ply on this passage from Leith to Kinghorn, which is a borough on the other side. In one of these our whole family embarked three days ago, excepting my sister who, being exceedingly fearful of the water, was left to the care of Mrs. Mitchelson. We had an easy and quick passage into Fife, where we visited a number of poor towns on the sea-side, including St. Andrew's, which is the skeleton of a venerable city; but we were much better pleased with some noble and elegant seats and castles, of which there is a great number in that part of Scotland. Yesterday we took boat again on our return to Leith, with fair wind and agreeable weather; but we had not advanced half-way when the sky was suddenly overcast, and the wind changing, blew directly in our teeth; so that we were obliged to turn, or tack the rest of the way. In a word, the gale increased to a storm of wind and rain, attended with such a fog, that we could not see the town of Leith, to which we were bound, nor even the castle of Edinburgh, notwithstanding its high situation. It is not to be doubted but that we were all alarmed on this occasion. And at the same time, most of the passengers were seized with a nausea that produced violent retchings. My aunt desired her brother to order the boatmen to put back to Kinghorn, and this expedient he actually proposed; but they assured him there was no danger. Mrs. Tabitha finding them obstinate, began to scold, and insisted upon my uncle's exerting his authority as a justice of the peace. Sick and peevish as he was, he could not help laughing at this wise proposal, telling her, that his commission did not extend so far, and, if it did, he should let the people take their own way; for he thought it would be great presumption in him to direct them in the exercise of their own profession. Mrs. Winifred Jenkins made a general clearance with the assistance of Mr. Humphry Clinker, who joined her both in prayer and ejaculation.—As he took it for granted that we should not be long in this world, he offered some spiritual consolation to Mrs. Tabitha, who rejected it with great disgust, bidding him keep his sermons for those who had leisure to hear such nonsense.—My uncle sat, collected in himself, without speaking; my man Archy had recourse to a brandy-bottle, with which he made so free, that I imagined he had sworn to die of drinking any thing rather than sea-water: but the brandy had no more effect upon him in the way of intoxication, than if it had been sea-water in good earnest.—As for myself, I was too much engrossed by the sickness at my stomach, to think of any thing else.—Meanwhile the sea swelled mountains high, the boat pitched with such violence, as if it had been going to pieces; the cordage rattled, the wind roared; the lightning flashed, the thunder bellowed, and the rain descended in a deluge—Every time the vessel was put about, we ship'd a sea that drenched us all to the skin.—When, by dint of turning, we thought to have cleared the pier head, we were driven to leeward, and then the boatmen themselves began to fear that the tide would fail before we should fetch up our lee-way: the next trip, however, brought us into smooth water, and we were safely landed on the quay, about one o'clock in the afternoon.— 'To be sure (cried Tabby, when she found herself on *terra firma*,) we must all have perished, if we had not been the particular care of Providence.'—'Yes, (replied my uncle) but I am much of the honest highlander's mind—after he had made such a passage as this: his friend told him he was much indebted to Providence;—"Certainly, (said Donald) but, by my saul, mon, I'se ne'er trouble Providence again, so long as the brig of Stirling stands." ' ———You must know the brig, or bridge of Stirling, stands above twenty miles up the river Forth, of which this is the outlet—I don't find that our 'squire has suffered in his health from this adventure; but poor Liddy is in a peaking way—I'm afraid this unfortunate girl is uneasy in her mind; and this apprehension distracts me, for she is really an amiable creature.

We shall set out to-morrow or next day for Stirling and Glasgow; and we propose to penetrate a little way into the Highlands, before we turn our course to the southward— In the mean time, commend me to all our friends round Carfax, and believe me to be, ever yours,

J. MELFORD.

EDINBURGH, *Aug.* 8.

To Dr. Lewis

I should be very ungrateful, dear Lewis, if I did not find myself disposed to think and speak favourably of this people, among whom I have met with more kindness, hospitality, and rational entertainment, in a few weeks, than ever I received in any other country during the whole course of my life.—Perhaps, the gratitude excited by these benefits may interfere with the impartiality of my remarks; for a man is as apt to be prepossessed by particular favours as to be prejudiced by private motives of disgust. If I am partial, there is, at least, some merit in my conversation from illiberal prejudices which had grown up with my constitution.

The first impressions which an Englishman receives in this country, will not contribute to the removal of his prejudices; because he refers every thing he sees to a comparison with the same articles in his own country; and this comparison is unfavourable to Scotland in all its exteriors, such as the face of the country in respect to cultivation, the appearance of the bulk of the people, and the language of conversation in general.——I am not so far convinced by Mr. Lismahago's arguments, but that I think the Scots would do well, for their own sakes, to adopt the English idioms and pronunciation; those of them especially, who are resolved to push their fortunes in South-Britain——I know, by experience, how easily an Englishman is influenced by the ear, and how apt he is to laugh, when he hears his own language spoken with a foreign or provincial accent —I have known a member of the house of commons speak with great energy and precision, without being able to engage attention, because his observations were made in the Scotch dialect, which (no offence to lieutenant Lismahago) certainly gives a clownish air even to sentiments of the greatest dignity and decorum.——I have declared my opinion on this head to some of the most sensible men of this country, observing, at the same time, that if they would employ a few natives of England to teach the pronunciation of our vernacular tongue, in twenty years there would be no difference, in point of dialect, between the youth of Edinburgh and of London.

The civil regulations of this kingdom and metropolis are taken from very different models from those of England, except in a few particular establishments, the necessary consequences of the union.——Their college of justice is a bench of great dignity, filled with judges of character and ability.—I have heard some causes tried before this venerable tribunal; and was very much pleased with the pleadings of their advocates, who are by no means deficient either in argument or elocution. The Scottish legislation is founded, in a great measure, on the civil law; consequently, their proceedings vary from those of the English tribunals; but, I think, they have the advantage of us in their method of examining witnesses apart, and in the constitution of their jury, by which they certainly avoid the evil which I mentioned in my last from Lismahago's observation.

The university of Edinburgh is supplied with excellent professors in all the sciences; and the medical school, in particular, is famous all over Europe.—The students of this art have the best opportunity of learning it to perfection, in all its branches, as there are different courses for the *theory of medicine* and the *practice of medicine;* for *anatomy, chemistry, botany,* and the *materia medica,* over and above those of *mathematics* and *experimental philosophy;* and all these are given by men of distinguished talents. What renders this part of education still more complete, is the advantage of attending the infirmary, which is the best instituted charitable foundation that I ever knew. Now we are talking of charities, here are several hospitals, exceedingly well endowed, and maintained under admirable regulations; and these are not only useful, but ornamental to the city. Among these, I shall only mention the general work-house, in which all the poor, not otherwise provided for, are employed, according to their different abilities, with such judgment and effect, that they nearly maintain themselves by their labour, and there is not a beggar to be seen within the precincts of this metropolis. It was Glasgow that set the example of this establishment, about thirty years ago.—Even the kirk of Scotland, so long reproached with fanatacism and canting, abounds at present with ministers celebrated for their learning, and respectable for their moderation.—I have heard their sermons with equal astonishment and pleasure.——The good people of Edinburgh no longer think dirt and cobwebs essential to the house of God ——Some of their churches have admitted such ornaments as would have excited sedition, even in England, a little more than a century ago; and psalmody is here practised and taught by a professor from the cathedral of Durham:——I should not be surprised, in a few years, to hear it accompanied with an organ.

Edinburgh is a hot-bed of genius——I have had the good fortune to be made acquainted with many authors of the first distinction; such as the two Humes, Robertson, Smith, Wallace, Blair, Ferguson, Wilkie, &c. and I have found them all as agreeable in conversation as they are instructive and entertaining in their writings. These acquaintances I owe to the friendship of Dr. Carlyle, who wants nothing but inclination to figure with the rest upon paper. The magistracy of Edinburgh is changed every year by election, and seems to be very well adapted both for state and authority.——The *lord provost* is equal in dignity to the *lord mayor of London;* and the *four bailies* are equivalent to the rank of aldermen.——There is a *dean of guild,* who takes cognizance of mercantile affairs; a treasurer; a townclerk; and the council is composed of deacons, one of whom is returned every year, in rotation, as representative of every company of artificers or handicraftsmen. Though this city, from the nature of its situation, can never be made either very convenient or very cleanly, it has, nevertheless, an air of magnificence that commands respect.——The castle is an instance of the sublime in scite and architecture.——Its fortifications are kept in good order, and there is always in it a garrison of regular soldiers, which is relieved every year; but it is incapable of sustaining a siege carried on according to the modern operations of war.——The castle hill, which extends from the outward gate to the upper end of the high street, is used as a public walk for the citizens, and commands a prospect, equally extensive and delightful, over the county of Fife, on the other side of the Frith, and all along the sea-coast, which is covered with a succession of towns that would seem to indicate a considerable share of commerce; but, if the truth must be told, these towns have been falling to decay ever since the union, by which the Scots were in a great measure deprived of their trade with France.—The palace of Holyrood-house is a jewel in architecture, thrust into a hollow where it cannot be seen; a situation which was certainly not chosen by the ingenious architect, who must have been confined to the site of the old palace, which was a convent. Edinburgh is considerably extended on the south side, where there are divers little elegant squares built in the English manner; and the citizens have planned some improvements on the north, which, when put in execution, will add greatly to the beauty and convenience of this capital.

The sea-port is Leith, a flourishing town, about a mile from the city, in the harbour of which I have seen above one hundred ships lying all together. You must know, I had the curiosity to cross the Frith in a passage boat, and stayed two days in Fife, which is remarkably fruitful in corn, and exhibits a surprising number of fine seats, elegantly built, and magnificently furnished. There is an incredible number of noble houses in every part of Scotland that I have seen.—Dalkeith, Pinkie, Yester, and lord Hopton's, all of them within four or five miles of Edinburgh, are princely palaces, in every one of which a sovereign might reside at his ease—I suppose the Scots affect these monuments of grandeur—If I may be allowed to mingle censure with my remarks upon a people I revere, I must observe, that their weak side seems to be vanity—I am afraid that even their hospitality is not quite free of ostentation.—I think I have discovered among them uncommon pains taken to display their fine linen, of which, indeed, they have great plenty, their furniture, plate, housekeeping, and variety of wines, in which article, it must be owned, they are profuse, if not prodigal—A burgher of Edinburgh, not content to vie with a citizen of London, who has ten times his fortune, must excel him in the expence as well as elegance of his entertainments.

Though the villas of the Scotch nobility and gentry have generally an air of grandeur and state, I think their gardens and parks are not comparable to those of England; a circumstance the more remarkable, as I was told by the ingenious Mr. Phillip Miller of Chelsea, that almost all the gardeners of South-Britain were natives of Scotland. The verdure of this county is not equal to that of England.—— The pleasure-grounds are, in my opinion, not so well laid out according to the *genius loci;* nor are the lawns, and walks, and hedges kept in such delicate order—The trees are planted in prudish rows, which have not such an agreeable natural effect, as when they are thrown into irregular groups, with intervening glades; and firs, which they generally raise around their houses, look dull and funereal in the summer season.——I must confess, indeed, that they yield serviceable timber, and good shelter against the northern blasts; that they grow and thrive in the most barren soil, and continually perspire a fine balsam of turpentine, which must render the air very salutary and sanative to lungs of a tender texture.

Tabby and I have been both frightened in our return by sea from the coast of Fife——She was afraid of drowning, and I of catching cold, in consequence of being drenched with sea-water; but my fears as well as her's, have been happily disappointed.——She is now in perfect health; I wish I could say the same of Liddy——Something uncommon is the matter with that poor girl; her colour fades, her appetite fails, and her spirits flag—She is become moping and melancholy, and is often found in tears——Her brother suspects internal uneasiness on account of Wilson, and denounces vengeance against that adventurer.——She was, it seems, strongly affected at the ball by the sudden

appearance of one Mr. Gordon, who strongly resembles
the said Wilson; but I am rather suspicious that she caught
cold by being overheated with dancing.—I have consulted
Dr. Gregory, an eminent physician of an amiable character,
who advises the highland air, and the use of goat-milk
whey, which, surely, cannot have a bad effect upon a patient
who was born and bred among the mountains of Wales—
The doctor's opinion is the more agreeable, as we shall find
those remedies in the very place which I proposed as the
utmost extent of our expedition—I mean the borders of
Argyle.

Mr. Smollett, one of the judges of the commissary court,
which is now sitting, has very kindly insisted upon our lodging at his country-house, on the banks of Lough-Lomond,
about fourteen miles beyond Glasgow. For this last city we
shall set out in two days, and take Stirling in our way, well
provided with recommendations from our friends at Edinburgh, whom, I protest, I shall leave with much regret. I
am so far from thinking it any hardship to live in this
country, that, if I was obliged to lead a town life, Edinburgh would certainly be the headquarters of

Yours always,

MATT. BRAMBLE.

EDIN. *August* 8.

To Sir Watkin Phillips, Bart. of Jesus college, Oxon.

DEAR KNIGHT,

I am now little short of the *Ultima Thule*, if this
appellation properly belongs to the Orkneys or Hebrides.
These last are now lying before me, to the amount of
some hundreds, scattered up and down the Deucalidonian
sea, affording the most picturesque and romantic prospect I
ever beheld——I write this letter in a gentleman's house,
near the town of Inverary, which may be deemed the capital

of the West Highlands, famous for nothing so much as for the stately castle begun, and actually covered in by the late duke of Argyle, at a prodigious expence—Whether it will ever be completely finished is a question.——

But, to take things in order——We left Edinburgh ten days ago; and the further North we proceed, we find Mrs. Tabitha the less manageable; so that her inclinations are not of the nature of the loadstone; they point not towards the pole. What made her leave Edinburgh with reluctance at last, if we may believe her own assertions, was a dispute which she left unfinished with Mr. Moffat, touching the eternity of hell torments. That gentleman, as he advanced in years, began to be sceptical on this head, till, at length, he declared open war against the common acceptation of the word *eternal*. He is now persuaded, that *eternal* signifies no more than an indefinite number of years; and that the most enormous sinner may be quit for *nine millions, nine hundred thousand, nine hundred and ninety-nine years of hell-fire;* which term or period, as he very well observes, forms but an inconsiderable drop, as it were, in the ocean of eternity—For this mitigation he contends, as a system agreeable to the ideas of goodness and mercy, which we annex to the supreme Being—Our aunt seemed willing to adopt this doctrine in favour of the wicked; but he hinted that no person whatever was so righteous as to be exempted entirely from punishment in a future state; and that the most pious Christian upon earth might think himself very happy to get off for a fast of seven or eight thousand years in the midst of fire and brimstone. Mrs. Tabitha revolted at this dogma, which filled her at once with horror and indignation—She had recourse to the opinion of Humphry Clinker, who roundly declared it was the popish doctrine of purgatory, and quoted scripture in defence of the *fire everlasting, prepared for the devil and his angels*—The reverend master Mackcorkendal, and all the theologists and saints of that persuasion were consulted, and some of them had doubts about the matter; which doubts and scruples had begun to infect our aunt, when we took our departure from Edinburgh.

We passed through Linlithgow, where there was an elegant royal palace, which is now gone to decay, as well as the town itself—This too is pretty much the case with Stirling, though it still boasts of a fine old castle in which the kings of Scotland were wont to reside in their minority —But Glasgow is the pride of Scotland, and, indeed, it might very well pass for an elegant and flourishing city in any part of Christendom. There we had the good fortune to be received into the house of Mr. Moore, an eminent surgeon, to whom we were recommended by one of our friends at Edinburgh; and, truly, he could not have done us more essential service—Mr. Moore is a merry facetious companion, sensible and shrewd, with a considerable fund of humour; and his wife an agreeable woman, well bred, kind, and obliging—Kindness, which I take to be the essence of good-nature and humanity, is the distinguishing characteristic of the Scotch ladies in their own country—Our landlord shewed us every thing, and introduced us to all the world at Glasgow; where, through his recommendation, we were complimented with the freedom of the town. Considering the trade and opulence of this place, it cannot but abound with gaiety and diversions————Here is a great number of young fellows that rival the youth of the capital in spirit and expence; and I was soon convinced, that all the female beauties of Scotland were not assembled at the hunters ball in Edinburgh————The town of Glasgow flourishes in learning as well as in commerce—Here is an university, with professors in all the different branches of science, liberally endowed, and judiciously chosen—It was vacation time when I passed, so that I could not entirely satisfy my curiosity; but their mode of education is certainly preferable to ours in some respects—The students are not left to the private instruction of tutors; but taught in public schools or classes each science by its particular professor or regent.

My uncle is in raptures with Glasgow—He not only visited all the manufactures of the place, but made excursions all around, to Hamilton, Paisley, Renfrew, and every other place within a dozen miles, where there was any thing remarkable to be seen in art or nature. I believe the exercise, occasioned by those jaunts, was of service to my sister Liddy, whose appetite and spirits begin to revive—Mrs. Tabitha displayed her attractions as usual, and actually believed she had entangled one Mr. Maclellan, a rich inkle-manufacturer, in her snares; but when matters came to an explanation, it appeared that his attachment was altogether spiritual, founded upon an intercourse of devotion, at the meeting of Mr. John Wesley; who, in the course of his evangelical mission, had come hither in person—At length, we set out for the banks of Lough-Lomond, passing through the little borough of Dumbarton, or (as my uncle will have it) Dunbritton, where there is a castle, more curious than any thing of the kind I had ever seen—It is honoured with a particular description by the elegant Buchanan, as an *arx inexpugnabilis*, and, indeed, it must have been impregnable by the antient manner of besieging. It is a rock of considerable extent, rising with a double top, in an angle formed by the confluence of two rivers, the Clyde and the Leven; perpendicular and inaccessible on all sides, except in one place where the entrance is fortified; and there is no rising-ground in the neighbourhood from whence it could be damaged by any kind of battery.

From Dumbarton, the West Highlands appear in the form of huge, dusky mountains, piled one over another; but this prospect is not at all surprising to a native of Glamorgan—We have fixed our headquarters at Cameron, a very neat country-house belonging to commissary Smollet, where we found every sort of accommodation we could desire——It is situated like a Druid's temple, in a grove of oak, close by the side of Lough-Lomond, which is a surprising body of pure transparent water, unfathomably deep in many places, six or seven miles broad, four and twenty miles in length, displaying above twenty green islands, covered with wood; some of them cultivated for corn, and many of them stocked with red deer——They belong to different gentlemen, whose seats are scattered along the banks of the lake, which are agreeably romantic beyond all conception. My uncle and I have left the women at Cameron, as Mrs. Tabitha would by no means trust herself again upon the water, and to come hither it was necessary to cross a small inlet of the sea, in an open ferry-boat——This country appears more and more wild and savage the further we advance; and the people are as different from the Low-land Scots, in their looks, garb, and language, as the mountaineers of Brecknock are from the inhabitants of Herefordshire.

When the Lowlanders want to drink a chearupping-cup, they go to the public house, called the Change-house, and call for a chopine of two-penny, which is a thin, yeasty beverage, made of malt; not quite so strong as the table-beer of England——This is brought in a pewter stoop, shaped like a skittle, from whence it is emptied into a quaff; that is, a curious cup made of different pieces of wood, such as box and ebony, cut into little staves, joined alternately, and secured with delicate hoops, having two ears or handles——It holds about a gill, is sometimes tipt round the mouth with silver, and has a plate of the same metal at bottom, with the landlord's cypher engraved.——The Highlanders, on the contrary, despise this liquor, and regale themselves with whisky; a malt spirit, as strong as geneva, which they swallow in great quantities, without any signs of inebriation. They are used to it from the cradle, and find it an excellent preservative against the winter cold, which must be extreme on these mountains——I am told that it is given with great success to infants, as a cordial in the confluent small-pox, when the eruption seems to flag, and the symptoms grow unfavourable——The Highlanders are used to eat much more animal food than falls to the share of their neighbours in the Low-country—They delight in hunting; have plenty of deer and other game, with a great number of sheep, goats, and black-cattle running wild, which they scruple not to kill as venison, without being much at pains to ascertain the property.

Inverary is but a poor town, though it stands immediately under the protection of the duke of Argyle, who is a mighty prince in this part of Scotland. The peasants live in wretched cabins, and seem very poor; but the gentlemen are tolerably well lodged, and so loving to strangers, that a man runs some risque of his life from their hospitality— It must be observed that the poor Highlanders are now seen to disadvantage—They have been not only disarmed by act of parliament, but also deprived of their ancient garb, which was both graceful and convenient; and what is a greater hardship still, they are compelled to wear breeches; a restraint which they cannot bear with any degree of patience: indeed, the majority wear them, not in the proper place, but on poles or long staves over their shoulders———They are even debarred the use of their striped stuff called Tartane, which was their own manu- facture, prized by them above all the velvets, brocades, and tissues of Europe and Asia. They now lounge along in loose great coats, of coarse russet, equally mean and cum- bersome, and betray manifest marks of dejection—Certain it is, the government could not have taken a more effectual method to break their national spirit.

We have had princely sport in hunting the stag on these mountains—These are the lonely hills of Morven, where Fingal and his heroes enjoyed the same pastime; I feel an enthusiastic pleasure when I survey the brown heath that Ossian wont to tread; and hear the wind whistle through the bending grass———When I enter our landlord's hall, I look for the suspended harp of that divine bard, and listen in hopes of hearing the aerial sound of his respected spirit—

The poems of Ossian are in every mouth—A famous anti-quarian of this country, the laird of Macfarlane, at whose house we dined a few days ago, can repeat them all in the original Gallick, which has a great affinity to the Welch, not only in the general sound, but also in a great number of radical words; and I make no doubt but that they are both sprung from the same origin. I was not a little sur-prised, when asking a Highlander one day, if he knew where we should find any game? he replied, 'hu niel Sas-senagh,' which signifies no English: the very same answer I should have received from a Welchman, and almost in the same words. The Highlanders have no other name for the people of the Low-country, but Sassenagh, or Saxons; a strong presumption, that the Lowland Scots and the Eng-lish are derived from the same stock———The peasants of these hills strongly resemble those of Wales in their looks, their manners, and habitations; every thing I see, and hear, and feel, seems Welch—The mountains, vales, and streams; the air and climate; the beef, mutton, and game, are all Welch—It must be owned, however, that this people are better provided than we in some articles—They have plenty of red deer and roebuck, which are fat and delicious at this season of the year—Their sea teems with amazing quantities of the finest fish in the world; and they find means to pro-cure very good claret at a very small expence.

Our landlord is a man of consequence in this part of the country; a cadet from the family of Argyle and hereditary captain of one of his castles—His name, in plain English, is Dougal Campbell; but as there is a great number of the same appellation, they are distinguished (like the Welch) by patronimics; and as I have known an antient Briton called Madoc ap-Morgan, ap-Jenkin, ap-Jones, our High-land chief designs himself Dou'l Mac-amish mac-'oul ich-ian, signifying Dougal, the son of James, the son of Dougal, the son of John—He has travelled in the course of his edu-cation and is disposed to make certain alterations in his

domestic œconomy; but he finds it impossible to abolish the
ancient customs of the family; some of which are ludicrous
enough—His piper, for example, who is an hereditary officer of the household, will not part with the least particle of
his privileges.———He has a right to wear the kilt, or ancient
Highland dress, with the purse, pistol, and durk—a broad
yellow ribbon, fixed to the chanter-pipe, is thrown over his
shoulder, and trails along the ground, while he performs
the function of his minstrelsy; and this, I suppose, is analogous to the pennon or flag which was formerly carried
before every knight in battle.———He plays before the laird
every Sunday in his way to the kirk, which he circles three
times, performing the family march which implies defiance
to all the enemies of the clan; and every morning he plays
a full hour by the clock, in the great hall, marching backwards and forwards all the time, with a solemn pace, attended by the laird's kinsmen, who seem much delighted
with the music—In this exercise he indulges them with a
variety of pibrachs or airs, suited to the different passions,
which he would either excite or assuage.

Mr. Campbell himself, who performs very well on the
violin, has an invincible antipathy to the sound of the Highland bag-pipe, which sings in the nose with a most alarming
twang, and, indeed, is quite intolerable to ears of common
sensibility, when aggravated by the echo of a vaulted hall—
He therefore begged the piper would have some mercy upon
him, and dispense with this part of the morning service———
A consultation of the clan being held on this occasion, it was
unanimously agreed, that the laird's request could not be
granted without a dangerous encroachment upon the customs of the family—The piper declared, he could not give
up for a moment the privilege he derived from his ancestors;
nor would the laird's relations forego an entertainment
which they valued above all others—There was no remedy;
Mr. Campbell, being obliged to acquiesce, is fain to stop his
ears with cotton; to fortify his head with three or four night-

caps, and every morning retire into the penetralia of his habitation, in order to avoid this diurnal annoyance. When the music ceases, he produces himself at an open window that looks into the court-yard, which is by this time filled with a crowd of his vassals and dependants, who worship his first appearance, by uncovering their heads, and bowing to the earth with the most humble prostration. As all these people have something to communicate in the way of proposal, complaint, or petition, they wait patiently till the laird comes forth, and, following him in his walks, are favoured each with a short audience in his turn. Two days ago, he dispatched above an hundred different solicitors, in walking with us to the house of a neighbouring gentleman, where we dined by invitation. Our landlord's house-keeping is equally rough and hospitable, and savours much of the simplicity of ancient times: the great hall, paved with flat stones, is about forty-five feet by twenty-two, and serves not only for a dining-room, but also for a bed-chamber to gentlemen-dependents and hangers-on of the family. At night, half a dozen occasional beds are ranged on each side along the wall. These are made of fresh heath, pulled up by the roots, and disposed in such a manner as to make a very agreeable couch, where they lie, without any other covering than the plaid—My uncle and I were indulged with separate chambers and down beds which we begged to exchange for a layer of heath; and indeed I never slept so much to my satisfaction. It was not only soft and elastic, but the plant, being in flower, diffused an agreeable fragrance, which is wonderfully refreshing and restorative.

Yesterday we were invited to the funeral of an old lady, the grand-mother of a gentleman in this neighbourhood, and found ourselves in the midst of fifty people, who were regaled with a sumptuous feast, accompanied by the music of a dozen pipers. In short, this meeting had all the air of a grand festival; and the guests did such honour to the entertainment, that many of them could not stand when we were reminded of the business on which we had met. The company forthwith taking horse, rode in a very irregular cavalcade to the place of interment, a church, at the distance of two long miles from the castle. On our arrival, however, we found we had committed a small oversight, in leaving the corpse behind; so we were obliged to wheel about, and met the old gentle-woman half way, being carried upon poles by the nearest relations of her family, and attended by the *coronach*, composed of a multitude of old hags, who tore their hair, beat their breasts, and howled most hideously. At the grave, the orator, or *senachie*, pronounced the panegyric of the defunct, every period being confirmed by a yell of the *coronach*. The body was committed to the earth, the pipers playing a pibroch all the time; and all the company standing uncovered. The ceremony was closed with the discharge of pistols; then we returned to the castle, resumed the bottle, and by midnight there was not a sober person in the family, the females excepted. The 'squire and I were, with some difficulty, permitted to retire with our landlord in the evening; but our entertainer was a little chagrined at our retreat; and afterwards seemed to think it a disparagement to his family, that not above a hundred gallons of whisky had been drank upon such a solemn occasion. This morning we got up by four, to hunt the roebuck, and, in half an hour, found breakfast ready served in the hall. The hunters consisted of Sir George Colquhoun and me, as strangers, (my uncle not chusing to be of the party) of the *laird in person, the laird's brother, the laird's brother's son, the laird's sister's son, the laird's father's brother's son,* and all their *foster brothers,* who are counted parcel of the family: but we were attended by an infinite number of *Gaellys,* or ragged Highlanders without shoes or stockings.

The following articles formed our morning's repast: one kit of boiled eggs; a second, full of butter; a third full of cream; an entire cheese, made of goat's milk; a large

earthen pot full of honey; the best part of a ham; a cold
venison pasty; a bushel of oat meal, made in thin cakes
and bannocks, with a small wheaten loaf in the middle for
the strangers; a large stone bottle full of whisky, another
of brandy, and a kilderkin of ale. There was a ladle chained
to the cream kit, with curious wooden bickers to be filled
from this reservoir. The spirits were drank out of a silver
quaff, and the ale out of horns: great justice was done to
the collation by the guests in general; one of them in particular ate above two dozen of hard eggs, with a propor-
tionable quantity of bread, butter, and honey; nor was
one drop of liquor left upon the board. Finally, a large roll
of tobacco was presented by way of desert, and every individual took a comfortable quid, to prevent the bad effects
of the morning air. We had a fine chace over the mountains, after a roebuck, which we killed, and I got home
time enough to drink tea with Mrs. Campbell and our
'squire. To-morrow we shall set out on our return for
Cameron. We propose to cross the Frith of Clyde, and take
the towns of Greenock and Port-Glasgow in our way.
This circuit being finished, we shall turn our faces to the
south, and follow the fun with augmented velocity, in
order to enjoy the rest of the autumn in England, where
Boreas is not quite so biting as he begins already to be on
the tops of these northern hills. But our progress from place
to place shall continue to be specified in these detached
journals of,

Yours always,

J. MELFORD.

ARGYLESHIRE, *Sept.* 3.

To Dr. Lewis

DEAR DICK,

About a fortnight is now elapsed, since we left the
capital of Scotland, directing our course towards Stirling,

where we lay—The castle of this place is such another as that of Edinburgh, and affords a surprising prospect of the windings of the river Forth, which are so extraordinary, that the distance from hence to Alloa by land, is but four miles, and by water it is twenty-four. Alloa is a neat thriving town, that depends in a great measure on the commerce of Glasgow, the merchants of which send hither tobacco and other articles, to be deposited in warehouses for exportation from the Frith of Forth. In our way hither we visited a flourishing iron-work, where, instead of burning wood, they use coal, which they have the art of clearing in such a manner as frees it from the sulphur, that would otherwise render the metal too brittle for working. Excellent coal is found in almost every part of Scotland.

The soil of this district produces scarce any other grain but oats and barley; perhaps because it is poorly cultivated, and almost altogether uninclosed. The few inclosures they have consist of paultry walls of loose stones gathered from the fields, which indeed they cover, as if they had been scattered on purpose. When I expressed my surprize that the peasants did not disencumber their grounds of these stones; a gentleman, well acquainted with the theory as well as practice of farming, assured me that the stones, far from prejudicial, were serviceable to the crop. This philosopher had ordered a field of his own to be cleared, manured and sown with barley, and the produce was more scanty than before. He caused the stones to be replaced, and next year the crop was as good as ever. The stones were removed a second time, and the harvest failed; they were again brought back, and the ground retrieved its fertility. The same experiment has been tried in different parts of Scotland with the same success—Astonished at this information, I desired to know in what manner he accounted for this strange phenomenon; and he said there were three ways in which the stones might be serviceable. They might possibly restrain an excess in the perspiration of the earth, analogous to colliquative sweats, by which the human body is sometimes wasted and consumed. They might act as so many fences to protect the tender blade from the piercing winds of the spring; or, by multiplying the reflexion of the sun, they might increase the warmth, so as to mitigate the natural chilness of the soil and climate—But, surely this excessive perspiration might be more effectually checked by different kinds of manure, such as ashes, lime, chalk, or marl, of which last it seems there are many pits in this kingdom: as for the warmth, it would be much more equally obtained by inclosures; one half of the ground which is now covered, would be retrieved; the cultivation would require less labour; and the ploughs, harrows, and horses, would not suffer half the damage which they now sustain.

These north-western parts are by no means fertile in corn. The ground is naturally barren and moorish. The peasants are poorly lodged, meagre in their looks, mean in their apparel, and remarkably dirty. This last reproach they might easily wash off, by means of those lakes, rivers, and rivulets of pure water, with which they are so liberally supplied by nature. Agriculture cannot be expected to flourish where the farms are small, the leases short, and the husbandman begins upon a rack rent, without a sufficient stock to answer the purposes of improvement. The granaries of Scotland are the banks of the Tweed, the counties of East and Mid-Lothian, the Carse of Gowrie, in Perthshire, equal in fertility to any part of England, and some tracts in Aberdeen-shire and Murray, where I am told the harvest is more early than in Northumberland, although they lie above two degrees farther north. I have a strong curiosity to visit many places beyond the Forth and the Tay, such as Perth, Dundee, Montrose, and Aberdeen, which are towns equally elegant and thriving; but the season is too far advanced to admit of this addition to my original plan.

I am so far happy as to have seen Glasgow, which, to the best of my recollection and judgment, is one of the prettiest towns in Europe; and, without all doubt, it is one of the most flourishing in Great Britain. In short, it is a perfect bee-hive in point of industry. It stands partly on a gentle declivity, but the greatest part of it is in a plain, watered by the river Clyde. The streets are straight, open, airy, and well paved; and the houses lofty and well built of hewn stone. At the upper end of the town, there is a venerable cathedral, that may be compared with York-minster or West-minster; and, about the middle of the descent from this to the Cross, is the college, a respectable pile of building, with all manner of accommodation for the professors and students, including an elegant library, and a observatory well provided with astronomical instruments. The number of inhabitants is said to amount to thirty thousand; and marks of opulence and independency appear in every quarter of this commercial city, which, however, is not with-out its inconveniences and defects. The water of their public pumps is generally hard and brackish, an imperfection the less excusable, as the river Clyde runs by their doors, in the lower part of the town; and there are rivulets and springs above the cathedral, sufficient to fill a large reservoir with excellent water, which might be thence distributed to all the different parts of the city. It is of more consequence to consult the health of the inhabitants in this article, than to employ so much attention in beautifying their town with new streets, squares, and churches. Another defect, not so easily remedied, is the shallowness of the river, which will not float vessels of any burthen within ten or twelve miles of the city; so that the merchants are obliged to load and unload their ships at Greenock and Port-Glasgow, situated about fourteen miles nearer the mouth of the Frith, where it is about two miles broad.

The people of Glasgow have a noble spirit of enter-prise—Mr. Moore, a surgeon, to whom I was recom-mended from Edinburgh, introduced me to all the principal merchants of the place. Here I became acquainted with

Mr. Cochran, who may be stiled one of the sages of this kingdom. He was first magistrate at the time of the last rebellion. I sat as member when he was examined in the house of commons, upon which occasion Mr. P—— observed he had never heard such a sensible evidence given at that bar. I was also introduced to Dr. John Gordon, a patriot of a truly Roman spirit, who is the father of the linen manufacture in this place, and was the great promoter of the city workhouse, infirmary, and other works of public utility. Had he lived in ancient Rome, he would have been honoured with a statue at the public expence. I moreover conversed with one Mr. G—ssf—d, whom I take to be one of the greatest merchants in Europe. In the last war, he is said to have had at one time five and twenty ships with their cargoes, his own property, and to have traded for above half a million sterling a-year. The last war was a fortunate period for the commerce of Glasgow—The merchants, considering that their ships bound for America, launching out at once into the Atlantic by the north of Ireland, pursued a track very little frequented by privateers, resolved to insure one another, and saved a very considerable sum by this resolution, as few or none of their ships were taken——You must know I have a sort of national attachment to this part of Scotland—The great church dedicated to St. Mongah, the river Clyde, and other particulars that smack of our Welch language and customs, contribute to flatter me with the notion, that these people are the descendants of the Britons, who once possessed this country. Without all question, this was a Cumbrian kingdom: its capital was Dumbarton (a corruption of Dumbritton) which still exists as a royal borough, at the influx of the Clyde and Leven, ten miles below Glasgow. The same neighbourhood gave birth to St. Patrick, the apostle of Ireland, at a place where there is still a church and village, which retain his name. Hard by are some vestiges of the famous Roman wall, built in the reign of Antonine, from the Clyde to the Forth, and fortified with castles, to restrain the incursions of the Scots or Caledonians, who inhabited the West-Highlands. In a line parallel to this wall, the merchants of Glasgow have determined to make a navigable canal betwixt the two Friths, which will be of incredible advantage to their commerce, in transporting merchandize from one side of the island to the other.

From Glasgow we travelled along the Clyde, which is a delightful stream, adorned on both sides with villas, towns, and villages. Here is no want of groves, and meadows, and corn-fields interspersed; but on this side of Glasgow, there is little other grain than oats and barley; the first are much better, the last much worse, than those of the same species in England. I wonder, there is so little rye, which is a grain that will thrive in almost any soil; and it is still more surprising, that the cultivation of potatoes should be so much neglected in the Highlands, where the poor people have not meal enough to supply them with bread through the winter. On the other side of the river are the towns of Paisley and Renfrew. The first, from an inconsiderable village, is become one of the most flourishing places of the kingdom, enriched by the linen, cambrick, flowered lawn, and silk manufactures. It was formerly noted for a rich monastery of the monks of Clugny, who wrote the famous *Scoti-Chronicon*, called *The Black Book of Paisley*. The old abbey still remains, converted into a dwelling-house, belonging to the earl of Dundonald. Renfrew is a pretty town, on the banks of Clyde, capital of the shire, which was heretofore the patrimony of the Stuart family, and gave the title of baron to the king's eldest son, which is still assumed by the prince of Wales.

The Clide we left a little on our left-hand at Dunbritton, where it widens into an æstuary or frith, being augmented by the influx of the Leven. On this spot stands the castle formerly called Alcluyd, washed by these two rivers on all sides, except a narrow isthmus, which at every spring-tide

is overflowed. The whole is a great curiosity, from the
quality and form of the rock, as well as from the nature
of its situation——We now crossed the water of Leven,
which, though nothing near so considerable as the Clyde, is
much more transparent, pastoral, and delightful. This
charming stream is the outlet of Lough-Lomond, and
through a tract of four miles pursues its winding course,
murmuring over a bed of pebbles, till it joins the Frith at
Dunbritton. A very little above its source, on the lake, stands
the house of Cameron, belonging to Mr. Smollett, so em-
bosomed in an oak wood, that we did not see it till we were
within fifty yards of the door. I have seen the Lago di
Garda, Albano, De Vico, Bolsena, and Geneva, and, upon
my honour, I prefer Lough-Lomond to them all, a preference which is certainly owing to the verdant islands that
seem to float upon its surface, affording the most inchanting
objects of repose to the excursive view. Nor are the banks
destitute of beauties, which even partake of the sublime.
On this side they display a sweet variety of woodland, corn-
field, and pasture, with several agreeable villas emerging as
it were out of the lake, till, at some distance, the prospect
terminates in huge mountains covered with heath, which
being in the bloom, affords a very rich covering of purple.
Every thing here is romantic beyond imagination. This
country is justly stiled the Arcadia of Scotland; and I don't
doubt but it may vie with Arcadia in every thing but climate.——I am sure it excels it in verdure, wood, and
water.—What say you to a natural bason of pure water,
near thirty miles long, and in some places seven miles broad,
and in many above a hundred fathom deep, having four
and twenty habitable islands, some of them stocked with
deer, and all of them covered with wood, containing immense quantities of delicious fish, salmon, pike, trout, perch,
flounders, eels, and powans, the last a delicate kind of fresh-
water herring peculiar to this lake; and finally communi-
cating with the sea, by sending off the Leven, through which

all those species (except the powan) make their exit and entrance occasionally?

Inclosed I send you the copy of a little ode to this river, by Dr. Smollett, who was born on the banks of it, within two miles of the place where I am now writing.—It is at least picturesque and accurately descriptive, if it has no other merit.—There is an idea of truth in an agreeable landscape taken from nature, which pleases me more than the gayest fiction which the most luxuriant fancy can display.

I have other remarks to make; but as my paper is full, I must reserve them till the next occasion. I shall only observe at present, that I am determined to penetrate at least forty miles into the Highlands, which now appear like a vast fantastic vision in the clouds, inviting the approach of,

> Yours always,
>
> MATT. BRAMBLE.

CAMERON, *Aug.* 28.

ODE TO LEVEN-WATER.

On Leven's banks, while free to rove,
And tune the rural pipe to love;
I envied not the happiest swain
That ever trod th' Arcadian plain.

Pure stream! in whose transparent wave
My youthful limbs I wont to lave;
No torrents stain thy limpid source;
No rocks impede thy dimpling course,
That sweetly warbles o'er its bed,
With white, round, polish'd pebbles spread;
While, lightly pois'd, the scaly brood
In myriads cleave thy crystal flood;
The springing trout in speckled pride;
The salmon, monarch of the tide;

The ruthless pike, intent on war;
The silver eel, and motled par.[1]

Devolving from thy parent lake,
A charming maze thy waters make,
By bow'rs of birch, and groves of pine,
And hedges flow'r'd with eglantine.

Still on thy banks so gayly green,
May num'rous herds and flocks be seen,
And lasses chanting o'er the pail,
And shepherds piping in the dale,
And ancient faith that knows no guile,
And industry imbrown'd with toil,
And hearts resolv'd, and hands prepar'd,
The blessings they enjoy to guard.

To Dr. Lewis

DEAR DOCTOR,

If I was disposed to be critical, I should say this house
of Cameron is too near the lake, which approaches, on one
side, to within six or seven yards of the window. It might
have been placed in a higher site, which would have afforded
a more extensive prospect and a drier atmosphere; but this
imperfection is not chargeable on the present proprietor,
who purchased it ready built, rather than be at the trouble
of repairing his own family-house of Bonhill, which stands
two miles from hence on the Leven, so surrounded with
plantation, that it used to be known by the name of the
Mavis (or thrush) Nest. Above that house is a romantic
glen or clift of a mountain, covered with hanging woods
having at bottom a stream of fine water that forms a num-

---

[1] The par is a small fish, not unlike the smelt, which it rivals
in delicacy and flavour.

ber of cascades in its descent to join the Leven; so that the scene is quite enchanting. A captain of a man of war, who had made the circuit of the globe with Mr. Anson, being conducted to this glen, exclaimed, 'Juan Fernandez, by God!'

Indeed, this country would be a perfect paradise, if it was not, like Wales, cursed with a weeping climate, owing to the same cause in both, the neighbourhood of high mountains, and a westerly situation, exposed to the vapours of the Atlantic ocean. This air, however, notwithstanding its humidity, is so healthy, that the natives are scarce ever visited by any other disease than the small-pox, and certain cutaneous evils, which are the effects of dirty living, the great and general reproach of the commonalty of this kingdom. Here are a great many living monuments of longævity; and among the rest a person, whom I treat with singular respect, as a venerable druid, who has lived near ninety years, without pain or sickness, among oaks of his own planting.—He was once proprietor of these lands; but being of a projecting spirit, some of his schemes miscarried, and he was obliged to part with his possession, which hath shifted hands two or three times since that period; but every succeeding proprietor hath done every thing in his power, to make his old age easy and comfortable. He has a sufficiency to procure the necessaries of life; and he and his old woman resided in a small convenient farm-house, having a little garden which he cultivates with his own hands. This ancient couple live in great health, peace, and harmony, and, knowing no wants, enjoy the perfection of content. Mr. Smollett calls him the admiral, because he insists upon steering his pleasure-boat upon the lake; and he spends most of his time in ranging through the woods, which he declares he enjoys as much as if they were still his own property—I asked him the other day, if he was never sick, and he answered, Yes; he had a slight fever the year before the union. If he was not deaf, I should take much pleasure in his conversation;

for he is very intelligent, and his memory is surprisingly retentive.——These are the happy effects of temperance, exercise, and good nature——Notwithstanding all his innocence, however, he was the cause of great perturbation to my man Clinker, whose natural superstition has been much injured, by the histories of witches, fairies, ghosts, and goblins, which he has heard in this country——On the evening after our arrival Humphry strolled into the wood, in the course of his meditation, and all at once the admiral stood before him, under the shadow of a spreading oak. Though the fellow is far from being timorous in cases that are not supposed preternatural, he could not stand the sight of this apparition, but ran into the kitchen, with his hair standing on end, staring wildly, and deprived of utterance. Mrs. Jenkins, seeing him in this condition, screamed aloud, 'Lord have mercy upon us, he has seen something!' Mrs. Tabitha was alarmed, and the whole house in confusion. When he was recruited with a dram, I desired him to explain the meaning of all this agitation; and, with some reluctance, he owned he had seen a spirit, in the shape of an old man with a white beard, a black cap, and a plaid night-gown. He was undeceived by the admiral in person, who, coming in at this juncture, appeared to be a creature of real flesh and blood.

Do you know how we fare in this Scottish paradise? We make free with our landlord's mutton, which is excellent, his poultry-yard, his garden, his dairy, and his cellar, which are all well stored. We have delicious salmon, pike, trout, perch, par, &c. at the door, for the taking. The Frith of Clyde, on the other side of the hill, supplies us with mullet, red and grey, cod, mackarel, whiting, and a variety of sea-fish, including the finest fresh herrings I ever tasted. We have sweet, juicy beef, and tolerable veal, with delicate bread from the little town of Dunbritton; and plenty of partridge, growse, heath cock, and other game in presents.

We have been visited by all the gentlemen in the neigh-

bourhood, and they have entertained us at their houses, not
barely with hospitality, but with such marks of cordial
affection, as one would wish to find among near relations,
after an absence of many years.

I told you, in my last, I had projected an excursion to
the Highlands, which project I have now happily executed,
under the auspices of Sir George Colquhoun, a colonel in
the Dutch service, who offered himself as our conductor
on this occasion. Leaving our women at Cameron, to the
care and inspection of Lady H———— C————, we set out
on horseback for Inverary, the county town of Argyle, and
dined on the road with the Laird of Macfarlane, the greatest genealogist I ever knew in any country, and perfectly
acquainted with all the antiquities of Scotland.

The Duke of Argyle has an old castle in Inverary, where
he resides when he is in Scotland; and hard by is the shell
of a noble Gothic palace, built by the last duke, which,
when finished, will be a great ornament to this part of the
Highlands. As for Inverary, it is a place of very little
importance.

This country is amazingly wild, especially towards the
mountains, which are heaped upon the backs of one another, making a most stupendous appearance of savage
nature, with hardly any signs of cultivation, or even of
population. All is sublimity, silence, and solitude. The people
live together in glens or bottoms, where they are sheltered
from the cold and storms of winter; but there is a margin
of plain ground spread along the sea side, which is well
inhabited and improved by the arts of husbandry; and this I
take to be one of the most agreeable tracts of the whole
island; the sea not only keeps it warm, and supplies it with
fish, but affords one of the most ravishing prospects in the
whole world; I mean the appearance of the Hebrides, or
Western Islands to the number of three hundred, scattered
as far as the eye can reach, in the most agreeable confusion.
As the soil and climate of the Highlands are but ill adapted

to the cultivation of corn, the people apply themselves chiefly to the breeding and feeding of black cattle, which turn to good account. Those animals run wild all the winter, without any shelter or subsistence, but what they can find among the heath. When the snow lies so deep and hard, that they cannot penetrate to the roots of the grass, they make a diurnal progress, guided by a sure instinct, to the sea-side at low water, where they feed on the *alga marina*, and other plants that grow upon the beach.

Perhaps this branch of husbandry, which requires very little attendance and labour, is one of the principal causes of that idleness and want of industry, which distinguishes these mountaineers in their own country—When they come forth into the world, they become as diligent and alert as any people upon earth. They are undoubtedly a very distinct species from their fellow subjects of the Lowlands, against whom they indulge an ancient spirit of animosity; and this difference is very discernible even among persons of family and education. The Lowlanders are generally cool and circumspect, the Highlanders fiery and ferocious: but this violence of their passions serves only to inflame the zeal of their devotion to strangers, which is truly enthusiastic.

We proceeded about twenty miles beyond Inverary, to the house of a gentleman, a friend of our conductor, where we stayed a few days, and were feasted in such a manner, that I began to dread the consequence to my constitution.

Notwithstanding the solitude that prevails among these mountains, there is no want of people in the Highlands. I am credibly informed that the duke of Argyle can assemble five thousand men in arms, of his own clan and surname, which is Campbell; and there is besides a tribe of the same appellation, whose chief is the Earl of Breadalbine. The Macdonalds are as numerous, and remarkably warlike: the Camerons, M'Leods, Frasers, Grants, M'Kenzies, M'Kays, M'Phersons, M'Intoshes, are powerful clans; so that if all the Highlanders, including the inhabitants of the Isles, were united, they could bring into the field an army of forty thousand fighting men, capable of undertaking the most dangerous enterprise. We have lived to see four thousand of them, without discipline, throw the whole kingdom of Great Britain into confusion. They attacked and defeated two armies of regular troops accustomed to service. They penetrated into the centre of England; and afterwards marched back with deliberation, in the face of two other armies, through an enemy's country, where every precaution was taken to cut off their retreat. I know not any other people in Europe, who, without the use or knowledge of arms, will attack regular forces sword in hand, if their chief will head them in battle. When disciplined, they cannot fail of being excellent soldiers. They do not walk like the generality of mankind, but trot and bounce like deer, as if they moved upon springs. They greatly excel the Lowlanders in all the exercises that require agility; they are incredibly abstemious, and patient of hunger and fatigue; so steeled against the weather, that in travelling, even when the ground is covered with snow, they never look for a house, or any other shelter but their plaid, in which they wrap themselves up, and go to sleep under the cope of heaven. Such people, in quality of soldiers, must be invincible, when the business is to perform quick marches in a difficult country, to strike sudden strokes, beat up the enemy's quarters, harrass their cavalry, and perform expeditions without the formality of magazines, baggage, forage, and artillery. The chieftainship of the Highlanders is a very dangerous influence operating at the extremity of the island, where the eyes and hands of government cannot be supposed to see an act with precision and vigour. In order to break the force of clanship, administration has always practised the political maxim, *Divide et impera*. The legislature hath not only disarmed these mountaineers, but also deprived them of their antient garb, which contributed in a great measure to keep up their military spirit; and their slavish tenures are all dissolved by act of parliament; so that they are at present as free and independent of their chiefs, as the law can make them: but the original attachment still remains, and is founded on something prior to the *feudal system*, about which the writers of this age have made such a pother, as if it was a new discovery, like the *Copernican system*. Every peculiarity of policy, custom, and even temperament, is affectedly traced to this origin, as if the feudal constitution had not been common to almost all the natives of Europe. For my part, I expect to see the use of trunk-hose and buttered ale ascribed to the influence of the *feudal system*. The connection between the clans and their chiefs is, without all doubt, *patriarchal*. It is founded on hereditary regard and affection, cherished through a long succession of ages. The clan consider the chief as their father, they bear his name, they believe themselves descended from his family, and they obey him as their lord, with all the ardour of filial love and veneration; while he, on his part, exerts a paternal authority, commanding, chastising, rewarding, protecting, and maintaining them as his own children. If the legislature would entirely destroy this connection, it must compel the Highlanders to change their habitation and their names. Even this experiment has been formerly tried without success—— In the reign of James VI a battle was fought within a few short miles of this place, between two clans, the M'Gregors and the Colquhouns, in which the latter were defeated: the Laird of M'Gregor made such a barbarous use of his victory, that he was forfeited and outlawed by act of parliament: his lands were given to the family of Montrose, and his clan were obliged to change their name. They obeyed so far, as to call themselves severally Campbell, Graham, or Drummond, the surnames of the families of Argyle, Montrose, and Perth, that they might enjoy the protection of those houses; but they still added M'Gregor to their new appellation; and as their chief was deprived of his estate, they robbed and plundered for his subsistence.—Mr. Cameron of Lochiel, the chief of that clan, whose father was attainted for having been concerned in the last rebellion, returning from France in obedience to a proclamation and act of parliament, passed at the beginning of the late war, payed a visit to his own country, and hired a farm in the neighbourhood of his father's house, which had been burnt to the ground. The clan, though ruined and scattered, no sooner heard of his arrival than they flocked to him from all quarters, to welcome his return, and in a few days stocked his farm with seven hundred black cattle, which they had saved in the general wreck of their affairs: but their beloved chief, who was a promising youth, did not live to enjoy the fruits of their fidelity and attachment.

The most effectual method I know to weaken, and at length destroy this influence, is to employ the commonalty in such a manner as to give them a taste of property and independence—In vain the government grants them advantageous leases on the forfeited estates, if they have no property to prosecute the means of improvement—The sea is an inexhaustible fund of riches; but the fishery cannot be carried on without vessels, casks, salt, lines, nets, and other tackle. I conversed with a sensible man of this country, who, from a real spirit of patriotism had set up a fishery on the coast, and a manufacture of coarse linen, for the employment of the poor Highlanders. Cod is here in such plenty, that he told me he had seen several hundred taken on one line, at one hawl——It must be observed, however, that the line was of immense length, and had two thousand hooks, baited with muscles; but the fish was so superior to the cod caught on the banks of Newfoundland, that his correspondent at Lisbon sold them immediately at his own price, although Lent was just over when they arrived, and the people might be supposed quite cloyed with this kind of diet ——His linen manufacture was likewise in a prosperous way, when the late war intervening, all his best hands were pressed into the service.

It cannot be expected, that the gentlemen of this country should execute commercial schemes to render their vassals independent; nor, indeed, are such schemes suited to their way of life and inclination; but a company of merchants might, with proper management, turn to good account a fishery established in this part of Scotland——Our people have a strange itch to colonize America, when the unculti-vated parts of our own island might be settled to greater advantage.

After having rambled through the mountains and glens of Argyle, we visited the adjacent islands of Ila, Jura, Mull, and Icolmkill. In the first, we saw the remains of a castle, built in a lake, where Macdonald, lord or king of the isles, formerly resided. Jura is famous for having given birth to one Mackcrain, who lived one hundred and eighty years in one house, and died in the reign of Charles the Second. Mull affords several bays, where there is safe anchorage: in one of which, the Florida, a ship of the Spanish armada, was blown up by one of Mr. Smollett's ancestors—About forty years ago, John duke of Argyle is said to have consulted the Spanish registers, by which it appeared, that this ship had the military chest on board— He employed experienced divers to examine the wreck; and they found the hull of the vessel still entire, but so covered with sand, that they could not make their way between decks; however, they picked up several pieces of plate, that were scattered about in the bay, and a couple of fine brass cannon.

Icolmkill, or Iona, is a small island which St. Columba chose for his habitation—It was respected for its sanctity, and college or seminary of ecclesiastics—Part of its church is still standing, with the tombs of several Scottish, Irish, and Danish sovereigns, who were here interred—These islanders are very bold and dexterous watermen, consequently the better adapted to the fishery: in their manners they are less savage and impetuous than their countrymen on the con-

tinent; and they speak the Erse or Gaelick in its greatest
purity.

Having sent round our horses by land, we embarked in
the distinct of Cowal, for Greenock, which is a neat little
town, on the other side of the Frith, with a curious harbour
formed by three stone jetties, carried out a good way into
the sea——Newport-Glasgow is such another place, about
two miles higher up—Both have a face of business and
plenty, and are supported entirely by the shipping of Glasgow, of which I counted sixty large vessels in these harbours——Taking boat again at Newport, we were in less
than an hour landed on the other side, within two short
miles of our head-quarters, where we found our women
in good health and spirits—They had been two days before
joined by Mr. Smollett and his lady, to whom we have such
obligations as I cannot mention, even to you, without blush-
ing.

To-morrow we shall bid adieu to the Scotch Arcadia,
and begin our progress to the southward, taking our way
by Lanerk and Nithsdale, to the west borders of England.
I have received so much advantage and satisfaction from this
tour, that if my health suffers no revolution in the winter,
I believe I shall be tempted to undertake another expedition
to the Northern extremity of Caithness, unencumbered by
those impediments which now clog the heels of,

Yours,
MATT. BRAMBLE.

CAMERON, Sept. 6.

To Miss Lætitia Willis, at Gloucester

MY DEAREST LETTY,

Never did poor prisoner long for deliverance, more
than I have longed for an opportunity to disburthen my
cares into your friendly bosom; and the occasion which

now presents itself, is little less than miraculous——Honest Saunders Macawly, the travelling Scotchman, who goes every year to Wales, is now at Glasgow, buying goods, and coming to pay his respects to our family, has undertaken to deliver this letter into your own hand——We have been six weeks in Scotland, and seen the principal towns of the kingdom, where we have been treated with great civility ——The people are very courteous; and the country being exceedingly romantic, suits my turn and inclinations——I contracted some friendships at Edinburgh, which is a large and lofty city, full of gay company; and, in particular, commenced an intimate correspondence with one miss R——t——n, an amiable young lady of my own age, whose charms seemed to soften, and even to subdue the stubborn heart of my brother Jery; but he no sooner left the place than he relpased into his former insensibility—— I feel, however, that this indifference is not the family constitution—I ne'er admitted but one idea of love, and that has taken such root in my heart, as to be equally proof against all the pulls of discretion, and the frosts of neglect.

Dear Letty! I had an alarming adventure at the hunters ball in Edinburgh——While I sat discoursing with a friend in a corner, all at once the very image of Wilson stood before me, dressed exactly as he was in the character of Aimwell! It was one Mr. Gordon, whom I had not seen before——Shocked at the sudden apparition, I fainted away, and threw the whole assembly in confusion——However, the cause of my disorder remained a secret to every body but my brother, who was likewise struck with the resemblance, and scolded after we came home—I am very sensible of Jery's affection, and know he spoke as well with a view to my own interest and happiness, as in regard to the honour of the family; but I cannot bear to have my wounds probed severely—I was not so much affected by the censure he passed upon my own indiscretion, as with

the reflection he made on the conduct of Wilson—He observed, that if he was really the gentleman he pretended to
be, and harboured nothing but honourable designs he would
have vindicated his pretensions in the face of day—This
remark made a deep impression upon my mind——I endeavoured to conceal my thoughts; and this endeavour had
a bad effect upon my health and spirits; so it was thought
necessary that I should go to the Highlands, and drink the
goat-milk-whey.

We went accordingly to Lough Lomond, one of the
most enchanting spots in the whole world; and what with
this remedy, which I had every morning fresh from the
mountains, and the pure air, and chearful company, I have
recovered my flesh and appetite; though there is something
still at bottom, which it is not in the power of air, exercise,
company, or medicine to remove——These incidents would
not touch me so nearly, if I had a sensible confidant to
sympathize with my affliction, and comfort me with wholesome advice—I have nothing of this kind, except Win
Jenkins, who is really a good body in the main, but very
ill qualified for such an office.—The poor creature is weak
in her nerves, as well as in her understanding; otherwise I
might have known the true name and character of that
unfortunate youth—But why do I call him *unfortunate?*
perhaps the epithet is more applicable to me for having listened to the false professions of —— But, hold! I have
as yet no right, and sure I have no inclination to believe any
thing to the prejudice of his honour—In that reflection I
shall still exert my patience—As for Mrs. Jenkins, she
herself is really an object of compassion—Between vanity,
methodism, and love, her head is almost turned. I should
have more regard for her, however, if she had been more
constant in the object of her affection; but, truly, she aimed
at conquest, and flirted at the same time with my uncle's
footman, Humphry Clinker, who is really a deserving
young man, and one Dutton, my brother's valet de chambre.

a debauched fellow; who, leaving Win in the lurch, ran away with another man's bride at Berwick.

My dear Willis, I am truly ashamed of my own sex——We complain of advantages which the men take of our youth, inexperience, insensibility, and all that; but I have seen enough to believe, that our sex in general make it their business to ensnare the other; and for this purpose, employ arts which are by no means to be justified——In point of constancy, they certainly have nothing to reproach the male part of the creation—My poor aunt, without any regard to her years and imperfections, has gone to market with her charms in every place where she thought she had the least chance to dispose of her person, which, however, hangs still heavy on her hands—I am afraid she has used even religion as a decoy, though it has not answered her expectation——She has been praying, preaching, and catechising among the methodists, with whom this country abounds; and pretends to have such manifestations and revelations, as even Clinker himself can hardly believe, though the poor fellow is half crazy with enthusiasm. As for Jenkins, she affects to take all her mistress's reveries for gospel—She has also her heart-heavings and motions of the spirit; and God forgive me if I think uncharitably, but all this seems to me to be downright hypocrisy and deceit—Perhaps, indeed the poor girl imposes on herself—She is generally in a flutter, and is much subject to vapours—Since we came to Scotland, she has seen apparitions, and pretends to prophesy——If I could put faith in all these supernatural visitations, I should think myself abandoned of grace; for I have neither seen, heard, nor felt any thing of this nature, although I endeavour to discharge the duties of religion with all the sincerity, zeal, and devotion, that is in the power of,

Dear Letty,
your ever affectionate,
LYDIA MELFORD.

GLASGOW, *Sept.* 7.

We are so far on our return to Brambleton-hall; and I would fain hope we shall take Gloucester in our way, in which case I shall have the inexpressible pleasure of embracing my dear Willis—Pray remember me to my worthy governess.

To Mrs. Mary Jones, at Brambleton-hall

DEAR MARY,

Sunders Macully, the Scotchman, who pushes directly to Vails, has promised to give it you into your own hand, and therefore I would not miss the opportunity to let you know as I am still in the land of the living: and yet I have been on the brink of the other world since I sent you my last letter.—We went by sea to another kingdom called Fife, and coming back, had like to have gone to pot in a storm. —What between the frite and sickness, I thought I should have brought my heart up; even Mr. Clinker was not his own man for eight and forty hours after we got ashore.— It was well for some folks that we scaped drownding; for mistress was very frexious, and seemed but indifferently prepared for a change; but, thank God, she was soon put in a better frame by the private exaltations of the reverend Mr. Macrocodile.—We afterwards churned to Starling and Grascow, which are a kiple of handsome towns; and then we went to a gentleman's house at Loff-Loming, which is a wonderful sea of fresh water, with a power of hylands in the midst on't.—They say as how it has n'er a bottom, and was made by a musician; and, truly, I believe it; for it is not in the coarse of nature.—It has got *waves without wind, fish without fins, and a floating hyland;* and one of them is a crutch-yard, where the dead are buried; and always before the person dies, a bell rings of itself to give warning.

O Mary! this is the land of congyration—The bell

knolled when we were there—I saw lights, and heard lamentations.—The gentleman, our landlord, has got another
house, which he was fain to quit, on account of a mischievous ghost, that would not suffer people to lie in their beds.
—The fairies dwell in a hole of Kairmann, a mounting
hard by; and they steal away the good women that are
in the straw, if so be as how there a'n't a horshoe nailed
to the door: and I was shewn an ould vitch, called Elspath
Ringavey, with a red petticoat, bleared eyes, and a mould
of grey bristles on her sin.—That she mought do me no
harm, I crossed her hand with a taster, and bid her tell my
fortune; and she told me such things—descriving Mr.
Clinker to a hair—but it shall ne'er be said, that I min-
chioned a word of the matter.—As I was troubled with fits,
she advised me to bathe in the loff, which was holy water;
and so I went in the morning to a private place along with
the house-maid, and we bathed in our birth-day soot, after the
fashion of the country; and behold whilst we dabbled in the
loff, Sir George Coon started up with a gun; but we clapt
our hands to our faces, and passed by him to the place where
we had left our smocks—A civil gentleman would have
turned his head another way.—My comfit is, he new not
which was which; and, as the saying is, *all cats in the
dark are grey.*——Whilst we stayed at Loff-Loming, he
and our two 'squires went three or four days churning
among the wild men of the mountings; a parcel of selvidges
that lie in caves among the rocks, devour young children,
speak Velch, but the vords are different. Our ladies would
not part with Mr. Clinker, because he is so stout and so
pyehouse, that he fears neither man nor devils, if so be
as they don't take him by surprise.—Indeed, he was once so
flurried by an operition, that he had like to have sounded.
—He made believe as if it had been the ould edmiral; but
the old edmiral could not have made his air to stand on end,
and his teeth to shatter; but he said so in prudence, that the
ladies mought not be afear'd. Miss Liddy has been puny,

and like to go into a decline—I doubt her pore art is too tinder—but the got's-fey has set her on her legs again.—You nows got's-fey is mother's milk to a Velch-woman. As for mistress, blessed be God, she ails nothing.—Her stomick is good, and she improves in grease and godliness; but, for all that, she may have infections like other people, and I believe, she wouldn't be sorry to be called *your lady-ship*, whenever Sir George thinks proper to ax the question —But, for my part, whatever I may see or hear, not a praticle shall ever pass the lips of,

Dear Molly,

Your loving friend,

WIN. JENKINS.

GRASCO, *Sept.* 7.

Remember me, as usual, to Sall.—We are now coming home, though not the nearest road.——I do suppose, I shall find the kitten a fine boar at my return.

To Sir Watkin Phillips, Bart. at Oxon.

DEAR KNIGHT,

Once more I tread upon English ground, which I like not the worse for the six weeks' ramble I have made among the woods and mountains of Caledonia; no offence to the *land of cakes, where bannocks grow upon straw.* I never saw my uncle in such health and spirits as he now enjoys. Liddy is perfectly recovered; and Mrs. Tabitha has no reason to complain. Nevertheless, I believe, she was, till yesterday, inclined to give the whole Scotch nation to the devil, as a pack of insensible brutes, upon whom her accomplishments had been displayed in vain.—At every place where we halted, did she mount the stage, and flourished her rusty arms, without being able to make one conquest. One of her last essays was against the heart of Sir George Colquhoun, with whom she fought all the weapons more than twice over.——She was grave and gay by turns—she moralized and methodized—she laughed, and romped, and danced, and sung, and sighed, and ogled, and lisped, and fluttered, and flattered—but all was preaching to the desart —The baronet, being a well-bred man, carried his civilities as far as she could in conscience expect, and, if evil tongues are to be believed, some degrees farther; but he was too much a veteran in gallantry, as well as in war, to fall into any ambuscade that she could lay for his affection —While we were absent in the Highlands, she practised also upon the laird of Ladrishmore, and even gave him the rendezvous in the wood of Drumscailloch; but the laird had such a reverend care of his own reputation, that he came attended with the parson of the parish, and nothing passed but spiritual communication.——After all these miscarriages, our aunt suddenly recollected lieutenant Lismahago, whom, ever since our first arrival at Edinburgh, she seemed to have utterly forgot; but now she expressed her hopes of seeing him at Dumfries, according to his promise.

We set out from Glasgow by the way of Lanerk, the county-town of Clydesdale, in the neighbourhood of which, the whole river Clyde, rushing down a steep rock, forms a very noble and stupendous cascade. Next day we were obliged to halt in a small borough, until the carriage, which had received some damage, should be repaired; and here we met with an incident which warmly interested the benevolent spirit of Mr. Bramble—As we stood at the window of an inn that fronted the public prison, a person arrived on horseback, genteelly, tho' plainly, dressed in a blue frock, with his own hair cut short, and a gold-laced hat upon his head.—Alighting, and giving his horse to the landlord, he advanced to an old man who was at work in paving the street, and accosted him in these words 'This is hard work for such an old man as you.'—So saying, he took the instrument out of his hand, and began to thump the pavement.—After a few strokes, 'Have you never a son (said

he) to ease you of this labour?' 'Yes, an please your honour,
(replied the senior) I have three hopeful lads, but, at present, they are out of the way.' 'Honour not me (cried the
stranger); it more becomes me to honour your grey hairs.
—Where are those sons you talk of?' The ancient paviour
said, his eldest son was a captain in the East Indies; and the
youngest had lately inlisted as a soldier, in hopes of prosper-
ing like his brother. The gentleman desiring to know what
was become of the second, he wiped his eyes, and owned,
he had taken upon him his old father's debts, for which he
was now in the prison hard by.

The traveller made three quick steps towards the jail,
then turning short, 'Tell me, (said he) has that unnatural
captain sent you nothing to relieve your distresses?' 'Call him
not unnatural (replied the other); God's blessing be upon
him! he sent me a great deal of money; but I made a bad
use of it; I lost it by being security for a gentleman that
was my landlord, and was stript of all I had in the world
besides.' At that instant a young man, thrusting out his head
and neck between two iron bars in the prison-window, exclaimed, 'Father! father! if my brother William is in life,
that's he!' 'I am!—I am!—(cried the stranger, clasping
the old man in his arms, and shedding a flood of tears)—I
am your son Willy, sure enough!' Before the father, who
was quite confounded, could make any return to this tenderness, a decent old woman bolting out from the door of a
poor habitation, cried, 'Where is my bairn? where is my
dear Willy?'—The captain no sooner beheld her, than he
quitted his father, and ran into her embrace.

I can assure you, my uncle, who saw and heard every thing
that passed, was as much moved as any one of the parties
concerned in this pathetic recognition——He sobbed, and
wept, and clapped his hands, and hollowed, and finally ran
down into the street. By this time, the captain had retired
with his parents, and all the inhabitants of the place were
assembled at the door.——Mr. Bramble, nevertheless, pressed

thro' the crowd, and entering the house, 'Captain (said he) I beg the favour of your acquaintance——I would have travelled a hundred miles to see this affecting scene; and I shall think myself happy if you and your parents will dine with me at the public house.' The captain thanked him for his kind invitation, which, he said, he would accept with pleasure, but in the mean time, he could not think of eating or drinking, while his poor brother was in trouble. He forthwith deposited a sum equal to the debt in the hands of the magistrate, who ventured to set his brother at liberty without farther process; and then the whole family repaired to the inn with my uncle, attended by the crowd, the individuals of which shook their townsmen by the hand, while he returned their caresses without the least sign of pride or affectation.

This honest favourite of fortune, whose name was Brown, told my uncle, that he had been bred a weaver, and, about eighteen years ago, had, from a spirit of idleness and dissipation, enlisted as a soldier in the service of the East-India company; that, in the course of duty, he had the good fortune to attract the notice and approbation of Lord Clive, who preferred him from one step to another, till he attained the rank of captain and pay-master to the regiment, in which capacities he had honestly amassed above twelve thousand pounds, and, at the peace, resigned his commission.——He had sent several remittances to his father, who received the first only, consisting of one hundred pounds; the second had fallen into the hands of a bankrupt; and the third had been consigned to a gentleman of Scotland, who died before it arrived; so that it still remained to be accounted for by his executors. He now presented the old man with fifty pounds for his present occasions, over and above bank notes for one hundred, which he had deposited for his brother's release. ——He brought along with him a deed ready executed, by which he settled a perpetuity of four-score pounds upon his parents, to be inherited by their other two sons after their decease.——He promised to purchase a commission for his youngest brother; to take the other as his own partner in a manufacture which he intended to set up, to give employment and bread to the industrious; and to give five hundred pounds, by way of dower, to his sister, who had married a farmer in low circumstances.——Finally, he gave fifty pounds to the poor of the town where he was born, and feasted all the inhabitants without exception.

My uncle was so charmed with the character of captain Brown, that he drank his health three times successively at dinner—he said, he was proud of his acquaintance; that he was an honour to his country, and had in some measure redeemed human nature from the reproach of pride, selfishness, and ingratitude.——For my part, I was as much pleased with the modesty as with the filial virtue of this honest soldier, who assumed no merit from his success, and said very little of his own transactions, though the answers he made to our inquiries were equally sensible and laconic. Mrs. Tabitha behaved very graciously to him until she understood that he was going to make a tender of his hand to a person of low estate, who had been his sweet-heart while he worked as a journeyman weaver.——Our aunt was no sooner made acquainted with this design, than she starched up her behaviour with a double proportion of reserve; and when the company broke up, she observed with a toss of her nose, that Brown was a civil fellow enough, considering the lowness of his original; but that Fortune, though she had mended his circumstances, was incapable to raise his ideas, which were still humble and plebeian.

On the day that succeeded this adventure, we went some miles out of our road to see Drumlanrig, a seat belonging to the duke of Queensberry, which appears like a magnificent palace erected by magic, in the midst of a wilderness.—— It is indeed a princely mansion, with suitable parks and plantations, rendered still more striking by the nakedness of the surrounding country, which is one of the wildest tracts in all Scotland.—This wilderness, however, is different from that of the Highlands; for here the mountains, instead of heath, are covered with a fine green swarth, affording pasture to innumerable flocks of sheep. But the fleeces of this country, called Nithsdale, are not comparable to the wool of Galloway, which is said to equal that of Salisbury plain. Having passed the night at the castle of Drumlanrig, by invitation from the duke himself, who is one of the best men that ever breathed, we prosecuted our journey to Dumfries, a very elegant trading town near the borders of England, where we found plenty of good provision and excellent wine, at very reasonable prices, and the accommodation as good in all respects as in any part of South-Britain.—If I was confined to Scotland for life, I would chuse Dumfries as the place of my residence. Here we made enquiries about captain Lismahago, of whom hearing no tidings, we proceeded by the Solway Frith, to Carlisle. You must know, that the Solway sands, upon which travellers pass at low water, are exceedingly dangerous, because, as the tide makes, they become quick in different places, and the flood rushes in so impetuously, that the passengers are often overtaken by the sea and perish.

In crossing these treacherous Syrtes with a guide, we perceived a drowned horse, which Humphry Clinker, after due inspection, declared to be the very identical beast which Mr. Lismahago rode when he parted with us at Feltonbridge in Northumberland. This information, which seemed to intimate that our friend the lieutenant had shared the fate of his horse, affected us all, and above all our aunt Tabitha, who shed salt tears, and obliged Clinker to pull a few hairs out of the dead horse's tail, to be worn in a ring as a remembrance of his master: but her grief and ours was not of long duration; for one of the first persons we saw in Carlisle, was the lieutenant *in propria persona*, bargaining with a horse-dealer for another steed, in the yard of the inn where we alighted.—Mrs. Bramble was the first that perceived him, and screamed as if she had seen a ghost; and, truly, at a proper time and place, he might very well have passed for an inhabitant of another world; for he was more meagre and grim than before.——We received him the more cordially for having supposed he had been drowned; and he was not deficient in expressions of satisfaction at this meeting.——He told us, he had enquired for us at Dumfries, and been informed by a travelling merchant from Glasgow, that we had resolved to return by the way of Coldstream.——He said, that in passing the sands without a guide, his horse had knocked up, and he himself must have perished, if he had not been providentially relieved by a return post-chaise.——He moreover gave us to understand, that his scheme of settling in his own country having miscarried, he was so far on his way to London, with a view to embark for North-America, where he intended to pass the rest of his days among his old friends the Miamis, and amuse himself in finishing the education of the son he had by his beloved Squinkinacoosta.

This project was by no means agreeable to our good aunt, who expatiated upon the fatigues and dangers that would attend such a long voyage by sea, and afterwards such a tedious journey by land——She enlarged particularly on the risque he would run, with respect to the concerns of his precious soul, among savages who had not yet received the glad tidings of salvation; and she hinted that his abandoning Great-Britain might, perhaps, prove fatal to the inclinations of some deserving person, whom he was qualified to make happy for life. My uncle, who is really a Don Quixote in generosity, understanding that Lismahago's real reason for leaving Scotland was the impossibility of subsisting in it with any decency upon the wretched provision of a subaltern's half-pay, began to be warmly interested on the side of compassion.——He thought it very hard, that a gentleman who had served his country with honour, should be driven by necessity to spend his old age, among the refuse

of mankind, in such a remote part of the world.——He discoursed with me upon the subject; observing, that he would
willingly offer the lieutenant an asylum at Brambleton-hall,
if he did not foresee that his singularities and humour of
contradiction would render him an intolerable house-mate,
though his conversation at some times might be both instructive and entertaining: but, as there seemed to be something
particular in his attention to Mrs. Tabitha, he and I agreed
in opinion, that this intercourse should be encouraged and improved, if possible, into a matrimonial union; in which case
there would be a comfortable provision for both; and they
might be settled in a house of their own, so that Mr.
Bramble should have no more of their company than he
desired.

In pursuance of this design, Lismahago has been invited
to pass the winter at Brambleton-hall, as it will be time
enough to execute his American project in the spring.——He
has taken time to consider of this proposal; mean while, he
will keep us company as far as we travel in the road to
Bristol, where he has hopes of getting a passage for America.
I make no doubt but that he will postpone his voyage, and
prosecute his addresses to a happy consummation; and sure,
if it produces any fruit, it must be of a very peculiar flavour.
As the weather continues favourable, I believe, we shall take
the Peak of Derbyshire and Buxton Wells in our way.——
At any rate, from the first place where we make any stay,
you shall hear again from

Yours always,
J. MELFORD.

CARLISLE, *Sep.* 12.

To Dr. Lewis

DEAR DOCTOR,

The peasantry of Scotland are certainly on a poor footing all over the kingdom; and yet they look better, and are

better cloathed than those of the same rank in Burgundy, and many other places of France and Italy; nay, I will venture to say they are better fed, notwithstanding the boasted wine of these foreign countries. The country people of North-Britain live chiefly on oat-meal, and milk, cheese, butter, and some garden-stuff, with now and then a pickled-herring, by way of delicacy; but flesh-meat they seldom or never taste; nor any kind of strong liquor, except two-penny, at times of uncommon festivity—Their breakfast is a kind of hasty pudding, of oat-meal or pease-meal, eaten with milk. They have commonly pottage for dinner, composed of cale or cole, leeks, barley or big, and butter; and this is reinforced with bread and cheese, made of skimmed-milk—At night they sup on sowens or flummery of oat-meal—In a scarcity of oats, they use the meal of barley and pease, which is both nourishing and palatable. Some of them have potatoes; and you find parsnips in every peasant's garden—They are cloathed with a coarse kind of russet of their own making, which is both decent and warm—They dwell in poor huts, built of loose stones and turf, without any mortar, having a fireplace or hearth in the middle, generally made of an old mill-stone, and a hole at top to let out the smoke.

These people, however, are content, and wonderfully sagacious—All of them read the Bible, and are even qualified to dispute upon the articles of their faith; which in those parts I have seen, is entirely Presbyterian. I am told, that the inhabitants of Aberdeenshire are still more acute. I once knew a Scotch gentleman at London, who had declared war against this part of his countrymen; and swore that the impudence and knavery of the Scots, in that quarter, had brought a reproach upon the whole nation.

The river Clyde, above Glasgow, is quite pastoral; and the banks of it are every where adorned with fine villas. From the sea to its source, we may reckon the seats of many families of the first rank, such as the duke of Argyle at Roseneath, the earl of Bute in the isle of that name, the earl of Glencairn at Finlayston, lord Blantrye at Areskine, the dutchess of Douglas at Bothwell, duke Hamilton at Hamilton, the duke of Douglas at Douglas, and the earl of Hyndford at Carmichael. Hamilton is a noble palace, magnificently furnished; and hard by is the village of that name, one of the neatest little towns I have seen in any country. The old castle of Douglas being burned to the ground by accident, the late duke resolved, as head of the first family of Scotland, to have the largest house in the kingdom, and ordered a plan for this purpose; but there was only one wing of it finished when he died. It is to be hoped that his nephew, who is now in possession of his great fortune, will complete the design of his predecessor—Clydesdale is in general populous and rich, containing a great number of gentlemen, who are independent in their fortune; but it produces more cattle than corn—This is also the case with Tweedale, through part of which we passed, and Nithsdale, which is generally rough, wild, and mountainous—These hills are covered with sheep; and this is the small delicious mutton, so much preferable to that of the London-market. As their feeding costs so little, the sheep are not killed till five years old, when their flesh, juices, and flavour are in perfection; but their fleeces are much damaged by the tar, with which they are smeared to preserve them from the rot in winter, during which they run wild night and day, and thousands are lost under huge wreaths of snow——'Tis pity the farmers cannot contrive some means to shelter this useful animal from the inclemencies of a rigorous climate, especially from the perpetual rains, which are more prejudicial than the greatest extremity of cold weather.

On the little river Nid, is situated the castle of Drumlanrig, one of the noblest seats in Great-Britain, belonging to the duke of Queensberry; one of those few noblemen whose goodness of heart does honour to human-nature—

I shall not pretend to enter into a description of this palace, which is really an instance of the sublime in magnificence, as well as in situation, and puts one in mind of the beautiful city of Palmyra, rising like a vision in the midst of the wilderness. His grace keeps open house, and lives with great splendour—He did us the honour to receive us with great courtesy, and detain'd us all night, together with above twenty other guests, with all their servants and horses to a very considerable number—The dutchess was equally gracious, and took our ladies under her immediate protection. The longer I live, I see more reason to believe that prejudices of education are never wholly eradicated, even when they are discovered to be erroneous and absurd. Such habits of thinking as interest the grand passions, cleave to the human heart in such a manner, that though an effort of reason may force them from their hold for a moment, this violence no sooner ceases, than they resume their grasp with an increased elasticity and adhesion.

I am led into this reflection, by what passed at the duke's table after supper. The conversation turned upon the vulgar notions of spirits and omens, that prevail among the commonalty of North-Britain, and all the company agreed, that nothing could be more ridiculous. One gentleman, however, told a remarkable story of himself, by way of speculation— 'Being on a party of hunting in the North, (said he) I resolved to visit an old friend, whom I had not seen for twenty years—So long he had been retired and sequestered from all his acquaintance, and lived in a moping melancholy way, much afflicted with lowness of spirits, occasioned by the death of his wife, whom he had loved with uncommon affection. As he resided in a remote part of the country, and we were five gentlemen with as many servants, we carried some provision with us from the next market town, lest we should find him unprepared for our reception. The roads being bad, we did not arrive at the house till two o'clock in the afternoon; and were agreeably surprised to find a very good dinner ready in the kitchen, and the cloth laid with six covers. My friend himself appeared in his best apparel at the gate, and received us with open arms telling me he had been expecting us these two hours—Astonished at this declaration, I asked who had given him intelligence of our coming? and he smiled without making any other reply—However, presuming upon our former intimacy, I afterwards insisted upon knowing; and he told me, very gravely, he had seen me in a vision of the second sight—Nay, he called in the evidence of his steward, who solemnly declared, that his master had the day before apprised him of my coming, with four other strangers, and ordered him to provide accordingly; in consequence of which intimation, he had prepared the dinner which we were now eating; and laid the covers according to the number foretold.' The incident we all owned to be remarkable, and I endeavoured to account for it by natural means. I observed, that as the gentleman was of a visionary turn, the casual idea, or remembrance of his old friend, might suggest those circumstances, which accident had for once realized; but that in all probability he had seen many visions of the same kind, which were never verified. None of the company directly dissented from my opinion; but from the objections that were hinted, I could plainly perceive, that the majority were persuaded there was something more extraordinary in the case.

Another gentleman of the company, addressing himself to me, 'Without all doubt, (said he) a diseased imagination is very apt to produce visions; but we must find some other method to account for something of this kind, that happened within these eight days in my neighbourhood——A gentleman of a good family, who cannot be deemed a visionary in any sense of the word, was near his own gate, in the twilight, visited by his grandfather, who has been dead these fifteen years—The spectre was mounted seemingly on the very horse he used to ride, with an angry and

terrible countenance, and said something, which his grandson, in the confusion of fear, could not understand. But
this was not all—He lifted up a huge horse whip, and
applied it with great violence to his back and shoulders, on
which I saw the impression with my own eyes. The apparition was afterwards seen by the sexton of the parish, hover-
ing about the tomb where his body lies interred; as the man
declared to several persons in the village, before he knew
what had happened to the gentleman—Nay, he actually
came to me as a justice of the peace, in order to make oath
of these particulars, which, however, I declined administer-
ing. As for the grandson of the defunct, he is a sober,
sensible, worldly minded fellow, too intent upon schemes of
interest to give in to reveries. He would have willingly
concealed the affair; but he bawled out in the first transport
of his fear, and, running into the house, exposed his back
and his sconce to the whole family; so that there was no
denying it in the sequel. It is now the common discourse
of the country, that this appearance and behaviour of the
old man's spirit, portends some great calamity to the family,
and the good-woman has actually taken to her bed in this
apprehension.'

Though I did not pretend to explain this mystery, I said,
I did not at all doubt, but it would one day appear to be a
deception; and, in all probability, a scheme executed by
some enemy of the person who had sustained the assault;
but still the gentleman insisted upon the clearness of the
evidence, and the concurrence of testimony, by which two
creditable witnesses, without any communication one with
another, affirmed the appearance of the same man, with
whose person they were both well acquainted—From Drumlanrig we pursued the course of the Nid to Dumfries, which
stands seven miles above the place where the river falls into
the sea; and is, after Glasgow, the handsomest town I have
seen in Scotland—The inhabitants, indeed, seem to have
proposed that city as their model; not only in beautifying

their town and regulating its police, but also in prosecuting their schemes of commerce and manufacture, by which they are grown rich and opulent.

We re-entered England, by the way of Carlisle, where we accidentally met with our friend Lismahago, whom we had in vain inquired after at Dumfries and other places— It would seem that the captain, like the prophets of old, is but little honoured in his own country, which he has now renounced for ever—He gave me the following particulars of his visit to his native soil—In his way to the place of his nativity, he learned that his nephew had married the daughter of a burgeois, who directed a weaving manufacture, and had gone into partnership with his father-in-law: chagrined with this information, he had arrived at the gate in the twilight, where he heard the sound of treddles in the great hall, which had exasperated him to such a degree, that he had like to have lost his senses: while he was thus transported with indignation, his nephew chanced to come forth, when, being no longer master of his passion, he cried, 'Degenerate rascal! you have made my father's house a den of thieves;' and at the same time chastised him with his horse-whip; then, riding round the adjoining village, he had visited the burying-ground of his ancestors by moon-light; and, having paid his respects to their *manes*, travelled all night to another part of the country—— Finding the head of the family in such a disgraceful situation, all his own friends dead or removed from the places of their former residence, and the expence of living increased to double of what it had been, when he first left his native country, he had bid it an eternal adieu, and was determined to seek for repose among the forests of America.

I was no longer at a loss to account for the apparition, which had been described at Drumlanrig; and when I repeated the story to the lieutenant, he was much pleased to think his resentment had been so much more effectual than he intended; and he owned, he might at such an hour, and in such an equipage, very well pass for the ghost of his father, whom he was said greatly to resemble————Between friends, I fancy Lismahago will find a retreat without going so far as the wigwams of the Miamis. My sister Tabby is making continual advances to him, in the way of affection; and, if I may trust to appearances, the captain is disposed to take opportunity by the forelock. For my part, I intend to encourage this correspondence, and shall be glad to see them united——In that case, we shall find a way to settle them comfortably in our own neighbourhood. I, and my servants, will get rid of a very troublesome and tyrannic gouvernante; and I shall have the benefit of Lismahago's conversation, without being obliged to take more of his company than I desire; for though an olla is a high-flavoured dish, I could not bear to dine upon it every day of my life.

I am much pleased with Manchester, which is one of the most agreeable and flourishing towns in Great-Britain; and I perceive that this is the place which hath animated the spirit, and suggested the chief manufactures of Glasgow. We propose to visit Chatsworth, the Peak, and Buxton, from which last place we shall proceed directly homewards, though by easy journies. If the season has been as favourable in Wales as in the North, your harvest is happily finished; and we have nothing left to think of but our October, of which let Barns be properly reminded. You will find me much better in flesh than I was at our parting; and this short separation has given a new edge to those sentiments of friendship with which I always have been, and ever shall be,

yours,
MATT. BRAMBLE.

MANCHESTER, *Sept.* 15.

To Mrs. Gwyllim, house-keeper at Brambleton-hall

MRS. GWYLLIM,

It has pleased Providence to bring us safe back to England, and partake us in many pearls by land and water, in particular the *Devil's Harse a pike*, and *Hoyden's Hole*, which hath got no bottom; and, as we are drawing huom-wards, it may be proper to uprise you, that Brambleton-hall may be in a condition to receive us, after this long gurney to the islands of Scotland. By the first of next month you may begin to make constant fires in my brother's chamber and mine; and burn a fagget every day in the yellow damask room: have the tester and curtains dusted, and the feather-bed and matrosses well haired, because, perhaps, with the blissing of haven, they may be yoosed on some occasion. Let the ould hogsheads be well skewred and seasoned for bear, as Mat is resolved to have his seller choak fool.

If the house was mine, I would turn over a new leaf ————I don't see why the sarvants of Wales shouldn't drink fair water, and eat hot cakes and barley cale, as they do in Scotland, without troubling the botcher above once a quarter —I hope you keep accunt of Roger's purseeding in rever-ence to the buttermilk. I expect my dew when I come huom, without baiting an ass, I'll assure you.——As you must have layed a great many more eggs than would be eaten, I do suppose there is a power of turks, chickings, and guzzling about the house; and a brave kergo of cheese ready for market; and that the owl has been sent to Crickhowel, saving what the maids spun in the family.

Pray let the whole house and furniture have a thorough cleaning from top to bottom, for the honour of Wales; and let Roger search into, and make a general clearance of the slit holes, which the maids have in secret; for I know they are much given to sloth and uncleanness. I hope you have worked a reformation among them, as I exhorted you in my last, and set their hearts upon better things than they can find in junkitting and caterwauling with the fellows of the country.

As for Win Jenkins, she has undergone a perfect meta-murphysis, and is become a new creeter from the ammuni-

tion of Humphrey Clinker, our new footman, a pious young
man, who has laboured exceedingly, that she may bring
forth fruits of repentance. I make no doubt but he will
take the same pains with that pert hussey Mary Jones, and
all of you; and that he may have power given to penetrate
and instill his goodness, even into your most inward parts,
is the fervent prayer of

Your friend in the spirit,
TAB. BRAMBLE.

Septr. 18.

To Dr. Lewis

DEAR LEWIS,

Lismahago is more paradoxical than ever.—The late
gulp he had of his native air, seems to have blown fresh
spirit into all his polemical faculties. I congratulated him
the other day on the present flourishing state of his country,
observing that the Scots were now in a fair way to wipe off
the national reproach of poverty, and expressing my satisfaction at the happy effects of the union, so conspicuous in
the improvement of their agriculture, commerce, manufactures, and manners—The lieutenant, screwing up his features into a look of dissent and disgust, commented on my
remarks of this effect—'Those who reproach a nation for
its poverty, when it is not owing to the profligacy or vice
of the people, deserve no answer. The Lacedæmonians were
poorer than the Scots, when they took the lead among all
the free states of Greece, and were esteemed above them
all for their valour and their virtue. The most respectable
heroes of ancient Rome, such as Fabricius, Cincinnatus, and
Regulus, were poorer than the poorest freeholder in Scotland; and there are at this day individuals in North-Britain,
one of whom can produce more gold and silver than the
whole republic of Rome could raise at those times when

her public virtue shone with unrivalled lustre; and poverty was so far from being a reproach, that it added fresh laurels to her fame, because it indicated a noble contempt of wealth, which was proof against all the arts of corruption—If poverty be a subject for reproach, it follows that wealth is the object of esteem and veneration——In that case, there are Jews and others in Amsterdam and London, enriched by usury, peculation, and different species of fraud and extortion, who are more estimable than the most virtuous and illustrious members of the community. An absurdity which no man in his senses will offer to maintain.——Riches are certainly no proof of merit: nay they are often (if not most commonly) acquired by persons of sordid minds and mean talents: nor do they give any intrinsic worth to the possessor; but, on the contrary, tend to pervert his understanding, and render his morals more depraved. But, granting that poverty were really matter of reproach, it cannot be justly imputed to Scotland. No country is poor that can supply its inhabitants with the necessaries of life, and even afford articles for exportation. Scotland is rich in natural advantages: it produces every species of provision in abundance, vast herds of cattle and flocks of sheep, with a great number of horses; prodigious quantities of wool and flax, with plenty of copse wood, and in some parts large forests of timber. The earth is still more rich below than above the surface. It yields inexhaustible stores of coal, freestone, marble, lead, iron, copper, and silver, with some gold. The sea abounds with excellent fish, and salt to cure them for exportation; and there are creeks and harbours round the whole kingdom, for the convenience and security of navigation. The face of the country displays a surprising number of cities, towns, villas, and villages, swarming with people; and there seems to be no want of art, industry, government, and police: such a kingdom can never be called poor, in any sense of the word, though there may be many others more powerful and opulent. But the proper use of those advantages, and the present prosperity of the Scots, you seem to derive from the union of the two kingdoms!'

I said, I supposed he would not deny that the appearance of the country was much mended; that the people lived better, had more trade, and a greater quantity of money circulating since the union, than before. 'I may safely admit these premises, (answered the lieutenant) without subscribing to your inference. The difference you mention, I should take to be the natural progress of improvement————Since that period, other nations, such as the Swedes, the Danes, and in particular the French, have greatly increased in commerce, without any such cause assigned. Before the union, there was a remarkable spirit of trade among the Scots, as appeared in the case of their Darien company, in which they had embarked no less than four hundred thousand pounds sterling; and in the flourishing state of the maritime towns in Fife, and on the eastern coast, enriched by their trade with France, which failed in consequence of the union. The only solid commercial advantage reaped from that measure, was the privilege of trading to the English plantations; yet, excepting Glasgow and Dumfries, I don't know any other Scotch towns concerned in that traffick. In other respects, I conceive the Scots were losers by the union.—They lost the independency of their state, the greatest prop of national spirit; they lost their parliament, and their courts of justice were subjected to the revision and supremacy of an English tribunal.'

'Softly, captain (cried I) you cannot be said to have lost your own parliament, while you are represented in that of Great-Britain.' 'True, (said he, with a sarcastic grin) in debates of national competition, the sixteen peers and forty-five commoners of Scotland, must make a formidable figure in the scale, against the whole English legislature.' 'Be that as it may (I observed) while I had the honour to sit in the lower house, the Scotch members had always the majority on their side.' 'I understand you, Sir, (said he) they generally side with the majority; so much the worse for their constituents. But even this evil is not the worst they have sustained by the union. Their trade has been saddled with grievous impositions, and every article of living severely taxed, to pay the interest of enormous debts, contracted by the English, in support of measures and connections in which the Scots had no interest nor concern.' I begged he would at least allow, that by the union the Scots were admitted to all the privileges and immunities of English subjects; by which means multitudes of them were provided for in the army and navy, and got fortunes in different parts of England, and its dominions. 'All these (said he) become English subjects to all intents and purposes, and are in a great measure lost to their mother-country. The spirit of rambling and adventure has been always peculiar to the natives of Scotland. If they had not met with encouragement in England, they would have served and settled, as formerly in other countries, such as Muscovy, Sweden, Denmark, Poland, Germany, France, Piedmont, and Italy, in all which nations their descendants continue to flourish even at this day.'

By this time my patience began to fail, and I exclaimed, 'For God's sake, what has England got by this union which, you say, has been so productive of misfortune to the Scots.' 'Great and manifold are the advantages which England derives from the union (said Lismahago, in a solemn tone). First and foremost, the settlement of the protestant succession, a point which the English ministry drove with such eagerness, that no stone was left unturned, to cajole and bribe a few leading men, to cram the union down the throats of the Scottish nation, who were surprisingly averse to the expedient. They gained by it a considerable addition of territory, extending their dominion to the sea on all sides of the island, thereby shutting up all back-doors against the enterprizes of their enemies. They got an accession of above a million of useful subjects, constituting a never-failing nursery of seamen, soldiers, labourers, and mechanics; a most valuable acquisition to a trading country, exposed to foreign wars, and obliged to maintain a number of settle ments in all the four quarters of the globe. In the course of seven years, during the last war, Scotland furnished the English army and navy with seventy thousand men, over and above those who migrated to their colonies, or mingled with them at home in the civil departments of life. This was a very considerable and seasonable supply to a nation, whose people had been for many years decreasing in num- ber, and whose lands and manufactures were actually suf- fering for want of hands. I need not remind you of the hackneyed maxim, that, to a nation in such circumstances, a supply of industrious people is a supply of wealth; nor repeat an observation, which is now received as an eternal truth, even among the English themselves, that the Scots who settle in South-Britain are remarkably sober, orderly, and industrious.'

I allowed the truth of this remark, adding that by their industry, œconomy, and circumspection, many of them in England, as well as in her colonies, amassed large fortunes, with which they returned to their own country, and this was so much lost to South-Britain.——'Give me leave, sir, (said he) to assure you, that in your fact you are mistaken, and in your deduction erroneous.——Not one in two hun- dred that leave Scotland ever returns to settle in his own country; and the few that do return, carry thither nothing that can possibly diminish the stock of South-Britain; for none of their treasure stagnates in Scotland—There is a continual circulation, like that of the blood in the human body, and England is the heart, to which all the streams which it distributes are refunded and returned: nay, in consequence of that luxury which our connexion with Eng- land hath greatly encouraged, if not introduced, all the produce of our lands, and all the profits of our trade, are engrossed by the natives of South-Britain; for you will find that the exchange between the two kingdoms is always against Scotland; and that she retains neither gold nor silver sufficient for her own circulation.——The Scots, not content with their own manufactures and produce, which would very well answer all necessary occasions, seem to vie with each other in purchasing superfluities from England; such as broad-cloth, velvets, stuffs, silks, lace, furs, jewels, furniture of all sorts, sugar, rum, tea, chocolate, and coffee; in a word, not only every mode of the most extravagant luxury, but even many articles of convenience, which they might find as good, and much cheaper in their own country. For all these particulars, I conceive, England may touch about one million sterling a year.——I don't pretend to make an exact calculation; perhaps, it may be something less, and perhaps, a great deal more. The annual revenue arising from all the private estates of Scotland cannot fall short of a million sterling; and, I should imagine, their trade will amount to as much more.——I know the linen manufacture alone returns near half a million, exclusive of the home-consumption of that article.——If, therefore, North-Britain pays a ballance of a million annually to England, I insist upon it, that country is more valuable to her in the way of commerce, than any colony in her possession, over and above the other advantages which I have specified: therefore, they are no friends, either to England or to truth who affect to depreciate the northern part of the united kingdom.'

I must own, I was at first a little nettled to find myself schooled in so many particulars.——Though I did not receive all his assertions as gospel, I was not prepared to refute them; and I cannot help now acquiescing in his remarks so far as to think, that the contempt for Scotland, which prevails too much on this side the Tweed, is founded on prejudice and error.——After some recollection, 'Well, captain, (said I) you have argued stoutly for the importance of your own country: for my part, I have such a regard for our fellow-subjects of North-Britain, that I shall be glad to see the day, when your peasants can afford to give all their oats to their cattle, hogs, and poultry, and indulge themselves with good wheaten loaves, instead of such poor, unpalatable, and inflammatory diet.' Here again I brought my self into a premunire with the disputative Caledonian. He said he hoped he should never see the common people lifted out of that sphere for which they were intended by nature and the course of things; that they might have some reason to complain of their bread, if it were mixed, like that of Norway, with saw dust and fish-bones; but that oatmeal was, he apprehended, as nourishing and salutary as wheat-flour, and the Scots in general thought it at least as savoury. —He affirmed, that a mouse, which, in the article of self-preservation, might be supposed to act from infallible instinct, would always prefer oats to wheat, as appeared from experience; for, in a place where there was a parcel of each, that animal had never begun to feed upon the latter till all the oats were consumed: for their nutritive quality, he appealed to the hale, robust constitutions of the people who lived chiefly upon oatmeal; and, instead of being inflammatory, he asserted, that it was a cooling sub-acid, balsamic and mucilaginous; insomuch that in all inflammatory distempers, recourse was had to water-gruel, and flummery made of oatmeal.

'At least, (said I) give me leave to wish them such a degree of commerce as may enable them to follow their own inclinations.'————'Heaven forbid! (cried this philosopher). Woe be to that nation, where the multitude is at liberty to follow their own inclinations! Commerce is undoubtedly a blessing, while restrained within its proper channels; but a glut of wealth brings along with it a glut of evils: it brings false taste, false appetite, false wants, profusion, venality, contempt of order, engendering a spirit of licentiousness, insolence, and faction, that keeps the community in continual ferment, and in time destroys all the distinctions of civil society; so that universal anarchy and uproar must ensue. Will any sensible man affirm, that the national advantages of opulence are to be sought on these terms?' 'No, sure; but I am one of those who think, that, by proper regulations, commerce may produce every national benefit, without the allay of such concomitant evils.'

So much for the dogmata of my friend Lismahago, whom I describe the more circumstantially, as I firmly believe he will set up his rest in Monmouthshire. Yesterday, while I was alone with him, he asked, in some confusion, if I should have any objection to the success of a gentleman and a soldier, provided he should be so fortunate as to engage my sister's affection. I answered without hesitation, that my sister was old enough to judge for herself; and that I should be very far from disapproving any resolution she might take in his favour.—His eyes sparkled at this declaration. He declared, he should think himself the happiest man on earth to be connected with my family; and that he should never be weary of giving me proofs of his gratitude and attachment. I suppose Tabby and he are already agreed; in which case, we shall have a wedding at Brambleton-hall, and you shall give away the bride.—It is the least thing you can do, by way of atonement for your former cruelty to that poor love-sick maiden, who has been so long a thorn in the side of

Yours,

MATT. BRAMBLE.

Sept. 20.

We have been at Buxton; but, as I did not much relish either the company or the accommodations, and had no occasion for the water, we stayed but two nights in the place.

To Sir Watkin Phillips, Bart. of Jesus college, Oxon.

DEAR WAT,

Adventures begin to thicken as we advance to the southward.—Lismahago has now professed himself the admirer of our aunt, and carries on his addresses under the sanction of her brother's approbation; so that we shall certainly have a wedding by Christmas. I should be glad you was present at the nuptials, to help me to throw the stocking, and perform other ceremonies peculiar to that occasion. ——I am sure it will be productive of some diversion; and, truly, it would be worth your while to come across the country on purpose to see two such original figures in bed together, with their laced night caps; he, the emblem of good cheer, and she, the picture of good nature. All this agreeable prospect was clouded, and had well nigh vanished entirely, in consequence of a late misunderstanding between the future brothers-in-law, which, however, is now happily removed.

A few days ago, my uncle and I, going to visit a relation, met with lord Oxmington at his house, who asked us to dine with him next day, and we accepted the invitation.——Accordingly, leaving our women under the care of captain Lismahago, at the inn where we had lodged the preceding night, in a little town, about a mile from his lordship's dwelling, we went at the hour appointed, and had a fashionable meal served up with much ostentation to a company of about a dozen persons, none of whom he had ever seen before.——His lordship is much more remarkable for his pride and caprice, than for his hospitality and understanding; and, indeed, it appeared, that he considered his guests merely as objects to shine upon, so as to reflect the lustre of his own magnificence.——There was much state, but no courtesy; and a great deal of compliment without any conversation.——Before the desert was removed, our noble entertainer proposed three general toasts; then calling for a glass of wine, and bowing all round, wished us a good afternoon. This was the signal for the company to break up, and they obeyed it immediately, all except our 'squire who was greatly shocked at the manner of this dismission.——He changed countenance, bit his lip in silence, but still kept his seat, so that his lordship found himself obliged to give us another hint, by saying, he should be glad to see us another time. 'There is no time like the present (cried Mr. Bramble); your lordship has not yet drank a bumper to *the best in Christendom.*' 'I'll drink no more bumpers to-day (answered our landlord); and I am sorry to see you have drank too many.—Order the gentleman's carriage to the gate.'—So saying, he rose and retired abruptly; our 'squire starting up at the same time, laying his hand upon his sword, and eyeing him with a most ferocious aspect. The master having vanished in this manner, our uncle bad one of the servants to see what was to pay; and the fellow answering, 'This is no inn,' 'I cry you mercy, (cried the other) I perceive it is not; if it were, the landlord would be more civil.—There's a guinea, however; take it, and tell your lord, that I shall not leave the country till I have had the opportunity to thank him in person for his politeness and hospitality.'

We then walked down stairs through a double range of lacqueys, and getting into the chaise, proceeded homewards. Perceiving the 'squire much ruffled, I ventured to disapprove of his resentment, observing, that as lord Oxmington was well known to have his brain very ill timbered, a sensible man should rather laugh, than be angry at his ridiculous want of breeding,—Mr. Bramble took umbrage at my presuming to be wiser than he upon this occasion; and told me, that as he had always thought for himself in every occurrence in life, he would still use the same privilege, with my good leave.

When we returned to our inn, he closeted Lismahago; and having explained his grievance, desired that gentleman to go and demand satisfaction of lord Oxmington in his name.—The lieutenant charged himself with this commission, and immediately set out a horseback for his lordship's house, attended, at his own request, by my man Archy Macalpine, who had been used to military service; **and** truly, if Macalpine had been mounted upon an ass, this couple might have passed for the knight of La Mancha and his 'squire Panza. It was not till after some demur that Lismahago obtained a private audience, at which he formally defied his lordship to single combat, in the name of Mr. Bramble, and desired him to appoint the time and place. Lord Oxmington was so confounded at this unexpected message, that he could not, for some time, make any articulate reply; but stood staring at the lieutenant with manifest marks of perturbation. At length, ringing a bell with great vehemence, he exclaimed, 'What! a commoner send a challenge to a peer of the realm!—Privilege! privilege!— Here's a person brings me a challenge from the Welshman that dined at my table—An impudent fellow—My wine is not yet out of his head.'

The whole house was immediately in commotion.—Macalpine made a soldierly retreat with the two horses; but the captain was suddenly surrounded and disarmed by the footman, whom a French valet de chambre headed in this exploit; his sword was passed through a close-stool, and his person through the horse pond.—In this plight he returned to the inn, half mad with his disgrace.—So violent was the rage of his indignation, that he mistook its object.—He wanted to quarrel with Mr. Bramble; he said, he had been dishonoured on his account, and he looked for reparation at his hands.—My uncle's back was up in a moment; and he desired him to explain his pretensions.—'Either compel lord Oxmington to give me satisfaction, (cried he) or give it me in your own person.' 'The latter part of the alternative is the most easy and expeditious (replied the 'squire, starting up): if you are disposed for a walk, I'll attend you this moment.'

Here they were interrupted by Mrs. Tabby, who had overheard all that passed.——She now burst into the room, and running betwixt them, in great agitation, 'Is this your regard for me (said she to the lieutenant) to seek the life of my brother?' Lismahago, who seemed to grow cool as my uncle grew hot, assured her he had a very great respect for Mr. Bramble, but he had still more for his own honour, which had suffered pollution; but if that could be once purified, he should have no further cause of dissatisfaction. ——The 'squire said, he should have thought it incumbent upon him to vindicate the lieutenant's honour; but, as he had now carved for himself, he might swallow and digest it as well as he could——In a word, what betwixt the mediation of Mrs. Tabitha, the recollection of the captain, who perceived he had gone too far, and the remonstrances of your humble servant, who joined them at this juncture, those two originals were perfectly reconciled; and then we proceeded to deliberate upon the means of taking vengeance for the insults they had received from the petulant peer; for, until that aim should be accomplished, Mr. Bramble swore, with great emphasis, that he would not leave the inn where we now lodged, even if he should pass his Christmas on the spot.

In consequence of our deliberations, we next day, in the forenoon, proceeded in a body to his lordship's house, all of us, with our servants, including the coachman, mounted a-horseback, with our pistols loaded and ready primed.—— Thus prepared for action, we paraded solemnly and slowly before his lordship's gate, which we passed three times in such a manner, that he could not but see us, and suspect the cause of our appearance.——After dinner we returned, and performed the same cavalcade, which was again repeated the morning following; but we had no occasion to persist in these manœuvres.——About noon, we were visited by the gentleman, at whose house we had first seen lord Oxmington.——He now came to make apologies in the name of his lordship, who declared he had no intention to give offence to my uncle, in practising what had been always the custom of his house; and that as for the indignities which had been put upon the officer, they were offered without his Lordship's knowledge, at the instigation of his valet de chambre.—'If that be the case, (said my uncle, in a peremptory tone) I shall be contented with lord Oxmington's personal excuses; and I hope my friend will be satisfied with his lordship's turning that insolent rascal out of his service.'—'Sir, (cried Lismahago) I must insist upon taking personal vengeance for the personal injuries I have sustained.'

After some debate, the affair was adjusted in this manner.——His lordship, meeting us at our friend's house, declared he was sorry for what had happened; and that he had no intention to give umbrage.—The valet de chambre asked pardon of the lieutenant upon his knees, when Lismahago, to the astonishment of all present, gave him a violent kick on the face, which laid him on his back, exclaiming in a furious tone, *'Oui je te pardonne, gens foutre.'*

Such was the fortunate issue of this perilous adventure, which threatened abundance of vexation to our family; for the 'squire is one of those who will sacrifice both life and fortune, rather than leave what they conceive to be the least speck or blemish upon their honour and reputation. His lordship had no soner pronounced his apology, with a very bad grace, than he went away in some disorder, and, I dare say, he will never invite another Welchman to his table.

We forthwith quitted the field of this atchievement, in order to prosecute our journey; but we follow no determinate course.——We make small deviations, to see the remarkable towns, villas, and curiosities on each side of our route; so that we advance by slow steps towards the borders of Monmouthshire: but in the midst of these irregular motions, there is no abberration nor eccentricity in that affection with which I am, dear Wat,

Yours always,

J. MELFORD.

Sept. 28.

To Dr. Lewis

DEAR DICK,

At what time of life may a man think himself exempted from the necessity of sacrificing his repose to the
punctilios of a contemptible world? I have been engaged
in a ridiculous adventure, which I shall recount at meeting;
and this, I hope, will not be much longer delayed, as we
have now performed almost all our visits, and seen every
thing that I think has any right to retard us in our journey
homewards——A few days ago, understanding by accident,
that my old friend Baynard was in the country, I would
not pass so near his habitation without paying him a visit,
though our correspondence had been interrupted for a long
course of years.

I felt my self very sensibly affected by the ideas of our
past intimacy, as we approached the place where we had
spent so many happy days together; but when we arrived at
the house, I could not recognize any one of those objects,
which had been so deeply impressed upon my remembrance
—The tall oaks that shaded the avenue, had been cut down,
and the iron gates at the end of it removed, together with
the high wall that surrounded the court yard. The house
itself, which was formerly a convent of Cistercian monks,
had a venerable appearance: and along the front that looked
into the garden, was a stone gallery, which afforded me
many an agreeable walk, when I was disposed to be con-
templative—Now the old front is covered with a screen of
modern architecture; so that all without is Grecian, and all
within Gothic—As for the garden, which was well stocked
with the best fruit which England could produce, there is
not now the least vestige remaining of trees, walls, or hedges
——Nothing appears but a naked circus of loose sand, with
a dry bason and a leaden triton in the middle.

You must know, that Baynard, at his father's death, had

a clear estate of fifteen hundred pounds a-year, and was in other respects extremely well qualified to make a respectable figure in the commonwealth; but, what with some excesses of youth, and the expence of a contested election, he in a few years found himself encumbered with a debt of ten thousand pounds, which he resolved to discharge by means of a prudent marriage—He accordingly married a miss Thomson, whose fortune amounted to double the sum that he owed—She was the daughter of a citizen, who had failed in trade; but her fortune came by an uncle, who died in the East-Indies—Her own parents being dead, she lived with a maiden aunt, who had superintended her education; and, in all appearance, was well enough qualified for the usual purposes of the married state——Her virtues, however, stood rather upon a negative, than a positive foundation— She was neither proud, insolent, nor capricious, nor given to scandal, nor addicted to gaming, nor inclined to gallantry —She could read, and write, and dance, and sing, and play upon the harpsichord, and smatter French, and take a hand at whist and ombre; but even these accomplishments she possessed by halves—She excelled in nothing. Her conversation was flat, her stile mean, and her expression embarrassed —In a word, her character was totally insipid. Her person was not disagreeable; but there was nothing graceful in her address, nor engaging in her manners; and she was so ill qualified to do the honours of the house, that when she sat at the head of the table, one was always looking for the mistress of the family in some other place.

Baynard had flattered himself, that it would be no diffi-cult matter to mould such a subject after his own fashion, and that she would chearfully enter into his views, which were wholly turned to domestic happiness. He proposed to reside always in the country, of which he was fond to a degree of enthusiasm; to cultivate his estate, which was very improvable; to enjoy the exercise of rural diversions; to maintain an intimacy of correspondence with some friends that were settled in his neighbourhood; to keep a comfortable house, without suffering his expence to exceed the limits of his income; and to find pleasure and employment for his wife in the management and avocations of her own family ——This, however, was a visionary scheme, which he never was able to realize. His wife was as ignorant as a new-born babe of every thing that related to the conduct of a family; and she had no idea of a country-life. Her understanding did not reach so far as to comprehend the first principles of discretion; and, indeed, if her capacity had been better than it was, her natural indolence would not have permitted her to abandon a certain routine, to which she had been habituated. She had not taste enough to relish any rational enjoyment; but her ruling passion was vanity, not that species which arises from self-conceit of superior accomplishments, but that which is of a bastard and idiot nature, excited by shew and ostentation, which implies not even the least consciousness of any personal merit.

The nuptial peal of noise and nonsense being rung out in all the usual changes, Mr. Baynard thought it high time to make her acquainted with the particulars of the plan which he had projected——He told her that his fortune, though sufficient to afford all the comforts of life, was not ample enough to command all the superfluities of pomp and pageantry, which, indeed, were equally absurd and intolerable——He therefore hoped she would have no objection to their leaving London in the spring, when he would take the opportunity to dismiss some unnecessary domestics, whom he had hired for the occasion of their marriage——She heard him in silence, and after some pause, 'So (said she) I am to be buried in the country!' He was so confounded at this reply, that he could not speak for some minutes: at length he told her, he was much mortified to find he had proposed any thing that was disagreeable to her ideas——'I am sure (added he) I meant nothing more than to lay down a comfortable plan of living within the bounds of our fortune, which is but moderate.' 'Sir, (said she) you are the best judge of your own affairs——My fortune, I know, does not exceed twenty thousand pounds——Yet, even with that pittance, I might have had a husband who would not have begrudged me a house in London—' 'Good God! my dear, (cried poor Baynard, in the utmost agitation) you don't think me so sordid—I only hinted what I thought—But, I don't pretend to impose—' 'Yes, sir, (resumed the lady) it is your prerogative to command, and my duty to obey—'

So saying, she burst into tears and retired to her chamber, where she was joined by her aunt——He endeavoured to recollect himself, and act with vigour of mind on this occasion; but was betrayed by the tenderness of his nature, which was the greatest defect of his constitution. He found the aunt in tears, and the niece in a fit, which held her the best part of eight hours, at the expiration of which, she began to talk incoherently about *death* and her *dear husband,* who had sat by her all this time, and now pressed her hand to his lips, in a transport of grief and penitence for the offence he had given——From thence forward, he carefully avoided mentioning the country; and they continued to be sucked deeper and deeper into the vortex of extravagance and dissipation, leading what is called a fashionable life in town—About the latter end of July, however, Mrs. Baynard, in order to exhibit a proof of conjugal obedience, desired of her own accord, that they might pay a visit to his country house, as there was no company left in London. He would have excused himself from this excursion which was no part of the œconomical plan he had proposed; but she insisted upon making this sacrifice to his taste and prejudices, and away they went with such an equipage as astonished the whole country——All that remained of the season was engrossed by receiving and returning visits in the neighbourhood; and, in this intercourse it was discovered that sir John Chickwell had a house-steward and one footman in livery more than the complement of Mr. Baynard's household. This remark was made by the aunt at table, and assented to by the husband, who observed that sir John Chickwell might very well afford to keep more servants than were found in the family of a man who had not half his fortune. Mrs. Baynard ate no supper that evening; but was seized with a violent fit, which completed her triumph over the spirit of her consort. The two supernumerary servants were added—The family plate was sold for old silver, and a new service procured; fashionable furniture was provided, and the whole house turned topsy turvy.

At their return to London in the beginning of winter, he, with a heavy heart, communicated these particulars to me in confidence. Before his marriage, he had introduced me to the lady as his particular friend; and I now offered in that character, to lay before her the necessity of reforming her œconomy, if she had any regard to the interest of her own family, or complaisance for the inclinations of her husband—But Baynard declined my offer, on the supposition that his wife's nerves were too delicate to bear expostulation; and that it would only serve to overwhelm her with such distress as would make himself miserable.

Baynard is a man of spirit, and had she proved a termagant, he would have known how to deal with her ; but, either by accident or instinct, she fastened upon the weak side of his soul, and held it so fast, that he has been in subjection ever since—I afterwards advised him to carry her abroad to France or Italy, where he might gratify her vanity for half the expence it cost him in England: and this advice he followed accordingly—She was agreeably flattered with the idea of seeing and knowing foreign parts, and foreign fashions; of being presented to sovereigns, and living familiarly with princes. She forthwith seized the hint which I had thrown out on purpose, and even pressed Mr. Baynard to hasten his departure; so that in a few weeks they crossed the sea to France, with a moderate train, still including the aunt: who was her bosom counsellor, and abetted her in all her oppositions to her husband's will——Since that period, I have had little or no opportunity to renew our former correspondence——All that I knew of his transactions, amounted to no more than that after an absence of two years, they returned so little improved in œconomy, that they launched out into new oceans of extravagance, which at length obliged him to mortgage his estate——By this time she had bore him three children, of which the last only survives, a puny boy of twelve or thirteen, who will be ruined in his education by the indulgence of his mother.

As for Baynard, neither his own good sense, nor the dread of indigence, nor the consideration of his children, has been of force sufficient to stimulate him into the resolution of breaking at once the shameful spell by which he seems enchanted——With a taste capable of the most refined enjoyment, a heart glowing with all the warmth of friendship and humanity, and a disposition strongly turned to the more rational pleasures of a retired and country life, he is hurried about in a perpetual tumult, amidst a mob of beings pleased with rattles, baubles, and gew-gaws, so void of sense and distinction, that even the most acute philosopher would find it a very hard task to discover for what wise purpose of providence they were created——Friendship is not to be found; nor can the amusements for which he sighs be enjoyed within the rotation of absurdity, to which he is doomed for life. He has long resigned all views of improving his fortune by management and attention to the exercise of husbandry, in which he delighted; and as to domestic happiness, not the least glimpse of hope remains to amuse his imagination. Thus blasted in all his prospects, he could not fail to be overwhelmed with melancholy and chagrin, which have preyed upon his health and spirits in such a manner, that he is now threatened with a consumption.

I have given you a sketch of the man, whom the other day I went to visit——At the gate we found a great number of powdered lacquies, but no civility—After we had sat a considerable time in the coach, we were told, that Mr. Baynard had rode out, and that his lady was dressing; but we were introduced to a parlour, so very fine and delicate, that in all appearance it was designed to be seen only, not inhabited. The chairs and couches were carved, gilt, and covered with rich damask, so smooth and slick, that they looked as if they had never been sat upon. There was no carpet upon the floor; but the boards were rubbed and waxed in such a manner, that we could not walk, but were obliged to slide along them; and as for the stove, it was too bright and polished to be polluted with sea-coal, or stained by the smoke of any gross material fire—When we had remained above half an hour sacrificing to the inhospitable powers in the *temple of cold reception,* my friend Baynard arrived, and understanding we were in the house, made his appearance, so meagre, yellow, and dejected, that I really should not have known him, had I met with him in any other place——— Running up to me, with great eagerness, he strained me in his embrace, and his heart was so full, that for some minutes he could not speak—Having saluted us all round, he perceived our uncomfortable situation, and conducting us into another apartment, which had fire in the chimney, called for chocolate———Then, withdrawing, he returned with a compliment from his wife, and, in the mean time, presented his son Harry, a shambling, blear-eyed boy, in the habit of a hussar; very rude, forward, and impertinent— His father would have sent him to a boarding-school, but his mamma and aunt would not hear of his lying out of the house; so that there was a clergyman engaged as his tutor in the family.

As it was but just turned of twelve, and the whole house was in commotion to prepare a formal entertainment, I foresaw it would be late before we dined, and proposed a walk to Mr. Baynard, that we might converse together freely. In the course of this perambulation, when I expressed some surprize that he had returned so soon from Italy, he gave me to understand, that his going abroad had not at all answered the purpose, for which he left England; that although the expence of living was not so great in Italy as at home, respect being had to the same rank of life in both countries, it had been found necessary for him to lift himself above his usual stile, that he might be on some footing with the counts, marquises, and cavaliers, with whom he kept company——He was obliged to hire a great number of servants, to take off a great variety of rich cloaths, and to keep a sumptuous table for the fashionable scoroccioni of the country; who, without a consideration of this kind, would not have payed any attention to an untitled foreigner, let his family or fortune be ever so respectable—Besides, Mrs. Baynard was continually surrounded by a train of expensive loungers, under the denominations of language-masters, musicians, painters, and ciceroni; and had actually fallen into the disease of buying pictures and antiques upon her own judgment, which was far from being infallible——At length she met with an affront, which gave her a disgust to Italy, and drove her back to England with some precipitation. By means of frequenting the dutchess of B——'s conversazione, while her grace was at Rome, Mrs. Baynard became acquainted with all the fashionable people of that city, and was admitted to their assemblies without scruple— Thus favoured, she conceived too great an idea of her own importance, and when the dutchess left Rome, resolved to have a conversazione that should leave the Romans no room to regret her grace's departure. She provided hands for a musical entertainment, and sent bighetti of invitation to every person of distinction; but not one Roman of the female sex appeared at her assembly—She was that night seized with a violent fit, and kept her bed three days, at the expiration of which she declared that the air of Italy would be the ruin of her constitution. In order to prevent this catastrophe, she was speedily removed to Geneva, from whence they returned to England by the way of Lyons and Paris. By the time they arrived at Calais, she had purchased such a quantity of silks, stuffs, and laces, that it was necessary to hire a vessel to smuggle them over, and this vessel was taken by a custom-house cutter; so that they lost the whole cargo, which had cost them above eight hundred pounds.

It now appears, that her travels had produced no effect upon her, but that of making her more expensive and fantastic than ever.——She affected to lead the fashion, not only in point of female dress, but in every article of taste and connoisseurship. She made a drawing of the new facade to the house in the country; she pulled up the trees, and pulled down the walls of the garden, so as to let in the easterly wind, which Mr. Baynard's ancestors had been at great pains to exclude. To shew her taste in laying out ground, she seized into her own hand a farm of two hundred acres, about a mile from the house, which she parcelled out into walks and shrubberies, having a great bason in the middle, into which she poured a whole stream that turned two mills, and afforded the best trout in the country. The bottom of the bason, however, was so ill secured, that it would not hold the water which strained through the earth, and made a bog of the whole plantation: in a word, the ground which formerly payed him one hundred and fifty pounds a year, now cost him two hundred pounds a year to keep it in tolerable order, over and above the first expence of trees, shrubs, flowers, turf, and gravel. There was not an inch of garden ground left about the house, nor a tree that produced fruit of any kind; nor did he raise a truss of hay, or a bushel of oats for his horses, nor had he a single cow to afford milk for his tea; far less did he ever dream of feeding his own mutton, pigs, and poultry: every article of housekeeping, even the most inconsiderable, was brought from the next market town, at the distance of five miles, and thither they sent a courier every morning to fetch hot rolls for breakfast. In short, Baynard fairly owned that he spent double his income, and that in a few years he should be obliged to sell his estate for the payment of his creditors. He said that his wife had such delicate nerves, and such imbecility of spirit, that she could neither bear remonstrance, be it ever so gentle, nor practise any scheme of retrenchment, even if she perceived the necessity of such a measure. He had therefore ceased struggling against the stream, and endeavoured to reconcile himself to ruin, by reflecting that his child at least would inherit his mother's fortune, which was secured to him by the contract of marriage.

The detail which he gave me of his affairs, filled me at once with grief and indignation. I inveighed bitterly against the indiscretion of his wife, and reproached him with his unmanly acquiescence under the absurd tyranny which she exerted. I exhorted him to recollect his resolution, and make one effectual effort to disengage himself from a thraldom, equally shameful and pernicious. I offered him all the assistance in my power. I undertook to regulate his affairs, and even to bring about a reformation in his family, if he would only authorise me to execute the plan I should form for his advantage. I was so affected by the subject, that I could not help mingling tears with my remonstrances, and Baynard was so penetrated with these marks of my affection, that he lost all power of utterance. He pressed me to his breast with great emotion, and wept in silence. At length he exclaimed, 'Friendship is undoubtedly the most precious balm of life! Your words, dear Bramble, have in a great measure recalled me from an abyss of despondence, in which I have been long overwhelmed—I will, upon honour, make you acquainted with a distinct state of my affairs, and, as far as I am able to go, will follow the course you prescribe. But there are certain lengths which my nature——The truth is, there are tender connexions, of which a batchelor has no idea—Shall I own my weakness? I cannot bear the thoughts of making that woman uneasy—'

'And yet, (cried I) she has seen you unhappy for a series of years—unhappy from her misconduct, without ever shewing the least inclination to alleviate your distress—' 'Nevertheless (said he) I am persuaded she loves me with the most warm affection; but these are incongruities in the composition of the human mind which I hold to be inexplicable.'

I was shocked at his infatuation, and changed the subject, after we had agreed to maintain a close correspondence for the future—He then gave me to understand, that he had two neighbours, who, like himself, were driven by their wives at full speed, in the high road to bankruptcy and ruin. All the three husbands were of dispositions very different from each other, and, according to this variation, their consorts were admirably suited to the purpose of keeping them all three in subjection. The views of the ladies were exactly the same. They vied in grandeur, that is, in ostentation, with the wife of Sir Charles Chickwell, who had four times their fortune; and she again piqued herself upon making an equal figure with a neighbouring peeress, whose revenue trebled her own. Here then was the fable of the frog and the ox, realized in four different instances within the same county: one large fortune, and three moderate estates, in a fair way of being burst by the inflation of female vanity; and in three of these instances, three different forms of female tyranny were exercised. Mr. Baynard was subjugated by practising upon the tenderness of his nature. Mr. Milksan, being of a timorous disposition, truckled to the insolence of a termagant. Mr. Sowerby, who was of a temper neither to be moved by fits, nor driven by menaces, had the fortune to be fitted with a helpmate, who assailed him with the weapons of irony and satire; sometimes sneering in the way of compliment; sometimes throwing out sarcastic comparisons, implying reproaches upon his want of taste, spirit, and generosity: by which means she stimulated his passions from one act of extravagance to another, just as the circumstances of her vanity required.

All these three ladies have at this time the same number of horses, carriages, and servants in and out of livery; the same variety of dress; the same quantity of plate and china; the like ornaments in furniture; and in their entertainments they endeavour to exceed one another in the variety, delicacy, and expence of their dishes. I believe it will be found upon enquiry, that nineteen out of twenty, who are ruined by extravagance, fall a sacrifice to the ridiculous pride and vanity of silly women, whose parts are held in contempt by the very men whom they pillage and enslave. Thank heaven, Dick, that among all the follies and weaknesses of human nature, I have not yet fallen into that of matrimony.

After Baynard and I had discussed all these matters at leisure, we returned towards the house, and met Jery with our two women, who had come forth to take the air, as the lady of the mansion had not yet made her appearance. In short, Mrs. Baynard did not produce herself, till about a quarter of an hour before dinner was upon the table. Then her husband brought her into the parlour, accompanied by her aunt and son, and she received us with a coldness of reserve sufficient to freeze the very soul of hospitality. Though she knew I had been the intimate friend of her husband, and had often seen me with him in London, she shewed no marks of recognition or regard, when I addressed myself to her in the most friendly terms of salutation. She did not even express the common compliment of, *I am glad to see you*; or, *I hope you have enjoyed your health since we had the pleasure of seeing you*; or some such words of course: nor did she once open her mouth in the way of welcome to my sister and my niece: but sat in silence like a statue, with an aspect of insensibility. Her aunt, the model upon which she had been formed, was indeed the very essence of insipid formality but the boy was very pert and impudent, and prated without ceasing.

At dinner, the lady maintained the same ungracious indifference, never speaking but in whispers to her aunt; and as to the repast, it was made up of a parcel of kickshaws, contrived by a French cook, without one substantial article adapted to the satisfaction of an English appetite. The pottage was little better than bread soaked in dishwashings, lukewarm. The ragouts looked as if they had been once eaten and half digested: the fricassees were involved in a nasty yellow poultice: and the rotis were scorched and stinking, for the honour of the fumet. The desert consisted of faded fruit and iced froth, a good emblem of our landlady's character; the table-beer, was sour, the water foul, and the wine vapid; but there was a parade of plate and china, and a powdered lacquey stood behind every chair, except those of the master and mistress of the house, who were served by two valets dressed like gentlemen. We dined in a large old Gothic parlour, which was formerly the hall. It was now paved with marble, and, notwithstanding the fire, which had been kindled about an hour, struck me with such a chill sensation, that when I entered it the teeth chattered in my jaws—In short, every thing was cold, comfortless, and disgusting, except the looks of my friend Baynard, which declared the warmth of his affection and humanity.

After dinner we withdrew into another apartment, where the boy began to be impertinently troublesome to my niece Liddy. He wanted a play-fellow, forsooth; and would have romped with her, had she encouraged his advances— He was even so impudent as to snatch a kiss, at which she changed countenance, and seemed uneasy; and though his father checked him for the rudeness of his behaviour, he became so outrageous as to thrust his hand in her bosom: an insult to which she did not tamely submit, though one of the mildest creatures upon earth. Her eyes sparkling with resentment, she started up, and lent him such a box in the ear, as sent him staggering to the other side of the room.

'Miss Melford, (cried his father) you have treated him

with the utmost propriety—I am only sorry that the impertinence of any child of mine should have occasioned this exertion of your spirit, which I cannot but applaud and admire.' His wife was so far from assenting to the candour of his apology, that she rose from table, and, taking her son by the hand, 'Come, child, (said she) your father cannot abide you.' So saying, she retired with this hopeful youth, and was followed by her gouvernante: but neither the one nor the other deigned to take the least notice of the company.

Baynard was exceedingly disconcerted; but I perceived his uneasiness was tinctured with resentment, and derived a good omen from this discovery. I ordered the horses to be put to the carriage, and, though he made some efforts to detain us all night, I insisted upon leaving the house immediately; but, before I went away, I took an opportunity of speaking to him again in private. I said every thing I could recollect, to animate his endeavours in shaking off those shameful trammels. I made no scruple to declare, that his wife was unworthy of that tender complaisance which he had shewn for her foibles: that she was dead to all the genuine sentiments of conjugal affection; insensible of her own honour and interest, and seemingly destitute of common sense and reflection. I conjured him to remember what he owed to his father's house, to his own reputation, and to his family, including even this unreasonable woman herself, who was driving on blindly to her own destruction. I advised him to form a plan for retrenching superfluous expence, and try to convince the aunt of the necessity for such a reformation, that she might gradually prepare her niece for its execution; and I exhorted him to turn that disagreeable piece of formality out of the house, if he should find her averse to his proposal.

Here he interrupted me with a sigh, observing that such a step would undoubtedly be fatal to Mrs. Baynard—'I shall lose all patience, (cried I) to hear you talk so weakly

—Mrs. Baynard's fits will never hurt her constitution. I believe in my conscience they are all affected: I am sure she has no feeling foɩ your distresses; and, when you are ruined, she will appear to have no feeling for her own.' Finally, I took his word and honour that he would make an effort, such as I had advised; that he would form a plan of œconomy, and, if he found it impracticable without my assistance, he would come to Bath in the winter, where I promised to give him the meeting, and contribute all in my power to the retrieval of his affairs—With this mutual engagement we parted; and I shall think myself supremely happy, if, by my means, a worthy man, whom I love and esteem, can be saved from misery, disgrace, and despair.

I have only one friend more to visit in this part of the country, but he is of a complexion very different from that of Baynard. You have heard me mention Sir Thomas Bullford, whom I knew in Italy. He is now become a country gentleman; but, being disabled by the gout from enjoying any amusement abroad, he entertains himself within doors, by keeping open house for all comers, and playing upon the oddities and humours of his company: but he himself is generally the greatest original at his table. He is very good-humoured, talks much, and laughs without ceasing. I am told that all the use he makes of his understanding at present, is to excite mirth, by exhibiting his guests in ludicrous attitudes. I know not how far we may furnish him with entertainment of this kind, but I am resolved to beat up his quarters, partly with a view to laugh with the knight himself, and partly to pay my respects to his lady, a good-natured sensible woman, with whom he lives upon very easy terms, although she has not had the good fortune to bring him an heir to his estate.

And now, dear Dick, I must tell you for your comfort, that you are the only man upon earth to whom I would presume to send such a long-winded epistle, which I could not find in my heart to curtail, because the subject interested the warmest passions of my heart, neither will I make any other apology to a correspondent who has been so long accustomed to the impertinence of

MATT. BRAMBLE.

Sept. 30.

To Sir Watkin Phillips, Bart. at Oxon.

DEAR KNIGHT,

I believe there is something mischievous in my disposition, for nothing diverts me so much as to see certain characters tormented with false terrors.——We last night lodged at the house of Sir Thomas Bullford, an old friend of my uncle, a jolly fellow, of moderate intellects, who, in spite of the gout, which hath lamed him, is resolved to be merry to the last; and mirth he has a particular knack in extracting from his guests, let their humour be ever so caustic or refractory.—Besides our company, there was in the house a fat-headed justice of the peace, called Frogmore, and a country practitioner in surgery, who seemed to be our landlord's chief companion and confidant.—— We found the knight sitting on a couch, with his crutches by his side, and his feet supported on cushions; but he received us with a hearty welcome, and seemed greatly rejoiced at our arrival.—After tea, we were entertained with a sonata on the harpsichord by lady Bullford, who sung and played to admiration; but Sir Thomas seemed to be a little asinine in the article of ears, though he affected to be in raptures, and begged his wife to favour us with an *arietta* of her own composing.—This *arietta*, however, she no sooner began to perform, than he and the justice fell asleep; but the moment she ceased playing, the knight waked snorting, and exclaimed, '*O cara!* what d'ye think, gentlemen? Will you talk any more of your Pargolesi and your Corelli?'—At the same time, he thrust his tongue in one cheek, and leered with one eye at the doctor and me, who sat on his left hand.———He concluded the pantomime with a loud laugh, which he could command at all times extempore.———Notwithstanding his disorder, he did not do penance at supper, nor did he ever refuse his glass when the toast went round, but rather encouraged a quick circulation, both by precept and example.

I soon perceived the doctor had made himself very necessary to the baronet.———He was the whetstone of his wit, the butt of his satire, and his operator in certain experiments of humour, which were occasionally tried upon strangers.— Justice Frogmore was an excellent subject for this species of philosophy; sleek and corpulent, solemn and shallow, he had studied Burn with uncommon application, but he studied nothing so much as the art of living (that is, eating) well ———This fat buck had often afforded good sport to our landlord; and he was frequently started with tolerable success, in the course of this evening; but the baronet's appetite for ridicule seemed to be chiefly excited by the appearance, address, and conversation of Lismahago, whom he attempted in all the different modes of exposition; but he put me in mind of a contest that I once saw betwixt a young hound and an old hedge-hog—The dog turned him over and over, and bounced and barked, and mumbled; but as often as he attempted to bite, he felt a prickle in his jaws, and recoiled in manifest confusion;———The captain, when left to himself, will not fail to turn his ludicrous side to the company, but if any man attempts to force him into that attitude, he becomes stubborn as a mule, and unmanageable as an elephant unbroke.

Divers tolerable jokes were cracked upon the justice, who eat a most unconscionable supper, and, among other things, a large plate of broiled mushrooms, which he had no sooner swallowed than the doctor observed, with great gravity, that they were of the kind called *champignons*, which in some constitutions had a poisonous effect.—Mr. Frogmore, star-

tled at this remark, asked, in some confusion, why he had
not been so kind as to give him that notice sooner.—He
answered, that he took it for granted, by his eating them so
heartily, that he was used to the dish; but as he seemed to
be under some apprehension, he prescribed a bumper of
plague water, which the justice drank off immediately, and
retired to rest, not without marks of terror and disquiet.

At midnight we were shewn to our different chambers,
and in half an hour, I was fast asleep in bed; but about
three o'clock in the morning I was waked with a dismal
cry of *Fire!* and starting up, ran to the window in my
shirt.—The night was dark and stormy; and a number of
people half-dressed ran backwards and forwards thro' the
court-yard, with links and lanthorns, seemingly in the utmost hurry and trepidation.—Slipping on my cloaths in a
twinkling, I ran down stairs, and, upon enquiry, found the
fire was confined to a back-stair, which led to a detached
apartment where Lismahago lay.——By this time, the
lieutenant was alarmed by bawling at his window, which
was in the second story, but he could not find his cloaths
in the dark, and his room-door was locked on the outside.
——The servants called to him, that the house had been
robbed; that, without all doubt, the villains had taken
away his cloaths, fastened the door, and set the house on
fire, for the stair-case was in flames.——In this dilemma
the poor lieutenant ran about the room naked like a squir-
rel in a cage, popping out his head at the window between
whiles, and imploring assistance.—At length, the knight in
person was brought out in his chair, attended by my uncle
and all the family, including our aunt Tabitha, who
screamed, and cried, and tore her hair, as if she had been
distracted.—Sir Thomas had already ordered his people to
bring a long ladder which was applied to the captain's window, and now he exhorted him earnestly to descend.—
There was no need of much rhetoric to persuade Lismahago, who forthwith made his exit by the window, roaring

all the time to the people below to hold fast the ladder.

Notwithstanding the gravity of the occasion, it was impossible to behold this scene without being seized with an inclination to laugh. The rueful aspect of the lieutenant in his shirt, with a quilted night-cap fastened under his chin, and his long lank limbs and posteriors exposed to the wind, made a very picturesque appearance, when illumined by the links and torches which the servants held up to light him in his descent.—All the company stood round the ladder, except the knight, who sat in his chair, exclaiming from time to time, 'Lord, have mercy upon us!—save the gentleman's life!—mind your footing, dear captain!—softly!—stand fast!—clasp the ladder with both hands!—there! ——well done, my dear boy!—O bravo!—an old soldier for ever!—bring a blanket——bring a warm blanket to comfort his poor carcase——warm the bed in the green room———give me your hand, dear captain—I'm rejoiced to see thee safe and sound with all my heart.' Lismahago was received at the foot of the ladder by his inamorata, who snatching a blanket from one of the maids, wrapped it about his body; two men-servants took him under the arms, and a female conducted him to the green room, still accompanied by Mrs. Tabitha, who saw him fairly put to bed.—During this whole transaction, he spoke not a syllable, but looked exceeding grim, sometimes at one, sometimes at another of the spectators, who now adjourned in a body to the parlour where we had supped, every one surveying another with marks of astonishment and curiosity.

The knight being seated in an easy chair, seized my uncle by the hand, and bursting into a long and loud laugh, 'Matt, (cried he) crown me with oak, or ivy, or laurel, or parsley, or what you will, and acknowledge this to be a *coup de maître* in the way of waggery—ha, ha, ha!—Such a *comisicata, scagliata, beffata*! *O, che roba*!—O, what a subject!——O, what *caricatura*!——O, for a Rosa, a Rembrandt, a Schalken!—Zooks, I'll give a hundred

guineas to have it painted!——what a fine descent from
the cross, or ascent to the gallows! what lights and shadows!
—what a groupe below!—what expression above!——what
an aspect!—did you mind the aspect?—ha, ha, ha!——and
the limbs, and the muscles——every toe denoted terror!—
ha, ha, ha!——then the blanket!—O, what *costume*! St.
Andrew! St. Lazarus! St. Barrabas!—ha, ha, ha!' 'After
all then, (cried Mr. Bramble very gravely) this was no
more than a false alarm.—We have been frightened out
of our beds, and almost out of our senses, for the joke's
sake.' 'Ay, and such a joke! (cried our landlord) such a
farce! such a *denouement*! such a *catastrophe!*'

'Have a little patience (replied our 'squire); we are
not yet come to the *catastrophe*; and pray God it may not
turn out a tragedy instead of a farce.——The captain is
one of those saturnine subjects, who have no idea of
humour.—He never laughs in his own person; nor can he
bear that other people should laugh at his expence—Besides,
if the subject had been properly chosen, the joke was too
severe in all conscience.' ' 'Sdeath! (cried the knight), I
could not have bated him an ace had he been my own
father; and as for the subject, such another does not present
itself once in half a century.' Here Mrs. Tabitha interposing, and bridling up, declared, she did not see that Mr.
Lismahago was a fitter subject for ridicule than the knight
himself; and that she was very much afraid, he would very
soon find he had mistaken his man.——The baronet was
a good deal disconcerted by this intimation, saying, that he
must be a Goth and a barbarian, if he did not enter into
the spirit of such a happy and humourous contrivance.—He
begged, however, that Mr. Bramble and his sister would
bring him to reason; and this request was reinforced by
lady Bullford, who did not fail to read the baronet a lecture upon his indiscretion, which lecture he received with
submission one one side of his face, and a leer upon the
other.

We now went to bed for the second time; and before I got up, my uncle had visited Lismahago in the green room, and used such arguments with him, that when we met in the parlour he seemed to be quite appeased.—He received the knight's apology with good grace, and even professed himself pleased at finding he had contributed to the diversion of the company.——Sir Thomas shook him by the hand, laughing heartily; and then desired a pinch of snuff, in token of perfect reconciliation—The lieutenant, putting his hand in his waistcoat pocket, pulled out, instead of his own Scotch mull, a very fine gold snuff-box, which he no sooner perceived than he said, 'Here is a small mistake.' 'No mistake at all (cried the baronet): a fair exchange is no robbery.—Oblige me so far, captain, as to let me keep your mull as a memorial.' 'Sir, (said the lieutenant) the mull is much at your service; but this machine I can by no means retain.—It looks like compounding a sort of felony in the code of honour.—Besides, I don't know but there may be another joke in this conveyance; and I don't find myself disposed to be brought upon the stage again. ——I won't presume to make free with your pockets, but I beg you will put it up again with your own hand.'——So saying, with a certain austerity of aspect, he presented the snuff-box to the knight, who received it in some confusion, and restored the mull, which he would by no means keep except on the terms of exchange.

This transaction was like to give a grave cast to the conversation, when my uncle took notice that Mr. Justice Frogmore had not made his appearance either at the night-alarm, or now at the general rendezvous. The baronet hearing Frogmore mentioned, 'Odso! (cried he) I had forgot the justice.—Pr'ythee, doctor, go and bring him out of his kennel.'—Then laughing till his sides were well shaken, he said he would shew the captain, that he was not the only person of the drama exhibited for the entertainment of the company. As to the night-scene, it could not affect the justice, who had been purposely lodged in the farther end of the house, remote from the noise, and lulled with a dose of opium into the bargain. In a few minutes, Mr. Justice was led into the parlour in his night-cap and loose morning-gown, rolling his head from side to side, and groaning piteously all the way.—'Jesu! neighbour Frogmore, (exclaimed the baronet) what is the matter?—you look as if you was not a man for this world——Set him down softly on the couch——poor gentleman!—Lord have mercy upon us!—What makes him so pale, and yellow, and bloated?' 'Oh, Sir Thomas! (cried the justice) I doubt 'tis all over with me——Those mushrooms I eat at your table have done my business——ah! oh! hey!' 'Now the Lord forbid! (said the other) what!—man, have a good heart—How does thy stomach feel?—hah?'

To this interrogation he made no reply; but throwing aside his night-gown, discovered that his waist-coat would not meet upon his belly by five good inches at least. 'Heaven protect us all! (cried Sir Thomas)—what a melancholy spectacle!—never did I see a man so suddenly swelled, but when he was either just dead, or just dying.——Doctor, can'st thou do nothing for this poor object?' 'I don't think the case is quite desperate (said the surgeon), but I would advise Mr. Frogmore to settle his affairs with all expedition; the parson may come and pray by him, while I prepare a glyster and an emetic draught.' The justice, rolling his languid eyes, ejaculated with great fervency, 'Lord, have mercy upon us! Christ, have mercy upon us!'—— Then he begged the surgeon, in the name of God, to dispatch—'As for my worldly affairs, (said he) they are all settled but one mortgage, which must be left to my heirs— but my poor soul! my poor soul! what will become of my poor soul?—miserable sinner that I am!' 'Nay, pr'ythee, my dear boy, compose thyself (resumed the knight); consider the mercy of heaven is infinite; thou can'st not have any sins of a very deep dye on thy conscience, or the devil's in't.' 'Name not the devil (exclaimed the terrified Frogmore), I have more sins to answer for than the world dreams of.—Ah! friend, I have been sly—sly—damn'd sly!——Send for the parson without loss of time, and put me to bed, for I am posting to eternity.'—He was accordingly raised from the couch, and supported by two servants, who led him back to his room; but before he quitted the parlour, he intreated the good company to assist him with their prayers.—He added, 'Take warning by me, who am suddenly cut off in my prime, like a flower of the field; and God forgive you, Sir Thomas, for suffering such poisonous trash to be eaten at your table.'

He was no sooner removed out of hearing, than the baronet abandoned himself to a violent fit of laughing, in which he was joined by the greatest part of the company; but we could hardly prevent the good lady from going to undeceive the patient, by discovering, that while he slept his waistcoat had been straitened by the contrivance of the surgeon; and that the disorder in his stomach and bowels was occasioned by some antimonial wine, which he had taken over night, under the denomination of plague-water. ——She seemed to think that his apprehension might put an end to his life: the knight swore he was no such chicken, but a tough old rogue, that would live long enough to plague all his neighbours.—Upon enquiry, we found his character did not intitle him to much compassion or respect, and therefore we let our landlord's humour take its course.—A glyster was actually administered by an old woman of the family, who had been Sir Thomas's nurse, and the patient took a draught made with oxymel of squills to forward the operation of the antimonial wine, which had been retarded by the opiate of the preceding night. He was visited by the vicar, who read prayers, and began to take an account of the state of his soul, when those medicines produced their effect; so that the parson was obliged to hold his nose while he poured forth spiritual consolation from his mouth. The same expedient was used by the knight and me, who, with the doctor, entered the chamber at this juncture, and found Frogmore enthroned on an easing-chair, under the pressure of a double evacuation. The short intervals betwixt every heave he employed in crying for mercy, confessing his sins, or asking the vicar's opinion of his case; and the vicar answered, in a solemn snuffling tone, that heightened the ridicule of the scene. The emetic having done its office, the doctor interfered, and ordered the patient to be put in bed again. When he examined the *egista*, and felt his pulse, he declared that much of the *virus* was discharged, and, giving him a composing draught, assured him he had good hopes of his recovery.——This welcome hint he received with the tears of joy in his eyes, protesting, that if he should recover, he would always think himself indebted for his life to the great skill and tenderness of his doctor, whose hand he squeezed with great fervour; and thus he was left to his repose.

We were pressed to stay dinner, that we might be witnesses of his resuscitation; but my uncle insisted upon our departing before noon, that we might reach this town before it should be dark.——In the mean-time, lady Bullford conducted us into the garden to see a fishpond just finished, which Mr. Bramble censured as being too near the parlour, where the knight now sat by himself, dozing in an elbow-chair after the fatigues of his morning atchievement,——In this situation he reclined, with his feet wrapped in flannel, and supported in a line with his body, when the door flying open with a violent shock, lieutenant Lismahago rushed into the room with horror in his looks, exclaiming, 'A mad dog! a mad dog!' and throwing up the window sash, leaped into the garden—Sir Thomas, waked by this tremendous exclamation, started up, and forgetting his gout, followed the lieutenant's example by a kind of instinctive impulse.——He not only bolted thro' the window like an arrow from a bow, but ran up to his middle in the pond before he gave the least sign of recollection. Then the captain began to bawl, 'Lord have mercy upon us!—pray, take care of the gentleman!——for God's sake, mind your footing, my dear boy!—get warm blankets—comfort his poor carcase—warm the bed in the green room.'

Lady Bullford was thunder-struck at this phænomenon, and the rest of the company gazed in silent astonishment, while the servants hastened to assist their master, who suffered himself to be carried back into the parlour without speaking a word.——Being instantly accommodated with dry clothes and flannels, comforted with a cordial, and replaced *in statu quo*, one of the maids was ordered to chafe his lower extremities, an operation in consequence of which his senses seemed to return and his good humour to revive. —As we had followed him into the room, he looked at every individual in his turn, with a certain ludicrous expression in his countenance, but fixed his eye in particular upon Lismahago, who presented him with a pinch of snuff, and when he took it in silence, 'Sir Thomas Bullford, (said he) I am much obliged to you for all your favours, and some of them I have endeavoured to repay in your own coin.' 'Give me thy hand (cried the baronet); thou hast indeed payed me *Scot and lot*; and even left a balance in my hands, for which, in presence of this company, I promise to be accountable.'—So saying, he laughed very heartily, and even seemed to enjoy the retaliation which had been exacted at his own expence; but lady Bullford looked very grave; and in all probability thought the lieutenant had carried his resentment too far, considering that her husband was valetudinary—but, according to the proverb, *he that will play at bowls must expect to meet with rubbers.*

I have seen a tame bear, very diverting when properly managed, become a very dangerous wild beast when teized for the entertainment of the spectators.—As for Lismahago, he seemed to think the fright and the cold bath would have a good effect upon his patient's constitution; but the doctor hinted some apprehension that the gouty matter might, by such a sudden shock, be repelled from the extremities and thrown upon some of the more vital parts of the machine.—I should be very sorry to see this prognostic verified upon our facetious landlord, who told Mrs. Tabitha at parting, that he hoped she would remember him in the distribution of the bride's favours, as he had taken so much pains to put the captain's parts and mettle to the proof.——After all, I am afraid our 'squire will appear to be the greatest sufferer by the baronet's wit; for his constitution is by no means calculated for night-alarms.—He has yawned and shivered all day, and gone to bed without supper; so that, as we have got into good quarters, I imagine we shall make a halt to-morrow; in which case, you will have at least one day's respite from the persecution of

J. MELFORD.

Oct. 3.

To Mrs. Mary Jones, at Brambleton-hall

DEAR MARY JONES,

Miss Liddy is so good as to unclose me in a kiver as fur as Gloster, and the carrier will bring it to hand—God send us all safe to Monmouthshire, for I'm quite jaded with rambling—'Tis a true saying, *live and learn*—O woman, what chuckling and changing have I seen!—Well, there's nothing sartain in this world——Who would have thought that mistriss, after all the pains taken for the good of her prusias sole, would go for to throw away her poor body? that she would cast the heys of infection upon such a carrying-crow a Lashmihago! as old as Mathewsullin, as dry as a red herring, and as poor as a starved veezel—O, Molly! hadst thou seen him come down the ladder, in a

shurt so scanty, that it could not kiver his nakedness!—The
young 'squire called him Dunquickset; but he looked for
all the world like Cradoc-ap-Morgan, the ould tinker, that
suffered at Abergany for steeling of kettle—Then he's
a profane scuffle, and, as Mr. Clinker says, no better than
an impfiddle, continually playing upon the pyebill and the
new-burth—I doubt he has as little manners as money; for
he can't say a civil word, much more make me a present
of a pair of gloves for good-will; but he looks as if he
wanted to be very forewood and familiar—O! that ever a
gentlewoman of years and discretion should tare her air,
and cry and disporridge herself for such a nubjack! as the
song goes—

> 'I vow she would fain have a burd
> That bids such a price for an owl.'

but, for sartain, he must have dealt with some Scotch musician to bring her to this pass——As for me, I put my trust
in the Lord; and I have got a slice of witch elm sowed
in the gathers of my under petticoat; and Mr. Clinker
assures me, that by the new light of grease, I may deify
the devil and all his works——But I nose what I nose—
If mistress should take up with Lashmyhago, this is no
sarvice for me—Thank God, there's no want of places;
and if it wan't for wan thing, I would—but, no matter—
Madam Baynar's woman has twenty good pounds a-year
and parquisites; and dresses like a parson of distinkson——
I dined with her and the valley de shambles, with bags and
golden jackets; but there was nothing kimfittable to eat,
being as how they lived upon board, and having nothing
but a piss of could cuddling tart and some blamangey, I
was tuck with the cullick, and a murcey it was that mistress
had her viol of assings in the cox.

But, as I was saying, I think for sartain this match will
go forewood; for things are come to a creesus; and I have

seen with my own hays, such smuggling——But I scorn
for to exclose the secrets of the family; and if it wance
comes to marrying, who nose but the frolick may go round
—I believes as how, Miss Liddy would have no reversion
if her swan would appear; and you would be surprised,
Molly, to receive a bride's fever from your humble sarvant
——but this is all suppository, dear girl; and I have sul-
lenly promised to Mr. Clinker, that neither man, woman,
nor child shall no that arrow said a civil thing to me in
the way of infection—I hope to drink your health at Brambleton-hall, in a horn of October, before the month be out
—Pray let my bed be turned once a-day, and the windore
opened, while the weather is dry; and burn a few billets
with some brush in the footman's garret, and see their
mattrash be dry as a bone; for both our gentlemen have
got a sad could by lying in damp shits at sir Tummas Ball-
fart's. No more at present, but my sarvice to Saul and the
rest of our fellow-sarvants, being,

Dear Mary Jones,
Always yours,
WIN. JENKINS.

Oct. 4.

To Miss Lœtitia Willis, at Gloucester

MY DEAR LETTY,

This method of writing to you from time to time,
without any hopes of an answer, affords me, I own, some
ease and satisfaction in the midst of my disquiet, as it in
some degree lightens the burthen of affliction: but it is at
best a very imperfect enjoyment of friendship, because it
admits of no return of confidence and good counsel——I
would give the whole world to have your company for a
single day—I am heartily tired of this itinerant way of life
—I am quite dizzy with a perpetual succession of objects

——Besides it is impossible to travel such a length of way, without being exposed to inconveniencies, dangers, and disagreeable accidents, which prove very grievous to a poor creature of weak nerves like me, and make me pay very dear for the gratification of my curiosity.

Nature never intended me for the busy world——I long for repose and solitude, where I can enjoy that disinterested friendship which is not to be found among crouds, and indulge those pleasing reveries that shun the hurry and tumult of fashionable society——Unexperienced as I am in the commerce of life, I have seen enough to give me a disgust to the generality of those who carry it on——There is such malice, treachery, and dissimulation, even among professed friends and intimate companions, as cannot fail to strike a virtuous mind with horror; and when Vice quits the stage for a moment, her place is immediately occupied by Folly, which is often too serious to excite any thing but compassion——Perhaps I ought to be silent on the foibles of my poor aunt; but with you, my dear Willis, I have no secrets; and, truly, her weaknesses are such as cannot be concealed. Since the first moment we arrived at Bath, she has been employed constantly in spreading nets for the other sex; and, at length, she has caught a superannuated lieutenant, who is in a fair way to make her change her name——My uncle and my brother seem to have no objection to this extraordinary match, which, I make no doubt, will afford abundance of matter for conversation and mirth; for my part, I am too sensible of my own weaknesses, to be diverted with those of other people——At present, I have something at heart that employs my whole attention, and keeps my mind in the utmost terror and suspence.

Yesterday in the forenoon, as I stood with my brother at the parlour window of an inn, where we had lodged, a person passed a horseback, whom (gracious Heaven!) I instantly discovered to be Wilson! He wore a white riding-coat, with the cape buttoned up to his chin; looking remarkably pale, and passed at a round trot, without seeming to observe us———Indeed, he could not see us; for there was a blind that concealed us from the view. You may guess how I was affected at this apparition—The light forsook my eyes; and I was seized with such a palpitation and trembling, that I could not stand. I sat down upon a couch, and strove to compose myself, that my brother might not perceive my agitation; but it was impossible to escape his prying eyes—He had observed the object that alarmed me; and, doubtless, knew him at the first glance—He now looked at me with a stern countenance; then he ran out into the street, to see what road the unfortunate horseman had taken—He afterwards dispatched his man for further intelligence, and seemed to meditate some violent design. My uncle, being out of order, we remained another night at the inn; and all day long Jery acted the part of an indefatigable spy upon my conduct—He watched my very looks with such eagerness of attention, as if he would have penetrated into the utmost recesses of my heart—This may be owing to his regard for my honour, if it is not the effect of his own pride; but he is so hot, and violent, and unrelenting, that the sight of him alone throws me into a flutter; and really it will not be in my power to afford him any share of my affection, if he persists in persecuting me at this rate. I am afraid he has formed some scheme of vengeance, which will make me completely wretched! I am afraid he suspects some collusion from this appearance of Wilson. ———Good God! did he really appear? or was it only a phantom, a pale spectre to apprise me of his death?

O Letty, what shall I do?—where shall I turn for advice and consolation?—shall I implore the protection of my uncle, who has been always kind and compassionate.—This must be my last resource.———I dread the thoughts of making him uneasy; and would rather suffer a thousand deaths than live the cause of dissension in the family.—I cannot conceive the meaning of Wilson's coming hither:———perhaps, it was in quest of us, in order to disclose his real name and situation:——but wherefore pass without staying to make the least enquiry?——My dear Willis, I am lost in conjecture.——I have not closed an eye since I saw him.——All night long have I been tossed about from one imagination to another.——The reflection finds no resting place.—— I have prayed, and sighed, and wept plentifully.——If this terrible suspence continues much longer, I shall have another fit of illness, and then the whole family will be in confusion.——If it was consistent with the wise purposes of Providence, would I were in my grave.——But it is my duty to be resigned.——My dearest Letty, excuse my weakness—excuse these blots——my tears fall so fast that I cannot keep the paper dry—yet I ought to consider that I have as yet no cause to despair——but I am such a fainthearted timorous creature!

Thank God, my uncle is much better than he was yesterday.——He is resolved to pursue our journey strait to Wales.——I hope we shall take Gloucester in our way— that hope chears my poor heart—I shall once more embrace my best beloved Willis, and pour all my griefs into her friendly bosom.——O heaven! is it possible that such happiness is reserved for

The dejected and forlorn

LYDIA MELFORD.

Oct. 4.

To Sir Watkin Phillips, Bart. of Jesus college, Oxon.

DEAR WATKIN,

I yesterday met with an incident which I believe you will own to be very surprising—As I stood with Liddy at the window of the inn where we had lodged, who should pass by but Wilson a-horseback!—I could not be mistaken in the person, for I had a full view of him as he advanced; I plainly perceived by my sister's confusion that

she recognized him at the same time. I was equally astonished and incensed at his appearance, which I could not
but interpret into an insult, or something worse. I ran out
at the gate, and, seeing him turn the corner of the street,
I dispatched my servant to observe his motions, but the
fellow was too late to bring me that satisfaction. He told
me, however, that there was an inn, called the Red Lion,
at that end of the town, where he supposed the horseman
had alighted, but that he would not enquire without further orders. I sent him back immediately to know what
strangers were in the house, and he returned with a report
that there was one Mr. Wilson lately arrived. In consequence of this information I charged him with a note
directed to that gentleman, desiring him to meet me in half
an hour in a certain field at the town's end, with a case
of pistols, in order to decide the difference which could
not be determined at our last rencounter: but I did not
think proper to subscribe the billet. My man assured me
he had delivered it into his own hand; and, that having
read it, he declared he would wait upon the gentleman
at the place and time appointed.

M'Alpine being an old soldier, and luckily sober at the
time, I entrusted him with my secret. I ordered him to be
within call, and, having given him a letter to be delivered
to my uncle in case of accident, I repaired to the rendezvous,
which was an inclosed field at a little distance from the
highway. I found my antagonist had already taken his
ground, wrapped in a dark horseman's coat, with a laced
hat flapped over his eyes; but what was my astonishment,
when, throwing off this wrapper, he appeared to be a person whom I had never seen before! He had one pistol
stuck in a leather belt, and another in his hand ready for
action, and, advancing a few steps, called to know if I
was ready—I answered, 'No,' and desired a parley; upon
which he turned the muzzle of his piece towards the earth;
then replaced it in his belt, and met me half way—When

I assured him he was not the man I expected to meet, he said *it might be so:* that he had received a slip of paper directed to Mr. Wilson, requesting him to come hither; and that as there was no other in the place of that name, he naturally concluded the note was intended for him, and him only—I then gave him to understand, that I had been injured by a person who assumed that name, which person I had actually seen within the hour, passing through the street on horseback; that hearing there was a Mr. Wilson at the Red Lion, I took it for granted he was the man, and in that belief had writ the billet; and I expressed my surprize, that he, who was a stranger to me and my concerns, should give me such a rendezvous, without taking the trouble to demand a previous explanation——He replied, that there was no other of his name in the whole country; that no such horseman had alighted at the Red Lion since nine o'clock, when he arrived—that having had the honour to serve his majesty, he thought he could not decently decline any invitation of this kind, from what quarter soever it might come; and that if any explanation was necessary, it did not belong to him to demand it, but to the gentleman who summoned him into the field—Vexed as I was at this adventure, I could not help admiring the coolness of this officer, whose open countenance prepossessed me in his favour.—He seemed to be turned of forty; wore his own short black hair, which curled naturally about his ears, and was very plain in his apparel—When I begged pardon for the trouble I had given him, he received my apology with great good humour.—He told me that he lived about ten miles off, at a small farm-house, which would afford me tolerable lodging, if I would come and take the diversion of hunting with him for a few weeks; in which case we might, perhaps, find out the man who had given me offence—I thanked him very sincerely for his courteous offer, which, I told him, I was not at liberty to accept at present, on account of my being engaged in a family party;

and so we parted, with mutual professions of good will and esteem.

Now tell me, dear knight, what am I to make of this singular adventure?—Am I to suppose that the horseman I saw was really a thing of flesh and blood, or a bubble that vanished into air?—or must I imagine Liddy knows more of the matter than she chuses to disclose?—If I thought her capable of carrying on any clandestine correspondence with such a fellow, I should at once discard all tenderness, and forget that she was connected with me by the ties of blood—But how is it possible that a girl of her simplicity and inexperience, should maintain such an intercourse, surrounded, as she is, with so many eyes, destitute of all opportunity, and shifting quarters every day of her life!—Besides, she has solemnly promised—No—I can't think the girl so base—so insensible to the honour of her family. What disturbs me chiefly, is the impression which these occurrences seem to make upon her spirits—These are the symptoms from which I conclude that the rascal has still a hold on her affection—surely I have a right to call him a rascal, and to conclude that his designs are infamous. But it shall be my fault if he does not one day repent his presumption——I confess I cannot think, much less write on this subject, with any degree of temper or patience; I shall therefore conclude with telling you, that we hope to be in Wales by the latter end of the month: but before that period you will probably hear again from

your affectionate

J. MELFORD.

Oct. 4.

To Sir Watkin Phillips, Bart. of Jesus college, Oxon.

DEAR PHILLIPS,

When I wrote you by last post, I did not imagine I should be tempted to trouble you again so soon: but I now sit down with a heart so full that it cannot contain itself; though I am under such agitation of spirits, that you are to expect neither method nor connexion in this address—— We have been this day within a hair's breadth of losing honest Matthew Bramble, in consequence of a cursed accident, which I will endeavour to explain.——In crossing the country to get into the post road, it was necessary to ford a river, and we that were a-horseback passed, without any danger or difficulty; but a great quantity of rain having fallen last night and this morning, there was such an accumulation of water, that a mill-head gave way, just as the coach was passing under it, and the flood rushed down with such impetuosity, as first floated, and then fairly over-turned the carriage in the middle of the stream——Lismahago and I, and the two servants, alighting instantaneously, ran into the river to give all the assistance in our power.——Our aunt, Mrs. Tabitha, who had the good fortune to be upper-most, was already half way out of the coach window, when her lover approaching, disengaged her entirely; but, whether his foot slipt, or the burthen was too great, they fell over head and ears in each others' arms. He endeavoured more than once to get up, and even to disentangle himself from her embrace, but she hung about his neck like a mill-stone, (no bad emblem of matrimony) and if my man had not proved a stanch auxiliary, those two lovers would in all probability have gone hand in hand to the shades below—— For my part, I was too much engaged to take any cog-nizance of their distress.——I snatched out my sister by the hair of the head, and, dragging her to the bank, recollected that my uncle had not yet appeared——Rushing again into the stream, I met Clinker hauling ashore Mrs. Jenkins, who looked like a mermaid with her hair dishevelled about her ears; but, when I asked if his master was safe, he forth-with shook her from him, and she must have gone to pot, if a miller had not seasonably come to her relief.——As for Humphry, he flew like lightening, to the coach, that was

by this time filled with water, and, diving into it, brought up the poor 'squire, to all appearance, deprived of life—It is not in my power to describe what I felt at this melancholy spectacle—it was such an agony as baffles all description! The faithful Clinker, taking him up in his arms, as if he had been an infant of six months, carried him ashore, howling most piteously all the way, and I followed him in a transport of grief and consternation—When he was laid upon the grass, and turned from side to side, a great quantity of water ran out at his mouth, then he opened his eyes, and fetched a deep sigh—Clinker perceiving these signs of life, immediately tied up his arm with a garter, and, pulling out a horse-fleam, let him blood in the farrier stile.—At first a few drops only issued from the orifice; but the limb being chafed, in a little time the blood began to flow in a continued stream, and he uttered some incoherent words, which were the most welcome sounds that ever saluted my ear. There was a country inn hard by, the landlord of which had by this time come with his people to give their assistance.—Thither my uncle being carried, was undressed and put to bed, wrapped in warm blankets; but having been moved too soon, he fainted away, and once more lay without sense or motion, notwithstanding all the efforts of Clinker and the landlord, who bathed his temples with Hungary water, and held a smelling-bottle to his nose. As I had heard of the efficacy of salt in such cases, I ordered all that was in the house to be laid under his head and body; and whether this application had the desired effect, or nature of herself prevailed, he, in less than a quarter of an hour, began to breathe regularly, and soon retrieved his recollection, to the unspeakable joy of all the bystanders. As for Clinker, his brain seemed to be affected.
—He laughed, and wept, and danced about in such a distracted manner, that the landlord very judiciously conveyed him out of the room. My uncle, seeing me dropping wet, comprehended the whole of what had happened, and asked

if all the company was safe?—Being answered in the affirmative, he insisted upon my putting on dry clothes; and, having swallowed a little warm wine, desired he might be left to his repose. Before I went to shift myself, I inquired about the rest of the family—I found Mrs. Tabitha still delirious from her fright, discharging very copiously the water she had swallowed. She was supported by the captain, distilling drops from his uncurled periwig, so lank and so dank, that he looked like Father Thame without his sedges, embracing Isis, while she cascaded in his urn. Mrs. Jenkins was present also, in a loose bed gown, without either cap or handkerchief; but she seemed to be as little *compos mentis* as her mistress, and acted so many cross purposes in the course of her attendance, that, between the two, Lismahago had occasion for all his philosophy. As for Liddy, I thought the poor girl would have actually lost her senses. The good woman of the house had shifted her linen, and put her into bed; but she was seized with the idea that her uncle had perished, and in this persuasion made a dismal out-cry; nor did she pay the least regard to what I said, when I solemnly assured her he was safe. Mr. Bramble hearing the noise, and being informed of her apprehension, desired she might be brought into his chamber; and she no sooner received this intimation, than she ran thither half naked, with the wildest expression of eagerness in her countenance—Seeing the 'squire sitting up in the bed, she sprung forwards and throwing her arms about his neck, exclaimed in a most pathetic tone, 'Are you —Are you indeed my uncle—My dear uncle!—My best friend! My father!—Are you really living? or is it an illusion of my poor brain!' Honest Matthew was so much affected, that he could not help shedding tears, while he kissed her forehead, saying, 'My dear Liddy, I hope I shall live long enough to shew how sensible I am of your affection—But your spirits are fluttered, child—You want rest—Go to bed and compose yourself—' 'Well, I will

(she replied)—but still methinks this cannot be real—The
coach was full of water—My uncle was under us all—
Gracious God!—You was under water—How did you get
out;—tell me that? or I shall think this is all a deception—'
'In what manner I was brought out, I know as little as you
do, my dear (said the 'squire); and, truly, that is a circumstance of which I want to be informed.' I would have given
him a detail of the whole adventure, but he would not
hear me until I should change my clothes; so that I had
only time to tell him, that he owed his life to the courage
and fidelity of Clinker; and having given him this hint,
I conducted my sister to her own chamber.

This accident happened about three o'clock in the afternoon, and in little more than an hour the hurricane was
all over; but as the carriage was found to be so much
damaged, that it could not proceed without considerable
repairs, a blacksmith and wheelwright were immediately
sent for to the next market-town, and we congratulated
ourselves upon being housed at an inn, which, though remote from the post-road, afforded exceeding good lodging.
The women being pretty well composed, and the men all
a-foot, my uncle sent for his servant, and, in the presence
of Lismahago and me, accosted him in these words—'So,
Clinker, I find you are resolved I shan't die by water—As
you have fished me up from the bottom at your own risque,
you are at least entitled to all the money that was in my
pocket, and there it is—' So saying, he presented him with
a purse containing thirty guineas, and a ring nearly of the
same value—'God forbid! (cried Clinker) your honour
shall excuse me—I am a poor fellow, but I have a heart—
O! if your honour did but know how I rejoice to see—
Blessed be his holy name, that made me the humble instrument—But as for the lucre of gain, I renounce it—I have
done no more than my duty—No more than I would have
done for the most worthless of my fellow-creatures—No
more than I would have done for captain Lismahago, or

Archy Macalpine, or any sinner upon earth—But for your worship, I would go through fire as well as water——' 'I do believe it, Humphry (said the 'squire); but as you think it was your duty to save my life at the hazard of your own, I think it is mine to express the sense I have of your extraordinary fidelity and attachment—I insist upon your receiving this small token of my gratitude; but don't imagine that I look upon this as an adequate recompence for the service you have done me—I have determined to settle thirty pounds a-year upon you for life; and I desire these gentlemen will bear witness to this my intention, of which I have a memorandum in my pocketbook.' 'Lord make me thankful for all these mercies! (cried Clinker, sobbing) I have been a poor bankrupt from the beginning—your honour's goodness found me, when I was—naked—when I was—sick and forlorn——I understand your honour's looks—I would not give offence—but my heart is very full —and if your worship won't give me leave to speak,— I must vent it in prayers to heaven for my benefactor.' When he quitted the room, Lismahago said, he should have a much better opinion of his honesty, if he did not whine and cant so abominably; but that he had always observed those weeping and praying fellows were hypocrites at bottom. Mr. Bramble made no reply to this sarcastic remark, proceeding from the lieutenant's resentment of Clinker's having, in pure simplicity of heart, ranked him with M'Alpine and the sinners of the earth——The landlord being called to receive some orders about the beds, told the 'squire that his house was very much at his service, but he was sure he should not have the honour to lodge him and his company. He gave us to understand that his master who lived hard by, would not suffer us to be at a public house, when there was accommodation for us at his own; and that, if he had not dined abroad in the neighbourhood he would have undoubtedly come to offer his services at our first arrival. He then launched out in praise

of that gentleman, whom he had served as butler, repre-
senting him as a perfect miracle of goodness and generosity.
He said he was a person of great learning, and allowed
to be the best farmer in the country:——that he had a lady
who was as much beloved as himself, and an only son, a
very hopeful young gentleman, just recovered from a dangerous fever, which had like to have proved fatal to the
whole family; for, if the son had died, he was sure the
parents would not have survived their loss——He had not
yet finished the encomium of Mr. Dennison, when this gentleman arrived in a post-chaise, and his appearance seemed
to justify all that had been said in his favour. He is pretty
well advanced in years, but hale, robust, and florid, with
an ingenuous countenance, expressive of good sense and
humanity. Having condoled with us on the accident which
had happened, he said he was come to conduct us to his
habitation, where we should be less incommoded than at
such a paultry inn, and expressed his hope that the ladies
would not be the worse for going thither in his carriage, as
the distance was not above a quarter of a mile. My uncle
having made a proper return to this courteous exhibition,
eyed him attentively, and then asked if he had not been at
Oxford, a commoner of Queen's college? When Mr. Dennison answered, 'Yes,' with some marks of surprise—'Look
at me then (said our 'squire) and let us see if you can
recollect the features of an old friend, whom you have not
seen these forty years.'——The gentleman, taking him
by the hand, and gazing at him earnestly,—'I protest, (cried
he) I do think I recall the idea of Matthew Loyd of
Glamorganshire, who was student of Jesus.' 'Well remembered, my dear friend, Charles Dennison, (exclaimed my
uncle, pressing him to his breast) I am that very identical
Matthew Loyd of Glamorgan.' Clinker, who had just
entered the room with some coals for the fire, no sooner
heard these words, than throwing down the scuttle on the
toes of Lismahago, he began to caper as if he was mad,

crying—'Matthew Loyd of Glamorgan!—O Providence!
—Matthew Loyd of Glamorgan!'——Then, clasping my
uncle's knees, he went on in this manner——'Your worship must forgive me—Matthew Loyd of Glamorgan!—
O Lord, Sir!—I can't contain myself!—I shall lose my
senses—' 'Nay, thou hast lost them already, I believe, (said
the 'squire, peevishly) prithee, Clinker, be quiet——What is
the matter?'——Humphry, fumbling in his bosom, pulled
out an old wooden snuff-box, which he presented in great
trepidation to his master, who, opening it immediately, perceived a small cornelian seal, and two scraps of paper—
At sight of these articles he started, and changed colour, and
casting his eye upon the inscriptions—'Ha!—how!—what!
—where (cried he) is the person here named?' Clinker,
knocking his own breast, could hardly pronounce these
words—'Here—here——here is Matthew Loyd, as the certificate sheweth—Humphry Clinker was the name of the
farrier that took me 'prentice'—'And who gave you these
tokens?' said my uncle hastily—'My poor mother on her
death-bed'——replied the other—'And who was your
mother?' 'Dorothy Twyford, an please your honour, heretofore bar-keeper at the Angel at Chippenham.'—'And
why were not these tokens produced before?' 'My mother
told me she had wrote to Glamorganshire, at the time of
my birth, but had no answer; and that afterwards, when
she made enquiry, there was no such person in that county.'
'And so in consequence of my changing my name and going abroad at that very time, thy poor mother and thou
have been left to want and misery—I am really shocked
at the consequence of my own folly.'—Then, laying his
hand on Clinker's head, he added, 'Stand forth, Matthew
Loyd—You see, gentlemen, how the sins of my youth rise
up in judgment against me—Here is my direction written
with my own hand, and a seal which I left at the woman's
request; and this is a certificate of the child's baptism,
signed by the curate of the parish.' The company were not

a little surprised at this discovery, upon which Mr. Dennison facetiously congratulated both the father and the son: for my part, I shook my new-found cousin heartily by the hand, and Lismahago complimented him with the tears in his eyes, for he had been hopping about the room, swearing in broad Scotch, and bellowing with the pain occasioned by the fall of the coalscuttle upon his foot. He had even vowed to drive the *saul* out of the body of that mad rascal: but, perceiving the unexpected turn which things had taken, he wished him joy of his good fortune, observing that it went very near his heart, as he was like to be a great toe out of pocket by the discovery—Mr. Dennison now desired to know for what reason my uncle had changed the name by which he knew him at Oxford, and our 'squire satisfied him, by answering to this effect:—'I took my mother's name, which was Loyd, as heir to her lands in Glamorgan-shire; but when I came of age, I sold that property, in order to clear my paternal estate, and resumed my real name; so that I am now Matthew Bramble of Brambleton-hall in Monmouthshire, at your service; and this is my nephew, Jeremy Melford of Belfield, in the county of Glamorgan.' At that instant the ladies entering the room, he presented Mrs. Tabitha as his sister, and Liddy as his niece. The old gentleman saluted them very cordially, and seemed struck with the appearance of my sister, whom he could not help surveying with a mixture of complacency and surprize——'Sister, (said my uncle) there is a poor relation that recommends himself to your good graces—The quondam Humphry Clinker is metamorphosed into Matthew Loyd; and claims the honour of being your carnal kinsman——in short, the rogue proves to be a crab of my own planting in the days of hot blood and unrestrained libertinism.' Clinker had by this time dropt upon one knee, by the side of Mrs. Tabitha, who, eyeing him askance, and flirting her fan with marks of agitation, thought proper, after some con-flict, to hold out her hand for him to kiss, saying, with a demure aspect, 'Brother, you have been very wicked: but I hope you'll live to see the folly of your ways—I am very sorry to say the young man, whom you have this day acknowledged, has more grace and religion, by the gift of God, than you with all your profane learning, and repeated opportunity—I do think he has got the trick of the eye, and the tip of the nose of my uncle Loyd of Flluydwellyn; and as for the long chin, it is the very moral of the governor's —Brother, as you have changed his name pray change his dress also; that livery doth not become any person that hath got our blood in his veins.'——Liddy seemed much pleased with this acquisition to the family.—She took him by the hand, declaring she should always be proud to own her connexion with a virtuous young man, who had given so many proofs of his gratitude and affection to her uncle.—Mrs. Winifred Jenkins, extremely fluttered between her surprize at this discovery, and the apprehension of losing her sweetheart, exclaimed in a gigling tone,—'I wish you joy, Mr. Clinker—Floyd—I would say—hi, hi, hi!—you'll be so proud you won't look at your poor fellow servants, oh, oh, oh!' Honest Clinker owned he was overjoyed at his good fortune, which was greater than he deserved—'But wherefore should I be proud? (said he) a poor object conceived in sin, and brought forth in iniquity, nursed in a parish workhouse, and bred in a smithy——Whenever I seem proud, Mrs. Jenkins, I beg of you to put me in mind of the condition I was in, when I first saw you between Chippenham and Marlborough.'

When this momentous affair was discussed to the satisfaction of all parties concerned, the weather being dry, the ladies declined the carriage; so that we walked all together to Mr. Dennison's house, where we found the tea ready prepared by his lady, an amiable matron, who received us with all the benevolence of hospitality.—The house is old fashioned and irregular, but lodgeable and commodious. To the south it has the river in front, at the distance of a hundred paces; and on the north, there is a rising ground covered with an agreeable plantation; the greens and walks are kept in the nicest order, and all is rural and romantic. I have not yet seen the young gentleman, who is on a visit to a friend in the neighbourhood, from whose house he is not expected 'till to-morrow.

In the mean time, as there is a man going to the next market-town with letters for the post, I take this opportunity to send you the history of this day, which has been remarkably full of adventures; and you will own I give you them like a beef-steak at Dolly's, *hot* and *hot*, without ceremony and parade, just as they come from the recollection of

Yours,

J. MELFORD.

To Dr. Lewis

DEAR DICK,

Since the last trouble I gave you, I have met with a variety of incidents, some of them of a singular nature, which I reserve as a fund for conversation; but there are others so interesting, that they will not keep in *petto* till meeting.

Know then, it was a thousand pounds to a sixpence, that you should now be executing my will, instead of perusing my letter! Two days ago, our coach was overturned in the midst of a rapid river, where my life was saved with the utmost difficulty, by the courage, activity, and presence of mind of my servant Humphry Clinker——But this is not the most surprising circumstance of the adventure——The said Humphry Clinker proves to be Matthew Loyd, natural son of one Matthew Loyd of Glamorgan, if you know any such person——You see, Doctor, that notwithstanding all your philosophy, it is not without some reason that the

Welchmen ascribe such energy to the force of blood—But we shall discuss this point on some future occasion.

This is not the only discovery which I made in consequence of our disaster—We happened to be wrecked upon a friendly shore——The lord of the manor is no other than Charles Dennison, our fellow-rake at Oxford—We are now happily housed with that gentleman, who has really attained to that pitch of rural felicity, at which I have been aspiring these twenty years in vain. He is blessed with a consort, whose disposition is suited to his own in all respects; tender, generous, and benevolent—She, moreover, possesses an uncommon share of understanding, fortitude, and discretion, and is admirably qualified to be his companion, confidant, counsellor, and coadjutrix. These excellent persons have an only son, about nineteen years of age, just such a youth as they could have wished that Heaven would bestow to fill up the measure of their enjoyment—In a word, they know no other allay to their happiness, but their apprehension and anxiety about the life and concerns of this beloved object.

Our old friend, who had the misfortune to be a second brother, was bred to the law, and even called to the bar; but he did not find himself qualified to shine in that province, and had very little inclination for his profession—He disobliged his father, by marrying for love, without any consideration of fortune; so that he had little or nothing to depend upon for some years but his practice, which afforded him a bare subsistence; and the prospect of an increasing family, began to give him disturbance and disquiet. In the mean time, his father dying, was succeeded by his elder brother, a fox-hunter and a sot, who neglected his affairs, insulted and oppressed his servants, and in a few years had well nigh ruined the estate, when he was happily carried off by a fever, the immediate consequence of a debauch. Charles, with the approbation of his wife, immediately determined to quit business, and retire into the country,

although this resolution was strenuously and zealously opposed by every individual, whom he consulted on the subject. Those who had tried the experiment, assured him
that he could not pretend to breathe in the country for less
than the double of what his estate produced; that, in order
to be upon the footing of a gentleman, he would be obliged
to keep horses, hounds, carriages, with a suitable number
of servants, and maintain an elegant table for the entertainment of his neighbours; that farming was a mystery,
known only to those who had been bred up to it from the
cradle, the success of it depending not only upon skill and
industry, but also upon such attention and œconomy as no
gentleman could be supposed to give or practise; accordingly, every attempt made by gentlemen miscarried, and not
a few had been ruined by their prosecution of agriculture—
Nay, they affirmed that he would find it cheaper to buy
hay and oats for his cattle, and to go to market for poultry,
eggs, kitchen herbs, and roots, and every the most inconsiderable article of house-keeping, than to have those articles
produced on his own ground.

These objections did not deter Mr. Dennison, because
they were chiefly founded on the supposition, that he would
be obliged to lead a life of extravagance and dissipation,
which he and his consort equally detested, despised, and
determined to avoid—The objects he had in view, were
health of body, peace of mind, and the private satisfaction
of domestic quiet, unallayed by actual want, and uninterrupted by the fears of indigence—He was very moderate in
his estimate of the necessaries, and even of the comforts
of life—He required nothing but wholesome air, pure water,
agreeable exercise, plain diet, convenient lodging, and decent
apparel. He reflected, that if a peasant without education,
or any great share of natural sagacity, could maintain a
large family, and even become opulent upon a farm, for
which he payed an annual rent of two or three hundred
pounds to the landlord, surely he himself might hope for

some success from his industry, having no rent to pay, but, on the contrary, three or four hundred pounds a year to receive—He considered, that the earth was an indulgent mother, that yielded her fruits to all her children without distinction. He had studied the theory of agriculture with a degree of eagerness and delight; and he could not conceive there was any mystery in the practice, but what he should be able to disclose by dint of care and application. With respect to household expence, he entered into a minute detail and investigation, by which he perceived the assertions of his friends were altogether erroneous—He found he should save sixty pounds a year in the single article of house-rent, and as much more in pocket-money and contingencies; that even butcher's-meat was twenty per cent. cheaper in the country than in London; but that poultry, and almost every other circumstance of house-keeping, might be had for less than one-half of what they cost in town; besides, a considerable saving on the side of dress, in being delivered from the oppressive imposition of ridiculous modes, invented by ignorance, and adopted by folly.

As to the danger of vying with the rich in pomp and equipage, it never gave him the least disturbance. He was now turned of forty, and, having lived half that time in the busy scenes of life, was well skilled in the science of mankind. There cannot be in nature a more contemptible figure than that of a man, who, with five hundred a year, presumes to rival in expence a neighbour who possesses five times that income—His ostentation, far from concealing, serves only to discover his indigence, and render his vanity the more shocking; for it attracts the eyes of censure, and excites the spirit of inquiry. There is not a family in the county, nor a servant in his own house, nor a farmer in the parish, but what knows the utmost farthing that his lands produce, and all these behold him with scorn or compassion. I am surprised that these reflections do not occur to persons in this unhappy dilemma, and produce a salutary effect; but the truth is, of all the passions incident to human nature, vanity is that which most effectually perverts the faculties of the understanding; nay, it sometimes becomes so incredibly depraved, as to aspire at infamy, and find pleasure in bearing the stigmas of reproach.

I have now given you a sketch of the character and situation of Mr. Dennison, when he came down to take possession of this estate; but as the messenger, who carries the letters to the next town, is just setting off, I shall reserve what further I have to say on this subject, till the next post, when you shall certainly hear from

Yours always,
MATT. BRAMBLE.

Oct. 8.

To Dr. Lewis

Once more, dear doctor, I resume the pen for your amusement.—It was on the morning after our arrival that, walking out with my friend, Mr. Dennison, I could not help breaking forth into the warmest expressions of applause at the beauty of the scene, which is really inchanting; and I signified, in particular, how much I was pleased with the disposition of some detached groves, that afforded at once shelter and ornament to his habitation.

'When I took possession of these lands, about two and twenty years ago, (said he) there was not a tree standing within a mile of the house, except those of an old neglected orchard, which produced nothing but leaves and moss.—It was in the gloomy month of November, when I arrived, and found the house in such a condition, that it might have been justly stiled the *tower of desolation*.—The court-yard was covered with nettles and docks, and the garden exhibited such a rank plantation of weeds as I had never seen before; —the window-shutters were falling in pieces;—the sashes broken;—and owls and jack-daws had taken possession of the chimneys.—The prospect within was still more dreary —All was dark and damp, and dirty beyond description;— the rain penetrated in several parts of the roof;—in some apartments the very floors had given way;—the hangings were parted from the walls, and shaking in mouldy remnants;—the glasses were dropping out of their frames;— the family-pictures were covered with dust;—and all the chairs and tables worm-eaten and crazy.——There was not a bed in the house that could be used, except one old-fashioned machine, with a high gilt tester and fringed curtains of yellow mohair, which had been, for aught I know, two centuries in the family.——In short, there was no furniture but the utensils of the kitchen; and the cellar afforded nothing but a few empty butts and barrels, that stunk so abominably, that I would not suffer any body to enter it until I had flashed a considerable quantity of gunpowder to qualify the foul air within.

'An old cottager and his wife, who were hired to lie in the house, had left it with precipitation, alledging, among other causes of retreat, that they could not sleep for frightful noises, and that my poor brother certainly walked after his death.—In a word, the house appeared uninhabitable; the barn, stable, and outhouses were in ruins; all the fences broken down, and the fields lying waste.

'The farmer who kept the key never dreamed I had any intention to live upon the spot—He rented a farm of sixty pounds, and his lease was just expiring.—He had formed a scheme of being appointed bailiff to the estate, and of converting the house and the adjacent grounds to his own use. —A hint of his intention I received from the curate at my first arrival; I therefore did not pay much regard to what he said by way of discouraging me from coming to settle in the country; but I was a little startled when he gave me warning that he should quit the farm at the expiration of his lease, unless I could abate considerably in the rent.

'At this period I accidentally became acquainted with a person, whose friendship laid the foundation of all my prosperity. In the next market-town, I chanced to dine at an inn with a Mr. Wilson, who was lately come to settle in the neighbourhood.—He had been lieutenant of a man of war, but quitted the sea in some disgust, and married the only daughter of farmer Bland, who lives in this parish, and has acquired a good fortune in the way of husbandry— Wilson is one of the best natured men I ever knew; brave, frank, obliging, and ingenuous——He liked my conversation, I was charmed with his liberal manner; and acquaintance immediately commenced, and this was soon improved into a friendship without reserve.—There are characters which, like similar particles of matter, strongly attract each other.—He forthwith introduced me to his father-in-law, farmer Bland, who was well acquainted with every acre of my estate, of consequence well qualified to advise me on this occasion.——Finding I was inclined to embrace a country life, and even to amuse myself with the occupation of farming, he approved of my design—He gave me to understand that all my farms were under-lett; that the estate was capable of great improvement; that there was plenty of chalk in the neighbourhood; and that my own ground produced excellent marle for manure. ——With respect to the farm, which was like to fall into my hands, he said he would willingly take it at the present rent; but at the same time owned, that if I would expend two hundred pounds in enclosure, it would be worth more than double the sum.

'Thus encouraged, I began the execution of my scheme without further delay, and plunged into a sea of expence, though I had no fund in reserve, and the whole produce of the estate did not exceed three hundred pounds a year— In one week, my house was made weather-tight, and thoroughly cleansed from top to bottom; then it was well ventilated by throwing all the doors and windows open, and making blazing fires of wood in every chimney from the kitchen to the garrets.——The floors were repaired, the sashes new glazed, and out of the old furniture of the whole house, I made shift to fit up a parlour and three chambers in a plain yet decent manner.——The court-yard was cleared of weeds and rubbish, and my friend Wilson charged himself with the dressing of the garden; bricklayers were set at work upon the barn and stable; and labourers engaged to restore the fences, and begin the work of hedging and ditching, under the direction of farmer Bland, at whose recommendation I hired a careful hind to lie in the house, and keep constant fires in the apartments.

'Having taken these measures, I returned to London, where I forthwith sold off my household-furniture, and, in three weeks from my first visit, brought my wife hither to keep her Christmas.——Considering the gloomy season of the year, the dreariness of the place, and the decayed aspect of our habitation, I was afraid that her resolution would sink under the sudden transition from a town life to such a melancholy state of rustication; but I was agreeably disappointed.——She found the reality less uncomfortable than the picture I had drawn.——By this time indeed, things were mended in appearance——The out-houses had risen out of their ruins; the pigeon-house was rebuilt, and replenished by Wilson, who also put my garden in decent order, and provided a good stock of poultry, which made an agreeable figure in my yard; and the house, on the whole, looked like the habitation of human creatures. ——Farmer Bland spared me a milch cow for my family and an ordinary saddle-horse for my servant to go to market at the next town.——I hired a country lad for a footman, the hind's daughter was my house-maid, and my wife had brought a cook-maid from London.

'Such was my family when I began house-keeping in this place, with three hundred pounds in my pocket, raised from the sale of my superfluous furniture.——I knew we should find occupation enough through the day to employ our time; but I dreaded the long winter evenings; yet, for those too we found a remedy:——The curate, who was a single man, soon became so naturalized to the family, that he generally lay in the house; and his company was equally agreeable and useful.——He was a modest man, a good scholar, and perfectly well qualified to instruct me in such country matters as I wanted to know.——Mr. Wilson brought his wife to see us and she became so fond of Mrs. Dennison, that she said she was never so happy as when she enjoyed the benefit of her conversation——She was then a fine buxom country lass, exceedingly docile, and as good-natured as her husband Jack Wilson; so that a friendship ensued among the women, which hath continued to this day.

'As for Jack, he hath been my constant companion, counsellor, and commissary.——I would not for a hundred pounds you should leave my house without seeing him.—— Jack is an universal genius—his talents are really astonishing:——He is an excellent carpenter, joiner, and turner, and a cunning artist in iron and brass.——He not only superintended my œconomy, but also presided over my pastimes— He taught me to brew beer, to make cyder, perry, mead, usquebaugh, and plague-water; to cook several outlandish delicacies, such as *ollas, pepper-pots, pillaws, corys, chabobs,* and *stufatas.*——He understands all manner of games from chess down to chuck-farthing, sings a good song, plays upon the violin, and dances a horn-pipe with surprising agility— He and I walked, and rode, and hunted, and fished together, without minding the vicissitudes of the weather; and I am persuaded, that in a raw, moist climate, like this of England, continual exercise is as necessary as food to the preservation of the individual.——In the course of two and twenty years, there has not been one hour's interruption or abatement in the friendship subsisting between Wilson's family and mine; and, what is a rare instance of good fortune, that friendship is continued to our children.——His son and mine are nearly of the same age and the same disposition; they have been bred up together at the same school and college, and love each other with the warmest affection.

'By Wilson's means, I likewise formed an acquaintance with a sensible physician who lives in the next market-town; and his sister, an agreeable old maiden, passed the Christmas holidays at our house.——Mean while I began my farming with great eagerness, and that very winter planted these groves that please you so much.——As for the neighbouring gentry, I had no trouble from that quarter during my first campaign; they were all gone to town before I settled in the country; and by the summer I had taken measures to defend myself from their attacks.——When a gay equipage came to my gates, I was never at home; those who visited me in a modest way, I received; and according to the remarks I made on their characters and conversation, either rejected their advances, or returned their civility——I was in general despised among the fashionable company, as a low fellow, both in breeding and circumstances; nevertheless, I found a few individuals of moderate fortune, who gladly adopted my stile of living; and many others would have acceded to our society, had they not been prevented by the pride, envy, and ambition of their wives and daughters.—— Those, in times of luxury and dissipation, are the rocks upon which all the small estates in the country are wrecked.

'I reserved in my own hands, some acres of ground adjacent to the house, for making experiments in agriculture, according to the directions of Lyle, Tull, Hart, Duhamel, and others who have written on this subject; and qualified their theory with the practical observations of farmer Bland, who was my great master in the art of husbandry.——In short, I became enamoured of a country life; and my success greatly exceeded my expectation——I drained bogs, burned heath, grubbed up furze and fern; I planted copse and willows where nothing else would grow; I gradually inclosed all my farms, and made such improvements that my estate now yields me clear twelve hundred pounds a year——All this time my wife and I have enjoyed uninterrupted health, and a regular flow of spirits, except on a very few occasions, when our chearfulness was invaded by such accidents as are inseperable from the condition of life.—— I lost two children in their infancy, by the small-pox, so that I have one son only, in whom all our hopes are centered. ——He went yesterday to visit a friend, with whom he has stayed all night, but he will be here to dinner.——I shall this day have the pleasure of presenting him to you and your family; and I flatter myself you will find him not altogether unworthy of our affection.

'The truth is, either I am blinded by the partiality of a parent, or he is a boy of a very amiable character; and yet his conduct has given us unspeakable disquiet.——You must know, we had projected a match between him and a gentleman's daughter in the next county, who will in all probability be heiress of a considerable fortune; but, it seems, he had a personal disgust to the alliance.——He was then at Cambridge, and tried to gain time on various pretences; but being pressed in letters by his mother and me to give a definitive answer, he fairly gave his tutor the slip and disappeared about eight months ago.——Before he took this rash step, he wrote me a letter, explaining his objection to the match, and declaring, that he would keep himself concealed until he should understand that his parents would dispense with his contracting an engagement that must make him miserable for life, and he prescribed the form of advertising in a certain newspaper, by which he might be apprized of our sentiments on this subject.

'You may easily conceive how much we were alarmed and afflicted by this elopement, which he had made without dropping the least hint to his companion Charles Wilson, who belonged to the same college.——We resolved to punish him with the appearance of neglect, in hopes that he would return of his own accord; but he maintained his purpose till the young lady chose a partner for herself; then he produced himself, and made his peace by the mediation of Wilson.—Suppose we should unite our families by joining him with your niece, who is one of the most lovely creatures I ever beheld.—My wife is already as fond of her as if she were her own child, and I have a presentiment that my son will be captivated by her at first sight.' 'Nothing could be more agreeable to all our family (said I) than such an alliance; but, my dear friend, candour obliges me to tell you, that I am afraid Liddy's heart is not wholly disengaged——there is a cursed obstacle——' 'You mean the young stroller at Gloucester (said he)—You are surprised that I should know this circumstance; but you will be more surprised when I tell you that stroller is no other than my son George Dennison—That was the character he assumed in his eclipse.' 'I am, indeed, astonished and overjoyed, (cried I) and shall be happy beyond expression to see your proposal take effect.'

He then gave me to understand that the young gentleman, at his emerging from concealment, had disclosed his passion for Miss Melford, the niece of Mr. Bramble, of Monmouthshire. Though Mr. Dennison little dreamed that this was his old friend Matthew Loyd, he nevertheless furnished his son with proper credentials, and he had been at Bath, London, and many other places in quest of us, to make himself and his pretensions known.—The bad success of his enquiry had such an effect upon his spirits, that immediately at his return he was seized with a dangerous fever, which overwhelmed his parents with terror and affliction; but he was now happily recovered, though still weak and disconsolate. My nephew joining us in our walk, I informed him of these circumstances, with which he was wonderfully pleased. He declared he would promote the match to the utmost of his power, and that he longed to embrace young Mr. Dennison as his friend and brother.—Mean while, the father went to desire his wife to communicate this discovery gradually to Liddy, that her delicate nerves might not suffer too sudden a shock; and I imparted the particulars to my sister Tabby, who expressed some surprize, not altogether unmixed, I believe, with an emotion of envy; for, though she could have no objection to an alliance at once so honourable and advantageous, she hesitated in giving her consent on pretence of the youth and inexperience of the parties; at length, however, she acquiesced, in consequence of having consulted with captain Lismahago.

Mr. Dennison took care to be in the way when his son arrived at the gate, and, without giving him time or opportunity to make any enquiry about the strangers, brought him up stairs to be presented to Mr. Loyd and his family—The first person he saw when he entered the room, was Liddy, who, notwithstanding all her preparation, stood trembling in the utmost confusion—At sight of this object he was fixed motionless to the floor, and, gazing at her with the utmost eagerness of astonishment, exclaimed, 'Sacred heaven! what is this!—ha!—wherefore—' Here his speech failing, he stood straining his eyes, in the most emphatic silence—'George, (said his father) this is my friend Mr. Loyd.' Roused at this intimation, he turned and received my salute, when I said, 'Young gentleman, if you had trusted me with your secret at our last meeting, we should have parted upon better terms.' Before he could make any answer, Jery came round and stood before him with open arms.—At first, he started and changed colour; but after a short pause, he rushed into his embrace, and they hugged one another as if they had been intimate friends from their infancy: then he payed his respects to Mrs. Tabitha, and advancing to Liddy, 'Is it possible, (cried he) that my senses do not play me false!—that I see Miss Melford under my father's roof —that I am permitted to speak to her without giving offence—and that her relations have honoured me with their countenance and protection.' Liddy blushed, and trembled, and faultered—'To be sure, sir, (said she) it is a very surprising circumstance——a great—a providential——I really know not what I say—but I beg you will think I have said what's agreeable.'

Mrs. Dennison interposing said, 'Compose yourselves, my dear children.—Your mutual happiness shall be our peculiar care.' The son going up to his mother, kissed one hand; my niece bathed the other with her tears; and the good old lady pressed them both in their turns to her breast.—The lovers were too much affected to get rid of their embarrassment for one day; but the scene was much enlivened by the arrival of Jack Wilson, who brought, as usual, some game of his own killing——His honest countenance was a good letter of recommendation.—I received him like a dear friend after a long separation; and I could not help wondering to see him shake Jery by the hand as an old acquaintance——They had, indeed, been acquainted some days, in consequence of a diverting incident, which I shall explain at meeting.—That same night a consultation was held upon the concerns of the lovers, when the match was formally agreed to, and all the marriage articles were settled without the least dispute.—My nephew and I promised to make Liddy's fortune five thousand pounds. Mr. Dennison declared, he would make over one half of his estate immediately to his son, and that his daughter-in-law should be secured in a jointure of four hundred—Tabby proposed, that, considering their youth, they should undergo one year at least, of probation before the indissoluble knot should be tied; but the young gentleman being very impatient and importunate, and the scheme implying that the young couple should live in the house, under the wings of his parents, we resolved to make them happy without further delay.

As the law requires that the parties should be some weeks resident in the parish, we shall stay here till the ceremony is performed.——Mr. Lismahago requests that he may take the benefit of the same occasion; so that next Sunday the banns will be published for all four together.—I doubt

I shall not be able to pass my Christmas with you at Bram-bleton-hall.—Indeed, I am so agreeably situated in this place, that I have no desire to shift my quarters; and I fore-see, that when the day of separation comes, there will be abundance of sorrow on all sides.—In the mean time, we must make the most of those blessings which Heaven be-stows.—Considering how you are tethered by your pro-fession, I cannot hope to see you so far from home; yet the distance does not exceed a summer-day's journey, and Charles Dennison, who desires to be remembered to you, would be rejoiced to see his old compotator; but as I am now stationary, I expect regular answers to the epistles of

Yours invariably,

MATT. BRAMBLE.

Oct. 11.

To Sir Watkin Phillips, Bart. at Oxon.

DEAR WAT,

Every day is now big with incident and discovery——
Young Mr. Dennison proves to be no other than that identi-cal person whom I have execrated so long, under the name of Wilson—He had eloped from college at Cambridge, to avoid a match that he detested, and acted in different parts of the country as a stroller, until the lady in question made choice of a husband for herself; then he returned to his father, and disclosed his passion for Liddy, which met with the approbation of his parents, though the father little imagined that Mr. Bramble was his old companion Matthew Loyd. The young gentleman, being impowered to make honourable proposals to my uncle and me, had been in search of us all over England, without effect; and he it was whom I had seen pass on horseback by the window of the inn, where I stood with my sister, but he little dreamed that we were in the house—As for the real Mr. Wilson, whom I

called forth to combat, by mistake, he is the neighbour and intimate friend of old Mr. Dennison, and this connexion had suggested to the son the idea of taking that name while he remained in obscurity.

You may easily conceive what pleasure I must have felt on discovering that the honour of our family was in no danger from the conduct of a sister whom I love with uncommon affection; that, instead of debasing her sentiments and views to a wretched stroller, she had really captivated the heart of a gentleman, her equal in rank and superior in fortune; and that, as his parents approved of his attachment, I was on the eve of acquiring a brother-in-law so worthy of my friendship and esteem. George Dennison is, without all question, one of the most accomplished young fellows in England. His person is at once elegant and manly, and his understanding highly cultivated. Tho' his spirit is lofty, his heart is kind; and his manner so engaging, as to command veneration and love, even from malice and indifference. When I weigh my own character with his, I am ashamed to find myself so light in the balance; but the comparison excites no envy—I propose him as a model for imitation—I have endeavoured to recommend myself to his friendship, and hope I have already found a place in his affection. I am, however, mortified to reflect what flagrant injustice we every day commit, and what absurd judgment we form, in viewing objects through the falsifying mediums of prejudice and passion. Had you asked me a few days ago, the picture of Wilson the player, I should have drawn a portrait very unlike the real person and character of George Dennison—Without all doubt, the greatest advantage acquired in travelling and perusing mankind in the original, is that of dispelling those shameful clouds that darken the faculties of the mind, preventing it from judging with candour and precision.

The real Wilson is a great original, and the best tempered, companionable man I ever knew—I question if ever he was angry or low-spirited in his life. He makes no pretensions to letters; but he is an adept in every thing else that can be either useful or entertaining. Among other qualifications, he is a complete sportsman, and counted the best shot in the county. He and Dennison, and Lismahago and I, attended by Clinker, went a-shooting yesterday, and made great havock among the partridges—To-morrow we shall take field against the woodcocks and snipes. In the evening we dance and sing, or play at commerce, love, and quadrille.

Mr. Dennison is an elegant poet, and has written some detached pieces on the subject of his passion for Liddy, which must be very flattering to the vanity of a young woman—Perhaps he is one of the greatest theatrical geniuses that ever appeared. He sometimes entertains us with reciting favourite speeches from our best plays. We are resolved to convert the great hall into a theatre, and get up the *Beaux Stratagem* without delay—I think I shall make no contemptible figure in the character of *Scrub;* and Lismahago will be very great in *Captain Gibbet*—Wilson undertakes to entertain the country people with *Harlequin Skeleton,* for which he has got a jacket ready painted with his own hand.

Our society is really enchanting. Even the severity of Lismahago relaxes, and the vinegar of Mrs. Tabby is remarkably dulcified, ever since it was agreed that she should take precedency of her niece in being first noosed: for, you must know, the day is fixed for Liddy's marriage; and the banns for both couples have been already once published in the parish church. The Captain earnestly begged that one trouble might serve for all, and Tabitha assented with a vile affectation of reluctance. Her inamorato, who came hither very slenderly equipt, has sent for his baggage to London, which, in all probability, will not arrive in time for the wedding; but it is of no great consequence, as every thing is to be transacted with the utmost privacy—Meanwhile, directions are given for making out the contracts of marriage, which are very favourable for both females; Liddy will be secured in a good jointure; and her aunt will remain mistress of her own fortune, except one half of the interest, which her husband shall have a right to enjoy for his natural life: I think this is as little in conscience as can be done for a man who yokes with such a partner for life.

These expectants seem to be so happy, that if Mr. Dennison had an agreeable daughter, I believe I should be for making the third couple in this country dance. The humour seems to be infectious; for Clinker, alias Loyd, has a month's mind to play the fool, in the same fashion, with Mrs. Winifred Jenkins. He has even sounded me on the subject; but I have given him no encouragement to prosecute this scheme—I told him I thought he might do better, as there was no engagement nor promise subsisting; that I did not know what designs my uncle might have formed for his advantage; but I was of opinion, that he should not, at present, run the risque of disobliging him by any premature application of this nature—Honest Humphry protested he would suffer death sooner than do or say any thing that should give offence to the 'squire: but he owned he had a kindness for the young woman, and had reason to think she looked upon him with a favourable eye; that he considered this mutual manifestation of good will, as an engagement understood, which ought to be binding to the conscience of an honest man; and he hoped the 'squire and I would be of the same opinion, when we should be at leisure to bestow any thought about the matter—I believe he is in the right; and we shall find time to take his case into consideration—You see we are fixed for some weeks at least, and as you have had a long respite, I hope you will begin immediately to discharge the arrears due to

Your affectionate,

J. MELFORD.

Oct. 14.

To Miss Lætitia Willis, at Gloucester

My dear, dear Letty,

Never did I sit down to write in such agitation as I now feel—In the course of a few days, we have met with a number of incidents so wonderful and interesting, that all my ideas are thrown into confusion and perplexity—You must not expect either method or coherence in what I am going to relate—my dearest Willis. Since my last, the aspect of affairs is totally changed!—and so changed!—but I would fain give you a regular detail——In passing a river about eight days ago, our coach was overturned, and some of us narrowly escaped with life—My uncle had well nigh perished——O Heaven, I cannot reflect upon that circumstance without horror—I should have lost my best friend, my father and protector, but for the resolution and activity of his servant Humphry Clinker, whom Providence really seems to have placed near him for the necessity of this occasion.—I would not be thought superstitious; but surely he acted from a stronger impulse than common fidelity—Was it not the voice of nature that loudly called upon him to save the life of his own father? for O Letty, it was discovered that Humphry Clinker was my uncle's natural son.

Almost at the same instant, a gentleman, who came to offer us his assistance, and invite us to his house, turned out to be a very old friend of Mr. Bramble.——His name is Mr. Dennison, one of the worthiest men living; and his lady is a perfect saint upon earth. They have an only son—who do you think is this only son?—O Letty!—O gra·cious heaven! how my heart palpitates, when I tell you that this only son of Mr. Dennison's, is that very identical youth who, under the name of Wilson, has made such ravage in my heart!—Yes, my dear friend! Wilson and I are now lodged in the same house, and converse together freely——His father approves of his sentiments in my favour; his mother loves me with all the tenderness of a parent; my uncle, my aunt and my brother, no longer oppose my inclinations—On the contrary, they have agreed to make us happy without delay; and in three weeks or a month, if no unforeseen accident intervenes, your friend Lydia Melford, will have changed her name and condition—I say, if *no accident intervenes*, because such a torrent of success makes me tremble!——I wish there may not be something treacherous in this sudden reconciliation of fortune—I have no merit—I have no title to such felicity. Far from enjoying the prospect that lies before me, my mind is harrassed with a continued tumult, made up of hopes and wishes, doubts and apprehensions—I can neither eat nor sleep, and my spirits are in perpetual flutter.—I more than ever feel that vacancy in my heart, which your presence alone can fill.—The mind, in every disquiet, seeks to repose itself on the bosom of a friend; and this is such a trial as I really know not how to support without your company and counsel——I must, therefore, dear Letty, put your friendship to the test—I must beg you will come and do the last offices of maidenhood to your companion Lydia Melford.

This letter goes inclosed in one to our worthy governess, from Mrs. Dennison, entreating her to interpose with your mamma, that you may be allowed to favour us with your company on this occasion; and I flatter myself that no material objection can be made to our request—The distance from hence to Gloucester, does not exceed one hundred miles, and the roads are good.—Mr. Clinker, alias Loyd, shall be sent over to attend your motions—If you step into the post-chaise, with your maid Betty Barker, at seven in the morning, you will arrive by four in the afternoon at the half-way house, where there is good accommodation. There you shall be met by my brother and myself, who will next day conduct you to this place, where, I am sure, you will find yourself perfectly at your ease in the midst of an agreeable society.—Dear Letty, I will take no refusal—if you have any friendship——any humanity——you will come. ——I desire that immediate application may be made to your mamma; and that the moment her permission is obtained, you will apprise

Your ever faithful,
LYDIA MELFORD.

Oct. 14.

To Mrs. Jermyn, at her house in Gloucester

DEAR MADAM,

Though I was not so fortunate as to be favoured with an answer to the letter with which I troubled you in the spring, I still flatter myself that you retain some regard for me and my concerns. I am sure the care and tenderness with which I was treated, under your roof and tuition, demand the warmest returns of gratitude and affection on my part, and these sentiments, I hope, I shall cherish to my dying day —At present, I think it my duty to make you acquainted with the happy issue of that indiscretion by which I incurred your displeasure.——Ah! madam, the slighted Wilson is metamorphosed into George Dennison, only son and heir of a gentleman, whose character is second to none in England, as you may understand upon inquiry. My guardian, my brother and I, are now in his house; and an immediate union of the two families is to take place in the persons of the young gentleman and your poor Lydia Melford.—You will easily conceive how embarrassing this situation must be to a young inexperienced creature like me, of weak nerves and strong apprehensions; and how much the presence of a friend and confident would encourage and support me on this occasion. You know, that of all the young ladies, Miss Willis was she that possessed the greatest share of my confidence and affection; and, therefore, I fervently wish to have the happiness of her company at this interesting crisis.

Mrs. Dennison, who is the object of universal love and esteem, has, at my request, written to you on this subject, and I now beg leave to reinforce her sollicitations.—My dear Mrs. Jermyn! my ever honoured governess! let me conjure you by that fondness which once distinguished your favourite Lydia! by that benevolence of heart, which disposes you to promote the happiness of your fellow-creatures in general! lend a favourable ear to my petition, and use your influence with Letty's mamma, that my most earnest desire may be gratified. Should I be indulged in this particular, I will engage to return her safe, and even to accompany her to Gloucester, where, if you will give me leave, I will present to you, under another name,

Dear Madam,
Your most affectionate
Humble servant,
And penitent,
Lydia Melford.

Oct. 14.

To Mrs. Mary Jones, at Brambleton-hall

O Mary Jones! Mary Jones!

I have met with so many axidents, suprisals, and terrifications, that I am in a pafeck fantigo, and believe I shall never be my own self again. Last week I was dragged out of a river like a drowned rat, and lost a bran-new nightcap, with a sulfer stay-hook, that cost me a good half-a-crown, and an odd shoe of green gallow monkey; besides wetting my cloaths and taring my smuck, and an ugly gash made in the back part of my thigh, by the stump of a tree— To be sure Mr. Clinker tuck me out of the cox; but he left me on my back in the water, to go to the 'squire; and

I mought have had a watry grave, if a millar had not brought me to the dry land——But, O! what choppings and changes girl—The player man that came after Miss Liddy, and frightened me with a beard at Bristol Well, is now matthewmurphy'd into a fine young gentleman, son and hare of 'squire Dollison—We are all together in the same house, and all parties have agreed to the match, and in a fortnite the surrymony will be performed.

But this is not the only wedding we are to have—Mistress is resolved to have the same frolick, in the naam of God! Last Sunday in the parish crutch, if my own ars may be trusted, the clerk called the banes of marridge betwixt Opaniah Lashmeheygo, and Tapitha Bramble, spinster; he mought as well have called her inkle-weaver, for she never spun and hank of yarn in her life—Young 'squire Dollison and Miss Liddy make the second kipple; and there might have been a turd, but times are changed with Mr. Clinker— O Molly! what do'st think? Mr. Clinker is found to be a pye-blow of our own 'squire, and his rite naam is Mr. Matthew Loyd (thof God he nose how that can be); and he is now out of livery, and wares ruffles—but I new him when he was out at elbows, and had not a rag to kiver his pistereroes; so he need not hold his head so high— He is for sartin very umble and compleasant, and purtests as how he has the same regard as before; but that he is no longer his own master, and cannot portend to marry with-- out the 'squire's consent—He says he must wait with pa- tience, and trust to Providence, and such nonsense—But if so be as how his regard be the same, why stand shilly shally? Why not strike while the iron is hot, and speak to the 'squire without loss of time? What subjection can the 'squire make to our coming together—Thof my father wan't a gentle- man, my mother was an honest woman—I did'n't come on the wrong side of the blanket, girl—My parents were marred according to the rights of holy mother crutch, in the face of men and angles—Mark that, Mary Jones.

Mr. Clinker (Loyd I would say) had best look to his tackle—There be other chaps in the market, as the saying is——What would he say if I should except the soot and sarvice of the young 'squire's valley? Mr. Machappy is a gentleman born, and has been abroad in the wars—He has a world of buck larning, and speaks French, and Ditch, and Scotch, and all manner of outlandish lingos; to be sure he's a little the worse for the ware, and is much given to drink; but then he's good-tempered in his liquor, and a prudent woman mought wind him about her finger—But I have no thoughts of him, I'll assure you——I scorn for to do, or to say, or to think any thing that mought give un-breech to Mr. Loyd, without furder occasion—But then I have such vapours, Molly—I sit and cry by myself, and take ass of etida, and smill to burnt fathers, and kindal-snuffs; and I pray constantly for grease, that I may have a glimpse of the new-light, to shew me the way through this wretched veil of tares—And yet, I want for nothing in this family of love, where every sole is so kind and so courteous, that wan would think they are so many saints in haven. Dear Molly, I recommend myself to your prayers, being, with my sarvice to Saul,

your ever loving,

and discounselled friend,

WIN. JENKINS.

Oct. 14.

To Dr. Lewis

DEAR DICK,

You cannot imagine what pleasure I have in seeing your hand-writing, after such a long cessation on your side of our correspondence—Yet, Heaven knows, I have often seen your hand-writing with disgust—I mean, when it ap-peared in abbreviations of apothecary's Latin—I like your hint of making interest for the reversion of the collector's place, for Mr. Lismahago, who is much pleased with the scheme, and presents you with his compliments and best thanks for thinking so kind of his concerns——The man seems to mend, upon further acquaintance. That harsh reserve, which formed a disagreeable husk about his character, begins to peel off in the course of our communication ——I have great hopes that he and Tabby will be as happily paired as any two draught animals in the kingdom; and I make no doubt but that he will prove a valuable acquisition to our little society, in the article of conversation, by the fire-side in winter.

Your objection to my passing this season of the year at such a distance from home, would have more weight if I did not find myself perfectly at my ease where I am; and my health so much improved, that I am disposed to bid defiance to gout and rheumatism——I begin to think I have put myself on the superannuated list too soon, and absurdly sought for health in the retreats of laziness——I am persuaded that all valetudinarians are too sedentary, too regular, and too cautious——We should sometimes increase the motion of the machine, to *unclog the wheels of life*; and now and then take a plunge amidst the waves of excess, in order to case-harden the constitution. I have even found a change of company as necessary as a change of air, to promote a vigorous circulation of the spirits, which is the very essence and criterion of good health.

Since my last, I have been performing the duties of friendship, that required a great deal of exercise, from which I hope to derive some benefit——Understanding, by the greatest accident in the world, that Mr. Baynard's wife was dangerously ill of a pleuritic fever, I borrowed Dennison's post-chaise, and went across the country to his habitation, attended only by Loyd (quondam Clinker) on horseback.——As the distance is not above thirty miles, I arrived about four in the afternoon, and meeting the physician at the door, was informed that his patient had just expired.—I was instantly seized with a violent emotion, but it was not grief.—The family being in confusion, I ran up stairs into the chamber, where, indeed, they were all assembled.—The aunt stood wringing her hands in a kind of stupefaction of sorrow, but my friend acted all the extravagancies of affliction——He held the body in his arms, and poured forth such a lamentation, that one would have thought he had lost the most amiable consort and valuable companion upon earth.

Affection may certainly exist independent of esteem; nay, the same object may be lovely in one respect, and detestable in another—The mind has a surprising faculty of accommodating, and even attaching itself, in such a manner, by dint of use, to things that are in their own nature disagreeable, and even pernicious, that it cannot bear to be delivered from them without reluctance and regret. Baynard was so absorbed in his delirium, that he did not perceive me when I entered, and desired one of the women to conduct the aunt into her own chamber.—At the same time I begged the tutor to withdraw the boy, who stood gaping in a corner, very little affected with the distress of the scene.— These steps being taken, I waited till the first violence of my friend's transport was abated, then disengaged him gently from the melancholy object, and led him by the hand into another apartment; though he struggled so hard, that I was obliged to have recourse to the assistance of his valet de chambre——In a few minutes, however, he recollected himself, and folding me in his arms, 'This, (cried he) is a friendly office, indeed!——I know not how you came hither; but, I think, Heaven sent you to prevent my going distracted—O Matthew! I have lost my dear Harriet!—my poor, gentle, tender creature, that loved me with such warmth and purity of affection—my constant companion of twenty years!—She's gone—she's gone for ever!—Heaven and earth! where is she?——Death shall not part us!'

So saying, he started up, and could hardly be withheld from returning to the scene we had quitted——You will perceive it would have been very absurd for me to argue with a man that talked so madly.——On all such occasions, the first torrent of passion must be allowed to subside gradually.——I endeavoured to beguile his attention by starting little hints and insinuating other objects of discourse imperceptibly; and being exceedingly pleased in my own mind at this event, I exerted myself with such an extraordinary flow of spirits as was attended with success.——In a few hours, he was calm enough to hear reason, and even to own that Heaven could not have interposed more effectually to rescue him from disgrace and ruin.——That he might not, however, relapse into weaknesses for want of company, I passed the night in his chamber, in a little tent bed brought thither on purpose; and well it was I took this precaution, for he started up in bed several times, and would have played the fool, if I had not been present.

Next day he was in a condition to talk of business, and vested me with full authority over his household, which I began to exercise without loss of time, tho' not before he knew and approved of the scheme I had projected for his advantage.——He would have quitted the house immediately; but this retreat I opposed.——Far from encouraging a temporary disgust, which might degenerate into an habitual aversion, I resolved, if possible, to attach him more than ever to his Houshold Gods.——I gave directions for the funeral to be as private as was consistant with decency; I wrote to London, that an inventory and estimate might be made of the furniture and effects in his town-house, and gave notice to the landlord, that Mr. Baynard should quit the premises at Ladyday; I set a person at work to take account of every thing in the country-house, including horses, carriages, and harness; I settled the young gentleman at a boarding school, kept by a clergyman in the neighbourhood, and thither he went without reluctance, as soon as he knew that he was to be troubled no more with his tutor, whom we dismissed.——The aunt continued very sullen, and never appeared at table, though Mr. Baynard payed his respects to her every day in her own chamber; there also she held conferences with the waiting-women and other servants of the family: but, the moment her niece was interred, she went away in a post-chaise prepared for that purpose: she did not leave the house, however, without giving Mr. Baynard to understand, that the wardrobe of her niece was the perquisite of her woman; accordingly that worthless drab received all the clothes, laces, and linen of her deceased mistress, to the value of five hundred pounds, at a moderate computation.

The next step I took was to disband that legion of supernumerary domestics, who had preyed so long upon the vitals of my friend: a parcel of idle drones, so intolerably insolent, that they even treated their own master with the most contemptuous neglect. They had been generally hired by his wife, according to the recommendation of her woman, and these were the only patrons to whom they payed the least deference. I had therefore uncommon satisfaction in clearing the house of these vermin. The woman of the deceased, and a chambermaid, a valet de chambre, a butler, a French cook, a master gardener, two footmen and a coachman, I payed off, and turned out of the house immediately, paying to each a month's wages in lieu of warning. Those whom I retained, consisted of the female cook, who had been assistant to the Frenchman, a house maid, an old lacquey, a postilion, and under-gardener. Thus I removed at once a huge mountain of expence and care from the shoulders of my friend, who could hardly believe the evidence of his own senses, when he found himself so suddenly and so effectually relieved. His heart, however, was still subject to vibrations of tenderness, which returned at certain intervals, extorting sighs, and tears, and exclamations of grief and impatience: but these fits grew every day less violent and less frequent,

till at length his reason obtained a complete victory over the
infirmities of his nature.

Upon an accurate enquiry into the state of his affairs, I
find his debts amount to twenty thousand pounds, for
eighteen thousand pounds of which sum his estate is mort-
gaged; and as he pays five per cent. interest, and some of
his farms are unoccupied, he does not receive above two hundred pounds a year clear from his lands, over and above
the interest of his wife's fortune, which produced eight
hundred pounds annually. For lightening this heavy burthen, I devised the following expedient—His wife's jewels,
together with his superfluous plate and furniture in both
houses, his horses and carriages, which are already adver-
tised to be sold by auction, will, according to the estimate,
produce two thousand five hundred pounds in ready money,
with which the debt will be immediately reduced to eighteen
thousand pounds—I have undertaken to find him ten thousand pounds at four per cent. by which means he will save
one hundred a-year in the article of interest, and perhaps
we shall be able to borrow the other eight thousand on the
same terms. According to his own scheme of a country life,
he says he can live comfortably for three hundred pounds
a-year; but, as he has a son to educate, we will allow him
five hundred; then there will be an accumulating fund of
seven hundred a-year, principal and interest, to pay off the
incumbrance; and, I think, we may modestly add three hundred, on the presumption of new-leasing and improving the
vacant farms: so that, in a couple of years, I suppose there
will be above a thousand a-year appropriated to liquidate a
debt of sixteen thousand.

We forthwith began to class and set apart the articles
designed for sale, under the direction of an upholder from
London; and, that nobody in the house might be idle, commenced our reformation without doors, as well as within.
With Baynard's good leave, I ordered the gardener to turn
the rivulet into its old channel, to refresh the fainting

Naiads, who had so long languished among mouldring roots, withered leaves, and dry pebbles—The shrubbery is condemned to extirpation; and the pleasure ground will be restored to its original use of corn-field and pasture—Orders are given for rebuilding the walls of the garden at the back of the house, and for planting clumps of firs, intermingled with beech and chestnut, at the east end, which is now quite exposed to the surly blasts that come from that quarter. All these works being actually begun, and the house and auction left to the care and management of a reputable attorney, I brought Baynard along with me in the chaise, and made him acquainted with Dennison, whose goodness of heart would not fail to engage his esteem and affection ——He is indeed charmed with our society in general, and declares that he never saw the theory of true pleasure reduced to practice before.—I really believe it would not be an easy task to find such a number of individuals assembled under one roof, more happy than we are at present.

I must tell you, however, in confidence, I suspect Tabby of tergiversation.—I have been so long accustomed to that original, that I know all the caprices of her heart, and can often perceive her designs while they are yet in embrio— She attached herself to Lismahago for no other reason but that she despaired of making a more agreeable conquest,— At present, if I am not much mistaken in my observation, she would gladly convert the widowhood of Baynard to her own advantage.—Since he arrived, she has behaved very coldly to the captain, and strove to fasten on the other's heart, with the hooks of overstrained civility.—These must be the instinctive efforts of her constitution, rather than the effects of any deliberate design; for matters are carried to such a length with the lieutenant, that she could not retract with any regard to conscience or reputation. Besides, she will meet with nothing but indifference or aversion on the side of Baynard, who has too much sense to think of such a partner at any time, and too much delicacy to admit a thought of any such connexion at the present juncture—. Meanwhile, I have prevailed upon her to let him have four thousand pounds at four per cent. towards paying off his mortgage. Young Dennison has agreed that Liddy's fortune shall be appropriated to the same purpose, on the same terms.——His father will sell out three thousand pounds stock for his accommodation.——Farmer Bland has, at the desire of Wilson, undertaken for two thousand; and I must make an effort to advance what further will be required to take my friend out of the hands of the Philistines. He is so pleased with the improvements made on this estate, which is all cultivated like a garden, that he has entered himself as a pupil in farming to Mr. Dennison, and resolved to attach himself wholly to the practice of husbandry.

Every thing is now prepared for our double wedding. The marriage-articles for both couples are drawn and executed; and the ceremony only waits until the parties shall have been resident in the parish the term prescribed by law. Young Dennison betrays some symptoms of impatience; but, Lismahago bears this necessary delay with the temper of a philosopher.——You must know, the captain does not stand altogether on the foundation of personal merit. Besides his half-pay, amounting to two and forty pounds a year, this indefatigable œconomist has amassed eight hundred pounds, which he has secured in the funds. This sum arises partly from his pay's running up while he remained among the Indians; partly from what he received as a consideration for the difference between his full appointment and the half-pay, to which he is now restricted; and partly from the profits of a little traffick he drove in peltry, during his sachemship among the Miamis.

Liddy's fears and perplexities have been much assuaged by the company of one Miss Willis, who had been her intimate companion at the boarding-school. Her parents had been earnestly sollicited to allow her making this friendly visit on such an extraordinary occasion; and two days ago she arrived with her mother, who did not chuse that she should come without a proper gouvernante. The young lady is very sprightly, handsome, and agreeable, and the mother a mighty good sort of a woman; so that their coming adds considerably to our enjoyment. But we shall have a third couple yoked in the matrimonial chain. Mr. Clinker Loyd has made humble remonstrance through the canal of my nephew, setting forth the sincere love and affection mutually subsisting between him and Mrs. Winifred Jenkins, and praying my consent to their coming together for life. I would have wished that Mr. Clinker had kept out of this scrape; but as the nymph's happiness is at stake, and she has had already some fits in the way of despondence, I, in order to prevent any tragical catastrophe, have given him leave to play the fool, in imitation of his betters; and I suppose we shall in time have a whole litter of his progeny at Bramble-ton-hall. The fellow is stout and lusty, very sober and con-scientious; and the wench seems to be as great an enthusiast in love as in religion.

I wish you would think of employing him some other way, that the parish may not be overstocked——you know he has been bred a farrier, consequently belongs to the faculty; and as he is very docile, I make no doubt but, with your good instruction, he may be, in a little time, qualified to act as a Welch apothecary. Tabby, who never did a favour with a good grace, has consented, with great re-luctance, to this match. Perhaps it hurts her pride, as she now considers Clinker in the light of a relation; but, I believe, her objections are of a more selfish nature. She declares she cannot think of retaining the wife of Matthew Loyd in the character of a servant; and she foresees, that on such an occasion the woman will expect some gratifica-tion for her past services. As for Clinker, exclusive of other considerations, he is so trusty, brave, affectionate, and alert, and I owe him such personal obligations, that he merits more than all the indulgence that can possibly be shewn him, by

Yours,

MATT. BRAMBLE.

Oct. 26.

To Sir Watkin Phillips, Bart. at Oxon.

DEAR KNIGHT,

The fatal knots are now tied. The comedy is near a close; and the curtain is ready to drop: but, the latter scenes of this act I shall recapitulate in order——About a fortnight ago, my uncle made an excursion across the country, and brought hither a particular friend, one Mr. Baynard, who has just lost his wife, and was for some time disconsolate, though by all accounts he had much more cause for joy than for sorrow at this event.——His countenance, however, clears up apace; and he appears to be a person of rare accomplishments.——But, we have received another still more agreeable reinforcement to our company, by the arrival of Miss Willis from Gloucester. She was Liddy's bosom friend at boarding-school, and being earnestly sollicited to assist at the nuptials her mother was so obliging as to grant my sister's request, and even to come with her in person. Liddy, accompanied by George Dennison and me, gave them the meeting half-way, and next day conducted them hither in safety. Miss Willis is a charming girl, and, in point of disposition, an agreeable contrast to my sister, who is rather too grave and sentimental for my turn of mind.—— The other is gay, frank, a little giddy, and always good-humoured. She has, moreover, a genteel fortune, is well born, and remarkably handsome.——Ah Phillips! if these qualities were permanent—if her humour would never change, nor her beauties decay, what efforts would I not make—But these are idle reflections—my destiny must one day be fulfilled.

At present we pass the time as agreeably as we can.—We have got up several farces, which afforded unspeakable entertainment by the effects they produced among the country people, who are admitted to all our exhibitions.—Two nights ago, Jack Wilson acquired great applause in Harlequin Skeleton, and Lismahago surprised us all in the character of Pierot,—His long lank sides, and strong marked features, were all peculiarly adapted to his part.——He appeared with a ludicrous stare, from which he had discharged all meaning: he adopted the impressions of fear and amazement so naturally, that many of the audience were infected by his looks; but when the skeleton held him in chace his horror became most divertingly picturesque, and seemed to endow him with such preternatural agility as confounded all the spectators. It was a lively representation of Death in pursuit of Consumption, and had such an effect upon the commonalty, that some of them shrieked aloud, and others ran out of the hall in the utmost consternation.

This is not the only instance in which the lieutenant has lately excited our wonder. His temper, which had been soured and shrivelled by disappointment and chagrin, is now swelled out, and smoothed like a raisin in plumb-porridge. From being reserved and punctilious, he is become easy and obliging. He cracks jokes, laughs and banters, with the most facetious familiarity; and, in a word, enters into all our schemes of merriment and pastime—The other day his baggage arrived in the waggon from London, contained in two large trunks and a long deal box not unlike a coffin. The trunks were filled with his wardrobe, which he displayed for the entertainment of the company, and he freely owned, that it consisted chiefly of the *opima spolia* taken in battle. What he selected for his wedding suit, was a tarnished white cloth faced with blue velvet, embroidered with silver: but, he valued himself most upon a tye-periwig, in which he had made his first appearance as a lawyer above thirty years ago. This machine had been in buckle ever since, and now all the servants in the family were employed to frizz it out for the occasion, which was yesterday celebrated at the parish church. George Dennison and his bride were distinguished by nothing extraordinary in their apparel. His eyes lightened with eagerness and joy, and she trembled with coyness and confusion. My uncle gave her away, and her friend Willis supported her during the ceremony.

But my aunt and her paramour took the pas, and formed, indeed, such a pair of originals, as, I believe all England could not parallel. She was dressed in the stile of 1739; and the day being cold, put on a manteel of green velvet laced with gold: but this was taken off by the bridegroom, who threw over her shoulders a fur cloak of American sables, valued at fourscore guineas, a present equally agreeable and unexpected. Thus accoutred, she was led up to the altar by Mr. Dennison, who did the office of her father: Lismahago advanced in the military step with his French coat reaching no farther than the middle of his thigh, his campaign wig that surpasses all description, and a languishing leer upon his countenance, in which there seemed to be something arch and ironical. The ring, which he put upon her finger, he had concealed till the moment it was used. He now produced it with an air of self-complacency. It was a curious antique, set with rose diamonds: he told us afterwards, it had been in his family two hundred years and was a present from his grand-mother. These circumstances agreeably flattered the pride of our aunt Tabitha, which had already found uncommon gratification in the captain's generosity; for he had, in the morning, presented my uncle with a fine bear's skin and a Spanish fowling-piece, and me with a case of pistols curiously mounted with silver. At the same time he gave Mrs. Jenkins an Indian purse, made of silk grass, containing twenty crown pieces. You must know, this young lady, with the assistance of Mr. Loyd, formed the third couple who yesterday sacrificed to Hymen. I wrote to you in my last, that he had recourse to my mediation, which I employed successfully with my uncle; but Mrs. Tabitha held out 'till the love-sick Jenkins had two fits of the mother; then she relented, and those two cooing turtles were caged for life——Our aunt made an effort of generosity in furnishing the bride with her superfluities of clothes and linen, and her example was followed by my sister; nor did Mr. Bramble and I neglect her on this occasion. It was, indeed, a day of peace-offering.——Mr. Dennison insisted upon Liddy's accepting two bank notes of one hundred pounds each, as pocket-money; and his lady gave her a diamond necklace of double that value. There was, besides, a mutual exchange of tokens among the individuals of the two families thus happily united.

As George Dennison and his partner were judged improper objects of mirth, Jack Wilson had resolved to execute some jokes on Lismahago, and after supper began to ply him with bumpers, when the ladies had retired; but the captain perceiving his drift, begged for quarter, alledging that the adventure, in which he had engaged, was a very serious matter; and that it would be more the part of a good Christian to pray that he might be strengthened, than to impede his endeavours to finish the adventure.——He was spared accordingly, and permitted to ascend the nuptial couch with all his senses about him.——There he and his consort sat in state, like Saturn and Cybele, while the benediction posset was drank; and a cake being broken over the head of Mrs. Tabitha Lismahago, the fragments were distributed among the bystanders, according to the custom of the antient Britons, on the supposition that every person who eat of this hallowed cake, should that night have a vision of the man or woman whom Heaven designed should be his or her wedded mate.

The weight of Wilson's waggery fell upon honest Humphry and his spouse, who were bedded in an upper room, with the usual ceremony of throwing the stocking. ——This being performed, and the company withdrawn, a sort of catterwauling ensued, when Jack found means to introduce a real cat shod with walnut-shells, which galloping along the boards, made such a dreadful noise as effectually discomposed our lovers.——Winifred screamed aloud, and shrunk under the bed-cloaths—Mr. Loyd, believing that Satan was come to buffet him *in propria persona*, laid aside all carnal thoughts, and began to pray aloud with great fervency.——At length, the poor animal, being more afraid than either, leaped into the bed, and meauled with the most piteous exclamation.——Loyd, thus informed of the nature of the annoyance, rose and set the door wide open, so that this troublesome visitant retreated with great expedition; then securing himself, by means of a double bolt, from a second intrusion, he was left to enjoy his good fortune without further disturbance.

If one may judge from the looks of the parties, they are all very well satisfied with what has passed—George Dennison and his wife are too delicate to exhibit any strong marked signs of their mutual satisfaction, but their eyes are sufficiently expressive—Mrs. Tabitha Lismahago is rather fulsome in signifying her approbation of the captain's love; while his deportment is the very pink of gallantry.——He sighs, and ogles, and languishes at this amiable object; he kisses her hand, mutters ejaculations of rapture, and sings tender airs; and, no doubt, laughs internally at her folly in believing him sincere.——In order to shew how little his vigour was impaired by the fatigues of the preceding day, he this morning danced a Highland sarabrand over a naked back-sword, and leaped so high, that I believe he would make no contemptible figure as a vaulter at Sadler's Wells. —Mr. Matthew Loyd, when asked how he relished his bargain, throws up his eyes, crying, 'For what we have received, Lord make us thankful: amen.'——His helpmate giggles, and holds her hand before her eyes, affecting to be ashamed of having been in bed with a man—Thus all these widgeons enjoy the novelty of their situation; but, perhaps their note will be changed, when they are better acquainted with the nature of the decoy.

As Mrs. Willis cannot be persuaded to stay, and Liddy is engaged by promise to accompany her daughter back to Gloucester, I fancy there will be a general migration from hence, and that most of us will spend the Christmas holidays at Bath; in which case, I shall certainly find an opportunity to beat up your quarters.——By this time, I suppose, you are sick of *alma mater*, and even ready to execute that scheme of peregrination, which was last year concerted between you and

Your affectionate
J. MELFORD.

Nov. 8.

To Dr. Lewis

DEAR DOCTOR,

My niece Liddy is now happily settled for life; and captain Lismahago has taken Tabby off my hands; so that I have nothing further to do, but to comfort my friend Baynard, and provide for my son Loyd, who is also fairly joined to Mrs. Winifred Jenkins.——You are an excellent genius at hints.——Dr. Arbuthnot was but a type of Dr. Lewis in that respect.———What you observe of the vestry-clerk deserves consideration.——I make no doubt but Matthew Loyd is well enough qualified for the office; but, at present, you must find room for him in the house.———His incorruptible honesty and indefatigable care will be serviceable in superintending the œconomy of my farm; tho' I don't mean that he shall interfere with Barns, of whom I have no cause to complain.——I am just returned with Baynard, from a second trip to his house, where every thing is regulated to his satisfaction.——He could not, however, review the apartments without tears and lamentation, so that he is not yet in a condition to be left alone; therefore I will not part with him till the spring, when he intends to plunge into the avocations of husbandry, which will at once employ and amuse his attention.——Charles Dennison has promised to stay with him a fortnight, to set him fairly afloat in his improvements; and Jack Wilson will see him from time to time; besides, he has a few friends in the country, whom his new plan of life will not exclude from his society.——In less than a year, I make no doubt, but he will find himself perfectly at ease both in his mind and body, for the one had dangerously affected the other; and I shall enjoy the exquisite pleasure of seeing my friend rescued from misery and contempt.

Mrs. Willis being determined to return with her daughter, in a few days, to Gloucester, our plan has undergone some alteration.——Jery has persuaded his brother-in-law to carry his wife to Bath; and I believe his parents will accompany him thither.——For my part, I have no intention to take that route.——It must be something very extraordinary that will induce me to revisit either Bath or London.—— My sister and her husband, Baynard and I, will take leave of them at Gloucester, and make the best of our way to Brambleton hall, where I desire you will prepare a good chine and turkey for our Christmas dinner.——You must also employ your medical skill in defending me from the attacks of the gout, that I may be in good case to receive the rest of our company, who promise to visit us in their return from the Bath.——As I have laid in a considerable stock of health, it is to be hoped you will not have much trouble with me in the way of physic, but I intend to work you on the side of exercise.——I have got an excellent fowling-piece from Mr. Lismahago, who is a keen sportsman, and we shall take the heath in all weathers.——That this scheme of life may be prosecuted the more effectually, I intend to renounce all sedentary amusements, particularly that of writing long letters; a resolution, which, had I taken it sooner, might have saved you the trouble which you have lately taken in reading the tedious epistles of

MATT. BRAMBLE.

Nov. 20.

To Mrs. Gwyllim, at Brambleton-hall

GOOD MRS. GWYLLIM,

Heaven, for wise porpuses, hath ordained that I should change my name and citation in life, so that I am not to be considered any more as manager of my brother's family; but as I cannot surrender up my stewardship till I have settled with you and Williams, I desire you will get your accounts ready for inspection, as we are coming home without further delay.——My spouse, the captain, being subject to rummaticks, I beg you will take great care to have the blew chamber, up two pair of stairs, well warmed for his reception.——Let the sashes be secured, the crevices stopt, the carpets laid, and the beds well tousled.——Mrs. Loyd, late Jenkins, being married to a relation of the family, cannot remain in the capacity of a sarvant; therefore, I wish you would cast about for some creditable body to be with me in her room——If she can spin, and is mistress of plain-work, so much the better——but she must not expect extravagant wages——having a family of my own, I must be more occumenical than ever. No more at present, but rests

Your loving friend,
TAB. LISMAHAGO.

Nov. 20.

To Mrs. Mary Jones, at Brambleton-hall

MRS. JONES,

Providinch hath bin pleased to make great halteration in the pasture of our affairs.——We were yesterday three kiple chined, by the grease of God, in the holy bands of mattermoney, and I now subscrive myself Loyd at your sarvice.—All the parish allowed that young 'squire Dallison and his bride was a comely pear for to see.—As for madam Lashmiheygo, you nose her picklearities—her head, to be sure, was fintastical; and her spouse had rapt her with a long marokin furze cloak from the land of the selvidges, thof they say it is of immense bally.—The captain himself had a huge hassock of air, with three tails, and a tum-tawdry coat, boddered with sulfur.—Wan said he was a monkey-bank; and the ould bottler swore he was the born imich of Titidall.——For my part, I says nothing, being as how the captain has done the handsome thing by me.—— Mr. Lloyd was dressed in a lite frog, and checket with gould binding; and thof he don't enter in caparison with great folks of quality, yet he has got as good blood in his veins as arrow privet 'squire in the county; and then his pursing is far from contentible.—Your humble sarvant had on a plain pea-green tabby sack, with my Runnela cap, ruff toupee, and side curls.—They said, I was the very moral of lady Rickmanstone, but not so pale—that may well be, for her ladyship is my elder by seven good years and more. —Now, Mrs. Mary, our satiety is to suppurate—Mr. Mill-fart goes to Bath along with the Dallisons, and the rest of us push home to Wales, to pass our Chrishmarsh at Bram-pleton-hall—As our apartments is to be the yellow pepper, in the thurd story, pray carry my things thither.——Present my cumpliments to Mrs. Gwyllim, and I hope she and I will live upon dissent terms of civility.—Being, by God's blessing, removed to a higher spear, you'll excuse my being familiar with the lower sarvents of the family; but, as I trust you'll behave respectful, and keep a proper distance, you may always depend upon the good will and purtection of

Yours,

W. LOYD.

Nov. 20.

FINIS

NOTES

P. 15, l. 34: *Dr. L——n.* Probably Dr. Diederick Wessel Linden, who, between 1751 and 1768, wrote several treatises on saline and chalybeate spring at Cheltenham, Llandrindrod, Bath, etc.

P. 16, l. 36: *the learned Dr. B——.* Probably Dr., afterwards Sir Edward, Barry (1696-1776), who wrote a book on the *Three Digestions of the human body* (1759).

P. 38, l. 30: *the same artist who planned the Circus. . . .* John Wood (1705 ?-1754) designed the North and South Parades and Queen's Square; his son, also named John, completed the Circus in 1764 and the Royal Crescent in 1769.

P. 42, l. 25: *the Master of Ceremonies.* Samuel Derrick (1724-1769), author of a few poems and some letters and editor of Dryden's Works. Boswell describes him as his 'first tutor in the ways of London . . . both literary and sportive.' Derrick had promised to introduce Boswell to Johnson but, though he was not able to do so, he 'had the merit of introducing him to Davies, the immediate introductor.' He is mentioned several times in the *Life of Johnson.* On one occasion 'Johnson, for sport perhaps, or from the spirit of contradiction, eagerly maintained that Derrick had merit as a writer. Mr. Morgann argued with him directly, in vain. At length he had recourse to this device. "Pray, sir (said he), whether do you reckon Derrick or Smart the best poet?" Johnson at once felt himself roused; and answered, "Sir, there is no settling the point of precedency between a louse and a flea." ' On another occasion Boswell expressed his opinion that his friend Derrick was but a poor writer, to which Johnson replied, 'To be sure, sir, he is; but you are to consider that his being a literary man has got for him all that he has. It has made him King of Bath.'

P. 50, l. 29: *our friend Ch——.* Dr. Rice Charleton, F.R.S., author of *A Treatise on the Bath Waters* (1754).

P. 56, l. 5: *the celebrated James Quin.* James Quin (1693-1766) was a celebrated actor of the eighteenth century, who at times rivalled Garrick in popular estimation. He was a close friend of the poet James Thomson, who refers to him, under the name of Esopus, in *The Castle of Indolence* (I. lxvii). Quin was vain, obstinate, quarrelsome and a gourmand, but was also able and witty. He first went to Bath at the beginning of the 1747-8 season, and from there wrote to Rich, the Manager

431

of Covent Garden Theatre, thus briefly, 'I am at Bath—yours, James Quin'; to which came the reply, 'Stay there and be damned—yours, John Rich.' He retired to Bath in 1751, and on his death was buried in the abbey church.

P. 59, l. 25: *purlieus of Puddledock*. At the end of Thames Street, London.

P. 77, l. 21: *one Paunceford*. The Paunceford-Serle incident is no doubt based on some ingratitude shown to Smollett by some individual from whom he expected a deserved consideration, but the details are unknown.

P. 88, l. 5: *Mr. T——*. William Taverner (1703-1772), a Proctor in Doctors Commons and Procurator-General of the Arches Court of Canterbury. In his own day he enjoyed a great reputation as an amateur artist. In our day he is interesting as an early water-colourist.

P. 89, l. 27: *G. H.——*. George Heathcote.

P. 110, l. 21: *Mrs. Cornelys's assembly*. Theresa Imer (1723-1797), under the name of Mme. Cornelys, managed subscription balls, masquerades and concerts at Carlisle House, Soho, between 1760 and 1772. She eventually became bankrupt and died in the Fleet prison.

P. 114, l. 1: *the duke of C——*. The Duke of Cumberland (1721-1765).

P. 114, l. 18: *the favourite yearl*. The Earl of Bute, who resigned the premiership in 1763.

P. 114, l. 24: *the grand pensionary*. William Pitt, Earl of Chatham.

P. 114, l. 32: *One of them, without a drop of red blood in his veins.* . . . Probably Henry Fox, Lord Holland: 'The other' is probably Earl Temple.

P. 115, l. 17: *the old duke of N——*. The Duke of Newcastle (1693-1768). He was Secretary of State under Walpole from 1724 to 1742, succeeded Pelham as First Lord of the Treasury in 1754, resigned two years later, formed a coalition with Pitt in 1757, resigned again in 1762, after which date his influence was lost. He was much ridiculed in his own day, not without grounds, as he was 'nervous,' pompous, always in a hurry and always behindhand.' He was always agitated, often rambling and confused, but was good-natured, laborious and free from avarice; he must also have had considerable skill in management of men and transaction of business to have endured so long a career.

P. 119, l. 34: *the British Museum*. The collections of Sir Hans Sloane, President of the Royal College of Physicians, 1719-1735, were purchased by the nation on his death in 1753 and placed in Montagu House, which later became the British Museum.

P. 127, l. 24: *pye bald ass*. A zebra which had been presented to Queen Charlotte and which was kept in St. James's Park.

P. 135, l. 5: *my friend C—— T——*. Charles Townshend (1725-1767), Chancellor of the Exchequer. The character of him given here would probably be accepted by most historians as accurate.

P. 147, l. 13: *to dine with S——.* Smollett himself. His house in the skirts of the town' was Monmouth House, in Lawrence Lane, Chelsea.

P. 166, l. 24: *Mr. W——'s preaching.* George Whitefield (1714-1770), leader of the Calvinistic Methodists. He founded two Tabernacles in London, one in Moorfields (1741) and another in Tottenham Court Road (1756).

P. 219, l. 13: *the M—— of G——.* John Manners, Marquis of Granby (1721-1770).

P. 245, l. 17: *Lord B——'s inglorious peace.* The Treaty of Paris (1763), by which Lord Bute became very unpopular.

P. 261, l. 26: *Dr. C——.* Alexander Carlyle (1722-1805), minister of Inveresk, leader of the Scottish 'Broad Church' party moderator of the general assembly (1770).

P. 267, l. 25: *Mr. R—— C——.* Robert Cullen, afterwards a lord of session under the title of Lord Cullen. He was a wit, a lover of good company and an accomplished mimic.

P. 270, l. 32: *the charming Miss R——n.* Miss Renton, niece of the Earl of Eglinton, who married a Mr. Telfer, one of Smollett's nephews.

P. 283, l. 9: *Mr. Phillip Miller* (1691-1771), an eminent gardener and supervisor of the Chelsea Botanic Garden.

P. 284, l. 4: *Dr. Gregory.* Probably John Gregory (1724-1773) Professor of Medicine at Edinburgh, who was well-known in literary circles in that city.

P. 286, l. 12: *Mr. Moore. John Moore,* physician and author of the once well-known novel *Zeluco.* He edited Smollett's Works and wrote a Memoir of him in 1797. Father of Sir John Moore-the hero of Coruña.

P. 287, l. 33: *commissary Smollett.* The novelist's cousin, James Smollett, one of the Commissaries of Edinburgh.

P. 298, l. 12: *Mr. G—ssf—d.* John Glassford, tobacco merchant and ship owner. Bailie of Glasgow.

P. 305, l. 10: *Lady H—— C——.* Lady Helen Colquhoun.

The Best of the World's Best Books
COMPLETE LIST OF TITLES IN
THE MODERN LIBRARY

A series of handsome, cloth-bound books, formerly available only in expensive editions.

MISCELLANEOUS

MODERN LIBRARY GIANTS

A series of sturdily bound and handsomely printed, full-sized library editions of books formerly available only in expensive sets. These volumes contain from 600 to 1,400 pages each.

THE MODERN LIBRARY GIANTS REPRESENT A
SELECTION OF THE WORLD'S GREATEST BOOKS

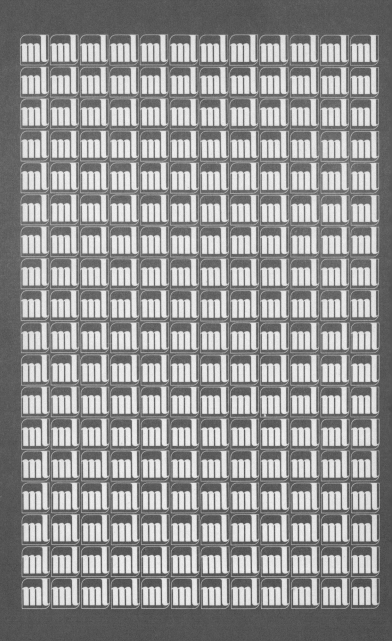